RESONANCE

About the Author

BORN AND RAISED in Dublin, Ireland, Celine Kiernan has spent the majority of her working life in the film business. She was trained at the Sullivan Bluth Studios, and her career as a classical feature character animator spanned over seventeen years. She spent most of her time working between Germany, Ireland and the USA.

Her popular Moorehawke Trilogy has been internationally acclaimed, and her novel *Into the Grey* was awarded both the Children's Books Ireland Book of the Year Award and Children's Choice Award in a single year. For more information about Celine, see her blog: celinekiernan.wordpress.com.

Also by Celine Kiernan

RESONANCE

Celine Kiernan

THE O'BRIEN PRESS
DUBLIN

First published 2015 by The O'Brien Press Ltd.,
12 Terenure Road East, Rathgar, Dublin 6, Ireland.
Tel: +353 1 4923333; Fax: +353 1 4922777
E-mail: books@obrien.ie
Website: www.obrien.ie

First published 2015 in Australia by Allen & Unwin.

ISBN 978-1-84717-577-9

1 3 5 6 4 2

15 17 19 20 18 16

Cover and text design by Sandra Nobes
Cover images: girl © Malgorzata Maj / Trevillion Images;
moth and cobwebs © Grace Kiernan; cracked ice © Strannik.fox / Shutterstock
Miss Ursula's performance on page 54 paraphrased from Shakespeare's *Macbeth*
Set in 10.5 pt Minister Light by Sandra Nobes

Printed and bound by Nørhaven, Denmark.
The paper in this book is produced using pulp from managed forests.

To Mam, I love you.
To Noel, Emmet and Grace,
always and with all my heart.

To Erica and Elise,
with eternal gratitude, love and respect.

Part I

The Collection

The Fading God

FOR A MOMENT, the Angel looked directly at him, and Cornelius' heart leapt with joy and dread.

Can you see me? he thought. *Do you know I am here?*

He took two steps downwards, hoping against all reason that the Angel had finally registered his presence, but the creature's fearsome, glowing face turned away almost immediately. It began to pace once more, its bright hands roaming the walls, those great luminous wings brushing the ceiling and the floor, and Cornelius cursed the surge of ridiculous hope that had flared within him. Of course the Angel had not seen him. The Angel saw nothing, heard nothing, except perhaps its own desolate thoughts.

Cornelius crouched on the damp step and watched the Angel pace.

Vincent's usual warning came to him, his wry voice clear and rich in Cornelius' mind: *You spend too much time in the creature's presence, cully. Come back up to us.*

Leave me be, he replied softly. *I shall only be a moment.*

Do not let it touch you. Don't forget what befell the crew.

{ 2 }

Cornelius huffed. As if he could forget. Even two centuries later, the ugly torment of the crew's deaths haunted him: their rapid loss of teeth and hair, the welter of sores blossoming on their skin.

Why must Vincent speak of it?

He closed his eyes, letting the Angel's presence soothe him.

Once, many decades after they had died, in a moment of melancholy, Cornelius had confided the crew's fate to Raquel. She had smiled and gently squeezed his hand. 'Come now, *meu caro*,' she'd said. 'You know as well as I that it was their punishment for having laid hands on an instrument of God.'

At the time Cornelius had nodded, but secretly he had not been so sure. After all, the crew had simply been following the orders that he and Vincent had given. If their fate was a punishment, should the Angel not also have tormented those who had paid for the net to be thrown? Those who now kept it prisoner?

Truth be told, Cornelius doubted the Angel ever truly understood what went on around it. Even all that time ago, as the nets had been cast about it, and those brave few had dragged it to the ground – even as it had been hauled, silent and struggling, over the blistering grass and down into the seeping depths of the tunnels – Cornelius suspected the Angel had had but the dimmest understanding of its plight.

Since then, Cornelius had been the only one with courage or curiosity enough to keep coming down here, and over the many decades he had come to suspect that the Angel was no more aware of his presence than he himself was of the air around him. To the Angel, human beings seemed as invisible and as inconsequential as the multitude of tiny particle-creatures that Vincent insisted lived in the air and water all around mankind.

Cornelius wondered if this was how humanity appeared to the immortal conscience of God. In his youth, his father had told him that God saw everything – that He judged everything. This had struck Cornelius with horror: the thought that God should look inside him and see the terrible weakness within. But now he wondered: Did God see him at all? If an angel, God's instrument on earth, could not register Cornelius' presence, then was he commensurately invisible to God himself? Was mankind, perhaps, no more to its divine Creator than a pot of maggots – a striving, squirming, formless mass, living tiny lives and dying insignificant deaths unmarked by that great, impervious mind?

Cornelius felt that would explain much, if it were so. It would *change* much: to be unseen, to be unjudged. Raquel would shake her head at that: she despised God as one would a brutal father whose children could never please him. In her philosophy, mankind existed only to be tested by God, to be punished by Him, and then destroyed.

Cornelius shrugged lower into his jacket. Perhaps she was right.

He watched the Angel move deeper into the humid reaches of the under-tunnels. As ever, its fingers probed the seams of the outer walls, its face held close to the seeping stones, as if the water of the moat beyond were whispering to it. Cornelius waited until it had retreated down the corridor before climbing the steps and gently closing the door to shut it in.

Centuries of habit made him draw the bolt, though as far as he knew the Angel had never tried to come forth. He placed his hand on the thickness of the door and imagined it in there, the warming light of its presence moving through the eternal darkness under the castle.

Its power was weakening. Cornelius had sensed this for a long time; had felt the ache creep up. Vincent, too, had felt it. But the younger ones had not, at least not until very recently – and then they had seemed to feel it all in a rush.

Cornelius sighed. It was time, once more, for festivals and song. But how might one go about such things now? In the old days here, long before Cornelius' time, things had been simple, apparently: people had given of themselves willingly, and with joy. In Cornelius' time, they had been easily duped and used up and never missed. Perhaps this new age held no such simplicity? Cornelius did not know. He would need to send out into the world, to find things out.

The world: he grew weary even thinking about it.

The prolonged exposure to the Angel's radiance had left a drifting after-image on his eyes, and Cornelius loitered by the door waiting for it to clear. Gradually the glowing presence faded from his vision and darkness closed in. Then slowly – much more slowly than usual – his surroundings reappeared; the walls and floor and rough-stoned ceiling redefined themselves in ghost-fire outlines and washes of shimmering green as his night vision restored itself.

Cornelius began the long trudge back. In the rooms above, the children had at last fallen silent. It was a relief. They had been shrieking all day, their rage such that it had wormed its way even down here, to the peace of the under-tunnels. They were hungry. All the family were hungry these days, but of course the children – like all young things – found it hardest to bear.

Cornelius reached his mind past their now silent presence to...there: Raquel, pacing, pacing – anxious, but full of faith. So much faith she had in him. He sought past her and found Vincent, a calm stillness in the house, anchoring him.

The others were there, too – Luke and the old ones and all the rest – all frightened, now, and drawn into themselves with uncertainty. Cornelius sensed them all. He loved them all. But it was for Vincent, always for Vincent, and for Raquel, of course – it was for them that he would find a way.

He had reached the stairs at last, and so began the climb, up to wearisome daylight, up to companionship, and to the waiting silence of the house.

VINCENT WAS STANDING in a wash of pale light by the arched window on the first-floor landing, gazing out across the estate. He was dressed with his usual careless grace, his loose white shirt untucked, his scarlet waistcoat unbuttoned, his cravat untied. He had a book in his hand, of course. No, not a book: one of his many periodicals. *Scientific America*? Something from the Royal Astronomical Society? Coming up the stairs, Cornelius tried to make it out.

Vincent did not look around; merely tilted his head to acknowledge Cornelius' presence and continued to gaze out the window. He was growing his hair again. Soon it would stand out from his head in that familiar shock of massy twists, the sight of which had always made Cornelius smile. *Shall you grow your beard again, too, Captain? Thread slow match into your braids like Edward Teach?*

Cornelius came to a sudden halt. Surely the last time they had seen each other, Vincent's hair had been cropped? His amusement fled as he struggled to put time into its proper order. How long had he just spent with the Angel? He stared at Vincent's dark face. His high cheekbones were like blades. When had he grown thin?

Vincent lifted his chin to indicate the gardens. 'Look,' he said.

Cornelius followed his gaze down the broad sweep of daisy-speckled lawns, past the bright green of the fluttering trees and across to the wide expanse of the boating pond.

It took him a moment to understand.

'It is frozen,' said Vincent.

He was right. Even at this distance, Cornelius could see it. The lush green of the grass nearest the pond was brittle with frost, the trees there beginning to don the autumn colours they had not worn for decades. How long had this been happening? Cornelius had no way of telling – he so rarely went outside.

Vincent watched him from the corner of his eye. 'The children have a rabbit,' he said.

Cornelius' stomach flipped.

'Luke gave it to them.'

'And you *allowed* this? Vincent, how could you? Why did you not take it from them?'

Vincent tutted. 'I couldn't stand their screeching any longer. Do not look at me like that, Cornelius. You are the one who brought them here; the least you could do is look after them yourself.' He glanced sideways again, obviously unhappy. 'It has been over an hour,' he said quietly.

With a groan of revulsion, Cornelius spun and dashed upstairs.

IN THE CHILDREN'S room, he knelt, took off his cravat and covered the poor animal's face with it – not wanting to look. The hoarse keening stopped, though the small body still trembled. Pain surged from it in waves, scouring the edges of Cornelius' consciousness with pity and shame. He lifted the creature in one piece, as best he could, and laid it at the bottom of a hatbox. He wanted to put the lid on but that seemed too cruel, so he simply rearranged the cravat over the twitching mess and carried the box from the room.

Even in their sleep, the children's faces turned to him as he passed by, drawn to the suffering of the creature within. It was a movement as unconscious as a flower following the sun.

Raquel was standing by the window of the adjoining room, staring fixedly out into the trees. She said nothing. He did not look at her as he carried his burden past.

HE TOOK THE gravel driveway in long, crunching strides. Despite his vile cargo, Cornelius registered the breeze, fresh and subtle against his skin, the scent of flowers and trill of birdsong. He had not been outside in…how long? Weeks? Yes, certainly weeks, possibly even months. Why had he forsaken this simple pleasure? It was too easy to forget how good it felt, simply being alive.

Still walking, he glanced back at the house. Vincent, a dim figure now in the distant window, placed his hand against the glass, his palm a stark pink against the blackness of his skin.

Pale vapours of mist closed in unexpectedly, obscuring the view. Cornelius looked down. The gravel at his feet was harsh with frost. To his right, the dark expanse of the pond stretched away in frozen silence. The birdsong was muffled here, as if he had left sound behind in the brighter reaches of the garden.

Something in the stillness made him falter. He stared out across the brooding ice, listening for he knew not what. There was a sense of held breath here. A sense of something sleeping, just about to stir. Cornelius shuddered, uncertain, almost frightened.

Then two shapes moved within the mist, sidling through the reeds at the edge of the ice, and he huffed with recognition and relief.

'Come, then,' he called. 'Come on.'

The shapes resolved themselves into the great shaggy forms of his dogs. They slunk towards him, their heads low between their massive shoulders, their eyes on the dripping box in his hands. For a moment, Cornelius thought of letting them have the rabbit – it would be an end to the poor thing, after all – but the idea that they might run off without eating it and bury it in the grounds was just too awful, so he snapped, 'No!'

The dogs backed down, trailing obediently behind him as he completed the frigid trek to the edge of the estate. Outside the gates, Cornelius stood with the box in his hands, looking up and down the foggy length of open road. There had been snow here, a light sprinkling of it, and the hedgerows were rimmed in hoarfrost though the sun was high in a clear sky. It must be winter.

The wretch in the box shifted and moaned, and Cornelius looked down at it. 'All right, dear,' he murmured. 'All right. It is nearly over now.'

He took his knife from his belt and crouched in the road. The dogs watched from the other side of the gates as he gently tipped the contents of the box onto the frozen earth. Cornelius could not bring himself to uncover the poor creature, so he chopped down through the spoiled silk, blindly separating head from spine, limb from twitching limb. He prayed that each cut would cease the feeble stirrings, but this was an estate creature born and bred. It had lived all its life within the benign radius of the Angel, and even there on outside ground, even there, it took an unconscionably long time to die.

The American Chap

THERE WAS A bulky travel bag dumped outside the theatre manager's office, and Joe nearly fell over it in the gloom. He was none too gently kicking it out of his way when an angry American voice cried out from within the office.

'He's *dead*? Whaddayah mean, he's dead?'

Someone was dead? Joe didn't know anyone was dead! Fascinated, he stepped into the gash of light and peered through the partially opened door. A stranger was silhouetted against the lamp on Mr Simmons' desk. A short enough fellow, dressed in a nice brown suit, he was broad-shouldered and strong-looking, his dark hair neatly oiled into waves. He shocked Joe by slapping Mr Simmons' desk.

'Explain yourself, sir! What exactly do you mean?'

Mr Simmons answered in his usual well bred drawl. 'Mr Weiss, despite your colonial delight in mangling the Queen's good English, I would not have thought you'd have such trouble understanding me. The Great Mundi is dead. I doubt I can be clearer than that.'

{ 11 }

Joe felt a tweak of disappointment. Oh, the Great Mundi. Was that all? Sure, the old magician had been dead three weeks already, of pneumonia. Everyone knew that.

'But I'm contracted as his assistant!' protested the American.

'Yes,' said Mr Simmons. 'Well. Awfully sorry about that.'

'It was to be a six-month tour, including the entire Christmas season here.'

'Hmm.'

'I've spent everything I had to get here. I gave up a good job. I bought a one-way ticket.' The American's voice suddenly changed to the exaggerated tones of a stage performer. 'I'm an excellent conjuror, sir! Allow me to astound you with some feats of legerdemain. As you can see, I have nothing up my sleeve, yet—'

'Mr Weiss,' interrupted Mr Simmons, 'as I've already told you, this theatre has its own troubles. With the fire and its subsequent expenses and delays, I can't even offer you the Great Mundi's spot on the bill. Had the poor man not died, he would have found himself as out of work as you are now, I'm afraid.'

'But what am I to *do*?'

There came the harsh scrape of a chair as Mr Simmons abruptly stood. Instinctively Joe stepped back, and tripped over the damned travel bag, his heavy lunch-pail clattering against the wall. The American whirled to glare at the door.

'Say!' he cried. 'Who's skulking out there?'

Joe's first impulse was to bolt, but the thought of Mr Simmons rushing out and catching him scurrying away was just too embarrassing. He pushed the door open. 'Just me,

Mr Simmons.' He lifted the lunch-pail. 'I come to share me dinner with Tina.'

The American belligerently looked him up and down. He was younger than Joe had first assumed – seventeen, maybe even sixteen – and his terrier-like ferocity was not in any way reduced by the fact that Mr Simmons, a full foot taller, could see right across the top of his head.

'Very well, Joseph,' said Mr Simmons. 'Thank you for letting me know that you are here.'

'Thank you, sir,' Joe said, turning to go.

'Joseph!'

In the gloom of the hallway, Joe sighed and hung his head. Simmons was all right, but he always had to have a little something to say. 'Yes, sir?'

'Be sure you don't entice Miss Kelly to dawdle; she has quite an amount of work to do.'

Joe gritted his teeth around another 'Yes, sir', took one last look at the American, and headed off down the corridor. *Entice her to dawdle*, he thought. *As if either of us had all day to be sitting on our arses doing nothing...*

The sight of the theatre did not improve his temper.

The proscenium arch and the stage itself had already been replaced. But the harsh smell of burnt wood and smoke lingered, and the orchestra pit was still a blackened hole. There was so much work to be done before the theatre could open again. The loss of business had hit the theatre cabbies hard – no one knew that better than Joe – but it was the artistes who would suffer most, being out of work this close to the lucrative Christmas season. It was such rotten luck.

Joe was just climbing the steps to the stage, his mind on the artistes, his brow furrowed with worry, when a fortuitous coincidence of time and weather stopped him in his tracks. First the sun came out, streaming through the uncovered skylights and flooding the stage with all its wintry brilliance. Then Tina stepped from the wings. Her arms were filled with the skirts and bodice of some elaborate costume, the heavy brocade sprinkled all over with gold and silver sequins. As soon as she left the shadows, the sun reflected off her, like in a kaleidoscope, and the gloomy interior came alive with a million dancing spangles of light.

Tina paused onstage, gazing upwards. Her face was all aglitter – her dark eyes, her strong jaw and nose, her loosely gathered mass of dark hair, all dazzling and bottom-lit with radiance from the dress.

'You look like a mermaid, Tina,' said Joe softly. 'You look like you're standing at the bottom of the sea.'

She turned to him in surprise, laughed, and ran to crouch at the edge of the stage. She was so close, her face so luminous with those golden scribbles of light, that Joe found himself momentarily short of words. 'You're…you're all glittery,' he managed at last.

'So are you.'

He indicated the shimmering costume. 'It's lovely.'

'It should be! It's taken me days to sew. Her Ladyship is waiting for the final fitting now.'

'It would look much nicer on you,' he said, glancing briefly into her eyes.

Tina laughed again, and shook the stiff brocade. 'This is an eighteen-inch waist, Joe Gosling! I'd need to be wired into a corset just to look sideways at it. The day I do *that* to meself, you can drown me in the canal.'

Joe huffed fondly. 'You fiery radical. Here, look what I

brought you.' He lifted his lunch-pail. 'Mutton stew from Finnegan's!'

Tina's smile twisted a little with an anxiety she couldn't quite hide.

'It's all right,' he assured her. 'A coach-load of toffs gave me a shilling-and-six tip last night. Mr Trott was too drunk to even notice. Mickey'll get his cut of me wages on payday as usual, and never be any the wiser there was more to be had.'

Tina reached for his arm. 'Joe, why don't you just get out of there? Get yourself some *nice* lodgings, with a nice landlady, who'll make a fuss of you? There's no need to be staying with that…with Mickey, now your mam is gone.'

He gently twisted his arm until she let go. 'I'm not ready.'

'Joe. You're *seventeen*. When will you be ready?'

That stung – Joe was surprised how badly. Did she think he hadn't the courage to leave? He almost blurted his plan at her there and then, almost shouted it. But in the end, he just glowered. 'Do you want to share me dinner or not?' he snapped.

Tina got the message. She smiled. 'The stew does smell lovely.'

Joe felt himself smiling back at her. He could never stay angry with Tina. 'Look what else I got.'

He reached into his jacket and slyly drew out the book. Tina practically squealed with delight.

'Oh, Joe, you rented a new one! What's it about? What's it called?'

'It's by that French lad you like, the one who wrote about Captain Nemo. This one's about people who go to the moon. See?' He showed her the cover, running his finger under the title, reading slowly so she could follow the words. '*From the Earth to the Moon,*' he said.

'To the moon,' breathed Tina. 'Just imagine.'

She said this very softly, looking at him all the while, and suddenly it was as if Joe's heart had dropped off the edge of a cliff. His smile became a grin, and he could no longer bring himself to look up from the book.

Tina stood in an abrupt rustle of satin and dazzle of sequins. 'Right!' she said. 'Just give me ten minutes with Her Majesty the Queen in there, and I'll be—'

Her abrupt silence made Joe look up sharply. She'd gone very still, her expression puzzled.

'Tina?'

She didn't answer. Instead, her eyes lifted to the darkened theatre behind him, a frown growing between those forthright eyebrows. She seemed to be listening to some faint, disturbing sound that only she could hear.

It was a look Joe hadn't seen in years, and it caused an all too familiar tightening in his belly, an old creeping feeling on the back of his neck. He glanced over his shoulder to the top of the steps, where Tina's attention was focused. There was nothing there. Just row upon row of shadowy seats and the bright, distant rectangle of the foyer door.

He was about to whisper, *What do you see?* when shapes moved within that bright rectangle – the distinctive shadow play of a person walking across the reflective floor of the foyer.

For a moment, Joe's heart shrivelled with the fearful conviction that it was Mickey the Wrench come to beat his share of the shilling and six from Joe's hide. But the figure that came to the foyer door had nothing like Mickey's bulldog silhouette. This man was tall and lean, and as he came into the auditorium, Joe saw him take a top hat from his head.

With the use of a cane, the man began to make his way down the steps. As he descended through the darkness towards them, Tina took a step back, as if afraid. Joe put himself between her and the approaching stranger. His hand tightened on the handle of his lunch-pail. He found himself thinking, *Stay away from her!*

The man came to the edge of the shadows. He put a gloved hand on the gate that led from the dress circle into the stalls, but he did not step into the light.

'Good afternoon,' he said.

At the sound of his voice, Joe felt his inexplicable aggression drain away, leaving just a dull and dreamy unease. He heard the click of Tina's high-heeled boots as she stepped forward.

'I'm looking for the manager,' said the man.

Joe felt his arm float upwards, his finger pointing. 'Mr Simmons is in his office. That door, then up the stairs.'

'Thank you,' said the man. 'I am much obliged.' He did not turn to leave, however, and there followed a strained silence as he observed them from the shadows. After a moment, he lifted his cane and pointed to the reflections still shivering across Tina's face and hair. 'What a bewitching effect,' he murmured. 'Quite...*moving*. You are an artiste, dear? You "tread the boards", as they say?'

There was a rustle by Joe's left ear, but no reply. 'She's a seamstress,' he said. 'She makes costumes.' Then, almost as if someone else were speaking: 'She's very good at it – there's no one better.'

The man was silent for a moment. 'And you?' he asked doubtfully. '*You* are an artiste?'

Joe snorted.

'He's a cab-man,' said Tina. 'He works in the depot out back, fixing the cabs and helping with the driving.'

At that, the man seemed to abruptly lose interest, and he turned without another word and walked away. There was a brief moment of light as he let himself into the corridor that led to Mr Simmons' office; then the door closed softly behind him, and all was shadow once more.

Joe hunched his shoulders, trying to rid himself of a discomfort he couldn't quite define. 'Well,' he said. 'He was a queer duck.'

'There's rumours of an impresario,' said Tina distantly. 'Come to fund a run of extravaganzas. I wonder if that was him.'

She didn't look too happy at the possibility. Joe couldn't say he disagreed.

As ALWAYS, ONCE work was done, Joe waited outside the theatre for Tina. Night was falling, the air already snapping with cold when she appeared like sunshine within the foyer. He held the door and she hurried out, pulling her shawl tight against the weather.

'Well?' he said. 'How's Her Majesty?'

She grimaced. 'She didn't get the part.'

'I *told* you. She's too old.'

'Joe! Miss Ursula is a wonderful artiste. Why shouldn't she play Ophelia? Mr Irving is over forty and he's still allowed to play Hamlet!'

Joe snorted. 'Miss Ursula is a touch more than *over forty*,

Tina.' Tina glowered, all pink-cheeked and angry within the frame of her blue bonnet, and Joe couldn't help but smile. He tried to imagine her playing Ophelia and just couldn't manage it. He couldn't picture Tina going prettily mad, strewing flowers and such – she'd more likely clatter Hamlet over the head with a frying pan.

'Hey,' Tina said, 'isn't that the out-of-work magician you were telling me about?' She pointed over Joe's shoulder. 'Gosh, he looks awful lost, poor lad. He looks awful hungry.'

Jesus, she got that same look on her face every time she saw a stray cat. Joe knew where this was leading. 'Here, let me carry that for you.' He took Tina's workbasket, purposely blocking her view of the American, who was loitering forlornly in the backstage alley, his bag at his feet. 'Come on, Tina. It's getting dark.'

Joe began herding Tina down the street with a hand on her elbow. This was a risky move when it came to Miss Martina Kelly. She'd been raised by fruit-stall shawlies, and could be fierce as a fishmonger when she wanted to be. She wasn't too keen on being herded around.

Sure enough, Tina dug her heels in, looked at Joe's hand, looked at his face, raised her eyebrows.

Joe released her elbow.

'Tina, he's a *complete stranger*.'

Tina's mouth tweaked up in amusement. She patted Joe's arm. 'Let's buy him a bag of chestnuts,' she said.

'EHRICH WEISS,' SAID the American, smiling a broad show-man's smile and tipping his hat. 'You can call me Harry – everyone does.'

'Martina Kelly. You can call me Tina. This is Joseph Gosling.'

The American offered his hand. Unsmiling, Joe shifted the workbasket, as if it were more than he could manage to carry it and his lunch-pail and shake hands at the same time. The showman's smile never flickered as the American returned his hand, unshaken, to his pocket.

'Heavy load you have there,' he said dryly.

Tina was looking him up and down with her usual smiling curiosity. 'Where you from, Harry?'

'Oh, here and there,' he said, clearly amused at her frank survey of his clothes. 'I travel a bit. But mostly I live in New York with my family.' He eyed Tina with an appreciation of which Joe did not even remotely approve, and Joe flatly cut in to the conversation.

'You Hungarian, Harry?'

The American looked surprised.

'Your accent,' said Joe. 'It sounds Hungarian.'

'Why, that's amazing! My parents *are* Hungarian. My brothers and I are American, of course, but Mama and Papa...well, we speak hardly any English at home.' He spread his hands, perhaps in indulgence at his parents' immigrant ways. We speak a kind of German – it's Mama and Papa's native language. Most strangers don't realise we're Hungarians. How on earth did you know?'

'Oh, Joe's very clever,' said Tina. 'Anyway, you talk like Saul, the auld Jew who runs the bookshop. He's a Hungarian.'

Harry's showman's smile stiffened just a little. 'The "auld Jew"?'

'Yes,' said Tina. 'Saul. He's Joe's best friend.'

Joe rolled his eyes. This was a favourite joke of Tina's,

Saul's shop being the only place in Dublin where Joe freely spent his money.

All at once there wasn't a trace of the showman in Harry's demeanour. 'Say,' he said, apparently surprised. 'Say, your friend, huh? Well, that's just *grand.*' Seemingly on impulse, he once again offered his hand.

There was something so warm about this gesture, something so genuinely pleased, that Joe had shifted the workbasket to his hip and was shaking Harry's hand before he remembered he didn't trust strangers.

'You had your supper yet?' asked Tina.

Harry flushed. 'Oh, sure,' he said. 'Sure I did.'

Sure you did, thought Joe, eyeing Harry's pinched face. *And a nice big dinner, too.*

'Mm hmm,' said Tina wryly. 'What did you have?'

'Uh…fish and…uh…butter and some bread.' Harry had to wipe the corners of his mouth just saying the words.

Tina tutted and shook her head. 'Stay here, Harry Weiss. I'll be back in a moment.' She ran lightly off around the corner of the alley, and the men were left looking at each other – Joe holding her flower-covered wicker basket on his hip, Harry trying to look as if he knew what was going on.

Joe sighed, knowing well how Tina worked. 'She's gone to send a message home,' he explained. 'You're being invited to supper.'

He was about to tell Harry that he needn't think the offer of a bowl of soup meant a free meal every day for the rest of his life when a low voice behind him froze the words in his mouth.

'Well, Joe. What's that in your hand?'

Joe hated the shameful surge of fear that flared within him. Harry must have read it clear as day, because his face hardened and he frowned an unspoken question: *You need help?*

Joe shook his head and turned. He had to suppress a start at how close Mickey the Wrench was. He was looming as always, swaying from side to side in that hypnotic way of his, his hands in his pockets, his big face grinning. 'What's that in your hand, Joe?' he repeated amiably. 'Looks like a lunch-pail. Didn't know you owned a lunch-pail, Joe.'

'It's from Finnegan's.' Joe scanned the alley. Mickey was alone. Good. 'I'm bringing it back to them for Mr Simmons.'

'Well, aren't you *nice*,' crooned Mickey. His blue-button eyes met Joe's, and there was no smile in them at all. 'Mr Simmons must have been *powerful* hungry today. What with ordering a pail of dinner from Finnegan's right on top of the heap of bacon and cabbage he lowered down him in Foy's. How much does a pail of dinner set you back in Finnegan's, Joe?'

'How the hell would I know?'

'Must be a shiny copper or two. Must be a right pretty penny.' Mickey tossed a glance at Harry. 'Why don't you run along now, son? Meself and the cousin here need to chat.'

Harry just flashed that showboat of a smile and shrugged. 'I'm comfy,' he said.

Mickey's grin flickered off, then on again. 'That so?' he said.

At the far end of the alley, someone opened the side door to the cabbies' depot. Dim light spilled out into the darkness, and Joe's heart dropped as Mickey's brothers, Daymo and Graham, stepped into view.

He pushed Tina's basket at Harry. 'Harry. Get lost.'

'Yeah,' grinned Mickey. 'Get lost, Harry.'

But Harry just closed his fists, his face set, and Joe realised with horror that he was going to stay.

Tina's voice stilled them all. 'Joseph Gosling!'

She was standing at the head of the alley, in the full light of the street lamps, her hands on her hips. She was purposely blocking foot-traffic, and Joe suppressed a little smile as several people glanced down the alley to see what she was staring at. God, she was clever.

'Are you walking me home or not?' she demanded.

Two dandies, filled with haughty amusement, paused to watch the gutter-boy get a drubbing from his girl. 'I'd hurry if I were you, my lad,' drawled one of them. 'Or you'll have no one to hold your hand on the tram!'

Joe snatched the basket from Harry's arms. 'Grab your bag,' he muttered and hurried out towards the bustle of the evening crowd. Mickey and his brothers stood watching from the shadows. Harry glowered back at them, and Joe hustled him on. 'Just keep walking, you eejit.'

THEY ROUNDED THE corner of the alley and were instantly mired in a swarm of screeching urchins. Buttoning their pockets, Harry and Joe fell into place on either side of Tina. She tightened her grip on her basket, and the three of them began pushing their way through the rancid chaos.

The urchins seemed enthralled by a beautiful two-horsed carriage parked on the street outside the theatre. The carriage was of a heavy old-fashioned type, built for long journeys, and the coachman occupied a roomy boot, complete with access gate. The scruffy little children who surrounded it were in a frenzied state of excitement.

'Lookit the blackfella!' they were shrieking. 'Lookit the blackfella!'

The cause of their hysteria turned out to be the carriage driver, a tall, slim black man who seemed nothing but patiently amused by the filthy little creatures surrounding his vehicle. As Joe, Tina and Harry passed by, the driver met Joe's eye and his easy smile faded. He sat forward with a frown.

At that moment, Mr Simmons came barrelling out of the theatre, waving his arms and yelling at the urchins. 'Oi! Clear off, the lot of you! Before I call the peelers!'

At the mention of the police, the swarm dispersed like grimy fog, up alleys, down side streets, over walls.

All hand-wringing concern, Mr Simmons turned to the gentleman who had followed him from the theatre. 'Please do accept my most profuse apologies, Lord Wolcroft. I can only hope they haven't scratched the paint or discommoded your horses.'

The gentleman shook his head as if to say, *Think nothing of it*. Smooth-shaven, his lean figure clad in an elegance of dove-grey morning coat, top hat and cape, he was the very picture of aloof aristocracy, despite the chalky pallor of his skin.

'Joe,' whispered Tina. 'That's the strange man from the auditorium. See his cane?'

Joe nodded absently, his attention still fixed on the carriage driver, who was regarding him with frowning interest. Abruptly, and without any kind of regard for his status, the driver leaned over and cut across Simmons' conversation with his master. 'Cornelius,' he demanded.

'Look at that boy.'

Mr Simmons was rendered momentarily speechless with horror, but the gentleman just turned in the direction pointed and gazed at Joe. The carriage driver did the same, and Joe found himself frozen in place, the unwilling object of their combined scrutiny.

'Do you see it?' said the carriage driver.

The gentleman tensed, as if suddenly realising what he was being asked. 'No,' he said sharply, turning away.

'Is it not Matthew?'

'Please, Vincent. *No.*'

'But...'

Abruptly, the gentleman retreated to the carriage and slammed the door. He turned his face from the window even as he snapped the blind shut. The driver spent another moment gazing at Joe; then he pulled the carriage into the street and drove away.

'Well,' drawled Harry, 'it's just like a penny drama! *The Finding of the Prodigal Son.* Play your cards right, *Matthew*, and you might be set to inherit a fortune.'

Joe huffed. 'He's bloody hard up for a son if he has to resort to the likes of me.'

'I don't like those men,' said Tina. 'There's something not right about them.'

'Miss Kelly!' Mr Simmons' voice had them snapping to attention like soldiers.

'Yes, Mr Simmons?'

'Is Miss Ursula still within?'

'Yes, Mr Simmons.'

'Very well. I shall speak with her. I want you back here bright and early tomorrow, Miss Kelly.' At Tina's puzzled look, the theatre manager almost smiled. 'There are to be auditions.'

'Auditions?'

This time Mr Simmons did smile. 'A tour, Miss Kelly! A fortuitously timed tour! An extravaganza for the Christmas season!'

Fran the Apples
and the Lady Nana

HARRY SINCERELY HOPED he wasn't headed for a smashed skull and emptied pockets in the slime of a Dublin alley. The places through which this vivacious girl and her slouching alley cat of a chap were leading him were so narrow and mean that it was difficult to believe they could exist this close to the well appointed theatre district. At some point along the way, the girl had covered her bright-blue bonnet with her shawl. Harry thought it right that she had – in these surroundings that bonnet would have seemed wrong, somehow; it would have seemed vulnerable. Her chap, striding silently at her side, had a cut-throat walk to him here, a stone-eyed *I'll-mind-my-business-if-you-mind-yours* expression, which Harry recognised all too well from the slums of New York.

'Say,' he murmured, fighting the urge to look back over his shoulder, 'have we much further to go?'

'No,' said Tina, smiling. 'We're right here.'

Harry followed Joe's example and scraped his shoes clean of horse muck and street filth at the boot-scrape; then he followed Tina up stone steps to the gloomy arch of a front door. As she squinted in the almost-dark to find the lock, Harry eyed the scarred wood and Tina's smile widened.

'It's a bit battered, isn't it? When we first started locking up, the dossers got angry and tried to kick it down. But we were sick to the teeth of them sleeping in the hall and pissing on the stairs, so we refused to give up. Every morning, Miss Price and Fran' – she glanced at him – 'that is, the landlady and my aunt Fran, they'd come out and fix the damage; then we'd lock it up all over again.'

She and Joe went inside. Darkness swallowed them as soon as they stepped from the threshold, and Harry hesitated. The house breathed out a rich, wholesome, welcoming smell, not at all what he'd expected – not the usual stench of a tenement. There was damp, certainly, and the unavoidable taint of human waste, but there was also the tang of apples and fresh turnips, the satisfying scent of bread, pipe-smoke, coal-fire and carbolic soap. This place almost smelled *good*. It almost smelled like home.

There was a *tap-a-tap-tap* way off down the hall, and Tina's voice called out in the darkness.

'Miss Price? It's Martina. I've come for me lamp.'

There came the cracking of a lock. A door opened, and there was Tina, outlined in candlelight. Harry saw that she was surrounded by a flock of metal prams. They were filled with old breadboards and baskets of fruit and vegetables, and Tina smiled against the backdrop of humpbacked shadows they threw against the wall. The ticking of clocks and mewing of cats filled the narrow hall as an inordinately tiny old woman peered around the door of her apartment.

'Come in now,' murmured Joe, surprisingly close in the dark, and Harry stepped inside.

The old woman squinted up at Tina. 'Frances said you'll have a boy with you. I don't care for boys, Miss Kelly. I don't care for them at all.'

'I know, Miss Price, but Mr Harry Weiss is a very quiet fellow, very mannerly and reserved.'

Stepping closer and removing his hat, Harry tried to look mannerly and reserved. The tiny woman scowled, clearly unimpressed. Joe stepped to Harry's side and the woman shrank back.

'Who's that?' she cried. 'Someone's lurking!'

'It's just me, Miss Price. Joe.'

The wrinkled old face melted into tenderness. 'Ah, Joe,' she crooned. 'I'm sorry. I thought you were a boy.'

Joe sighed, and Harry had to bite his lips against a smile.

'Well,' said the tiny woman, 'if Joe's with you...' She reached to a shelf by the door, touched a taper to a wick. 'Here you go, Miss Kelly,' she said, lifting down a heavy oil lamp. 'No need to fetch a pail of water or bring up coal; Fran did it all when she got home.' She handed the lamp to Tina, smiled fondly at Joe, scowled suspiciously at Harry, then shut the door in their faces.

'Be ready to be on display,' whispered Tina, and she hoisted the lamp and led them upstairs.

Doors opened on every landing. Women's faces appeared. Framed in candlelight, they clucked and cooed with questions. Tina greeted them all without stopping, the lamp held high so they could get a good look at Harry. 'Howyeh, Miss Mulvey. Howyeh, Miss Crannock. Howyeh, Norah, how's Sarah? Ah, that's lovely. Yeh, this is the boy. No, he's only staying for dinner...Yeh, from the theatre. Yeh, he's Joe's friend.'

Joe snorted quietly at that one. Harry nodded to each passing face, and smiled and did his best to look charming. *Are there no men here at all?* he thought.

Finally Tina took them up a last narrow flight of steps. 'None of them will sleep a wink 'til you're gone,' she whispered. 'They'll be gossiping about you for weeks.'

She touched Harry on the arm. He turned to look at her, and was surprised at the anxiousness in her expression. She leaned close. 'You can say you're a magician, Harry, if you like. Nana used to love a good magic trick, so she did. But please don't go doing any mind-reading or fortune-telling or anything like that, all right?' She flicked a glance over his shoulder at Joe, then back again. 'My aunt wouldn't approve.'

Harry was taken aback. 'Okay,' he said. 'Sure. I wouldn't want to upset anyone.'

Tina smiled and straightened, obviously relieved. She went to open the door, hesitated and turned once again. Her voice was lightly teasing this time, her eyes bright. 'Watch out for Daniel O'Connell,' she warned. 'He bites.'

With that, she pushed open the door and led the way into warm light, the scent of candles and the heady smell of food.

'BET YOU'VE NEVER seen such a lovely little room as this, have you, Harry?' The network of wrinkles that made up the Lady Nana's face formed itself into a broad and toothless grin. 'It's a proper little home, isn't it? A real gem.'

She clamped her gums onto her pipe and stroked

Daniel O'Connell's wiry fur with a work-seamed hand. The terrier bared his teeth at Harry from the comfort of the old woman's lap. Harry was pretty sure the little savage had bitten straight through his tendon. He indulged a brief fantasy of catapulting the dog out the window, then beamed his very best smile at the Lady Nana. 'It's a *darned* pretty home, ma'am,' he said. 'I've never *seen* prettier.'

On the opposite side of the fire, Tina exchanged an eye-rolling glance with Joe and went on with her knitting. By her side, the silent, dark-eyed woman she had introduced as Fran the Apples squinted narrowly, as if suspecting Harry of lying. He wasn't. He thought the little room was charming, with its well scrubbed floorboards, glittering metal bedstead, and host of religious pictures on the walls. Even the huge statue of the Virgin Mary, with her multitude of warmly melting candles, had a serene comfort to her that made Harry feel welcome. Of course, the feed of stew that nestled in the pit of his stomach had a lot to do with it. Harry rubbed his ankle and smiled contentedly around him.

'How's your leg, Harry?' smirked Joe. 'Still a bit sore?'

Harry grimaced at him.

Joe grinned. He was standing at the room's only table, pouring black beer into enamel mugs. After dinner, to the women's delight and Harry's admiration, the thin young man had produced two big bottles of the stuff, one from each of the hidden pockets inside his jacket, and he was now dividing the contents between three mugs and two large jam jars.

'Ah, thank you, Joe!' sighed the Lady Nana, accepting her mug of beer. 'Nothing like a little porter to build you up for the cold.' She raised her mug. 'To Miss Price!' she cried.

'We were blessed the day we found her,' agreed Fran the Apples. 'Blessed. You don't catch *her* upping the rent every time we buy a new bedspread or fix a broken window.'

'Amen,' said Tina, and they all raised their drinks.

Harry couldn't help but notice that Joe did so with a certain wry reluctance. 'To Miss Price,' Joe said. 'Despite what she thinks of *boys*.'

'Ah now, you can't blame her,' said Nana, tipping her mug so Daniel O'Connell could take his share. 'Sure, aren't men the ruin of the tenements? Never short their beer money while their women and childer starve.'

'I'm not like that,' said Joe softly.

'Ah, you're not at all, Joe,' crooned the Lady. 'You're not at all.' She reached and squeezed his chapped hand. 'And don't you pay for it? Don't they give you a terrible time? You poor gossun.'

Joe flushed. 'I do all right.' He flicked a glance at Harry, and Harry couldn't help but prickle in sympathy for his pride.

'But there's no avoiding it,' mused Nana. 'Men are bowsies, pure and simple.'

'Ah, Nan,' admonished Tina, glancing at Fran the Apples, who was frowning into her beer.

'Not all men are like that, Nana,' said Fran.

'Oh, ho!' crowed the Lady Nana. 'I know who you're thinking of! But you give him time, Frances love! They're all gents until they have their boots under your table; *then* you see the man in them! Useless shower of gurriers.'

'Say now,' cried Harry, 'that's just not true! My pa for one. He isn't like that. He works *hard*, and he'd do anything for my ma! It's not always a man's fault when times are tough!'

A stunned silence fell over the women. Joe shifted

uncomfortably, his eyes flicking to the Lady Nana, and Harry instantly regretted his outburst – he didn't know these people; he didn't know the delicate balances of their relationship.

'Of course,' he ventured, 'my pa might be a *rare* specimen of a man.'

'Well,' murmured the Lady Nana apologetically, 'it's more the drink, you know. The drink's a terror for emptying a man's pockets. I'm sure your pa's a grand fella for staving off the drink, Harry. Just like Joe here…and yourself, no doubt.'

'Are you all theatre folk, Harry?' asked Fran the Apples. 'Your dad and your mam and all?'

Tina lowered her knitting. 'Is your dad an artiste, Harry?'

'Uh…' Harry hesitated. On his travels, he had learned that there was an astonishing amount of kindness in this world – but he'd also learned firsthand how easy it was to find oneself out in the cold. The statue of the Virgin Mary gazed placidly at him over Tina's head, her plaster face set in sweet inquiry. *Well?* she seemed to ask. *What* does *Papa do?*

Harry glanced at Joe. *Joe's best friend*, that was what Tina had called Saul. *Joe's best friend.* Harry set down his jam jar. 'Uh, no,' he said, 'my pa's not an artiste. He's a rabbi, actually. In New York.'

'Whassat?' asked the Lady Nana, her brow furrowed. 'A rabbit?'

Joe released one of his now familiar sighs. 'Not a rabbit, Nan,' he explained patiently. 'A *rabbi*. A Jew priest.'

'Oh,' said Fran the Apples, her head turning sideways in frowning uncertainty.

'Oh!' said Tina, her eyes bright with questions.

'Ah,' nodded the Lady Nana. 'A Jewman.'

'Yes,' said Harry carefully. 'A Jew.'

'Ah, there's nothing like a good Jewman,' said Nana. 'Next to the pawn, there's nothing like him.' She nodded sagely, petting the sleepy Daniel O'Connell. 'You can always make a deal with them, you see. Not like them lousy loan sharks. It's very rare a woman'll get a black eye off a Jewman.'

'Your folks must be rich, then, are they, Harry?' asked Tina, leaning forward in genuine inquiry.

It was Harry's turn to sigh. 'Not that I've ever noticed.'

'Oh,' she said, disappointed. 'Ah, well. I suppose you can't *all* be.' She went back to her knitting.

'Joe knows a Jew,' said Fran. 'Says he's a very *nice* kind of fellow. Maybe you know him, Harry?'

As Harry shook his head to say no, he didn't know Joe's Jew friend, Joe met his eye. Harry couldn't help but smile at the rueful apology in the young man's face. *They mean no harm.*

Harry shrugged. *It's all right, I'm not offended.*

Joe nodded and raised his jam jar of porter in silent salute.

Somewhere downstairs, deep in the heart of the tenement house, someone began playing a violin. Fran the Apples settled back. 'There you go,' she said quietly. 'Miss Crannock's at it again.'

'Lovely,' murmured Nana, re-lighting her pipe.

Tina tilted her head to listen. 'Max Bruch,' she said. 'Concerto No. 1 in G minor.' She sighed, her knitting forgotten again, her expression dreamy. Harry couldn't help but smile at how Joe was watching her, his eyes gentle with affection. 'Oh!' she said suddenly. 'Joe!'

Joe jumped and blushed.

'Your book!' Tina cried. 'He rented a new book, Nan! Joe, read your book!'

Joe set down his jam jar and fumbled in his pockets for his 'new book'. All anticipation, the women rearranged themselves into positions better suited for attentive listening. Daniel O'Connell opened his one eye and growled at Harry. Harry raised his jam jar of porter.

L'chaim to you, too, you little jerk.

He stretched back, enjoying the fire. Even considering the fact that he was jobless, penniless and miles from home, this wasn't too shabby. Not too shabby at all. Joe opened his book, and Harry smiled.

And for once in my life, he thought, *I'm not the poor schmuck singing for his supper.*

Waiting in the Dark

Vincent stood at the hotel window and watched the moon rise above the city, illuminating the trees of a small park across the street. It brought him back to a night over two hundred years earlier, when he'd first arrived in this country. He had left the ship hidden at anchor behind some remote islands, and as his crew sculled the boarding boats through the flat, slow-moving plains of the estuary, the shallow water had reflected a similar moon in all its idiocy.

They had emerged from the reeds onto the wide river that would carry them to the manor house, and Luke had turned anxiously to him. 'You *will* get my land back, won't you, Captain? You'll rid us of Wolcroft's bloody reign?'

Vincent did not recall answering, but he remembered Cornelius had grinned, a sharp white flash in the shadows of his tricorn hat. 'We will win you back your land, dear,' he'd murmured, his fingers closing tight on Luke's shoulder. 'As long as you have told us true, of course, and brought the Captain to his cure.'

'Captain?' The uncertain whisper dragged Vincent down through centuries and back to the confines of the hotel room. The scent of coal and candle-wax overpowered the memory of salt and free air. The heavy furniture crowded in. At the sudden rush of confinement, Vincent flung wide the window and leaned far out. Closing his eyes, he seared his lungs with sea-tinged air.

'Captain?' whispered Cornelius again. 'Is something wrong?'

Vincent hung his head. *Yes. I am suffocated. I am trapped.*

He did not share this thought. It would only serve to distress his friend, who lay curled in a shivering ball on the sofa behind him.

'I…I know how this looks,' whispered Cornelius, 'but it is not what you think. I have not succumbed to my old vice.'

'I know that. I do not condemn you.'

'It is my own fault. Without the Angel's presence, I am weak. I revert to wicked thoughts, and I am punished.'

Vincent could not help the flare of irritation this brought him. 'Is that so? And should my disease reoccur? Would that be because I am wicked? Will that also be a punishment?'

'Captain, no! I would never for a moment think that!'

'Then cease to think it of yourself. You've spent too long away from the Bright Man, Cornelius. That is all. Your body has replaced one dependence for another, and now it suffers as it used to suffer when you tried to forgo the opium. This has nothing to do with God. Your body is simply screaming at you for more of what it craves.'

Behind him, Cornelius went deathly still. 'No,' he whispered eventually. 'You are wrong. The Angel has made me a better man. Its presence has strengthened me. It has stopped me from thinking of…I am no longer dependent on…I never *fall*, Captain! I am a *better man*! I—'

Ashamed, Vincent strode to the couch and grabbed his friend's clammy hand. 'Hush,' he said. 'Pay no heed to me. I am a fool. A head full of science and no heart at all.'

Cornelius clung tight, a drowning man. He whispered, 'I ache, Vincent!'

'We will be home soon, cully.'

'I am overcome.'

'What of it? You have but to ask, and I would go out now and purchase a vial of whatever it is will make you better. I—'

Cornelius groaned. 'Stop. Stop before I say yes.'

'I have known you through thick and thin, Cornelius. Whatever you perceive your failings to be, you have never failed me. You are a strong man. Rest easy in yourself. You will be home soon.'

The grip on his hand only increased. 'Don't let me sleep.'

Vincent straightened without speaking and, after a desperate moment, Cornelius released his hand, allowing him to return to the window. A cold breeze billowed the curtains, and Vincent inhaled it, closing his eyes. 'It is good to be close to the sea again. I had forgot how alive it smells.'

'Jolly times we had back then, eh, Captain? Under our old ragged flag.'

'Jolly times,' agreed Vincent.

'We were great men for the cutlass and the axe,' added Cornelius, beginning to smile. 'Fierce coves.'

Vincent grinned. 'The scourge of Nevis. Lousy with gold and silver, and all the things a sword could fetch us.'

'We were wicked.'

'We were free!' Vincent's grin faded. 'Though may chance we misremember even that.' He put his hand to the pain that was dull but growing in his chest: a small, insidious foretaste of things to come.

Cornelius straightened, suddenly alert. 'You are in distress? But you've spent barely a week away! We've taken much longer trips before, and with no ill effect to your health.'

'My last trip was a while ago, cully, and the creature was much stronger then. Its power is fading fast, and perhaps does not linger within us as it used to.' He glanced wryly at Cornelius. 'You should check the mirror. Your hair has begun to grey. Next, your fine face will line. Raquel will not recognise you on your return. She will cry, "Who is this old man in Cornelius' clothes? Cast him out! Cast him out!"'

The jest seemed to cause Cornelius a moment of pain.

Vincent sighed. 'I tease, cully. You do not look old.'

Cornelius pulled himself upright on the sofa. 'At home, we will both feel better,' he said. 'As soon as the Angel is restored, all will be mended.'

Vincent grimaced at the word 'angel'. He had never approved of Raquel and Cornelius' beliefs. As ever, Cornelius paid no mind to his disapproval and Vincent let it go.

'Speaking of superstitions,' he said, 'you still insist on this fool's meet tomorrow?' At Cornelius' nod, Vincent huffed. 'I thought you had left the throwing of bones and reading of entrails long behind you, cully. What makes you wish to consult the ether now, when we both wisened to the folly of such pursuits a century ago?'

'This theatre crone has quite the reputation as a seer, Captain. The new method she uses – this spirit board – it is apparently very effective. Should she prove more than just another charlatan, I should very much like to bring her back with us. I should like her to commune with the Angel. If we can speak with it, learn more accurately what it needs, this irritating dependence on extravaganzas and the intrusion of strangers into our peaceful home may yet prove unnecessary.'

Vincent shook his head, parted the curtains, and looked, once again, into the street. 'There is only one proven way to sustain the creature. You know this. There is no speaking to it.'

'The first soothsayer spoke to it.'

'Really? You recall this as fact? Over two hundred years have come and gone since then, Cornelius. I can barely recall the events of eighty years past, let alone two centuries. Let us not fall back on half-forgotten superstitions, shall we? Let us stick to that which we ourselves have proven to work.'

Too much talking and Vincent's lungs rebelled. It was just a gentle cough, but, without thinking, he found himself checking his palm for blood. It was a gesture from another lifetime, risen to the surface now with the threatened onset of his disease. He instantly regretted it. Cornelius' concern was palpable from across the room.

'We will fix this, Captain.'

Vincent nodded and dropped the curtain back into place. 'We will…and in the only way we know how. You meet with your soothsayers and entrail-readers tomorrow, cully, if you so desire. I wish you joy of the encounter. But do not neglect the real reason for our journey here. It is our one assured hope, and I will not have you derail it based on the ravings of a centuries-dead bedlamite who presumed to speak with angels and claimed a *demon* slept in the lake.' He pulled on his overcoat, heading for the door.

'You...you are leaving?'

'I cannot sit in this hotel room all night, Cornelius. I have business I must attend to.'

Cornelius leapt to his feet. 'But...it is cold out there. Your health! Surely there is nothing so important that...'

Vincent went very still, and Cornelius came to a halt. After a long, silent moment, Vincent placed his hat upon his head and opened the door. 'I wish to get Raquel some fabric,' he said. 'Something pretty, for a dress. Something bright. The draper will not see a man such as me on his premises before dark.'

'But I would have done this for you! You should not have to suffer the scorn of such fools!'

Vincent laughed softly. 'The chittering of insects and grunt of pigs is no insult to a man who knows his worth, cully.' He glanced sideways at his friend. 'It will be like old times, to explore a strange port. You will not join me? Stretch your legs?'

At Cornelius' hesitation, Vincent sighed again. 'No. Of course not. Very well, then. Stay here. I shall see you later.'

Cornelius went to speak, but Vincent closed the door on whatever objection he might have expressed, and made his way through the silence of carpeted hallways and out into the sharp winter night.

A Night's Wage Lost

As Joe led the way down through the darkness of Tina's house, Harry surprised him by starting a conversation. 'I liked how you read that story,' he said.

Joe waited for the sly dig. None came, and Joe had to admit it didn't sound like Harry was taking the piss. He took a chance on saying, 'Thanks.' Then, without really knowing why, he added, 'I like reading for the ladies.'

'They can't read, huh?'

'Not a word, but they'd add and subtract the eyes out of your head.'

He heard Harry chuckle. 'I'd say they would,' he said. 'There was a lot more science in that book than I'd thought women would appreciate, though – do you think they understood it?'

Joe came to an abrupt halt, causing Harry to bump into him. 'Did *you* understand it?' he asked coldly.

'Say, I didn't mean any insult. It's just…you know…all those terms: hyperbolas, parabolas, ellipses. Did you understand them?'

Joe had to smile at that. 'No,' he admitted. 'I hadn't a clue.'

Harry laughed, a relieved sound in the echoing dark, and Joe began descending the steps again. 'I marked the pages, though,' he said. 'I'll ask Saul in the morning, and he'll explain.'

'If Saul doesn't know,' said Harry, clattering along behind him, 'I'll write and ask my pa. He knows a *lot*. Then, even if I'm far away, I'll send you the letters so you'll know the answers, too.'

Joe almost stopped again at that – at the unexpected pleasure of it. 'I'd like that,' he said.

They let themselves out into the street, and the cold clamped itself around them like a fist. Joe shrugged deeper into his jacket as they trotted down the steps.

'Honestly though, Joe,' said Harry, 'you're like a different person when you read. You did a terrific job of the accents.'

'I was copying you with the accents. So that's what America is like, huh? Everyone shooting off guns and waving their wooden legs about?'

'More or less – though I've never met anyone with a silver nose, more's the pity.'

It was Joe's turn to chuckle. He was astonished to realise that he was enjoying himself – that he'd been enjoying himself all evening. He had never before had such a discussion with a man his own age: a discussion free of slyness and barbs. It was a good feeling.

'It's darned cold,' complained Harry. 'Tina should have given you that muffler she's knitting.'

Joe touched his throat where Tina had wrapped the red wool muffler around his neck to measure its length. That had been another nice surprise, to find she was doing that for him. 'Ah sure, it's not quite ready,' he murmured. 'I can wait.'

A familiar noise made them both look back down the foggy street. It was the coalman, Daniel Barrett, leading his drayhorse home. Joe took Harry's arm, bringing him to a stop.

'Watch,' he whispered.

As usual, Daniel Barrett clucked his horse to a halt in the middle of the road. Then, casually, as if he'd given it no thought at all, the big man fished in the pocket of his coal-stained jacket and produced his tobacco tin. As Daniel bent his head to fill and light his pipe, Joe nudged Harry and jerked his chin to indicate a slash of light high in Tina's tenement. A curtain had been pulled partially aside, and a slim figure could be seen peering out.

'Fran,' whispered Joe.

Daniel Barrett leaned back against his horse and gazed up at the window where Fran the Apples stood. The horse, well used to this routine, sighed and shook her heavy head. Daniel exhaled a thin stream of blue smoke, his eyes never leaving the unresponsive sliver of light high in the darkness above him.

Joe felt the old familiar sadness rise up in him. 'Come on,' he said, tugging Harry's arm. 'Leave him to his dreams.'

They strolled on. After a while, Joe surprised himself by saying, 'He's a good man, you know, Mr Barrett. Works hard. Owns his own dray. Lives clean. A real good fella.'

Harry glanced sideways at him. 'There's nothing can be done if the feelings aren't there, Joe.'

Joe shook his head. Fran the Apples loved Daniel Barrett, Joe was certain of it. He'd seen the look on her face when the big, quiet man came smiling to her stall for a chat and to buy an apple. When Daniel Barrett was around, Fran the

Apples looked like the young woman she really was. But Fran would never leave the Lady Nana, and Nana would never leave Miss Price's. Not if it meant returning to the squalor of a normal tenement – why would she? She'd be mad to.

'Why doesn't he go on up to her?' asked Harry. 'Lay on the old charm.' He tilted his head as he said this, and did a smoothly gliding dance step that ended with him rolling his hat down his outstretched arm. 'Ladies *looove* the charm,' he crooned.

Joe couldn't help but smile. Oily American git. He shoved his hands in his pockets and glanced back the way they'd come. 'He won't win her by standing in the street smoking, anyway. You need to work harder than that.'

'That's your plan of conquest, is it?' smirked Harry, jamming his hat back on his head. 'You plan to work so hard the girls will swoon?'

Joe just grinned as he led the way through the foggy dark. Harry seemed to take this as an admission of intent. 'Oh, as before ho!' he cried. 'Do you think, perhaps, that if you do enough night shifts, a certain brown-eyed miss will notice that you are a *boy*, Mr Gosling? OW! Watch those bony elbows!'

'Only if you watch your flapping mouth.'

They walked on in silence, Joe's hands in his pockets, Harry shifting the bag on his shoulders, his eyes all the time roaming the streets as they made their way back towards the river. Joe had to admit he liked the way this fellow kept track of where they were. He didn't think it would take Harry long to find his own way around.

It was almost a disappointment when Harry came to a halt and said, 'Well, here's where we part ways.'

'You're sure you've somewhere to stay, Harry? I could bring you round to Saul. He wouldn't see you stuck for a friendly lodging.'

'Nah! I'm fine, honest Injun.'

Something in Harry's expression made Joe falter. He dug deep and closed his fingers around his last remaining sixpence. *Don't you bloody dare!* screeched his mind. *Not for a bloody stranger!* He actually felt panic rising in his chest as he began to withdraw the money. 'You got enough cash on you, Harry?'

'Of course I've got cash!' cried Harry, backing off in theatrical horror. 'Do I look like some kinda bum?'

Joe laughed. He pushed the sixpence back into his pocket. 'Do like I told you tomorrow, all right? Go talk to the carpenter's gaffer. They're in dire need of help to finish the stage.'

Harry waved his assent as he walked away, already half swallowed by fog.

DOWN AT THE quays the wind hammered sleet into Joe's face, and he couldn't help but grin. This weather was going to be great for business. The toffs would be murdering each other for the want of a cab home. Ducking his head against the ferocious wind, Joe took a right onto the bridge and began to hurry across. He wasn't certain he should go home after work tonight, though. Truth was, Mickey had looked bad today: that grin. If some shleeveen had told him about the extra money…Joe shuddered.

Perhaps it would be best to sleep at the depot. It wouldn't be the first time, and probably wouldn't be the last. Joe tightened his grip on the sixpence in his pocket. Another four months. That's what Saul had said. Four short months, and then they'd have enough. All Joe had to do was hang on; all he had to do was keep quiet and work hard, and—

Something big knocked into him, and he was thrown hard against the stone railing of the bridge. 'Hey, watch it!' he cried, jerking an elbow into the ribs of whatever drunk had barrelled into him.

A large hand grabbed his wrist. A voice hissed in his ear: 'Watch it yourself, you little rat shit.' And Joe knew he was in trouble.

Someone punched the back of his head, and his face smacked stone as his body was slammed against the balustrade. A big man pressed his whole weight against Joe and held him as unseen hands invaded the pockets of his trousers and jacket. Joe lifted his head, and another punch slammed his face against stone. His vision exploded with stars. Blood ran hot over his eye.

They took his sixpence. They took Saul's book. They took the last crust of bread he'd saved from his dinner. The shame of helplessness stung almost as much as the blows.

You bastards, he thought, struggling hard. *You bastards. I hope you rot.*

'That's it? That's all he's got? A lousy sixpence and a mouldy book?'

At the sound of Mickey's voice, Joe stopped struggling. It was as if something inside him turned off, something drained away, and he was left cold and numb, and empty in his chest. He barely felt it when someone punched the back of his head again, barely felt the extra twist Mickey gave his arm before releasing him to slump against the balustrade.

Saul's book was flung into the air. Joe watched it tumble through the gaslight, the pages fanning and shivering as it sailed past the rail to plummet to the river.

To the Moon, whispered Tina.

To the Moon, Joe thought.

'Better fetch it,' said Mickey.

Joe blinked at him, not understanding. Then Mickey's grin sliced through the numbness, and Joe knew. He spun, panicked, but it was too late – his cousins grabbed him. Silently, they heaved him up and over the balustrade, and dropped him to the darkness below.

JOE HAD NO recollection of the fall – just that one moment he was in the buffeting air; then his nose and ears were filled with water, as he fought the sucking grip of the river. A scream exploded from him in soundless bubbles.

It was so dark! A freezing void of blackness, pulling him down.

Something huge loomed. Trailing slime brushed his face. Then he was inhaling air. Gasping, he thrashed against the sheer cliff of the quay wall, his windmilling arms and legs churning the water, which went into his mouth and his eyes and caught against what little breath he had.

The slime-drenched wall of the quay slipped and slid under the numb scrabble of his fingers. Then he was under, his mouth filled with putrid water, the weight of his clothes pulling him down. He was blind in the dark. Which direction was up? Where was the surface?

He had never learned to swim.

His head hit stone, and he was out in the thrashing air again: the foam and the chaos. There was a crack of cold-dulled pain as his elbow hit stone. His ribs impacted with the brutal edge of a weed-slicked shelf.

The boat steps!

Joe flung out an arm, trying to grab hold. But his hand simply slithered back, completely numb of feeling. The water swelled, and he was rolled, helpless, from the steps, his arms and legs dead from the cold.

Sleet bit his lips as his face turned one more time to the wind.

As he sank, he saw boots carefully descending the steps. He saw the trailing billow of a royal-blue overcoat. A hand as black as coal reached, and was lost as water closed against the light.

JOE OPENED HIS eyes to something pallid and lifeless lying in front of his face. A dead fish. Vaguely disgusted, Joe tried to push it away. His fingers barely twitched, and he realised he was looking at his own hand. His gaze drifted past it to the mud-spattered hem of a royal-blue overcoat. A man was crouched on the filthy steps beside him, leaning away, straining to snag something from the water. He succeeded and sat back on his heels, looking down at what he'd retrieved. He grunted.

'This is a good book,' he said. His voice was very deep and rich. When he turned, Joe recognised him as the carriage driver from the theatre. 'This is yours, Matthew? I do not recall you being inclined to read.'

He held up Saul's dripping copy of *From the Earth to the Moon*. The book was swollen with water. A fat, bloated frog of a book. The sight of it made Joe giggle.

The carriage driver frowned and brought his face level with Joe's. 'Matthew?'

'Have t'get t'work…'

Clumsily, Joe attempted to push himself to his feet. He barely made it to his knees. The carriage driver stood to help. He had been taking the brunt of the wind, and as soon as he moved the cold sliced through Joe's soaked clothes, right down to the bone. Joe moaned, and the man took his arm. His grip was vice-like and devil-hot, a band of furnace-heat through the sodden fabric of Joe's jacket.

'You need to get warm, Matthew. You have been away too long to suffer this cold without ill effect.'

Joe began to struggle up the steps. 'Need…get…t'*work*,' he croaked. ''e'll leave… 'thout me.' His lips were growing too numb to move.

The carriage driver supported him up the steps with an arm around his waist, Saul's sodden book in his free hand. 'Come back to the hotel,' he urged. 'Come talk to Cornelius.'

The heat from him was intense, unnatural, cloying. Even through the crippling pain of the cold, Joe felt suffocated by it. He elbowed his way free, gasping, and staggered towards the bridge. The man followed, his voice raised against the wind. 'Matthew!' he cried. 'He has been miserable since you left. Give him a chance. He meant none of what he said!'

Joe tried to run, but his legs were wet concrete; the man easily caught up. 'Here,' he said. Joe flinched at a sudden whipping flutter of cloth. Then came beautiful warmth – glorious warmth – as the man's blue overcoat settled around him like a cloak. The man tried to support him again, that strange, trapped feeling closing in. 'Let go!' Joe yelled, shoving him away.

The carriage driver stepped back, his hands up in defeat. The wind tugged at his fine white shirt, fluttered his crimson necktie, jerked at the tails of his scarlet waistcoat. 'Keep the coat,' he said.

'Don't touch me again,' said Joe as he backed away, his hand up in warning.

'Keep the coat,' repeated the carriage driver.

Joe backed across the bridge, then turned clumsily and stumbled his way down the quays towards the warren of Temple Bar. The man did not follow.

Auditions

Harry found Tina in the wings, her arms grimly folded, watching the auditions from the shadows backstage. 'Hey,' he whispered. 'How's Joe feeling?'

Tina shrugged unhappily. 'He says he's grand. He says he just needs to lie down awhile.'

'Nice of Miss Ursula to let him use her dressing-room.'

'She's a nice lady,' murmured Tina. 'Under it all…'

She drifted to silence, her eyes on the performers onstage, her mind miles away. She was obviously eaten up with worry.

Harry had been impressed by her lack of fussing. When Joe had turned up for morning break, and they'd seen the state his cousins had reduced him to, Harry had wanted to punch something. Despite his claims, Joe had looked anything but 'grand'. He had looked so far from grand – his heated cheeks stark in his chalky face – that Harry had been scared for him. It was all too familiar: too uncomfortably close to memories of Harry's brother Armin. Of Armin's horrible last days.

'Here we go,' whispered Tina. A sister act, Milly and Patsy Harris, had taken to the stage. All frills and curls and bows, they were just launching into a syrup-drenched rendition of *Old Dog Tray*. 'Miss Ursula's on after these two. She's doing the Scottish play.'

'She won't be chosen,' said Harry. Tina frowned at him, and he shrugged. 'She won't,' he insisted. 'I've been watching all morning. They're only going for the dog and pony acts – the tumblers, the contortionists – the real carnie entertainment. That couple who sing opera? Out. The man who recites poems? Out! The only artiste chosen who had anything like a bit of the highbrow to him was the piano player.'

'Professor Henman?'

Harry nodded. 'If your Miss Ursula presents them with Shakespeare, she's—'

'Next!' came the call from the auditorium.

The little girls onstage faltered in mid-song. Their mother fluttered anxiously in the far wings. 'W…would you like a different tune, sir?' called Milly, peering past the brightness of the limes to the darkness beyond. 'We do a lovely version of—'

'You're too young. Next!'

'We—'

'NEXT, damn your eyes! NEXT!'

The little girls leapt in shock at the unexpected roar. Patsy burst into tears, and they fled to their mother's scandalised arms.

'Never mind, m'dears,' whispered Miss Ursula as they stumbled past her in the far wings. 'It has happened to the best of us.' She spread her arms, and the glitter on her magnificent costume haloed her in light as she swept onto the stage.

'Oh God,' groaned Harry. 'She's ancient! What's she thinking in that dress?'

'Shh, Harry. Listen to her.'

The old lady stopped mid-stage, her kohl-ringed eyes glaring out at the surrounding darkness. There was silence. She lifted her arm. 'Come,' she ordered. 'Come, you spirits that tend on mortal thoughts; unsex me here. Fill me from my crown unto my toe, top-full of direst cruelty.'

She paused, searching the dark air of the auditorium, as if waiting for the spirits to come forth as ordered, and she looked so compelling that Harry felt himself lean forward – drawn in.

Miss Ursula pressed her hand to her heart. 'Make thick my blood. Stop up the access and passage to remorse, so that no compunctious visitings of nature shall shake my fell purpose, nor keep peace between the effect and it. Come to my woman's breasts. Take my milk for gall, you murdering ministers, wherever in your sightless substances you wait on nature's mischief.'

Another long silence followed as the old woman awaited an answer from the ringing void. The light from her dress shivered against her papery skin and gave her face all the authority of age as, once again, she held her arm out to the darkness and commanded it.

'Come, thick night, and pall thee in the dunnest smoke of hell, that my keen knife see not the wound it makes, nor heaven peep through the blanket of the dark, to cry unto me, "Hold."'

A whisper came from the darkness. 'No.'

The old woman paused, frowning as if uncertain of what she had heard.

'No,' whispered the voice in the darkness again, and then, as if in panic, it shouted: 'No! No! Off!'

Tina stepped forward, Harry at her side, both of them appalled by this terrible reaction to what had been a mesmerising performance.

'Get off!' cried the now unmistakable voice of Lord Wolcroft. 'Get off the stage, you old *crone*! AND TAKE OFF THAT DAMNED DRESS!'

Miss Ursula froze for the briefest of moments. Then she graced her audience with a stiff bow and swept from the stage.

'Miss U,' cried Tina, rushing to her. But Miss Ursula simply held a hand out in dismissal, and then continued on down the steps to the backstage corridor, where her costume caught whatever dim light it could and cast it in glitter onto the shabby ceiling and walls before she rounded the corner and was out of sight.

'Poor lady,' whispered Tina. 'Poor, poor…' She made a helpless gesture. Then, suddenly, she was angry – she was raging – and Harry had to step away from her as she kicked the sandbags with a ferocity he hadn't witnessed in her before.

Harry cast about for words of comfort, but before he could even speak Tina had contained herself, her arms wrapped tight around her chest, her breathing deep in the light-filtered half dark.

'Joe knew,' she said. 'He told me Miss U was too old. He said that's all the world can see of her now. How old she is. And he was *right*.'

She compressed her mouth and eyes against more rage. 'Joe,' she whispered.

'He'll be fine,' soothed Harry.

'Have you *seen what they did to him*?'

'He'll be *fine*, Tina. He's a tough guy.'

'He's never going to escape them, Harry. I don't think he knows how much he *needs* to escape. How much *I* need him to—' She cut herself off, took another deep breath, as if telling herself to calm down. 'You've no idea the kind of place Joe lives, Harry; the place we both come from. You can't imagine the people we grew up with, the street we grew up on. It's like a trap, and everyone he knows is caught in it. They all say they hate it, but they'd rather see each other *dead* than free of it.'

'You did okay,' said Harry quietly.

'But I had *Fran*, didn't I? I had the Lady Nana. No one tells them what to do. They just said, "Feck the lot of yehs," and we dragged ourselves out of there. But Joe…poor Joe. He has no one. Only stones weighing him down. Only a snare he can't seem to—'

She made a sharp noise suddenly, and turned for the steps.

'Tina, where are you going?'

'This is not going to happen anymore, Harry. I've decided. Joe's not going back. I'm not letting him. I'm going to his gaff right now, while he's asleep. I'm going to get his things. I'm bringing them back here, and he's *never* going back.'

'Say! You can't just make the chap's decisions like that!'

'Oh, can I not?'

Harry rushed to the top of the steps. 'Tina!' he hissed. '*Tina*, you're making a huge mistake.'

But she was already gone.

Practicalities

VINCENT HAD NEGLECTED the first round of auditions in favour of inquiring after Matthew at the stables where he worked. Returning to the theatre no better off for accurate information, he was surprised to find the backstage door blocked by a girl. She wore a bright-blue bonnet and scarf, and was in the process of angrily buttoning a yellow tartan coat. She glanced up at the sudden influx of wintry light as Vincent came in, and rather than push his way past, he gestured that she should finish what she was doing.

'Thank you, mister,' she said. 'I'll be out of your way now.'

Vincent liked the way she looked him directly in the eye when she said this, her grim efficiency as she tugged on her gloves. Her hair and eyes were almost as dark as Raquel's, her skin as creamy-fresh as Raquel's had been when they'd first met.

'You're Lord Wolcroft's man,' she said.

Suddenly it struck him who she was. 'You are the seamstress.'

She nodded, confused.

'Cornelius told me of you: a pretty girl carrying a pretty dress that shimmered like the sea.'

Her sudden discomfort was charming, her disconcerted frown a delight. Vincent had an urge, suddenly, like a flash of old heat, to see this pretty girl in that pretty dress – to shine a light upon her and make her sparkle like the sea. How well Cornelius knew him.

The girl shifted, obviously nervous under his frank examination of her, but she restrained herself from looking around for help. Vincent admired that. 'I have been looking for the stable boy,' he said. 'Joe, as you call him. He hasn't returned from his luncheon, apparently. I believe you are his friend?'

She nodded uncertainly.

'How long have you known him? The stable boy?'

'A…a long time. Since we were children.'

He quelled a flash of irritation. 'Come now. No lies. How long?'

She just stared at him, and Vincent sighed. 'I want you to give him a message,' he said. 'Tell him I am not fooled by his rough clothes and speech. Tell him I *know* who he is.'

Vincent leaned close. The girl shrank back as he spoke low into her ear. 'I had not been certain at first, but when I saw those men accost him – throw him to the water like that, like so much trash – I knew. Tell him this cannot continue. Tell him that his mother and I miss him. Tell him…tell him that we should both be *much happier* were he home.'

The girl remained motionless, her small hands clenched. Their faces were very close. She smelled faintly of violets. After a moment she glanced up and met his eyes. There was a real core of steel beneath her fear, a genuine ferocity that thrilled him in a way he had not felt in years. Vincent had no doubt that if he tried to touch her, she would fight.

The thought made him chuckle. Drawing back, he gestured that he would like to pass. The girl pressed close to the wall, and he moved on.

CORNELIUS WAS JUST where Vincent had left him, sitting in the middle row of the dress circle, by the aisle. There was a tray with fine china cups, a silver coffee pot and good pastries on the seat beside him. They had not been there when Vincent had left for the stables. It would seem that the theatre was going all-out to fete their impresario.

The stage manager was leaning over from the aisle, murmuring and pointing things out on the performance list, but Cornelius was only half-listening, his attention focused on the stage steps as if doggedly awaiting Vincent's return from backstage. The stage manager continued to speak as Vincent approached, but Cornelius flung up a hand to silence him. The manager straightened, his face stiff with disapproval as Vincent slipped past him and reclaimed his seat at Cornelius' side.

'The next performances shall start within the hour,' said the manager. 'If that is to your pleasure, Lord Wolcroft.'

'Auditions,' corrected Vincent.

The manager's jaw twitched. 'Beg pardon?' he asked tightly.

Vincent took his time, pouring himself a coffee and taking a pastry before looking at him. 'They are auditions,

Mr Simmons. We have not yet decided which performers shall be chosen – so they are *auditions*.' He took a large bite of the pastry and chewed, holding the manager's eye.

'Be sure they do start within the hour,' said Cornelius softly. 'We do not have all day.'

Vincent watched the manager leave, then spat the mouthful of chewed pastry into his hand and dropped it to the plate. He swilled the coffee around his mouth; savoured the almost forgotten process of swallowing.

Cornelius eyed all of this with horror. 'What in God's name do you think you're doing?'

'I have never done anything in God's name, cully.' Vincent chanced another small mouthful of coffee and swallowed, suddenly in tremendously good form.

'You shall make yourself *ill*.'

'May chance, but you know, I believe I might actually have begun to enjoy myself.'

Cornelius' scowl made him grin. Nevertheless, Vincent placed the cup on its saucer and spread his hands in surrender. 'I am done,' he promised. 'No more.'

Cornelius eyed the cup as if he would like to smash it, and, despite his amusement, Vincent felt a pang of guilt. He knew this uncharacteristic shortness of temper was a direct result of Cornelius' physical distress.

Never mind, cully, he thought. *Soon you will be home and this torment will end.*

Cornelius nodded tightly.

I saw the little seamstress, added Vincent, attempting to soothe him.

'And?'

She is delightful.

Cornelius brightened. *I knew it! I knew you would enjoy her. Never fear, Captain, I shall obtain her for you.*

Vincent thought about this a moment, then waved his hand. *No,* he said. *Leave her.*

Cornelius stared.

Vincent struggled to articulate his reasons. The girl was, as Cornelius had described her, oddly moving. Caught in the chiaroscuro of that gloomy corridor, she had been arresting in a way that went beyond prettiness. It was almost as though she emitted an aura – a magnetic field, perhaps – and Vincent found it particularly compelling. It was foolishness to leave her behind. Yet…Vincent thought again of Raquel, of Raquel's decline, the calcification of her once passionate, if fragile, vivacity, and he realised he did not want that vibrant girl diminished. He did not want her used. It was as simple as that. *Besides,* he thought to himself, *she is Matthew's friend. What would he think?*

'Let her go,' he murmured. 'The ballet chorus will suffice for me.'

Cornelius grimly turned his attention to the list of players he held in his lap. He pretended to read, but his entire body was stiff with offence. Vincent sighed. Cornelius never did react well to the rejection of a gift. In an attempt to move the situation along, he leaned across to read the performance list.

'Raquel will adore that little piano player.'

'She did once love the piano…'

'And the dog act is an inspired choice. And the woman with the monkey. Both will certainly appeal to the children.'

The corner of Cornelius' mouth twitched with distaste, and Vincent threw his hands up in frustration. 'Oh, come now! You cannot mean to have second thoughts about the animals?'

'You know what the children are capable of.'

'Cornelius, we are not discussing *torture* here. Simply a shorter than usual life – a speedier conclusion to the inevitably limited time on earth faced by all mortal creatures.'

'I cannot stand the idea of an animal suffering,' said Cornelius softly. 'Mankind deserves all it gets, for the most part, but animals…Animals are entirely innocent and incapable of cruelty.'

'You must never have witnessed a cat toy with a mouse then, friend.'

Cornelius shrugged. He continued to stare at the list, his fine face troubled, and Vincent knew where his mind was. When Cornelius had carried that bloodstained hatbox past him on the stairs, the waves of pain coming from it had fizzed against Vincent's skin. The despair – even from such a tiny creature, so little aware of its own existence – had been astounding.

When Vincent had made his way to the playroom, there had been a pool of blood on the floorboards, pairs of scissors, an orderly collection of bloodstained hatpins. He had gazed at the multitude of bloody boot-prints that tracked to and from the sleeping children. Apparently they had got up many times during the poor creature's ordeal – to adjust something on its body, perhaps, before taking their places again to watch. Vincent had to admit he had been shocked at that – it had turned even his stomach. He had had second thoughts, then, about having allowed this to happen. About having left it for Cornelius to handle.

Cornelius' quiet voice intruded on this memory. 'She had not even tried to stop them, Captain. The door to their room was unlocked, and yet…'

Yes, Raquel had been sitting motionless at the sewing-room window, her hands clenched in her lap, her eyes fixed on the path down which Cornelius was disappearing. Vincent had stared at her until she had turned to meet his gaze. Her expression had been a challenge. Everything about her was dark these days – her dark eyes, her heavy coils of braided hair, the dark-green of her dresses. These new, severe fashions suited her now in a way the old ones no longer could. Even the paleness of her creamy skin seemed to exist as a complement to the darkness.

She had tightened her hands and lifted her chin. *Spare me your disapprobation, Vicente. They are Cornelius' creatures, not mine.*

Vincent stretched his arm across the back of the seat, clutched his friend's shoulder and squeezed. 'Raquel is not what she once was. It is perhaps best not to expect too much of her…especially in relation to the children.'

'I do not understand,' whispered Cornelius. 'I do not understand this wanton cruelty within them.'

'We cannot help what moves them, cully. So…' He tapped the list. 'Monkeys and dancing poodles and parrots on sticks. The more the merrier. We can but hope they do their job. If they do not, well, perhaps we can arrange a dogfight?'

It had been meant to amuse, but Cornelius made a sharp sound of disgust. 'Don't be revolting! How can even you be so profane as to suggest such twisted amusements might sustain an angel!'

Vincent released his shoulder. 'This from the man who planned to display an innocent girl like a bauble, that I might have my enjoyment of her. In your philosophy, that is worthy food for angels, is it? Cornelius, it would be so refreshing to have just *one* conversation that does not end up marooned within your hopeless superstitions. Do you think it is at all possible, friend, that you might just this once reconcile yourself to a discussion of the practicalities without hiding behind your usual romantic self-deceit?'

There was a stretch of scalding silence, then Cornelius drew himself up. 'Speaking of self-deceit,' he said, 'did you retrieve your overcoat?'

Vincent sat back. He did not reply.

Cornelius would not relent. 'You have spoken with that boy? It is clear to you, now, that he is just like all the others? That he is not—'

Vincent leapt to his feet, cutting him off in mid-sentence. He vacillated for a moment, ready to stalk away. Then, without warning, he found himself roaring towards the stage. 'Ahoy there! Simmons! Are we to wait all day and night on your damned pleasure?'

The stage manager came into the light, shielding his eyes to try to see who had shouted. Uncertain, he called, 'A…another thirty minutes, Lord Wolcroft? Will another thirty minutes be acceptable?'

Vincent did not reply. Instead, he arranged the tails of his jacket behind him and expressionlessly resumed his seat. Not looking at Cornelius, he lifted another pastry and took a large bite.

Onstage, the manager continued to squint into the lights, his whiskers bristling in anxiety. 'Lord Wolcroft?' he ventured.

'*Yes*,' snapped Cornelius, his attention on Vincent's grim consuming of cake. 'Yes. Thirty minutes. Just hurry it up, you swab, or I'll gut you myself.'

The Purse

TINA WHISPERED IN his mind, *Did you not trust me, Joe?* and Joe answered, amazed, *Tina? You said you weren't meant to speak to me like this anymore.* She fell silent, and Joe woke confused and achey, not sure if it had been a dream.

She was standing at the foot of Miss Ursula's little sofa, looking down at him where he lay. She had a strange, wary expression on her face. For a moment Joe thought he must still be asleep, it was so odd. Then he saw the bundle she held and he recognised his spare shirt, his razor, his blanket, his book and his pencil. He struggled to his feet at the realisation that everything he owned in the world was held in Tina's arms.

'Have you been to my gaff?' he cried.

At that moment, Harry rushed through the dressing-room door, calling out in a hushed backstage shout, 'Tina! They told me you were back! Did you get his—' He halted at the realisation that Joe was awake. 'Oh,' he said. 'Joe…uh, hey there.'

Joe ignored him. At first he was simply filled with horror that Tina had been *there*. She'd gone *there*. Then the implication of what she had in her arms hit him, and panic set in. Oh God. What had she done?

She held the things out to him, and he snatched them from her arms. Rooting quickly through the meagre pile, relief flooded him. It wasn't there. Thank God. She hadn't found it. 'Did Mickey see you take these?' he said.

Tina shook her head, her face grim and watchful.

'I'm bringing these home, Tina. I'll be there and back before they get in from the morning shift. No one need know—'

'The whole street saw me. There's no keeping it a secret.'

He looked her up and down, suddenly aware of the mud spattering her coat, the mess of her hair. 'What happened?'

'Never mind that. The women just threw some dirt.'

'Jesus, Tina,' he whispered. 'I can't believe you went to that place.'

'Don't go back, Joe.'

He groaned. 'You don't understand.'

She stepped close, that strange, hard expression on her face. She gripped his arm. 'Don't go back,' she said. 'Do as I'm asking you, for once in your damned life, and don't go back.'

She was so earnest, so *set*-looking, he almost lifted his hand to touch her. 'I have to,' he said softly. 'I...Tina, I have a plan.'

'I've never heard of any plan. You'd think you'd have told me there was a plan.'

'I'll tell you in a little while,' he said, his eyes searching hers. 'I just...I just want everything to be certain first.'

In an unexpected gesture, Tina laid her cold hand on his heated cheek. He shut his eyes, his lips parting in pleasure, and she shifted her palm to his forehead. 'You're awful warm,' she whispered. 'I think you're very sick.'

'I'll be all right.'

And he would, too. So long as his secret was safe, and his plan was on track, everything would be all right.

The blood froze in him at Tina's next words.

'I found something under the floorboards in your gaff, Joe. In the corner where you sleep. Hidden under your blanket. I dislodged the board when I was taking down your shirt, and I saw it.'

He opened his eyes. *Oh no, Tina. No.*

'Margaret Reynolds' kids had followed me up to the room. They saw me lift it out; they saw me open it up. They thought it was treasure.'

'Oh Jesus, Tina. Tell me no.'

Tina reached into her pocket and withdrew his mother's purse. She held it out to him. 'I'm really hoping this is yours, Joe. I really am. Otherwise I've just robbed your cousins of nearly eighty pounds, and I don't fancy our chances of surviving when they find out.'

Harry came to peer over her shoulder. He glanced at Joe, then back to the money, and Joe knew what he was thinking: how had a raggedy-arsed street-rat like him got his hands on so much treasure? Without taking his eyes from Harry's face, Joe took the cracked leather purse and shoved it into the inside pocket of his jacket. He sat back down on the sofa, folding his arms.

Harry continued to stare at him, his gaze as piercing as a hypnotist's. 'I've never seen so much cash in my life,' he said. 'Where did you steal it?'

Before Joe could answer, Tina stepped between them,

her burgundy skirts filling his view. There was a sharp slap. When she came to sit by Joe's side, Harry was clutching his cheek and glaring. 'Say!' he cried.

'Tina,' gasped Joe, 'there was no need for—'

'You can shut up and all, Joe Gosling. The only reason I haven't slapped *you* is because you're sick.'

She sat rigidly staring at nothing for a moment, her cheeks pink, her expression furious. Then she reached and grabbed Joe's hand. He flinched in anticipation of more unaccountable female violence. But Tina just dragged his hand onto her lap and held it there, clutched between her own. It was the first time she had done this since they were children, and Joe marvelled at how small her hand was within his big chapped paw. He chanced gently closing his fingers on hers.

'All these years I've been worrying over you and crying over you, and thinking you were starving. All these years I thought them bloody gougers were stealing half your money every week and leaving you without.' Tina compressed her lips and shook her head, seemingly too angry to go on – but still she held on to Joe's hand.

'They *are* stealing half me money,' he said softly. 'But only from the wages they know about.'

She looked sideways at him, and he smiled. 'I've had three jobs since I was seven years old, Tina Kelly. I don't get drunk. I never smoked—'

'You eat less than a cat,' she whispered. 'You never wear a coat.'

'Mickey sold me coat,' he reminded her.

'Jesus, Joe,' she whispered. '*Jesus.*' She closed her eyes and held his hand to her mouth, squeezing it tight. He felt the heat of her breath on his fingers as she gritted her teeth against some strong emotion. A desire to hit him, maybe – or hug him? He hoped the latter.

'You could have been having a lovely time all these years!' she cried suddenly.

'I want more than that.'

'You could have been in a *nice* lodging. With a *nice* landlady.'

'Pissing away me money on rent and frivolities, with nowhere to stash me savings without some busybody snuffling around when I'm in work. What the lads don't know has never hurt me, Tina. They'd never a bloody clue there was anything more than fleas and mouse shit under me blankets. Until today, that is.' There was a moment of silence between them. Then he said, without much hope, 'Maybe the kids won't say anything?'

'They ran off up the street screaming for Mickey.'

Joe grimaced at her, but he wasn't angry. Not really. He was just tired suddenly, bone-tired and weary to his soul. He'd been careful such a long time. Mickey had never considered him much worth pissing on – but now? Tina had just shoved him straight into the spotlight, stark and vulnerable, with a fistful of money in each hand. He sighed. 'What am I going to do?'

'Eighty pounds is a lot of money to have saved,' said Harry. 'Three jobs or not.' He was still staring at Joe with that fixed intensity, demanding an explanation.

Joe was tempted to cut him dead with a sneer. To hell with Harry if he thought Joe was a thief. But Tina was squinting sideways at him now, doing the figures in her head, and Joe knew she deserved more than a gutter-boy's guff and bluster.

'Me da saved most of it,' he said. 'He spent his whole life saving, it seems. After he died, and me ma moved us in with *them*, she taught me how to hide the money from them and how to keep secretly adding to the purse. And after she was dead…I just kept doing it.'

'But why, Joe?' asked Tina. *'Why?'*

Joe saw it in her face, the horror at all the things his mam had endured, all the hardships she'd made him endure in that squalid room in the care of those brutes, when the two of them could at least have had their own place. He shook his head.

'I don't know what Ma and Da were saving for. Sometimes I wonder if *they* even knew. Maybe they'd have just kept on saving until they died of old age. Year after year, shoving money into that purse under the floorboards. It getting fatter and them getting thinner. I wonder if they'd have died having never done anything at all…'

'They *did*,' said Tina. 'They died with all that money, and never did anything. And now you—'

'No, *not me*,' cried Joe. 'I *know* what I'm doing with it. For a long time I didn't. I just kept squirrelling it away week after week like me ma had shown me, and I didn't know what the hell I was doing it for – but I know now, Tina.' He gently squeezed her hand. 'I've known for ages what all them years of shite were for.'

'A future,' breathed Harry, his face illuminated with fervent understanding.

Joe nodded. 'Not just tuppence-worth of comfort that's pissed away in an hour. A *proper* future; one worth sacrificing for. I have a plan.'

Harry leapt to his feet. 'So do I!' he cried. 'And it's not

to be a darned carpenter. What the heck was I thinking? I hope I'm not too late.'

'Where are you going?'

'To get my place in those auditions. I won't get to be a magician sitting on my ass dreaming about it!' He dived for the door.

'Break a leg!' called Tina.

Harry paused, then ran back. He grabbed Joe's hand and shook it. 'Don't go back to that cesspool, Joe. There's more than one way to skin a cat, and there are plenty of places to sleep in this theatre until you get yourself sorted.'

'I can't do that!'

'Why, of course you can. Free rent? No bedbugs? Come on, Gosling.' He winked. 'You wouldn't believe how easy it is to get past a locked door.'

Joe had to smile, so earnest were those fierce blue eyes and that handshake. He lost the smile pretty damned quick when Harry leaned across the table and kissed Tina on her mouth.

'Just for luck!' he cried, already running out the door.

Tina put her fingers to her lips, her cheeks cherry-red.

'Hey,' said Joe. 'You needn't look so delighted!'

She turned to him with smiling eyes. She opened her mouth to say something.

Mr Sheridan's scandalised voice cut her off. 'God preserve us!' His massive bulk filled the dressing-room door, his horrified eyes fixed on their joined hands. '*Miss Kelly!* This is *not* your own private *courting parlour!*'

They leapt up and apart like scalded cats. Sheridan crowded Joe out into the back corridor, pushed him out into the alley, and slammed the door on his face.

Unbalanced and empty after the warm company of the dressing-room, Joe dithered, uncertain of what to do. He looked down at his hand, which Tina had, only moments before, held clutched in her own. Snowflakes drifted from the gloomy sky and fell like small kisses onto his palm. Joe closed his fingers over them.

The door slammed open behind him, and he turned to find Tina leaning out into the cold.

Her breath streamed out when she hissed his name. 'Joe!'

He stood like an idiot, grinning at her, his fingers still closed over the feel of her palm on his.

She thrust out her arm. 'Give it to me!' Then again, impatiently: 'Give it to me, you eejit! Unless you want them nicking it!'

It took him a moment to understand. Then he dug the purse from his pocket and handed it over.

'I'll keep it safe for you,' she whispered, and then, incredibly, she kissed him – her lips soft and surprisingly cool, her breath a warm cloud around them in the snowy air – before ducking inside and slamming the door.

Séance

Dear Mama,

Here I am, only two days ashore and already a phenomenon! The manager says he has never seen such skill of prestidigitational art. He has ordered posters printed with my name in top billings – Harry Weiss, the Great Houdini! How's that for your boy, Ma? I will be sending you billings from all over the world soon.

I hope you aren't still sore at Pa for having slipped me the fare – as you can see, I have returned most of it with this letter! Your boy finds himself very well-in, and set up nice and cosy already, Ma! The Irish are not, as you'd feared they would be, unkind to those not of the Catholic persuasion, and I am well lodged, with a cosy room (a fireplace and wardrobe and full board!) and an introduction to the community over here. My week's wage goes a long way over here, so I can cheerfully send my mama and my papa back their investment in me without any dent in my pocket!

Harry nibbled his pencil and squinted in the dim backstage light, thinking hard. If he could find a penny-printer willing to press a single handbill, he could include a flyer with his stage name on it – The Great Houdini! – that would thrill Ma to no end.

He looked at the little stack of money he was enclosing with the letter. It was all the savings he had. He had intended sending his first week's wage home as part-payment for the boat fare. There was no first week's wage on the horizon now, of course, but Harry couldn't stand the thought of wandering about with a pocketful of cash while his ma was tearing her hair out trying to pay the rent.

He smiled at the thought of her opening the envelope and all the money showering out. Then she'd unfold the handbill, see his name on the top, and turn and show it to all the others.

Mein Ehrich! she'd say. *The Great Houdini!*

Yes, he'd go tomorrow and get that bill printed up. Grinning, he set pencil to paper again. *I am enclosing a copy of the bill Mr Simmons (stage manager) has had printed up. As you can see, I am using my new stage name—*

'Harry?'

Tina stepped into the wings. Harry shoved the letter and pencil in his pocket as she offered him the steaming mug she carried. 'Oh, say!' he whispered. 'Thanks! How's Mr Gosling?'

She sat on the sandbags beside him. 'He just finished his shift. I snuck him into Miss U's room. He's promised to have a bit of a rest.'

'He'll be back to himself before you know it,' said Harry.

'Mm hmm.'

'You really should go home, Tina. Joe and I don't have a heck of a lot to lose here, but it won't do you any good to be caught hanging about after lockup like this.'

She cut him a sideways look that conveyed just about all she had to say on the subject of her leaving. 'How'd you do in the auditions?' she asked.

Harry sighed. 'Not well,' he said.

'You and poor Miss Ursula both.'

Miss Ursula. Harry hadn't seen her since her dignified exit from the stage. 'Will she be all right?' he asked Tina.

She gave him that sideways look again – of course the old lady was not going to be all right. 'The theatre's no place to grow old, Harry.'

It was a bald statement, and both of them knew the horrible truth of it too well. To fill the silence that followed, Harry took his cards from his pocket and began practising riffle and faro shuffles in the near dark.

Tina watched him. 'Will *you* be all right, Harry?'

He shrugged. 'I guess I shouldn't have tried the magic act without an assistant. But I'd no shills for the mind-reading, couldn't even get them *interested* in the card tricks...I should have just done some fortune-telling and left it at that.'

'I used to tell fortunes. When I was a little kid.'

'Oh?'

'Fran made me stop. She didn't like how they used to come true.'

Harry grinned. 'Some people take it very seriously.'

There was an uncertain pause. 'I think I scared her.'

Oh, thought Harry. *That's sad.* 'Well, like I said, some people take it very seriously.'

'Joe was never scared of me. Joe...Joe's been very good to me, Harry.'

Harry thought of Joe's thin, street-wary face, his moments of unexpected gentleness. Silence weighed down on them once more. Harry let the cards run through his fingers, back-palmed the locator ace, cut it single-handed into the middle of the pack.

The abrupt rustle of Tina's skirts startled him, and he looked up as she surged to her feet. He thought maybe she'd heard Joe coming, but she just stood there, staring towards the moon-washed stage. 'Harry?' she whispered. 'Someone's coming.'

The tone of her voice had him stowing the deck and rising cautiously to her side. 'What do you mean?'

'Someone…that man. That *man* is coming. Lord Wolcroft.'

Before Harry could say, *How could you possibly know that?* the theatre lights went on, making him jump.

'He's here!' hissed Tina. 'Oh, Harry! He's here! What'll we do?'

There were voices in the auditorium now: the sound of people murmuring to each other as they neared the stage. Harry grabbed Tina and swivelled her towards the ladder to the catwalks. 'Climb up! Hurry! Just leave the darned cup! Climb up, before they catch you and you lose your job!'

Tina grabbed the hem of her heavy skirt, hoisted it over her knees and scrambled up the ladder with surprising agility. She had only just reached the top, with Harry climbing after her, when the first footsteps rang out on the stage.

Miss Ursula's plummy voice said, 'The witching hour approaches! If you do not object, Lord Wolcroft, I shall light the candles and lay out the spirit board so that when the others arrive, we may commence at once to commune with the dead.'

Tina leaned over the top of the catwalk's sandbag wall. Harry scrambled to her side. There was a terrific view of the stage, but Tina did not seem interested. Instead, she was craning her neck to see down the back stairs, and Harry realised that she was watching for Joe.

'Say,' whispered Harry. 'You knew that dandy was coming before the lights even went on. How did you know it was him?'

Tina shrugged. 'Sometimes I just know things.' She switched her attention to Cornelius Wolcroft, genuine unease creasing her face. 'I don't like him, Harry, or that man who works for him. There's something wrong with them.'

Unaware of their scrutiny, Lord Wolcroft was strolling around, shaking hands with the various bohemian-looking gents and ladies to whom Miss Ursula was introducing him. Despite his beautiful clothes, he looked terrible, with great dark rings under his eyes and a dewy sheen of sweat on his pasty skin. Harry wondered: was the man an opium fiend? He certainly had the look. 'Miss Ursula's getting on fine with him, considering the way he treated her earlier.'

'We find our uses as we may.'

'Pardon?'

'That's what Miss U always says. She's being what she calls "diplomatic".'

Harry watched the old woman graciously introduce Wolcroft to each newcomer. *She must be a fine actress*, he thought. If Wolcroft had bellowed at *him* like that, Harry sure as heck wouldn't have come back later just to smile and take his arm.

'Lord Wolcroft, Lord of Fargeal, I believe,' drawled a gentleman, shaking Wolcroft's hand.

Wolcroft smiled tightly. 'Among other things,' he said.

'I took the liberty of looking you up in the lists. Yours is an impressively *old* title, I must say. A peer of *England*, I believe, and not simply of this Emerald Isle? It is rare indeed to find a family with such an unbroken line of descent in this turbulent country.' Still holding Cornelius Wolcroft's hand, the gent turned to a scarf-draped woman by his side and exclaimed: 'Apparently, m'dear, there has been a Cornelius Wolcroft at the head of the family since the late sixteen hundreds!'

'You must be a very retiring family, sir, for us not to have heard of you sooner,' the woman said with a smile. 'Do you and the Lady Wolcroft never move in society?'

'There is not yet a Lady Wolcroft, m'dear,' answered her companion. 'The Lord of Fargeal is still footloose. Ain't I right, My Lord? Though at thirty-five years of age, one might suggest you are old enough to at least *consider* the prospect of marriage – give yourself time to produce a crop of little Wolcrofts before you are too old to enjoy the process!'

Lord Wolcroft lifted his lip ever so slightly and extricated his hand from the man's grip. The man seemed undeterred. 'Ou_ _a__lies share business history, you know – both having dabbled in sugar and slaves.' He laughed at Miss Ursula's pained frown. 'Ah, Ursula's come over all Quaker on us! Never fear, old girl, the slaving days are long gone. And thankfully some of us were wise enough to diversify before America stole the sugar business right out from under us, ain't that so, My Lord? I believe some of your ancestors had holdings in Saint Kitts?'

'Nevis,' Lord Wolcroft corrected.

'Nevis! You're mostly in shipping now, I believe? Brighton, India, the West Indies?'

There was a rolling of eyes from his female companion. 'Must you constantly harp on about business, Phillip?'

'As a matter of fact, Lord Wolcroft and I share an acquaintance in London. My nephew is an investor in one of your companies, I believe, sir. As such, he must deal quite regularly with your man of business?'

At Wolcroft's attempt to physically withdraw from this interrogation, another man hemmed him in. 'Oh, Lord Wolcroft has no *man* of business. All his accounts are handled by a *woman*. Is that not so, Lord Wolcroft? Your business is entirely managed by your...well, what would one call her? Your *bookkeeper*? Your *assistant*?' The man raised an eyebrow. 'Certainly she lives with you.'

The others glanced knowingly at each other.

Lord Wolcroft looked decidedly queasy. 'My business associate, Raquel, handles all my accounts,' he said. 'She is a most gifted woman.'

'Oh, your *associate*,' smirked one of the women.

'Yes,' snapped Wolcroft. 'My *business* associate. Raquel.'

'Raquel,' said one of the men. 'Raquel...' He tasted the word, his brow creased in mock surprise. 'Why, that's a *very* unconventional name. I don't think I know *anyone* of that name – except, perhaps, my tailor's daughter.'

The man's smile became a sneer, and anger rose in Harry's chest. 'He means she's Jewish,' he whispered.

'Harry,' tutted Tina. 'How would you know that just from—'

'How many Raquels do *you* know, Tina?'

She drew back. Her expression told him that she knew none.

Onstage, Wolcroft had gone dangerously still, his eyes hard as glass, his hand clenched around the silver top of his cane. 'The hour grows late,' he said softly.

Miss Ursula clasped her hands nervously and began shooing the participants towards the waiting table and chairs. Harry whistled beneath his breath. 'Well,' he said. 'That look sent them scattering. For all that he dresses like a *faygele*, I wouldn't like to tangle with Lord Wolcroft.'

'Oh no,' whispered Tina. 'They're starting the séance.'

'Ah, don't be scared, kid. I can tell you, it's gonna be rubbish – and I'm not just saying that because I now hate their *antisemitisch* guts. Look at the slapdash way the paraphernalia is scattered about the stage. And what's with all the lights? That's no way to build up an atmosphere. Whoever this medium is, they'd better have some patter, I tell you, because so far this show's on a short slide to Bumsville.'

'Harry, are you even speaking English?'

'They're *amateurs*. It's obvious they've no idea how to set up a show.'

'It's not a *show*, Harry. It's a *séance*.'

Harry groaned. *Oy gevalt*. She was a *believer*.

Onstage, the old woman was exhorting everyone to hold hands and open their hearts to positive thoughts and energies. 'I shouldn't be here,' Tina insisted, sounding panicked. 'I shouldn't be anywhere near a spirit board.'

'Aw, come on. It's all just entertainment. You're *theatre*, kid! You should know this.'

She was shaking her head, trying to push past him towards the ladder. 'I shouldn't be here.'

Harry gripped her arm. 'Look, there's nothing you'll see or hear that I can't explain for you, okay? I've done it all: messages from the dead, apparitions, spirit boards...You wouldn't *believe* the things I could convince you of, given the right set-up.' He pulled Tina back to his side. 'Look,' he urged again. 'Keep watching! I'll explain it all as it unfolds.'

Miss Ursula's voice rose up; the usual tremulous warble of a spiritualist, calling her spirit guide to come forth. 'Dora? Are there any eternal beings present? Any roaming spirits who require our aid?'

Harry froze as, deep below, in the pit of the backstage stairwell, a pair of pinprick lights sparked to life. At the same time, the old lady hesitated, as if aware of a sudden charge in the air. 'Dora?' she asked uncertainly. 'Are…are you there?'

The twin lights moved, bobbing in the darkness as they drifted up from the black. They blinked off and then on again, coming closer, and Harry gripped a handful of Tina's blouse as he realised that they were eyes. Eyes! Glowing and moving in the darkness, *ascending* in the darkness, as if their owner were staring upwards while climbing the stairs below.

'Tina,' he whispered. 'What's that? Down there. Look!'

But Tina was not listening to him. Her attention was fixed on Lord Wolcroft, who had sat forward at the séance table, his face sharp with concentration. He was staring up at Tina and Harry as if he could see them crouched there in the shadows.

Miss Ursula was now positively effervescent with excitement. 'Oh! Oh my!' she cried. 'Oh my, we have contact! Everyone, place your fingers on the spirit glass! Gently now! Gently!'

The assembled dilettantes did not do as they were told. Instead, they watched, rapt, as the small crystal glass began making its own way around the table. The *click, click, clickity* of its progress on the inlaid wood of the spirit board was very clear in the stunned silence.

The pinpricks of light reached the top of the stairs. Their owner stepped from the darkness, and Harry found himself staring down into the eyes of Lord Wolcroft's carriage driver. The tall man was looking up at the catwalk, his face transfixed with wonder. Heedless of the drop, Tina was leaning far out over the edge of the catwalk, her own eyes huge, her fingers gouged into the gritty fabric of the sandbags, and Harry realised with a jolt that the carriage driver was not, in fact, staring at him, but at her.

Lord Wolcroft rose to his feet at the séance table, his eyes also riveted on Tina.

On the spirit board, the little glass revolved faster and faster, its faceted surface glittering in the wavering light of the candles. It spiralled to the centre of the board, where it spun on its own axis like a top. Then, without warning, it rose straight into the air. Miss Ursula shrieked, and the hitherto awed spiritualists leapt back in fear. Undeterred, the glass continued its glittering ascent until it was spinning at their eye level, small and sparkling and beautiful, shooting arrows of light and rainbows into the faces of the watchers.

Lord Wolcroft stared through the darkness into the eyes of the girl above, his lips parted, his face, like that of the carriage driver, infused with joy. 'At last,' he whispered. 'We have found another.'

And, as if in agreement, the dark-skinned man in the shadows whispered, 'Yes.'

Tina made the strangest noise in the back of her throat: a choking sort of gurgle. Harry was dimly alarmed by it, but he couldn't seem to take his eyes from the carriage driver, who had crossed the backstage to stand directly below them.

Still gazing up at Tina, the man lifted his hand, as if to catch a thrown coin. Harry heard a distant *pat*, *pat*, *pat* as something dropped into his upraised palm.

The flock of dilettantes were frozen, apparently mesmerised by the glitter of the airborne crystal. For a brief moment, Lord Wolcroft looked from face to terror-struck face. Then he sighed, reached across, and plucked the spinning glass from the air.

'None of this is important,' he said.

There was an instant surge of relief. People smiled sheepishly, as if to say, *Well, of course not.*

'It is time to go home,' murmured Wolcroft, and they immediately began a merry chattering and gathering of overcoats. Only Miss Ursula seemed aware of the situation, her fingers pressed to her mouth, her eyes on the glass that glittered in Wolcroft's hand.

'I...I've never...' she whispered. 'I don't...'

Wolcroft took her by the arm. He smiled down into her anxious face. 'There is nothing to worry about, dear.' She relaxed. Wolcroft began to lead her from the stage. 'About the Christmas show, Miss Lyndon. I think you shall travel with me ahead of the other performers, to act as my advisor.'

'Advisor,' she breathed.

'Indeed. I am no expert in setting up a production, I'm afraid. You shall be a fount of usefulness in advance of your associates' arrival.'

'Oh, I can be very useful.'

'Of course, you shall bring your staff,' he said, guiding her down the steps to the auditorium.

'My...my staff?' said Miss Ursula.

'Indeed – your maid, your girl-servant. You would be shocked, Miss Lyndon, at the number of people these days who find it acceptable to travel without staff. A woman of your breeding, of course, shall wish to travel properly, with your companion in tow, as a lady should.'

'Oh yes,' said Miss Ursula dreamily. 'Oh yes, my companion…'

'And you shall bring only your finest clothes, dear. No doubt you have some lovely dresses. Tell me about them…'

They strolled off, arm in arm, apparently forgotten by the others, who, one by one, began to drift away.

Soon only the carriage driver remained, standing in the wings, gazing down at his palm. Harry, leaning far out across the sandbags, was aware of Tina's arm pressed hot and trembling against his own, and that she was still making a strange and gurgling sound. He wanted to turn to her, to ask what the matter was, but he couldn't seem to move his head or tear his eyes from the tall, dark-skinned man below. Somewhere far off, he could hear water running – a thin, distant sound, as if someone had left a tap dribbling into a sink.

The carriage driver looked up. Harry flinched as a rich, deep voice sounded in his head.

Don't just sit there, boy. Help her.

His words seemed to release some iron-tight grip, and Harry collapsed against the sandbags. The sound of running water was much closer than he'd thought: a light, steady fall, pattering against canvas. The roof must be leaking.

Harry turned his swimming head to check on Tina. She was staring at the stage, her eyes huge, her teeth clenched tight. Her nose was pouring blood. It ran in impossible gouts from each nostril, streaming onto her clawed hands and down into the darkness below. Her lower face was drenched in it.

As Harry clutched her shoulders and dragged her back from the edge he thought, very clearly: *He caught her blood. The carriage driver. He reached out his hand and caught her blood.* And then, with a sharp sense of panic he thought, *How am I going to get her down the ladder?*

Safe and Warm

OE DREAMT THAT Mickey the Wrench was chasing him. As Joe scrabbled featureless walls, weak and hot and desperate for breath, Mickey ambled along behind, carrying the big staff he used to beat the fighting dogs, swinging it from side to side, from side to side. Eventually there was nowhere left to run, and Joe waited like a child, his face pressed to the corner of a blind alley, unable to turn, unable to hide as Mickey advanced, taking his time, swinging the staff, his grin a living presence in the dark.

A DEEP VOICE called him from his desperation. 'Sit up.'

Strong hands gripped his shoulders and dragged him upwards, propping him against something soft. The change in position loosened something in Joe's chest and he took a breath.

He was too hot; too hot and there was no air.

He opened his eyes to find two green points of light floating over him. He reached for them. They drew back, and his fingers brushed skin: a face.

'Your eyes,' he whispered. 'They glow in the dark.'

Something lay briefly against his forehead, hot and dry – a hand? The deep voice said, 'You are ablaze, Matthew. Tell me you have not succumbed to my disease.'

Joe just stared up into the green lights, fascinated by the fans and whorls and patterns he saw within them. 'I know you,' he said.

The hand withdrew. 'Yes. You know me. What are you doing, huddled like a vagrant in this corner?'

'Not doing any harm. I'll leave when I've had me rest.'

There came a sigh of impatience. 'I've had enough of this. I am taking you home.'

'Miss Price won't let me stay. I'm a boy.'

A moment of silence was followed by a smooth upwards movement, and the green points of light were suddenly far above, looking down on him. The voice, when it came again, was cold and firm: 'I shall be taking you home, Matthew. Reconcile yourself to it. Cornelius or no, I shall not be denied.'

The green lights disappeared. There was a large movement in the cramped room – a heavy swish of cloth – and Joe realised it was Ursula Lyndon's costumes being taken from their hangers.

Joe sighed. 'Don't be robbing stuff, mister. The auld wan hasn't a farthing – it'll ruin her if you take them dresses.'

The door opened, then closed. Dusty silence settled once again on the room.

Too tired to care, Joe shut his eyes, waiting for the next dream. There was a scuffling in the corridor outside, and the click of the latch as someone opened the dressing-room door. *Oh, what now?* he thought wearily. *Can't a fella get some kip?*

A match flared and warm light filled the room. He opened

his eyes to see Harry lighting the lamp. Joe was just about to whisper hello when Tina turned from shutting the door and her blood-smeared face sent him struggling to his feet.

Tina lifted a hand to halt him. 'It wasn't Harry's fault.'

'Wasn't his...' Joe rounded on Harry. 'What the *hell* did you do to her?'

'I didn't do anything. It was the spirit board. Tina got scared and—'

'A spirit board!' cried Joe. 'Tina shouldn't be anywhere *near* a spirit board!' This shout seemed to rob his legs of their power. Harry reached for him as he staggered, but Joe shoved him aside. 'What were you doing making Tina use a spirit board, Harry?'

'What was *I* doing? Now *listen here*, Tina was—'

'I'm right here!' cried Tina. 'Stop fighting over me like two dogs with a rag.'

The two of them drew back, ashamed, and Tina shoved between them, stumbling to the sofa, where she sat and cradled her head in her hands.

'You shouldn't be using the board,' murmured Joe. 'You know that.'

'It wasn't her,' said Harry. 'It was the actress. She put on quite a show. Tina got scared and—'

'Harry,' mumbled Tina without lifting her head from her hands, 'if you say I was scared again, I'll kick you right in your arse.'

Joe sat beside her. Tentatively, he put his hand on her back. 'Did you see something, Tina? Was there a voice?'

She squeezed her eyes tight. 'The door opened again, Joe. I could see again – a kind of light, this time, all tangled up in those men.'

Harry crouched in front of them, his face vivid with curiosity. 'What's going on?'

Joe glared. *Never you mind, Harry Weiss.*

'There's something wrong with me,' mumbled Tina.

'There's nothing wrong with you!' insisted Joe.

'Ah, Joe,' she said softly. 'You know there is.' She looked up at Harry. 'There's something wrong with me. Up here.' She tapped her temple. 'I got a fever when I was small; it gave me fits. I heard voices. I saw things. I saw things for a long time after. People thought I was funny in the head.'

Joe turned his face away, not wanting to remember little Tina, thin as a twig, wrapped in a blanket on the front steps, smiling at nothing and following things with her eyes.

'What kinds of things?' asked Harry.

'Threads of light...' she whispered. 'Animals that tumble. Big floaty things with arms like eels. They talk to me in feelings...' To Joe's horror she reached as if to touch something. He grabbed her.

'Tina! Come back!'

She flinched and deflated, cradling her head again. 'I'm only remembering, Joe. Don't shout.'

'Sorry.' He lifted his hand, wanting to stroke her hair, not daring to. 'I'm sorry.'

She moaned. 'My mind hurts, Joe. I feel sick.'

Harry met his eyes. *What do we do?*

Joe shook his head, not knowing. Without looking up, Tina took his hand.

A soft noise out in the hall dragged Joe's attention to the door. To his horror, he realised Harry had left the lamp sitting on the floor. The light would be seeping out through the cracks, making it obvious to anyone in the corridor that someone was in here. Joe cursed under his breath as the door swung quietly open.

You could have blown him over when Daniel Barrett stepped into the room.

The big man looked pained, his shoulders hunched with embarrassment. He opened his mouth to speak; then he caught sight of Tina's bloodstained face, and his eyes went hard.

'Miss Kelly!' he said.

'She's there?' whispered a voice from the hall.

Joe's heart dropped. Oh God. Fran the Apples.

The little woman shoved her way past Daniel Barrett. Her face dropped when she saw Tina. 'Oh, *acushla*!'

'It wasn't Joe's fault,' mumbled Tina.

Fran's expression closed like a trap. Joe opened his mouth to say, *It's true! I didn't do it*. But Fran was already elbowing him aside and grabbing Tina. 'I told you, Joe Gosling. I *told* you! I *gave* you your chances!'

Tina gasped as Fran pulled her to her feet.

'No, Fran!' cried Joe. 'Don't!'

Before he knew what he was doing, he had grabbed Tina's other arm and tried to pull her from Fran's grip. His only thought was, *Don't take her from me!* but Fran wouldn't let go, and Tina ended up caught between the two of them, her face screwed up in pain.

'Say,' cried Harry, 'you're hurting her.'

Tina's nose began to bleed again.

Daniel Barrett filled Joe's vision. He put a huge hand on Joe's chest and bent to look into his face. 'Stop,' he said. '*Now.*'

'It wasn't me, Daniel,' whispered Joe. 'I didn't do it.'

'You let Miss Tina go, now, and we can discuss this in the morning.'

The soft fabric of Tina's sleeve slipped from Joe's fingers. He heard her moan as Fran hustled her to the door. 'It wasn't Joe, Fran. It wasn't him.' And then, just before her voice faded from hearing, she gasped, 'Oh, Fran! I'm going to be sick!'

Daniel Barrett backed to the door, his hand up, his eyes on Joe. His expression was a conflict of pity and disapproval. 'Miss Fran would never have let her stay out all night, Joe. Miss Tina should have known that.'

Joe, overwhelmed with the knowledge that everything was slipping away, lifted his empty hands.

'I didn't *do* anything.'

Daniel Barrett nodded, as if to say, *Sure, sure.* 'Don't be worrying, now,' he said. 'We'll go out the way we came in. We won't tell anyone you're here.'

He shut the door. The click of the latch was as final as goodbye.

'Say...' said Harry uncertainly. 'Say...it'll be okay, Joe.'

Joe shook his head.

'Why don't you sit down, huh? You look like you're going to fall. Sit down and I'll...I'll make us some tea!'

All false enthusiasm, Harry went to Ursula's dressing table, where he filled the kettle and lit the stove, trying to kill the silence with bustle. Joe just returned to the sofa and put his head in his hands. After a while, Harry stopped pretending everything would be all right and came and sat by his side.

'I've never seen anything like it,' he whispered. 'Tina. The blood. It just *poured* out of her.'

Joe groaned. 'I know. I've seen it before. Fran will blame me.'

'Don't be dumb! How could she possibly—'

'Because I bought Tina a spirit board, Harry. First time it happened, it was because I bought her a spirit board.'

'In America we bring our girls *flowers*, Joe. You should try it.'

'Would you just listen?'

Harry lifted his hands. 'Sorry. Go on...'

'When Tina and me were small, she and the Lady Nana and Fran lived across the street from me. If Tina stood in her window and I stood in mine we could see each other, and we used to play a kind of game...' Joe paused, remembering his hand on the filthy glass, Tina's tiny figure in the window opposite, suspended above the street. 'It must've started when we were really tiny,' he said softly, 'because it was always just something me and Tina did...our own little thing.'

He glanced quickly at Harry. 'Anyway, the game was that Tina would think of a word. She'd concentrate real hard on it, then I'd breathe on the window and draw a picture of what she'd thought.'

Harry's doubt showed in his face, and Joe tutted.

'Tina would think a *word*, Harry. I'd hear it in my head, then I'd draw it on the window.'

'Joe,' said Harry gently. 'That's impossible.'

'When we were eleven, she wanted to see what would happen if we used a spirit board: if maybe she'd be able to hear *my* thoughts, or if she could put her words into someone else's head. Fran was raging at the idea – everyone already thought Tina was peculiar, on account of, you know, the fits she'd had. Fran didn't want them saying she was a witch, too. But Tina just kept begging me to bring a spirit board, and eventually I did, and...' Joe shook his head.

'She had another fit, Harry. We were on our own. She fell down. Her nose poured blood. I thought she was going to die.' He met Harry's eye, the horror of that moment still raw. 'Fran wouldn't let me back for three months. *Three months.* Tina persuaded her, in the end. But I swore to Fran – I swore, Harry – that I'd never do it again. She *warned* me…I won't get her back, Harry. I've lost her.'

'No, you haven't.'

Joe dropped his head back into his hands. 'Course I have. Fran'll lock her up in that sweet little gaff. Tina won't be able to see me again.'

Harry stood up. 'Joe,' he said softly. 'You've gotta be the stupidest human being I ever met.'

Joe straightened. 'Hey,' he said, genuinely hurt.

Harry fetched Tina's basket from where she'd left it by the door and laid it on the ground by Joe's feet.

Joe gazed at it, puzzled. 'This is full of food.'

'Of course it's full of food, you *dumkop*! Tina brought it for you. She risked her *job* for you. She was willing to defy that terrifying Apples woman and spend the *night* here for you. Do you really think she's gonna let a stupid nosebleed stand between you?'

'It's not just a nosebleed, Harry!'

'Yeah, yeah.' Harry nudged the basket with his toe. 'Come on, I'm starved. Open the darned thing while I make the tea.'

Joe rubbed his mouth with his hand and frowned down into the crammed basket. Tina had put his purse there, nestled among the brown-paper parcels of sandwiches and cake. Gently, almost reverently, Joe touched it with his fingertips. He stayed like that for a moment, bent over the basket, his fingers resting on the purse, watching as Harry busied himself once again with the cups and kettle and tea. Then he made up his mind.

'I'm going to own me own cab, Harry.'

Harry looked around in surprise, and Joe felt himself blush, deep and hot and uncertain.

'I…I haven't told anyone that before. Not even Tina. The man I work for – Mr Trott – he's up to his neck in gambling debts. He's always behind on payments. They were going to burn his cab, as a lesson. But Saul knows the gougers who own the book, and he persuaded them that we can buy the cab. We've four months of saving left, and then I'll own it. Saul'll be me partner, but only a silent partner. I'll be working for meself, Harry. I'll *own the cab*.'

Harry just stared open-mouthed, until doubt and then horrible embarrassment flooded Joe's chest. 'Well…' he mumbled, covering the purse and straightening. 'I suppose that doesn't seem like much when you're going to be the greatest magician in the world.'

'Why, Joe, it's the most amazing thing I've ever heard!'

Joe squinted warily at him.

'I mean it! You're going to be an entrepreneur, Joe! Heck, you *are* an entrepreneur!'

Joe smiled, pleased. 'Don't be daft.'

Harry began to pace. 'You'll have to get signs made!' He made a sweeping arc in the air. 'Giant gold letters: *Gosling Cabs. Quality at your service.*'

Joe gazed at the empty space Harry had just filled with words. 'Oh, I like that. *Gosling Cabs. Quality at your service…*' He settled his head back onto the sofa, his eyes focused on that bright spot in the future. 'Yeah, I like that…'

'Tell you what,' cried Harry, 'I'll only ever use Gosling cabs when I'm touring here. You can paste advertising posters on the doors' – he made that sweeping movement again, conjuring words – *The Great Houdini Uses Gosling Cabs. So Should YOU!*'

'The Great Houdini Uses Gosling Cabs,' murmured Joe. *'So Should…*Wait, the Great Houdini?'

'Sure! That's my stage name,' said Harry. *'Houdini!* In honour of Robert-Houdin, the greatest magician to ever grace the stage. It means "like Houdin" in French. That's what a pal of mine told me. If you add an "ee" sound to the end of a word, it means "like" in French.' Harry puffed up his chest, clearly very pleased with himself and his faultless knowledge of the French language.

Joe thought deeply for a moment. 'An "ee" sound. I suppose that makes sense.'

'Sure it does,' said Harry, turning to fetch the tea. 'Orang*ey* – like an orange. Float*y* – like floating.'

Joe couldn't bring himself to reply. His eyes had drifted shut, and he was suddenly very comfortable sitting there with his head laid back and his legs stretched out. Even his chest felt better. *Maybe Harry is right*, he thought. *Maybe everything is going to be 'okay'.* He heard Harry shifting things about in the basket of food.

'Sneaky,' he murmured without opening his eyes. 'Like a sneak.'

'Smelly,' Harry retorted. 'Like a smell.'

Joe smiled.

Friendly, he thought, as he drifted downwards. *Like a friend.*

A Matter of Persuasion

Harry startled awake, sending sandwich wrappings and crumbs tumbling to the floor. Sheesh, when had he fallen asleep? The sofa beside him was empty, Joe nowhere to be seen.

Out in the dark corridor Harry found that the door to the alley had been left open. Maybe Joe had gone for a piss? The night outside was still. Snow drifted downwards, reflecting the gaslight of the nearby streets.

'Joe?'

A muffled shout dragged Harry's attention to a stark rectangle of light at the far end of the alley. The side door of the depot was open. Another shout came from there, and Harry ran towards the sound. He had no thought of what he expected to find, but as he slid in through the depot door and saw Joe felled by a punch to the belly, Harry's vision filled with red.

He roared and leapt, knocking Joe's attacker sideways with one blow. A shape moved behind him, and he had to duck as something whistled above his head – a staff or a walking stick, swung hard enough to kill. Harry spun.

Something slammed hard across his shoulders, and he went down. The cobbles impacted his face. Horse piss and stale water stole his breath.

A man roared, 'Who the fuck's *this* bugger?'

Another answered, 'Divil knows.'

'Mickey?' asked someone. 'Do you know this shleeveen?'

Joe's voice answered, breathless and thin. 'He's the theatre watchman's pal – you'd better let him go. He'll be missed.'

He was crouched in the dirty hay of the stall, his face the colour of chalk, glaring up at the broad, bull-necked man Harry recognised as Mickey the Wrench. 'I'm telling you,' he gasped, 'you can let that lad go. He won't say anything.' He looked to Harry. 'Sure you won't? If they let you go, you'll go right back in to the watchman and have your cup of cocoa, and you won't say anything.'

Harry climbed slowly to his feet. Mickey the Wrench looked him up and down, a flat, dead expression in his eyes. He bounced a thick, black wooden staff in his hand.

Harry glanced sideways at the man who'd beaten him to the ground: Daymo, one of Joe's other cousins. He held a similar heavy stick. The man Harry had punched was retrieving his own staff from where it had been flung from his hand. A fourth man, no doubt Joe's cousin Graham, shuffled about behind Harry's back.

Harry spat blood onto the cobbles. 'Oh, you're a real tough bunch, aren't you?' he said. 'Four of you, armed with bludgeons, to take on one man.'

'Jesus, Harry,' groaned Joe. 'Just *go*.'

Without changing his expression at all, Mickey the Wrench raised himself onto his tiptoes, swung his staff up and over, and brought it down full force on Joe's back. Joe collapsed into the hay with hardly a sound and lay there gaping like a fish.

'Shut up, Joe,' murmured Mickey the Wrench.

Harry roared, and flew for Mickey's throat. He was brought down with a numbing blow to the backs of his legs. The air was pressed from his lungs as someone knelt their full weight on him, and he was pinned, helpless. Mickey didn't pay this so much as a moment's attention. He just crouched by Joe and watched him struggle for breath in the hay. 'Now, Joe,' he said. 'What's this about money?'

Joe's mouth opened and closed, his face turning scarlet as he tried to get his shocked lungs to work. Mickey regarded him with detached patience. After a moment, he tapped Joe lightly on the forehead with his staff. 'Joe. Money, please.'

'You *bastard*!' wheezed Harry. 'Leave him alone!'

'Now, now,' murmured a voice just above Harry's head. 'Show a bit of respect.' Then this same person ground the butt of their staff hard into the hollow behind Harry's ear.

Harry almost screamed. He'd never felt anything so painful in his life. At some point, the man's weight lifted from his back and the staff stopped crushing his skull, and Harry was able to scramble to all fours. But the pain still splintered his brain, and it took a while before he registered the series of strange wracking barks tearing the air behind him. He turned and peered through watering eyes to where the four men were standing staring down at Joe with similar expressions of uncertainty.

'Stop that,' ordered Mickey.

But Joe just hacked another series of brutal coughs and

then arched his back. The air whooped in a strange way as it entered his lungs. Harry climbed to his feet, terrified by the bloody spit on Joe's lips, the glassy terror in his eyes. To his horror, Mickey the Wrench raised his stick again, snarling furiously at Joe: '*Stop that messing!*'

Harry launched himself between them. Quick as a snake-strike, Mickey butted him between his eyes. Harry was down in the hay before he could even think. He rolled to his back. The other men closed in on him and Joe, and with a sudden spear of despair Harry realised he wasn't going to win this battle.

How had Joe ever survived these men?

Mickey grinned and raised his arm high. But before he could bring the staff slamming down to brain Harry, a rich, deep voice spoke from the far end of the depot. 'You shall leave those boys alone.'

All the men except Mickey obediently lowered their weapons. Oddly passive, they turned towards the voice. Mickey simply rested his weapon across his wide shoulders and, without taking his eyes from Harry, said, 'Hello, darkie. Come to fetch your master's carriage?'

The carriage driver stepped into the light. His dark eyes moved from man to man, before settling on Mickey the Wrench. 'You shall leave now,' he said.

To Harry's amazement, Mickey's three henchmen nodded and made to go. Mickey, however, just chuckled – a low and dangerous sound. 'We'll leave when we're good and ready,' he said.

His voice seemed to snag something in his companions, and they paused, their faces creased in frowning puzzlement, as if torn between his command and the driver's.

'We've harnessed up your master's carriage,' said Mickey. 'And all his pretty packages are stowed like he wanted, so you can just haul your inky-black arse up into that box, drive out that arch, and bugger off down to the bog-hole of nowhere you came from. *This*' – he indicated Harry and Joe – 'is no concern of yours.'

The carriage driver's expression changed from distaste to fascination, and he regarded Mickey as if he were some strange new species of creature. 'Such independence. Is this due to the Bright Man's recent lack of power, perhaps? Or are you some anomaly in and of yourself?'

A fleeting moment of doubt showed in Mickey's face. The carriage driver laughed softly at his confusion, then glanced at Harry and Joe. Harry saw his eyes widen as he recognised the young man gasping for air on the ground at Mickey's feet. 'Matthew!' he cried, striding forward.

'Hey!' bellowed Mickey. 'Did you hear what I said? This isn't your business!'

At his voice, the men accompanying him jerked to life, raising their staffs. The carriage driver simply motioned his hand – *move aside* – and they subsided. Mickey could only stare as the man strode past and into the stable where Joe lay.

The driver crouched beside Harry, and between them, they heaved Joe onto his back. At the rough movement, Joe grabbed a panicked hold of Harry's jacket. He was panting short desperate hacks of air, his lips and nostrils tinted pink with blood.

'He can't breathe!' cried Harry.

'What is the matter?' asked the driver. 'Is it the consumption? Has he succumbed to an attack?'

Consumption. Harry's mind recoiled from the dreaded word. 'No.' He jabbed a finger at Mickey. 'It was *him*. He hit Joe on the back – hard. He hurt him. Hurt his lungs somehow.' He grabbed the carriage driver's hand and pressed it to Joe's side. The man's expression fell, his face reflecting Harry's own horror at the lopsided feel of Joe's breathing – at how only one side of Joe's chest was expanding with each breath.

The driver's carriage cloak fluttered about him as he surged to his feet.

Mickey took a step back, his black wooden staff clenched in his hand. 'Don't even think it, darkie. Me and my boys will break you like a twig.'

The carriage driver shook his head. 'A pack animal. Like most cowards. I have always wondered, coward, does your kind even exist when you are alone?'

Mickey looked to his companions. The carriage driver glanced their way. Quick as lightening, Mickey jerked back his staff, intending to jab the man's temple. Before Harry could even yell a warning to the driver, he had whipped out a hand, caught Mickey's wrist on the downward arc, and twisted. The staff flew from Mickey's fingers.

The driver, side-stepping in a flare of cloak, spun, twisting Mickey's arm behind his back. He was magnificent – a blur of stunning grace. He grabbed the back of Mickey's bull-neck with his free hand and pressed down, forcing Mickey to his knees.

Terrified, Mickey cried out, 'Lads! Help me!'

The driver tutted, looking up at the conflicted men. 'Oh, but look at their faces,' he crooned. 'So dirty. Their mothers would be appalled.' The men, ashamed and uncomfortable, began rubbing at their cheeks with childish concentration. 'You shall wash yourselves,' decided the driver. 'In the trough.'

To Mickey's horror and the driver's chuckling delight, the three men made a dive for the horse trough. There, they dropped to their knees and began a hectic sluicing and scrubbing at their faces.

The driver hauled Mickey to his feet. 'Let us see, animal, how well you survive without a pack of dogs at your heels.' He began herding Mickey across the depot floor, to get a better look at his companions.

'Harry,' Joe hissed, scrabbling for Harry's attention. 'Can't...breathe...'

Harry helped him sit a little higher. Together they watched in horror and fascination as the men splashed and gasped and strove with the water in the trough.

'Mesmerism,' whispered Harry. 'But how? I've never seen anything like it...'

Joe said nothing. His attention was fixed on Mickey. Mickey, who Harry guessed had dominated most of Joe's life with violence and terror; who must never have seemed anything other than indomitable. Mickey, who now crouched, hunched and helpless within the carriage driver's grip, watching as his thugs made fools of themselves in the filthy water of a horse's trough.

'Not enough,' the carriage driver told the splashing men. 'You need to soak the dirt off.' The dripping men paused, gazing up at him. 'You shall *soak* the dirt off,' he said.

Mickey's eyes widened in understanding. 'No, lads!' he cried. But his men had already plunged their heads deep into the horse trough. 'You're killing them!'

'Tut,' said the driver. 'Haven't you ever drowned unwanted pups? It ain't a bad way to go, all told. I've inflicted far worse. As, no doubt, have you.'

'Let them go,' gasped Joe. His words were barely a hiss, but the carriage driver glared across at him, as if Joe had yelled. There was a sudden dark rage in that glare, utterly shocking in contrast to his previous chuckling good humour. 'They'll drown,' gasped Joe.

'They will indeed,' snapped the driver, and Harry realised with a jolt that he meant to carry this strange game through to its bitterest end. He fully intended killing these men.

With no more effort than if he were lifting a child, the driver hauled Mickey to his feet. 'Come along to the fire, friend!' he cried. 'You are cold. I shall heat you up!'

At the brazier, he rubbed Mickey's shoulder and murmured soothingly in his ear until Mickey, his expression a horrified mingling of desire and fear, at last seemed to succumb to his suggestion and lowered his face towards the flames.

Desperate, Joe yelled, 'Let them GO!' The effort wrung him out, his breath reduced to a wheeze.

The driver turned from Mickey. 'Let them go?' he said.

At the trough, Daymo's toes began drumming the cobbles. His knuckles went white against the rim. Still he didn't lift his head. Beside him, quietly and with no effort to remove his head from the water, the nameless man pissed himself.

'I'll tip it over!' yelled Harry. He scrambled around to the trough and began heaving. It was a big trough, full to the brim, and he felt the tendons standing out on his neck as he strained into the lift.

At the fire, Mickey thrust out his hand as if to hold himself away from the flames. His fingers sizzled as they closed around the rim of the metal brazier. His eyes bugged in pain, his teeth bared to the gum. Still he kept his hand there, as if holding himself in check with it; as if it were the only thing preventing him from plunging his face into the burning coals.

The driver seemed to have completely lost interest in him, however, and was striding towards Joe. He passed by the trough just as Harry managed to tip it, and the drowning men spilled like fish from a barrel in his wake. Daymo and the henchman flopped and gasped, but Graham slid to the cobbles loose and sodden, dead as yesterday.

'You're…killing them,' gasped Joe. 'Let them…go.'

Something within the driver seemed to snap entirely at that, and he released a great howl of rage. 'Let them go? Let them…What are you *doing* here, Matthew? You have broken your mother's heart! You *broke her heart*! And I allowed it. Decades, I held my patience. *Decades*. Thinking you simply needed to gather your pride – thinking you needed to settle your mind. I respected you. I trusted you to return. *But you did not*. I have been seeking you forever, boy! Over and over, mistaking others…and now where do I find you? Here! *Here!* Debased and huddled and degraded as you have no right to be. Subjecting yourself to the tyranny of this scum. How *dare you*. How *dare you be living this life*?'

Harry flung himself past the driver and onto the ground by Joe. Grabbing handfuls of Joe's jacket, he pulled him into his arms as if to protect him from the man who paced before him now, clutching his hair, apparently speechless with rage.

'Let…them…go,' gasped Joe again.

The driver sneered. 'Oh, you have not changed, Matthew. Even after so wicked an exposure to mankind's crapulent brutality. You are just the same.'

Joe lifted himself from Harry's grip, as if willing the words from himself. 'Mister...I'm not...*Matthew*. Stop...killing...*me cousins*.' Abruptly his face drained of all remaining colour, his eyes lost focus, and he fell back. 'Oh, shite,' he whispered, his hand to his chest. 'Oh, shite.'

He went completely limp in Harry's arms.

The driver leapt as if to grab him, and Harry hunched over Joe's body. 'Leave him alone!'

'But I will help him.'

When Harry continued to hold on, the driver shocked him by smiling gently. 'I could order you to release him,' he said. 'I suspect you know this.' From the other end of the depot, there came a loud hiss, the acrid stench of burning hair, and Mickey the Wrench released a scream. The driver's eyes, only inches from Harry's own, glimmered green in the flickering light of the stable lamps. ' I am honouring you with choice, boy, because I saw you defend Matthew. Because I suspect you are his friend.'

Harry swallowed hard. 'What if I won't let you take him?'

'Then he will die here, surrounded by evil men who have abused him, and who deserved the retribution he saved them from. Is that what you wish for him?'

Harry released his grip.

The driver lifted Joe as easily as if he were a baby, and crossed with him to the waiting carriage. 'The survivors will not remain insensate for long,' he called. 'You had best run while you can.' Then he was taking his place in the driver's box, Joe pale and unmoving on the seat beside him. He shook the reins, and the horses lurched forward, filling the depot with the ring and clatter of hooves.

'Where are you taking him?' shouted Harry, running to catch up. 'Where are you taking him? He needs a doctor!'

The great wheels flashed past, missing him by inches. Then he was behind the carriage, running through the noise and chaos of its departure as it sped out into the cold grey murk of the pre-dawn street. Soon it would be gone, with Joe as its prisoner, unconscious, helpless and alone.

Harry didn't even pause for breath. Without thought, without planning, he just leapt. The ropes of the luggage-rack burned his palms as he hauled himself up. The tarpaulin was slick beneath his scrabbling hands. Then he was wedged into the packages beneath the canvas, burrowing and squirming into the great pile of luggage on the roof. Irrevocably committed to a plan he had yet to even think of, he huddled in the precarious and swaying dark as the growl of the wheels on the cobbles drowned out all other sound.

Two Small Stops
along the Way

VINCENT URGED THE horses up the wide double street that
would take him around the block to the theatre entrance.
The boy was motionless on the seat beside him. He would
be dead soon. Vincent had seen many a collapsed lung in
his time. In his experience not even the healthiest of men
came back from such a wound, and it had been obvious that
Matthew was dangerously ill even before those animals had
beaten him.

Seeing the boy in this condition had provoked such an
upsurge of emotion. Vincent had not felt that way in…in
how long? *Have I been asleep?* he thought. *It feels as though I
have been asleep.*

'I found you just in time, did I not, Matthew? Never
mind, I shall get you home soon enough. I shall reconcile
you and Cornelius to each other, and all will be well.' He
glanced again at the boy's thin face. 'I will have to clean
you up before your mother sees you, though. You are barely
recognisable as you are.' There was the briefest moment, the

tiniest itchy flicker, of doubt. He pushed it aside. This *was* Matthew, Vincent was certain of it. There would be no more embarrassing mistakes.

He cracked the reins and whistled the horses on. It would be good to be on the open road again, to urge the horses into a frenzy and simply let loose. Snowflakes slanted from the brightening sky. He opened his mouth and they melted like tiny moments of clarity on his tongue.

By the devil, it was excellent to be alive!

Without thinking, he breathed deep, and pain snagged dull and wicked in his lungs. His old friend, making itself known: the wasting sickness, the consumption, tuberculosis, whatever you chose to call the disease that was once again threatening to disassemble him one cell at a time.

You and me, Matthew, he thought. *Home and healed...*

And then? asked his mind slyly. *Home and healed...and then? Silence, and dust, and stillness once more...*

Vincent frowned into the wind. 'Cornelius spends so much time underground since you left. I am amazed he has not begun to glow in the dark. As for dear Raquel...your mother spends hours at her work table, Matthew, yet I do not think she ever sews. In your time, we were always out and about, do you recall? At the village, on the river, in the woods. When did that change?'

Matthew did not reply. He had slid to one side, his head angled awkwardly within the corner of the high-backed seat. Vincent took off his hat and gently placed it on the boy's tousled head. 'Things will improve when you return home,' he whispered.

The empty streets echoed as the carriage took a corner and the theatre came into sight. Cornelius was standing beneath the stained-glass porch of the entrance, making last-minute arrangements with the stage manager. He looked wretched, his face paler than the coming dawn, his eyes sunken in shadow.

Poor Cornelius. With so many trips up and down to the city – researching the theatre, arranging the arson – and so much time away from his beloved 'angel', it was no wonder he was coming undone.

'We must get him home, Matthew, before he falls asunder. Now, do excuse this small indignity.'

The boy's eyes widened in horror as Vincent jerked him down to lie on the seat and pulled the lap blanket up to cover his face. Vincent patted him through the fabric. 'We cannot have him seeing you until you are both ready to admit your feelings,' he said.

The manager, seemingly anxious that Lord Wolcroft might slip on the newly fallen snow, took Cornelius' elbow. Cornelius tensed, his hand tightening on his sword-cane, and Vincent straightened in concern; Cornelius hated to be touched when in this state – men had died for doing so. But Cornelius simply shook free and made his own way to the carriage, choosing to use the cane as an aid to walking, rather than putting it to its other, more lethal form of employ.

The manager hovered, desperate to please. 'You are certain your man remembers the way, Lord Wolcroft?' he asked. 'I can send a boy with you, if you feel he may need some help?'

Cornelius speared the man with a look. 'Captain,' he snarled, 'this creature believes you are too stupid to hold his instructions in your head. He wants to know if you need a child's help to find your way. What do you think? Do you need a child's help to find your way?'

Vincent couldn't help being amused. 'I need no help to find my way. Thank you very kindly for the offer.'

The manager huffed and tugged his waistcoat, not certain how to respond. When Cornelius had climbed into the carriage and slammed the door, Vincent took a coin from his pocket. 'Here,' he said, flipping it to the manager. 'For your trouble.'

The man caught it without thinking. His face blazed as he realised he had just taken a tip from a carriage driver – a darkie one at that. Then his mouth fell open as he recognised the coin as a gold sovereign. Vincent laughed – the man's mingled shock, horror and greed were just too comical. He was still laughing as he pulled the carriage into the street and drove off.

THEY COLLECTED THE actress first. She lived on one of those square little parks surrounded by decaying houses that this city seemed to have in abundance. Her home was a shabby little three-storey hostel, the snow-crusted sign reading 'St Martha's Boarding House for Ladies'.

Vincent took all this in from the driver's seat as the old woman crept out and gently shut the door. She was quite obviously slinking away. She owed rent, no doubt. Poor thing – Vincent thought she looked quite frail and tiny outside the confines of the theatre. He smiled at the thought of her in that glittering dress. Cornelius must have been appalled at the sight of her, wrapped in the trimmings he had intended for the fresh and lovely seamstress. How he must have bellowed!

The actress entered the carriage. Vincent gathered the reins as the door snicked quietly behind her. Cornelius' cane rapped the roof, and they were on their way once more.

THE SEAMSTRESS'S STREET was even seedier than the old woman's. Soot-stained, broken, mean, it was nevertheless transformed by the falling snow. Vincent found it almost beautiful. He remained in his seat, intent on enjoying the serenity as Cornelius and the actress went to collect the girl.

At the top of the steps, however, Cornelius stumbled, and the actress put an arm around his waist to steady him. He reacted badly, of course. He was not intentionally violent – Vincent had never seen Cornelius behave violently towards a woman – but the shock of that unexpected grip around his waist startled him and he cried out, shoving the old woman aside.

She almost tumbled down the steps.

Both parties brushed it off, content to murmur polite-nesses. Nevertheless, Vincent left the carriage and went to join them, ready to intervene should his friend's condition get the best of him. The actress nodded as he came up the steps, no doubt assuming that he'd come to protect his frail master.

Cornelius rapped on the tenement's scarred door, and a very tiny old woman with a cat in her arms flung up the sash on the nearest window. She was wearing a nightcap and a wrap, and didn't seem at all surprised by the odd trio standing on her doorstep.

'I'm landlady of this house,' she said, 'and you can take your missionary work elsewhere. No one here needs saving.'

'I am looking for Miss Kelly,' said Cornelius. 'The seamstress.'

That took her aback. She looked them up and down anew. 'You're not the Sally Army, then?'

The actress drew herself up. 'I am Miss Ursula Lyndon,' she said. 'I am accompanying Lord Wolcroft here to his manor in the country. Miss Kelly is my...she is to be my...'

'Your *companion*,' snapped Cornelius.

'I didn't hear anything about that,' said the landlady.

'Are you the girl's mother?' he asked.

'I am *not*.'

'*Then what business is it of yours, you old harridan?* Let us *in*!' Cornelius began pounding the door with his cane, the sound echoing like gunshots up and down the silent street.

'Stop that!' cried the landlady. 'How dare you!'

Vincent grabbed Cornelius' arm, his fingers biting deep. He gave the landlady a soothing look. 'You shall let us in,' he murmured.

To his immense surprise, the woman's scowl only deepened. 'Now you listen here,' she said. 'Money and privilege may ride roughshod over most of the broken backs in this damned country, but a fancy suit and a title gets your master no purchase with me. I *own* this house, and he can go spit if he thinks he can throw his weight around here. Miss Kelly is *sick*, Lady Nana and Fran the Apples aren't *here*, no one said anything to me about *callers*, and you can all go hang yourselves for being so *rude*.'

Vincent actually felt himself gape. What was wrong with these creatures? First that ruffian in the stables, and now this tiny wrinkled old prune of a women. He had never met people so immune.

'You shall let us *in*,' he insisted.

The landlady made no move for the door.

Cornelius shook off Vincent's hand, staring in amazement at the old woman. He turned to meet Vincent's eye. *Together?* he thought.

But gently, advised Vincent.

As one, they said, 'Let us in.'

Without a change of expression, the landlady withdrew from the window. Several cats leapt to take her place, prowling the windowsill and meowing their disapproval. In the ensuing wait, Ursula Lyndon laughed uncertainly. 'A veritable Cerberus,' she said, 'guarding her Persephone.'

Cornelius scowled, but Vincent found it quite witty. 'We shall avoid the pomegranates,' he said. Instead of sharing his amusement, the actress seemed shocked that he'd understood the reference, and then embarrassed that he had spoken. Vincent allowed his face to go cold and turned away.

The locks grumbled and the scarred door opened. The landlady peered out. She was confused and wary; Vincent could tell she was already doubting her actions. He stepped forward, discreetly putting his shoulder into the gap, ready to force his way in if necessary.

He thought, *These people have changed, Cornelius.*

Some of them. They are more difficult to persuade.

They feel like…Do you recall the feel of the old aristocracy?

Inside his head, Vincent heard Cornelius' bitter laugh. *So this is what the new age brings, Captain? A multitude of little kings, each ruler of their own small world.* With a huff, Cornelius brushed past the old women and into the hall.

Vincent smiled. If there was one thing Cornelius knew, it was how to outmanoeuvre the aristocracy. Shooing the actress ahead of him, Vincent stepped inside, closed the door and looked around. It was a dismal place, the narrow hall a strange tangle of baby-carriages and stacks of boards.

'Oh,' said the actress, eyeing the battered prams. 'Are you fruit dealers?'

The landlady proudly drew herself up. 'All my ladies are women of business.'

Vincent went to the base of the stairs and peered up into the dim reaches of the narrow house. Light filtered from a distant skylight, casting wan illumination on well scrubbed steps, damp-stained walls, chipped and flaking plaster.

'Where is everyone?'

The landlady tutted. 'Early mass. It's the new priest's first service. Everyone wants a look at him.'

'All of them?'

'Whole damned church-ridden street. Bloody fools.'

Cornelius met Vincent's eye again. An empty house on a street of empty houses – what luck.

The actress, who had been gazing about in awe, laid her hand on the landlady's arm. 'You *own* this entire house?' she asked.

'Every nail and board.'

'To own one's own home,' murmured Ursula Lyndon. 'How wonderful.'

'Every woman needs property of her own. Otherwise she's little more than property herself.'

'I have my career,' said the actress. 'I am no one's property.'

The women squinted keenly at each other, as if suddenly aware of some secret kinship. From over Vincent's shoulder, Cornelius spoke softly – almost inaudibly. 'We should like to see the seamstress now, please.' The women gave no indication of having heard him, but the landlady began leading the way upstairs, speaking to the actress as she went.

'My father left me this house,' she said. 'It caused ructions in his family. *Ructions*. They were determined no fallen woman's bastard brat would lay its grimy paws on their property. For three years Mama languished in an institution as they tried to prove her insane…'

'An institution!' The actress paused, her eyes wide, then she hurried to catch up as the landlady disappeared onto the first landing. Quietly, Vincent and Cornelius followed on behind.

A dog began barking as they climbed through the house: the angry territorial yap of a terrier. The landlady grimaced. 'You'll need to watch your ankles in here,' she said as they mounted the last of the narrowing stairs. She put the key in the lock of the door behind which the creature was barking, but then she frowned, staring at it.

'Wait. What am I…' She looked up at the door, then turned to stare at the two men who stood on the steps below her. By her side, the actress fidgeted, puzzled and unhappy. Behind the door, the dog barked and barked and barked.

Cornelius groaned, *I am weary, Captain. They are old and brittle. Let us just push them aside.*

As if in response to this, the lock clicked and the door opened. The seamstress emerged, her hair a dark cloud around her pale face, her dark eyes wary. She was barefoot, her nightdress white as snow. She was like a flower that had blossomed since Vincent had last seen her. Still the same girl, to all intents and purposes, but…brighter, somehow.

Shining. It was as if a light had been switched on inside her. The two old women seemed suspended in confusion, all skirts and ribbons, bonnets and frowns. The girl stepped between them, her little dog in her arms, her eyes on Vincent.

'Where are you taking him?' she asked.

Where was he taking whom? Surely she did not mean the dog?

Joe, she clarified. *Where are you taking Joe?* Vincent jolted as he realised she'd spoken inside his head. He slipped a glance at Cornelius. *I'm not talking to him, mister. He's not the one who took Joe.*

Sure enough, Cornelius gave no indication that he had heard the girl's voice. He was sagged against the banister, at the end of his energy after the stairs, the entirety of his attention expended on the growling dog. Vincent turned back to the seamstress.

You have Joe outside, she said. *He's frightened.*

He is ill. I am taking him home.

Joe doesn't have a home.

Cornelius pushed himself from the banister and laboured up the last of the steps to proffer his hand to the dog. The little brute responded with another frenzy of noise.

The seamstress kept her eyes on Vincent. *Where are you taking Joe?* she demanded again.

Come with me and see for yourself.

I'll scream. If you try and take Joe. I'll scream. People will come. They'll make you let him go.

Vincent sighed. *No one will come. You know this. And even if they did...*

He gestured to the dog in her arms. It had stopped

barking and was stretching towards Cornelius' hand, sniffing curiously. 'That's the boy,' whispered Cornelius as the dog snuffed, then nuzzled, then licked his shaking fingers. 'See?' he smiled. 'I'm not so bad.'

Wide-eyed, the girl looked from her suddenly docile guardian back to Vincent.

You are quite alone, he said.

I...I'll stop you myself.

Vincent found himself abruptly irritated with this stubborn child. Perhaps it was her unexpected intrusion into his head. Perhaps it was simply that he'd had enough defiance for one day. Without giving it any thought at all, he pushed at the girl's resistance in a way he had never done before – using his mind, instead of his voice.

You shall *come with* us, he commanded. *And you* shall *be quiet.*

He felt a shock of impact between them, as solid as if they'd hit each other square in the face. The girl's head snapped back, her eyelids fluttered, and a thin line of blood trickled, bright and sudden, from her nose. All internal communication with her went silent.

Cornelius laughed, delighted, as her battle-scarred little dog leapt straight into his arms.

At the sight of the blood, the actress came to life. 'Oh, my dear,' she cried, pressing a lace handkerchief to the girl's nose. 'Oh, it's the excitement. Perhaps your landlady should put a key down the back of your shirt?'

Vincent, feeling dazed, steadied himself against the wall. 'Take...take her inside and dress her,' he said. The girl did not protest as the older women guided her into the room. But until the very last moment, her eyes remained locked with his, and deep within them he saw a furious struggle as she tried to fathom what she was doing and why.

'Dress her warmly,' he said. 'It is snowing.'

CORNELIUS INSISTED ON carrying the dog downstairs. Somehow he managed the cane, the creature, the winding shadows and his own addled condition, and reached the ground hall without accident. The two old women followed, chattering birdlike as they supported the seamstress, snow-pale and dazed, between them.

When Vincent opened the front door and cold light washed the hall, the shock seemed to clear the girl's mind somewhat. She hesitated, pulling the women to a halt. The sight of Cornelius leaning at the bottom of the stairs murmuring into the adoring face of her dog appeared to upset her.

It is all right, thought Vincent, laying his hand on her arm. *See how content the little fellow is?*

The girl looked to the actress. 'Miss U?'

The woman nodded happily. 'We're off on business, my dear. You're to be my companion.'

The girl's eyes drifted to the carriage, and to the blanket that lay bundled on the driver's seat.

'Joe,' she whispered.

The actress tutted as she and the landlady led the girl down the steps. 'Joe!' she said. 'You girls and your boys! Absence makes the heart grow fonder, m'dear. *Joe* won't die for a few days' want of your company.'

The women's skirts swept a clear path through the accumulating snow. The girl's bright tartan coat was a brief and glorious splash of colour against the glossy black of the carriage; then she and the actress were inside.

As the landlady came scurrying back up the steps, shivering in her nightgown and wrap, Vincent surveyed the street. The snow was all sullied with footprints. They seemed fresh. It would be best to go.

Cornelius seemed intent on taking the dog, and Vincent had to gently prise it from him.

'Come now, cully. You do not want this poor thing subjected to the children's games.'

Once out of Cornelius' arms, the animal struggled free and ran upstairs. Vincent listened to the skitter of its nails as it searched the flights above. The landlady was watching him closely, her small hands knotted, her expression eloquent of the struggle for clarity within her.

'The seamstress has gone on respectable business,' he told her.

The old woman's face cleared. 'Miss Kelly is *very* respectable,' she agreed. 'And honest. A most useful girl.'

'Useful,' said Vincent. 'Indeed.'

Taking the old woman by her shoulders, he guided her to the door of her room and waited until she had gone inside. As he was leaving, the skitter of nails on wood signalled the return of the little dog. It came to a halt on the landing, its head cocked as it scanned the now empty hall. Vincent kept his eye on it as he closed the front door. It watched him, its expression questioning. Only after he had shut the door did it finally, belatedly, begin to bark.

Regrets

TIME TURNED TO water for Joe once the driver pulled the cover over him. He wanted air. He wanted so badly to bare his heated face to the falling snow. But his body seemed to have given up, and it just lay there, docile beneath the blanket, while the carriage jolted through the streets.

I'm dying, he thought.

After a stifling eternity, a familiar light had begun growing in the dimness of his mind: a candle coming towards him in the dark. Joe had smiled. The coarse fabric snagged his dry lips as he spoke her name. He barely noticed coming to a halt, nor the creak and shift of the passengers disembarking. He was just so happy to have that light in his mind – the comfort and the joy of her presence.

Joe, she said. *What have they done to you?*

He reached out and clung to her, for once in his life open and unguarded. She reached out, too, and for the first time held him in the fullness of her embrace.

I'm scared, Tina. I'm so scared.

Where are you, Joe?

Joe listened, trying to focus his swimming concentration on his surroundings. There were voices, dully muffled: a conversation of some kind, then angry banging, someone hammering wood. Silence followed – a protracted length of quiet in which Joe floated.

Tina said, *There are men coming for me*, and Joe's eyes snapped open as he realised where he must be. There came a furtive scratching. The carriage swayed as someone shifted about. The blanket was snatched back, and Joe found himself gazing up at dark-blue eyes, an angry halo of hair, the dove-grey sky filtering snow all around.

Harry.

Over his friend's shoulder, Joe recognised the familiar, beloved façade of Tina's home.

'Can you walk, Joe?'

Joe jerked in a weak lungful of air, but it was impossible to make a sound.

Harry shoved an arm under his shoulders. 'Come on, I don't think we've much time.' He tried to lift him. Pain flared. Joe made a desperate sound, and Harry stopped. 'Joe, you gotta try, pal. I can't lift you down unless you try.'

Joe glanced desperately over Harry's shoulder. *Look. Look!*

Puzzled, Harry followed his gaze. It took a moment – perhaps because it was daytime now, and snowing – but in the end he recognised it.

'Oh no,' he whispered. 'No. Not here…'

HARRY WENT RUNNING from door to door, trying to find help. Joe lay like a corpse, staring up into the disintegrating sky, and spoke to Tina in a way that had never been possible before: not just her words in his head, but his in hers, a conversation. And all the time she burned bright in his mind, like a lighthouse, like a beacon; as if something within her had been set on fire.

When she understood how beaten he was, she responded with horror, with rage, and with that core of steel he'd always adored. There was a terrifying sense of her stepping forward, of her crossing a threshold; of her looking up at some great, unvanquishable foe. Then there was nothing. She was gone.

Harry scrambled back onto the seat. 'There's no one around, Joe!' Their eyes met, the hopelessness of the situation clear to both of them.

Joe hissed one word: 'Run.'

'I *can't*, Joe. I can't leave you. I don't know where they're going!'

There was no more air. *Run*, thought Joe.

Harry took his hand. 'Joe, I gotta cover you up again.' Joe moaned in horror. 'Sorry, pal. I'm so sorry. But they can't know I was here.' He reached for the blanket, still holding Joe's hand. As he covered Joe's face, he whispered, 'I'm sticking with you, Joe. You hear me? I'm sticking with you, and as soon as I'm able, I'll get some help.' For a brief moment, their hands clamped tight; then Harry pulled away, scrambling across the seat, and Joe was alone.

Tina? he thought. *Are you there?*

He thought of the contents of that cracked purse and all the days they could have had together with it. He thought of all the times she'd offered to take him out – to the theatre or the races – and the pride that had made him refuse. *We should have gone to Bray*, he told her. *We should have taken the train to Kingstown.*

Useless, useless regrets – as useless as the crumbled wads of filthy money he'd crammed away all these years.

But I had me plan, he thought. *Surely that was worth something?*

He shut his eyes, and closed his hand around the memory of hers.

I wish I'd kissed you sooner, Tina. I wish I'd told you it all.

Everything was floating away, all the sounds, all the feelings, everything dim and feathered all around with black. A door opened somewhere far off. Women chattered, their words indistinct. The carriage swayed and juddered as people climbed aboard.

Joe barely heard the driver's gate latch click, nor registered the heavy movements as someone settled down beside him.

The driver's voice came from far, far away. 'Let us go home,' he said. The carriage lurched to life with a slap of the reins, they jolted forward, and after that there was nothing.

Kindness

Cornelius released the blind and pressed his heated face to the dewy glass. They were beyond the city limits already. Outside, a great expanse of sand dunes stretched away beneath a storm of tumultuously falling snow. He hoped they would make it home before the country roads were blocked.

The Angel burned in his mind with all its promise of calmness and clarity. The prospect of returning to its presence made Cornelius groan, an expression of pain and need.

Why am I suffering? he thought. *In this old, horrible way?* This was a condition he had always associated with the sins of shore leave. In the first weeks back at sea, he had always suffered thusly. Cornelius had accepted it then as his penance for the debauchery of land: the well deserved scourging of his body after yet another blue-eyed boatman had caused him to give in to weakness, and days of opium indulgence had silenced the ensuing guilt. But why was he like this *now*? He searched his memory for something he might have done – some lapse of body or sin of the mind that might have—

A light touch on his bare hand startled him and he jerked to life, already in the process of unsheathing his sword-cane. The crone sat back, her hands up, surprisingly composed in the face of a semi-bared blade. The girl at her side watched on, curious yet detached, as if from the well-end of a dream. She was a vision of creamy youth, her full-skirted yellow tartan coat bright as a Christmas bauble against the dark leather padding of the interior.

When had they been taken into the carriage? Cornelius had only the vaguest recollection of it. He sheathed the few inches of drawn blade, his hands trembling.

'Are you ill, sir?' asked the actress. 'Is there anything I can do?'

Cornelius pressed himself into the seat cushions. Oh God, she was so old: Raquel would be livid that he had brought such ugliness to the house.

'Shall I call out to your driver?' she asked. 'Tell him to stop?'

'Be quiet!' he cried. 'Can't you just be quiet, damn you! Is that so much to ask?'

Surprisingly, the woman's expression remained infused with understanding. 'I have a little medicine,' she said softly. 'If you need it.'

She withdrew a small brown glass bottle from the châtelaine purse on her waist and unstoppered it. The bitter-sweet scent of laudanum filled the carriage. The actress leaned forward and pressed the bottle into his shaking hand. 'I know what it is like,' she murmured, 'to get headaches.'

Cornelius gripped the bottle tight. 'You...you shall sit back,' he said. The actress sat back. 'Do not look at me.' She turned her eyes to the window. Cornelius thrust out his arm. 'Put this away.'

Handing the bottle back was like forcing his own flesh to tear, but once it was done, he felt stronger.

A sound rose above the jolting of the carriage and the roar of the storm: a howling, as wild and ungovernable as the sea. The women turned their eyes upwards, unnerved. But Cornelius knew this sound well, had heard it many times in his past. It was Vincent, the wind in his teeth, the storm in his face, spitting in the eye of the world. Vincent, standing at the reins of the carriage, as he had once stood at the masthead of their ship, howling his defiance to nature and heaven and the God in whom he professed not to believe.

Cornelius closed his eyes and listened. The sound, and his own recent act of self-control, tethered and soothed him – reminded him of all he had achieved. He turned his face to the glass and watched as jealous waves spent themselves against the stones of an estuary wall. The wind hurled snow into the distance. The carriage jolted, the shore dropped from sight, and they were once again hemmed in by hedgerows and walls. Overhead, Vincent's voice fell silent.

Cornelius smiled. *Roar all you wish*, he told the retreating voice of the sea. *You no longer own him. He is no longer yours.*

Part II

The Bright Man

The Dooryard
of the Flayed Badger

VINCENT COULD JUST about recall the very, very distant reaches of his youth, when he would help his father drive the slaves from his ship and deliver them to Cornelius' father's plantation high on the slopes of Nevis. After the money had been exchanged, and Vincent's father had ordered any unwanted goods back down to the harbour market for sale to the lesser plantation owners, he would take Vincent, and often Cornelius too, riding in the hills to collect herbs. He'd been a remarkable man, in so many ways, his father – there were not many other ship captains who also acted as surgeon. Then again, Vincent's father had never been one to trust his precious cargo to the care of another.

Vincent had never cared much back then for stopping and grubbing about in the roots. His father had often scolded him for driving his horse too hard and too fast; for forgetting to allow it rest. Vincent recalled the impatience this had made him feel, the frustration. To his fierce joy, he had no such problem with the horses he drove before him now. They had travelled almost two hundred miles since leaving the confines of the city, and showed no sign of tiring. Their endless headlong race down road and country lane was as close as Vincent had come in decades to the implacable rush of a ship. Despite the cold-induced ache in his lungs, he almost wished this journey would never end.

All through yesterday's long race from Dublin, he had managed to stay ahead of the storm, and only now, with pale light bleaching the horizon, had the snow caught up with them again. Vincent knew it would not be long before these narrow lanes were clogged, but he was not worried. At this speed, it was less than an hour to the village and then less again to the estate house. They were almost home. There he would present Raquel with a gift far better than bolts of fabric: a boy, newborn from the dirty hay of a stable – her son resurrected from a manger in the snow. And with him, new life. New purpose. A return to what had been. How delicious.

'Just wait until you see the theatre your mother has had constructed for the spectacular, Matthew. It rivals any I have ever seen. It reduces that flea's pit your seamstress friend inhabits to a Punchinello's chequered booth!'

The sun rose over the familiar flat stretches of bog, the wind-crippled huddle of trees, the endless spines of dry-stone wall. When the cobbles of the village clattered beneath the wheels, Vincent slowed the carriage so as not to desecrate the peace too badly. The wind had dropped, and snow drifted slowly down in silence, giving the close-pressed cottages and well tended market square an air of gentleness and serenity. Familiar faces showed at window and half door. There were nods, and the touching of hats, and Vincent responded in kind as he let the horses take their ease passing through.

He braked in the dooryard of the Flayed Badger, and Peadar Cahill came to hold the horses. 'Your Honour,' he said, squinting up with his usual shy smile. 'Good trip?'

Vincent climbed from the box. 'Very good. Excellent, in fact!'

Peadar flicked a hopeful glance at the carriage. 'Is Himself within?'

'Cornelius is a little fragile, Peadar. It might be best to leave him for the moment.'

The man's broad face fell. 'Oh,' he said. 'We...we had hoped you'd stop for a bit of a *céilí*, sir. It's been such a long time since you were in the village.'

Vincent regarded him curiously as he removed his gloves. 'I have only recently begun to realise that. Up at the estate, I had not seemed to feel the time passing, but this trip has served to clear my head somewhat, and I was wondering...how long do you suppose it has been since the family was out and about?'

Peadar scratched the pale stubble on his chin. 'Master Luke and I were trying to figure it when he came down to arrange accommodations for the players, sir. I reckon it must be a fair long time since you and I last stood here and had a chinwag.'

'Do you?' said Vincent softly.

'I reckon it might be nigh on fifty year – if not more.'

Fifty years? Vincent thought it over. 'I think you might be right,' he whispered.

'It got terrible quiet for ye without Master Matthew, I reckon,' said Peadar, not meeting Vincent's eye. 'I reckon the heart gradually went out of things for the family after he left.'

Vincent restrained himself from looking back at the driver's box. 'Perhaps that will change soon.'

'Perhaps it will. Certainly there'll be a bit of life around and about when the players come.'

The players. Of course. 'We want only the best for them, Peadar. You understand?'

'Of course, sir. Mother and I are doing the rooms up lovely for them here. Rest assured, their last days will be the best you could imagine.' He fleetingly met Vincent's eye. 'They're...they're good, sir, are they? They're entertaining?'

'They are everything you could wish, Peadar. A riot of flamboyance.'

'Riot of flamboyance,' breathed Peadar.

Vincent glanced behind him. All around the market square there were faces at windows, people watching from porch and corner.

'We're finding it hard, sir,' Peadar admitted. 'We're terrible hungry of late, and the older ones...' Peadar went quiet, choosing not to detail the older villagers' sufferings. Vincent noticed for the first time the pinched look around the man's eyes, the stoop to his broad back. Peadar held up his hand. The fingers were slightly crooked. 'I'm getting old man's pains, sir.'

Vincent gently gripped his arm. 'This is but a temporary hitch, friend. All will be well soon.' Breaking the moment, he slapped Peadar's shoulder with his gloves. 'I assume you had no trouble securing provisions?'

'Pardon me, sir?'

'Miss Raquel was to order supplies, Peadar. For our house guests.'

At the words 'house guests', the man's confusion deepened.

'We sent a message,' exclaimed Vincent. 'Tell me the damned thing arrived!'

Peadar was only half-listening. 'A…a messenger from outside came and went, sir. But no order came down from the big house. I…' He stepped to the side, all the better to view the carriage door. 'You have guests in there? I had no idea.'

Vincent groaned. Apparently Raquel had decided to be awkward about this unexpected deviation from the plans. An awkward Raquel was an unpleasant Raquel. Things were not likely to be comfortable for the actress and the girl.

'We shall just have to cobble together a meagre supply from what you have, Peadar. Someone shall have to travel out into the world for the rest.'

'We haven't got no food,' said Peadar absently, drifting closer to the carriage. 'Not due to be delivered until the players come. Haven't got no candles either – nor chopped any firewood. Haven't got anything outsiders might have want of. Not yet.'

Vincent felt a small, sharp headache flare between his eyes. He reached for his purse, already running up lists in his head. 'You will have to send out for supplies immediately, Peadar. You know what outsiders are like for feeling the cold and needing their food and such things.'

But Peadar wasn't listening. He was gazing up at the carriage door, his hand raised as if to try the latch. His mouth was open slightly, in wonder. 'Are they players, sir?' he whispered. 'Might they play for us?'

Alarmed, Vincent thrust the purse back into his pocket. He grabbed the man's shoulder, was about to snap, *They are not for you,* when the carriage door opened and the seamstress stepped out.

Vincent felt a powerful, unexpected surge at the sight of her. It was all he could do not to run and grab her. What he would do then he did not know; all he knew was that he *wanted* her.

She burns, he thought. *She burns.*

She had been transformed. Shining with an invisible light, she made Vincent want to shade his eyes, though there was no reason for him to do so.

Peadar made a soft, drawn-out 'oooh' and went to step forward. This brought Vincent back to himself somewhat, and he tightened his grip on the man's shoulder. 'Get back inside,' he told the girl.

She glanced at him before stepping warily from the footplate into the snow. She was a void to him, a silence; there was no hint of the internal communication they had shared at the house. *I have broken her*, he thought. Keeping her back pressed to the gleaming wood of the carriage and her dark eyes fixed on him, the girl began edging her way to the driver's box. 'Please help us,' she said to Peadar. 'He took my friend.'

From all over the village, folk were coming from house and yard, drifting towards her, their expressions dreamy. 'Get back *inside*!' Vincent cried.

A cracked voice spoke from the door of the inn: 'So bright.' Vincent turned to find Peadar's mother tottering towards them. She had always been ancient and wizened, but Vincent was shocked at how twisted her poor body had become; at the very great difficulty she had in walking. 'Rose,' he whispered. 'What has become of you?'

She pushed past him, her eyes fixed on the girl. She flung up her crooked hands. 'So bright! She burns so bright!'

The seamstress had reached the driver's gate and was struggling with the latch. 'Help us,' she said. 'We're from Dublin. He took my friend.'

A young woman came running from behind the horses, black curls sprinkled with snow, face rosy with expectation. It was Sheila Morgan, the blacksmith's daughter. Her friend Agnes Dwyer was with her, and she grabbed the seamstress, startling her.

'Twirl her for us,' cried Sheila. 'Let us see her!'

The seamstress broke free with a cry, pushing them away. Agnes grabbed her again.

'Does she dance? Make her dance!'

People were coming from all sides now, the entire village – thirty people in all – fawning and pawing. Some of them were moaning with desire. Jameson Morgan bellowed, 'Make her sing!'

Vincent began pushing them aside. 'Get back!'

'No!' snarled Peadar, shoving him. 'We're *hungry*!' The brutal desire in his face slammed Vincent back down through centuries. It overwhelmed him with forgotten horror, and with fear for the girl.

Over Peadar's shoulder, he saw her pull free of Agnes' grip again and scramble into the driver's box. Sighing with pleasure, Agnes let the girl's brightly coloured coat-skirts pass though her hands. Sheila Morgan grabbed her, but the girl kicked her into Agnes' arms and slammed the gate shut on them.

The villagers crowded past Vincent, moaning, 'Sing! Sing! Dance.' The carriage rocked under their combined weight. The girl fell to the floor of the box and out of Vincent's sight.

'She is not a player!' he cried, pulling folk aside. 'She is nothing! Get back!'

Fergus Morgan began climbing the gate. 'Stand up, miss! Let us see you!'

Vincent grabbed him by the collar and heaved him from the box. 'She is *nothing*! A labourer! A seamstress! Nothing!' He put his back to the gate, thrusting his arms out against the advancing tide of villagers. They pressed against him, dragging heedlessly at him with desperate strength. His feet slipped on the icy ground, and he felt himself go down beneath the relentless weight of their hunger.

Someone yelled – a hoarse, angry cry – and all went abruptly still. A familiar voice said, 'Stand back,' and the people did, their faces grave, their attention fixed on the door of the carriage.

Vincent pulled himself upright as Cornelius climbed unsteadily to the ground. He was on his last reserves, his hair straggling loose around his pasty face, his elegant frame bent. Vincent knew it was this that had tamed the crowd: the sight of Himself so horribly worn by his time outside; the sight of him undone. They shuffled backwards, shamed by his condition, which was so obviously worse than their own.

Cornelius clung to the door of the carriage and leaned heavily on his cane. 'Are you all right, Captain?'

Vincent nodded, straightening his cloak. He glanced into the driver's box. The girl was huddled against the far wall.

'We are hungry,' murmured Rose.

Cornelius hobbled out from the shadow of the carriage. 'Look at me,' he snapped. 'Do you suppose I am *not*? Do you suppose I do not share your every *pang*?' He revolved in a slow, painful circle, making certain to meet every eye. 'We must control ourselves!'

'She burns so bright,' whispered Peadar.

'She is a *seamstress*!' yelled Cornelius. 'That is *all*!' His unaccustomed rage made those nearest him shrink back. 'Is this what you shall do when the actual players arrive? Use them up on the spot? Squander their fire in the muddy dooryard of the Flayed Badger?' He slammed his cane onto the snow-crusted cobbles. 'Tell me you are not going to do that to me! Not after all I have been through!'

There were murmurs of denial, the shuffling of feet. Cornelius allowed them to marinate in their own shame for a moment; then he waved an arm to dismiss them. 'Let this poor girl be,' he said. 'She is nothing, and there is so much better to come.'

The crowd began to reluctantly disperse. 'Do not let me down,' he called. 'When the players arrive, do not waste them on a moment's greed, when, with a little patience, they will keep us going for so much longer.'

Vincent met his eye as the last of the crowd drifted away. *They are right, Cornelius. She does burn.*

I know.

I can barely look at her. Even now I want to throw myself upon her. What power is this?

Cornelius shook his head. *It has grown stronger the closer we get to home. Even the crone sensed it. She became so agitated by the girl's presence that I had to tell her to sleep.* His eyes slid to the driver's box. *Is she harmed?*

Just shaken. Get back inside. I will fetch her in to you.

She does not do as she is told, Captain. She may struggle.

Vincent shrugged wryly. *What choice has she, cully? I doubt she will stay here after our friends' alarming enthusiasm.*

As Cornelius made his pained way back into the carriage, Vincent glanced around the market square. The villagers had retreated to door and window again. Peadar was watching from the porch of the inn. Vincent stared at him until he lowered his eyes; then he braced himself against the girl's strange magnetism and opened the gate.

She was sitting on the floor, the skirts of her coat puffed cheerfully around her. She had uncovered Matthew and was gazing into his face. As Vincent crouched beside her she whispered, 'You took him, mister. You took him. I'll kill you.'

Vincent reached and gently loosened her fingers from their grip on Matthew's hand. She made two angry fists but said nothing as Vincent took the blanket and covered him once again. This time, the boy did not flinch as the coarse fabric came up to blot out the light. He simply kept staring up at the cloud-laden sky, his face slack and peaceful, his dead eyes filled with snow.

The Big House

Pᴀsᴛ ᴛʜᴇ ᴀʙᴀɴᴅᴏɴᴇᴅ church, the high stone wall that surrounded the estate's private lands began flashing by the window. *Almost home.* Cornelius knotted his fists, his mind speeding ahead as if his will could make the miles lessen. The Angel was a luminous presence at the edge of his senses now, the delicate aura of its power already tangible. Too distant yet to ease his pain, it only made him want to leap from the speeding carriage and run, screaming, the rest of the way.

Hurry, Captain, please.

Vincent did not reply.

The girl watched from the opposite seat, her hands clenched in her lap. Cornelius wanted to throw something over her so that she would stop hurting his eyes with her invisible light. She was weeping, the tears welling up and rolling down her face unheeded as she regarded him with an almost manic intensity. Every now and again her gaze would drift upwards, as if watching some invisible thing rise from his shoulders or his hair. Then her attention would snap back to his face.

Cornelius dredged his voice from some creaky place within him. 'What do you see?'

She clenched her hands tighter. 'Don't you know? Can't you see it?'

He shook his head. The girl hesitated. Her eyes roamed all around his edges – not looking at *him* exactly, but at something which seemed to surround him. She lifted her hand, uncurling a finger to point. Before she could speak, the carriage was plunged into a gloom so deep that the light was blotted almost entirely. The world outside had disappeared! There was nothing to be seen but featureless grey.

I am dead, thought Cornelius. *Dead and dropped to hell.*

They had driven into a fogbank. The realisation filled him with embarrassment and relief. Had he cried out? If so, he hoped Vincent had not overheard.

Within moments the carriage slowed, then stopped. There came the familiar sound of the estate's great iron gates being opened. Cornelius leaned his head against the window. The wrought-iron canopy of the gate arch was just visible above. In the fog it seemed unattached to any earthly support, its heavy filigree floating in the swarming grey, the massive gate pillars and small keeper's lodge invisible.

Vincent's voice called down from atop the carriage, his words flattened by the damp. 'You've been waiting.'

Luke's gruff monotone replied: 'Aye. Was in the lodge. Pull her through.'

The Angel's presence sang a note higher as they crossed the threshold, and Cornelius shut his eyes. *So close.* The fog pressed, sly and inquisitive, against the glass as the unseen gates were dragged shut. There came the harsh metallic *screel* of the chain being drawn, the snap of the padlock. Cornelius watched the girl's hand creep across to find that of the sleeping crone's. Luke's shadow passed the window and she flinched. Cornelius clenched his own hands against a sudden bout of shivering.

Please, Vincent, he thought. *Please, take me home.*

There came the familiar sway as Luke put his weight onto the footplate, meaning to step up into the driver's cab. 'You're in trouble with your missus, Captain,' he groused. 'She's not happy at all.'

Vincent said, 'Get into the carriage if you want a lift.'

Even through the haze of his suffering, Cornelius was shocked by that rudeness. He turned his face towards the ensuing silence, as if he could see through carriage and fog to read Luke's expression.

Vincent spoke again. 'I do not have all day, Luke! Do you want a lift to the house or not?'

There came the sound of the driver's gate being slammed. 'I'll walk,' snarled Luke.

The words had barely been spoken when the carriage jerked to life. They took off at immense speed, the drive spitting gravel beneath the wheels. The trees, the boathouse, the furthest stretches of the pond, all were lost behind the grey face of the fog. It felt like an eternity before Cornelius felt the bump and clatter of the cobbled stretch leading to the river. There was a jolt, and the sound of the wheels became hollow as they crossed the bridge; then gravel hissed under the wheels again as they sped the last half mile beneath the poplars.

The light grew, the fog cleared, and they were travelling past broad sweeps of daisy-speckled lawn. The trees fluttered their greenery in graceful bounty above. Birds sang in summer profusion. The scent of roses filled the carriage.

The Angel's power sang high and clear, its proximity an

embrace, and Cornelius almost wept in bliss. Home. Thank God. Home.

Outside, Raquel – all crinoline and flouncing overskirts – was pushing one of her baby-carriages across the misty grass. She pretended not to notice their arrival and continued her haughty progress without looking their way.

As the carriage rounded the last long curve of driveway, Cornelius realised he was going to be sick. Like the first rush of an opium-pipe after a long time at sea, the abrupt return to the Angel's power was making him ill. He reached for the door and almost flung himself from it before remembering that they were still travelling at a tremendous rate.

Stop, Vincent! he thought. Then he shouted it. 'Stop!'

The house slammed into view. The carriage came to an abrupt halt, and Cornelius threw himself out the door. His legs did not respond as he would have wanted them to, and he fell to the gravel, the harsh stones biting his knees. From the corner of his eye he saw Raquel startle at the sight of him, saw her step away from the baby-carriage. She began to run towards him. But Cornelius knew how he must look, how ill and wretched and ugly, and he knew she would not be able to face him. He lurched to his feet.

Raquel came to a halt at the edge of the drive, her toes touching the gravel, her expression conflicted. She struggled hard. With only yards between them, Cornelius saw her try to will herself across to him. He waved her concern aside – *No bother, my darling, no bother* – and staggered for the house.

'Raquel,' yelled Vincent. 'Escort our guests inside.' The tone of his voice brought Cornelius to a halt. Why was he speaking to her like that? 'Raquel!' yelled Vincent again. 'I have no time to waste! Escort our guests inside.'

At the word 'guests', Raquel's mouth tightened. She did not move. Exasperated, Vincent discarded the reins, about to leap from the driver's box.

Distressed that his friends might be reunited on such sour terms, Cornelius called out, 'Wait, wait...I shall...' Waving Vincent to stay where he was, he stumbled back around the carriage and flung open the door. The girl had moved to shield the old woman's body with her own. Her eyes were everywhere at once, darting from his face to the house, to Raquel and back again, as if tracing a web of lines only she could see.

'Come out,' demanded Cornelius, desperate now to be gone. 'This is the end of your journey.'

He saw her force herself to focus. 'You...' she whispered. She lifted the old woman's hand. 'You told her to sleep. Now she won't wake up.'

Goddamn it. 'Miss Lyndon! Wake yourself!'

The old woman jerked awake and regarded him with startled blue eyes.

'Out!' he cried.

The girl emerged slowly, like a pretty animal from its cage. She was not so dazzling here as in the village. It was the proximity of the Angel, perhaps – like a candle flame in sunlight, the girl was eclipsed by its aura. But she still emanated a bright power; still one felt the urge to squint. At the sight of her, Raquel took two fascinated steps onto the gravel. Then the old woman appeared within the dark frame of the carriage and Raquel stopped dead, her wonder turned to horror.

The girl helped the crone to disembark. They were scarcely out the door when Vincent slapped the reins, causing the horses to start forward with a jerk. The carriage took the corner, its wheels spraying gravel. Then it was gone, heading for the stable yards at the rear of the house.

'Must...' mumbled Cornelius, stumbling up the steps. 'So sorry, my dear...guests...' He waved his hand as he headed in the door. 'Be nice...'

And he stumbled away, leaving the guests to their own devices and the chilly uncertainty of Raquel's care.

The Terrible Voice

As soon as he was alone Vincent slid to the floor of the driver's box and tore the blanket from Matthew. The horses knew their own way, and they trotted into the yard and under the carriage-house arch without guidance as he gathered the boy into his arms. Matthew's body was cold and pliable, a loose-limbed collection of meaningless flesh and bone. His skin was blue-tinged with frost.

Intently, Vincent took the boy's face between his hands. He stared for a long time at the thin and barely recognisable features. There was no life; no movement but Vincent's own breath stirring the ragged strands of dirty-blond fringe. But Matthew was still there. Vincent knew it. Matthew was *there*. 'You hold fast, boy,' he whispered. Then he ducked his shoulder, flung the boy across his back and leapt from the carriage.

The horses whinnied as he ran past, shied as he kicked open the door to the orchard. And then he was out in the open air, dashing through the knee-deep grass of the neglected kitchen garden, stumbling away from the newer portions of the house towards the ruins of the castle, the old moat and the dark, open maw of the under-tunnels.

Vincent could barely remember the last time he had used these steps. Not even at the very beginning, when he'd had the crew drag the creature down here and batten it fast in the darkness – not even when his curiosity had been at its very highest – had he much ventured below the ground. Truth was, he did not like enclosed spaces. Vincent knew this originated in his childhood abhorrence of the packed and stinking cargo-holds of his father's ships, but even so clear an understanding of the cause of his unease could not help him conquer it. So he avoided the tunnels, and only ever ventured below if Cornelius spent too long underground and Raquel requested he be fetched out.

Yet here I am, he thought, *once again submitting myself to the deeps.*

As he shifted the fragile weight of the boy on his shoulder and wended his slow way downwards, Vincent thought wryly that only three people in the entire history of his adult life could have enticed him to do this. Raquel, Cornelius and Matthew – what a fool he had become for them.

'Now, Matthew,' he said, 'you are a long and lanky bundle these days, and these stones are slick. I should be most happy to see you dance a jig when we reach level ground, but pray do not be tempted to stir until then.'

The echoes that whispered back at him seemed to tighten the already close space, and Vincent immediately began to speak again.

'Cornelius…Cornelius will have run straight for the Bright Man, of course, but do not worry. He will have taken the house steps; we shall not stumble across each other in the dark. He is most likely sitting right now on the other side of the tunnels, only a few yards from the lower door, gazing up at his *angel*. In your day he would have had to venture much deeper to find it, but the creature never seems to wander far from the door now. It is almost as if it cannot bear to be any further from Cornelius than he can from it.'

Vincent paused, his hand on the wall, this knowledge suddenly very clear to him. The Bright Man had indeed taken to loitering near the lower door. Vincent knew this because Cornelius had been easier and easier to find recently – slumped only yards from the door, often on the steps themselves, while the creature paced or leaned or lay close by.

It is almost as if the creature is waiting for him, thought Vincent. *Could it be that two centuries of proximity had finally made Cornelius visible to it?* Vincent allowed this idea to percolate as he carried the boy deeper.

'Perhaps Cornelius' curious dependence is no longer one-sided, Matthew. I must detail my recent theories on mutualism to you. What think you of the idea that we are as indispensable to the creature as it is to us? That it – all unknowing to itself – now craves the proximity of creatures it does not even see?'

If Matthew had an opinion on this, he did not choose to share it.

They were deep underground now. Vincent could sense the waters of the moat pressing against the wall to his right, exuding moisture into the stones. Fed via natural channels from the waters of the boating pond, it ran all the way around the estate, enclosing the entire complex of ruins and the manor house itself within its cool green borders.

Vincent respected the moat as the last unchanged bastion of the estate's defences. It served to remind him of all that Cornelius had achieved when, two centuries ago, in the heart of famine and plague and war, he had convinced the original Wolcroft to sheath his sword and silence his cannon. In reconciling tenantry to landlord, Cornelius had succeeded in replacing parapet and drawbridge with manor house and garden, and in the process had shaped this crumbling fortress into a home.

'Into *our* home, Matthew. It all came a little too lightly to you, I suppose. But perhaps now you've seen something of the world, you might understand exactly what he has built for us here, and work a little harder to hold your patience with him. Ah...' Vincent came to a halt at the entrance of the Bright Man's cave.

'Here we are,' he said, laying Matthew onto the gritty sand. 'The site of your restoration.'

The cave was small – hardly larger than one of the estate's cellars – but even so small a space was a relief after the close confines of the tunnels. Vincent squatted for a moment, his hand on Matthew's motionless chest, gazing out across the ghost-fire shimmer of the pool that took up most of the cave's floor. Wisps of vapour rose from the warm stone walls. The air was alive with the soft *plinks* of dripping water and the resulting whispered echoes. Matthew's head had lolled to the side, his face turned to the pool. The water reflected a trembling rim of light onto his hollow features.

'This pool means something to the Bright Man, Matthew. It is drawn to this place. Soon I will fetch Cornelius upstairs, and when he is gone I am certain the creature will come here and spend some time with you.'

Vincent rose to his feet. The Bright Man's strange footprints punctuated the sandy shore all around them, but they were concentrated most heavily on the far side of the water, at the mouth of the tunnel that led to the lower door. According to Cornelius, the Bright Man habitually sat or squatted or lay by the side of this pool, gazing into the water. Cornelius said it *listened* to the water. Vincent had no idea why he should put it like that.

He glanced down at the motionless boy, nodded, and turned back the way he had come. 'I shall be locking the grill behind me,' he called, taking the iron key from his pocket. 'If you wake, do not panic. I shall not leave you alone with the creature any longer than I feel is necessary.'

A sound made him pause at the threshold of the cave. At first it did not even feel like a sound. It was more a trembling in his chest, the barest irritation of his heart, and he paused only to see if it was really there. Then it rose, a great howl of sensation, as if emanating from some depth of his body, as if produced by his own body: an inhuman feeling, conveying inhuman pain, but conveying pain nonetheless – an emotion so consuming it made Vincent want to tear his chest in order to reach his own heart.

Vincent knew – he *knew* – that this was the Bright Man. For the very first time, the Bright Man had a voice.

He turned back and ran for the lower door. Leaping Matthew's body, his boots sent ripples across the surface of the pool. The walls and ceiling came alive in geometries of fire as he dashed through the shallows. Vincent plunged into the far tunnel, his footsteps puncturing those of the Bright Man's as he followed their path.

AT THE LOWER door, the creature seemed in the process of trying to escape. Its spider-like hands roamed the surface of the iron-bound wood as if seeking a crack large enough to slip through. The great appendages Cornelius referred to as wings but that Vincent saw as tentacles – those spreading fans of eel-like protuberances that emanated from its hips and shoulders – were writhing in agitation, their tips probing frantically at ceiling and walls. Its massive head was low between its shoulders, swinging to and fro like that of a chained bear, and its voice – its *voice*! Vincent was certain it would drive him mad with grief.

He fought forward through the noise, his hands clamped to his ears.

Cornelius was pressed to the wall at the base of the steps, his arms braced against the stones, his eyes wide and filled with reflected brilliance as he stared up at the Bright Man. Vincent marvelled that he could tolerate the creature's searing presence. 'Cully!' he cried. 'Come away from it!'

Cornelius turned to him, his expression an ecstasy of wonder. 'He is singing. Can you hear him?'

Vincent gripped Cornelius by the shoulders. 'Can't you *feel* it? In your heart? In your lungs? This is a deadly sound!'

Indeed, the voice was resonating horribly within him: all the tiny particles that made him up – the atoms, the molecules – were shivering. Vincent could feel the vibration worrying at his damaged lungs, tearing old scars.

'Cornelius,' he gasped. He was clutching his friend now, where at first he had been trying to pull him away. 'Cornelius…'

Cornelius frowned. Through the fog of his bliss, some small understanding seemed to reach him.

'Are you in pain?' he asked.

Vincent gagged. It felt as if a clot had formed in his

throat. He coughed, and Cornelius' waistcoat was spattered in blood.

Dimly, Vincent felt strong arms grab him. From far away Cornelius shouted, 'Hold fast!' He felt himself being dragged up the steps towards the creature. Horrified, he tried to resist. Cornelius shook him. 'Trust me!'

They stopped side by side with the creature. Squinting up into the blinding luminosity of its face, Vincent thought he could make out features: the ridge of a heavy brow that seemed to wrap the entire skull; the long, shadowed arc of nostrils. But details came and went in blistering waves, and he could not be certain of what he saw. The Bright Man's proximity seemed to unravel his reason.

'Mind his wings!' Cornelius stretched forward, reaching for the latch, and Vincent looked up into the living archway of the creature's tentacles, lacing and unlacing, restlessly testing the ceiling and walls.

Careful not to come into contact with the creature's poisonous flesh, Cornelius slowly opened the door against the Bright Man. As ever, it showed no resistance to physical force, but the pitch of its voice changed, its grief becoming puzzlement as it was pressed against the wall.

'Quickly, Captain! Do not let it touch you.' Cornelius shoved Vincent up the steps ahead of him. 'Go on! I will follow.'

Outlined against the light, he slipped through the door after Vincent and began pulling it shut behind them. The Bright Man's tentacles seemed reluctant to retreat, and they probed the gap like the arms of some incandescent sea anemone. But Cornelius was merciless. Slowly he closed the door, forcing the arms to recoil, until finally the last glowing filament withdrew, the latch clicked, and they were once again in darkness.

Darkness but not silence. To Vincent's horror, the creature's voice rose in despair, once again unpicking the substance of his lungs. Agonised, he began an uncoordinated ascent of the tunnels. Then Cornelius' arm was around his waist, and they scrambled together until they reached the stairs, then climbed until they could no longer hear that anguished song.

'I can stop now,' gasped Vincent. 'I can stop.'

Cornelius released him and Vincent sank to his knees. The moisture pooling on the steps soaked the fabric of his trousers. His hands splashed into warm water as he rested his forehead against the stone.

Heedless of the damp, Cornelius sat beside him, gazing back the way they'd come. 'It was trying to get out,' he said, amazed.

Still breathless, Vincent nodded. He could feel the damage to his lungs beginning to reverse itself: the creature's healing aura counteracting its destructive power, now that he was beyond the range of its voice. 'The girl,' he managed. 'It must be the girl…'

The flat discs of phosphorescence that were Cornelius' eyes widened in understanding. He turned to Vincent in delight. In the darkness, the glowing planes of his slim, mobile face were even more expressive than in the light. 'But of *course*,' he whispered. 'It was attempting to commune with her.'

Vincent grinned. 'Shall we go see how she fares?'

Cornelius stood in a rush. Helping Vincent to his feet, he began hurrying him up the stairs. 'I do hope, Captain, that she retains her wits longer than the last seer. It is always such a chore to deal with the insane.'

The Children

Harry figured that Mama had come in during the
night and laid their overcoats on the bed the way she often
did when the weather was cold. It was so darned cosy. Dash
was a solid length of sleeping warmth to his right. To the
left, Leo was snoring like a hog. Somewhere beyond those
two, his other brothers, Nat and Will, would be adding
their warmth to the congregation, all of them pressed like
sardines into their narrow little bed. There was no sound
of their parents moving about yet, nor of Gladys in her cot
by the fire – perfect peace for once in the Weisses' crowded
apartment.

There was no way Harry was going to wake up yet.

Dash sighed, a great gusty blast of air right down the
back of Harry's neck. 'Aw, sheesh, *Dash*! What the heck've
you been eating?'

At that moment Leo yawned a similarly vile gust of
stench into his face, and Harry's memory came rushing back:
Joe, the carriage, Tina. He recalled the frantic storm of their
arrival; the carriage driver's frenzied departure; his own half-
frozen squirm from beneath the tarpaulin; crawling to the

safety of a hay-filled horse stall; unconsciousness. And now…

Harry opened his eyes to a gaping mouthful of teeth, a huge tongue, the pulsing gullet of the largest dog in the world.

The dog yawned into his face once more, flung its foreleg across Harry's chest, and lay its grizzled head on Harry's shoulder. On Harry's other side, another similarly massive dog took a moment to gaze into his eyes before settling back down.

Harry lay motionless in his pile of hay, staring up at the web-festooned rafters of the stable as the two huge dogs commenced snoring on either side of him. He listened to his heart hammer in his ears, and tried to take long, calm breaths.

Where was he exactly? What had happened to Joe? Where was Tina? He remembered very little of the journey except the bruising rattle of the carriage and the pain of the cold. He glanced down at the fists he had clenched on his chest. Carefully – without disturbing the dogs – he flexed his fingers. They hurt, but he could feel them. He had only the dimmest sensation of his toes.

A scuffle of sound drew his attention to the top of the stall's dividing wall and Harry was startled to find himself looking into the eyes of a small child. It was a boy of perhaps ten years of age, lying along the top of the wall. He was gazing down at Harry, his chin resting on his hands as if he had been watching for quite some time.

'Hello,' whispered Harry. 'Are these your dogs?'

The boy pursed his lips but did not answer. He was a very handsome child, blond, with bright-blue eyes and clear, healthy-looking skin. He was dressed in a smart little outfit of brown wool knickerbockers and a waistcoat, with a clean white shirt beneath. He kicked his booted feet behind him as he looked Harry up and down. 'You are not a stick-man,' he said eventually.

'Um...' Harry shifted beneath the weight of the sleeping dogs. 'Can...can you call off your dogs?'

'He speaks most peculiar.'

This comment came from a corner of the stall, and both Harry and the boy shifted their attention to its source. A small girl sat on a pile of hay, her knees drawn up to her chin, her hands clasped delicately around her legs. Though perhaps a year or so younger than the boy, she was the female image of him, right down to the questioning tilt of her blonde head and the wide blue innocence of her eyes.

'He's not from the village,' she said.

The boy returned his attention to Harry. '*Is* he a stick-man, though?' he asked.

'Everyone who's ever come before have been stick-men,' said the girl.

'Or stick-women. Or stick-children.' The little boy smiled when he said this, and something in the quality of his expression made Harry's stomach clench a little tighter.

'Stick-women and children and men,' sang the little girl. She jumped to her feet in a flounce of pale-blue skirts. The movement made Harry flinch, but the girl simply scrambled up the wall and sat by the boy's legs, swinging her little feet to and fro. 'Stick-children and women and men,' she sighed. 'So very easy to break.'

'He does not look easy to break,' murmured the boy.

The girl giggled. At her piping laugh, the dog at Harry's shoulder jerked awake. Harry felt it tense as it registered the presence of the children. The second dog whimpered. Laying their ears flat, both animals lowered their heads, eyeing the children with what could only be translated as fear.

Say now, thought Harry. *I've had my fill of this.*

He went to rise. The boy held out his little hand. 'You stay right there,' he said.

The hell I will! thought Harry. But to his horror, he found he didn't move. It wasn't even as if he'd tried and failed to succeed. He just didn't stand up. He wanted to, he kept meaning to, but his body simply didn't, and so he remained right where he was.

The boy lowered himself from the wall and hunkered down by Harry's side. The dogs jerked, as if to lurch to their feet, but the child laid his hand on the nearest one's neck. 'Stay,' he murmured. The animals stayed.

The child looked Harry up and down, taking in every detail of his clothes and face and hair. He stroked the dog's powerful shoulders as he did so. The dog trembled beneath his touch.

'Did you *wander in*?' asked the girl from her perch atop the wall.

'All stick-men *wander in*,' the boy informed Harry. 'A long time ago, stick-men were always wandering in. Whole families of them, like scarecrows, crying and begging for food.'

The little girl pouted. 'But Vincent and Pap always drive them on before we get a chance to play.'

'Not always,' corrected the boy. 'Sometimes we find one.' He smiled down at Harry.

The little girl hunched her shoulders in glee. 'Then we keep it,' she said.

'We haven't found a stick-man in *ages*,' breathed the little boy. He unbuttoned Harry's jacket and began to root in his pockets. 'I don't think you *are* a stick-man, though. You're too fat; you've too many things.'

Harry watched in helpless silence as the child took his pocketknife, examined it, laid it aside. He watched him take his pocket watch, and his last shining tuppence; watched as the boy's small fingers undid the buttons on his waistcoat. He felt the unnatural heat of small hands through the fabric of his shirt as the firm flesh of his stomach and chest was examined.

'You're very muscly,' observed the boy.

On the wall, the little girl hugged herself and kicked her legs. 'Will I fetch my scissors?' she asked. 'Will I fetch Mama's needles and pins?'

The boy met Harry's frantic eyes. 'Oh, I'm sorry,' he said. 'You may speak if you like.'

Harry's head lifted from the ground in fury. 'You touch me again, kid, and I'll beat you to a bloody pulp! Give me my damned watch back!'

The girl broke into gales of laughter. 'Oh, I adore the way he speaks! Say something else, fat stick-man!'

'Let me up off this floor, you brats, or, I'm telling yah, I'll—'

The boy leaned close. Harry recoiled at the cold, cruel curiosity in his wide blue eyes.

'You'd what?' asked the boy, genuinely interested. 'What would you do?'

'He'd beat us to a bloody pulp,' the little girl reminded him quietly.

The boy rose to his feet and stood with his hands on his

hips. 'A bloody pulp is not difficult. All it takes is a big rock and some time.'

'Or a hammer,' said the little girl. 'Hammers are fun.'

Harry gazed up at them both, fear a bright taste in his mouth. He tried and, once again, failed to rise.

The boy grinned. 'Don't move, fat stick-man. I'll be back in a moment.' He disappeared from view. Harry tried to turn his head, to keep the boy in sight, but his body simply did not respond, and he found himself stuck gazing up at the girl. She had shifted position, twisting her body as she watched her brother wander around the carriage house.

'No, not that,' she said. 'It is much too heavy – how would you carry it?'

Out of sight somewhere, the boy grunted in agreement. Something clunked as he laid it down.

Harry concentrated on his treacherously motionless hands, willing them to move. If he could manage to control just one arm, just one, then he could punch the little bastard right in his face. *I'll show you what 'bloody pulp' means*, he thought. *Come on, it's all a matter of will. Come* on!

The little girl said, 'Ooh, I like *that* one! Let's try that!'

Harry's heart began to race. His fingers twitched against his chest, but that was all. With a spike of despair, he remembered how impervious Mickey the Wrench had been to the carriage driver's suggestions, and how little difference it had made in the end.

I can't even get my ass up off the ground! he thought. *These kids can't be more than ten, and I'm about to let them cut me to pieces.*

Furious, he tried again to clench his fist. One punch. One goddamned punch was all he needed.

The sound of metal trailing across cobbles rang out in the stillness. On either side of him, the dogs whined.

'Can I try first?' said the little girl.

'No,' said the boy. 'But you can have his eyes.'

Something inside Harry screamed at that – some hectic, terrified thing. He tried to jerk into action. His body betrayed him with stillness. 'You'll be sorry if you hurt me,' he cried. 'You'll regret it.'

The sound of trailing metal grew loud as the boy re-entered the stall. 'Look what I found!' he exclaimed, as if expecting Harry to be pleased. It was a pitchfork, its prongs thin and sharp and wicked.

'Let me! Let me!' cried the girl, and she fell from the wall in a tumble of skirts. One of the dogs began a high, terrified moaning, and the little girl scowled, all her laughing sweetness gone. *You be quiet*, you dirty, *dirty* dog!'

Harry almost wept at the expression on her face. The huge dog howled in terror.

A thickly accented, Irish country voice spoke by the stall door. 'What are you two doing? You know you're not allowed to play with Himself's dogs.'

The children turned in sulky resentment to a man whose mud-caked boots Harry could just see from the corner of his eye.

'What have you got?' asked the voice.

'It's just a stick-man, Luke.'

'There are no more stick-men. You know that. The Hunger's been over for nigh on half a century.'

The boots came closer. Harry looked up into a tanned,

weather-beaten face, whiskered cheeks, and suspicious eyes under heavy brows.

'Help me,' gasped Harry. 'The pitchfork.'

'Maybe he's a tramp, Luke,' suggested the girl.

The man regarded Harry with reserved curiosity. 'Maybe,' he said.

'Can we keep him?'

The man looked uncertain. Then he nodded.

'No,' said Harry. His fingers twitched again, jerking against his rapidly beating heart.

The man was already turning away. 'Just let yon dogs be,' he said. 'And don't tell your pap I let you keep the tramp – I got enough grief over what ye done to that rabbit.'

'Don't!' cried Harry. 'You'll be in trouble!'

The man turned back, apparently entertained at the idea.

Grinning, the little boy crouched by Harry's side. 'And who would we be in trouble with, tramp? Who are *you*, that anyone would care?'

It was an action so natural to Harry, so often practised and re-practised, that it was over before he'd even thought of it: his left hand fluttered, drawing the audience's eye; his right picked the child's pocket; and with a flourish, Harry produced his own tuppence from behind the boy's ear.

It was the simplest of tricks, childish in its mundanity, but it made the boy gasp in wonder. The man sank to his haunches by the boy's side. The little girl clapped her hands over a giggle.

'I am the Great Houdini,' said Harry. 'Lord Wolcroft hired me. I'm for the Christmas show.'

THE MAN CALLED Luke dragged Harry by the scruff of his neck through a weed-clogged stable yard and around to the back of a huge and austerely beautiful house. Multi-paned windows watched him stumbling past. Granite cherubs peered impassively from distant eaves.

Reflected in the windows, Harry could see the boy following behind, a picture of sweetly childish manliness in his little suit, trailing the pitchfork. Its metal tines sang against the ground, leaving twin tracks in the clean white gravel of the path. The girl skipped along, twirling Harry's penknife in her hand. Harry tore his eyes from her and twisted his head against Luke's unnaturally strong grip, looking up into his face.

'They were gonna torture me with that pitchfork. You were gonna let them.'

The man grunted. 'Sacrifices must be made. Even Abraham had to give something in exchange for Isaac.'

They rounded a corner, and came up the side of the house. The tines of the pitchfork shrilled against the uneven flagstones of a sun terrace. On Harry's right, through high glass doors, he could see a library. On his left, a sunken garden held blood-red roses to the cloudy sky. There was something wrong with this picture, but Harry's brain refused to move past the sound of the pitchfork.

'The children's games make the Angel stronger,' muttered Luke. 'Seems to be I'm the only one as will admit it.'

Harry stopped listening. This man was quite obviously deranged. They neared the front of the house, and he could see a broad sweep of lawn, edged with fluttering trees. This rolled down to a small lake, partially swallowed by a bank of fog. Harry's eyes jumped from feature to feature, judging distances, escape routes, hiding places.

There was a woman on the lawn, tall and ornately dressed, grimly pushing a pram towards the house. Tina was standing by the front steps. All her attention seemed fixed on the lake at the far end of the lawns. The old actress from the theatre was with her, her eyes on the woman with the pram, who was now passing onto the drive.

'Missus!' yelled Luke. 'This one claims he belongs to the show!'

Though she seemed to be the one he was addressing, the woman sped up, clearly headed for the front steps. 'No one in the house!' she cried. 'I told Cornelius that. No one in the house!'

Luke dragged Harry after her. 'Now you look here, missus! Does this one belong to Himself or not? If he don't, I'm giving him to the childer. To hell with the consequences!'

The woman stopped at the bottom of the steps. Almost reluctant, she looked around at the two children who had come up beside Harry and Luke.

The boy bowed politely from his hip. 'Good evening, Mama.'

'This stick-man is *very* entertaining,' the little girl informed her. 'Ask him to fetch you a penny!'

The woman flicked a troubled glance at Harry.

Luke, meanwhile, seemed mesmerised by Tina. 'By God, missus. *What is she?*'

The woman's dark eyes slid sideways. 'You see it too? I think she belongs to Cornelius.'

'You…you'd best take her inside then, missus. You'd best look after her if she belongs to Himself.'

Ursula Lyndon looked uncomfortable at this. 'Now see here,' she murmured.

'Miss Kelly doesn't belong to nobody!' cried Harry.

Tina seemed not to notice the conversation, or if she did, she seemed not to care. Her eyes roamed the fog-shrouded lake. 'There's something down there,' she said. 'Like an empty space.'

The little girl was regarding her with piercing curiosity. 'Isn't she *pretty*,' she said. 'Doesn't she have pretty hair?' She smiled across at the woman and twirled Harry's knife. 'Would you like me to fetch you her hair, Mama?'

With a cry, the woman spun away and shoved the pram ahead of her up the steps. Its many frills and flounces bounced violently, but no crying came from within.

Luke shook Harry by the collar. 'What about this boy, missus?'

The woman paused on the top step. She could not seem to look directly at Harry, and only took him in with sideways glances. She was very beautiful, with her dark hair and eyes, her strong profile. Harry had no doubt in his mind that this was the famous Raquel. 'What age are you?' she asked. There was the faintest remnant of an accent in her words, breathy and sibilant, Spanish perhaps.

'I'm almost seventeen, ma'am.'

This caused her to look directly at him. 'Seventeen,' she said. She looked him up and down, a yearning wonder in her face. 'Yet nothing like him.' She seemed to recollect herself at that, gave a frowning glance to the children, then nodded to Luke. 'Allow him in.'

She crossed the porch with the bearing of a queen, her dark skirts whispering. Once she entered the house, she was lost from sight, but Harry could still hear the pram, its tyres squeaking as she travelled the rooms within.

The little boy looked puzzled. 'Can't we have him, then?'

'You can't have any of 'em,' grumbled Luke. 'They belong to your pap. Come on.' He gestured that they should follow him. 'I'll see what I can find ye in the traps.'

The children trailed after him, sulky but obedient, the little boy still dragging his pitchfork. Before rounding the corner, Luke paused. 'Best get yourselves into the house,' he told Harry. 'I'm going to release the dogs.'

As soon as the man was gone, Harry ran to Tina. 'Come on!' he cried. '*Now*. We gotta find Joe and go!'

Ursula Lyndon gripped his arm. 'What about the dogs?'

Harry thought of the enormous, battle-scarred creatures in the barn, and his stomach did a little flip.

'Young man,' said Ursula, 'I realise that uncouth fellow has given you a scare, but gamekeepers don't take kindly to trespassing. Now it's clear you are part of Lord Wolcroft's festivities, I'm sure your troubles are over.' She squinted at him, suddenly uncertain. 'Did you come in the carriage? I don't recall...' She seemed to struggle with her thoughts, as if realising there were a lot of things she didn't recall. 'I...I have been invited here as an advisor to Lord Wolcroft. Miss Kelly is...is my companion. Yes. Miss Kelly and I shan't be going anywhere, young man. Indeed, I wouldn't advise you set off on foot. How would you ever get through the snow?'

Snow? Slowly, Harry looked around him. Where the hell was the snow?

Ursula followed his gaze. She clasped her hands. 'What has become of the weather?' she whispered.

'I'm not leaving Joe,' said Tina.

'Do you know where he is?' cried Harry. 'Let's get him!'

She was tense as a knotted fist, and she stepped back from his touch. 'Joe...Joe's dead.'

Dead? No! 'When?' cried Harry. 'Where?'

But Tina didn't seem to hear him at all. 'Joe's dead,' she repeated softly. 'I'm not leaving him. You should go, though. Don't...don't go to the village. I think the people there are...Take Miss Ursula.'

She turned away. Walking careful as a drunk, she made her way up the steps. Harry watched her enter the house, his mind reeling.

'Young man?' Miss Ursula tapped his arm. 'Young *man*, what on earth is happening? Why is everyone behaving so peculiarly?'

'We need to go!' cried Harry. 'Tina!' He ran up the steps, then paused, turning to Miss Ursula. 'Wait here, okay, lady? Holler if anyone comes back.'

'Holler?'

'If someone comes, try not to listen to them. Just holler a warning, then block your ears and run.'

'Run?' she cried, as he entered the house. 'Are you deranged?'

THE RECEPTION HALL was dominated by a stuffed horse. The huge creature had been mounted on a wooden platform facing the entrance, its dusty eyes fixed on the landscape outside, its powerful body poised as if contemplating a trot around the lake. Harry skirted it warily, following the click of Tina's heels to the corridor beyond.

The hallway was muted with shadow, its walls lined with display cabinets. Stuffed birds and animals crowded the glass shelves, their bodies permanently twisted in frozen imitation of life. Beneath the scrutiny of so many tiny gazes, within the silence of the house, Harry found himself unwilling to call out. He passed through blocks of mote-filled sunlight falling through open doors. There was no stir of life in the revealed rooms.

He found Tina in the ticking quiet of a library. Through the high French doors he recognised the terrace across which Luke had dragged him and, beyond that, the sunken rose garden. The clock-tower of the stable block was just visible above the trees.

'Tina,' he whispered. 'You can't stay here.'

She paced the bookshelves, her hands opening and closing. 'It's here,' she whispered. 'It's here.'

'*Tina!*'

She turned to him, regarding him with hectic eyes.

'We have to *go*,' he said.

She shook her head, her gaze once again roaming the crowded walls. 'Joe.'

Oh God, Joe. 'Are you sure he's dead? Did…did you see a body?'

'I *saw* him. Oh, Harry, *I saw him*. He was all alone. His eyes were full of snow.' She pressed her fists to her temples and gasped. 'But he's here. He's right here! I can't leave him…'

'But *where* did you see him? What—'

'*Stop talking, Harry!* You're making it *worse*. There's so much *noise*. All the *singing*. All the *lights*! If you just let me *think*! If you just let me *listen*…' She trailed off, her entire body abruptly relaxing. 'Oh,' she whispered. 'It stopped singing.'

The room seemed very still now that she had stopped pacing. Harry was almost afraid to move, in case he set her off again. There was a small movement in the hall, and Harry spun to find Raquel standing on the threshold of the library. She cradled a baby doll in her arms, and her dark eyes were fixed on Tina.

Suddenly Harry had had enough. 'What did your god-damned friends do to Tina? Look at her! She's out of her mind!'

Raquel dismissed him with a glance.

'They're coming,' Tina whispered. 'Up from below ground.'

Raquel nodded. 'Vicente fetches him up for me some-times.'

There were rapid footsteps in the hall and Ursula Lyndon appeared, wide-eyed and breathless. 'There *are* dogs, you know! They're enormous.'

At the sight of the old woman, Raquel sidled into the room, the doll raised as if to shield her. 'Not in my house!' she cried.

'I...I am sure they won't come in,' soothed Ursula. Her eyes flitted to Tina, whose attention was still focused on the bookshelves.

'In *my* house,' insisted Raquel, 'the old ones are *upstairs*. We don't have to *see* them.'

These people are nuts, thought Harry. *Full-blown, howl-at-the-moon nuts.* His gaze met Ursula's, and he saw the same understanding in her eyes.

Tina breathed out suddenly, a sound of discovery and satisfaction. 'Ah, I knew it!'

At the exact spot where she had been staring, there came

the sound of a key in a lock. A latch clicked within the wall of shelves, and a false front, complete with books, swung outwards. The space within was so dark that it seemed to swallow light. The man it contained was invisible until he stepped forward.

'Cornelius,' said Raquel, her expression warming with relief and joy.

Lord Wolcroft smiled at her. Harry thought he was transformed; his face younger, his bearing infinitely more graceful than before. 'Dearest,' he murmured, advancing to kiss Raquel's hand. He chucked the doll beneath its chin. 'Sophie,' he said, as if in greeting. 'Have you been good for your mama while I was away?'

His jacket and trousers were stained with damp, his waistcoat spattered with what looked suspiciously like blood. Raquel noticed this with a frown, and Wolcroft tilted his head to acknowledge her disapproval.

'I am a touch dishevelled,' he agreed. 'For which I apologise.' His cool grey eyes took in the occupants of the room. 'You'll have met our lovely—'

At the sight of Harry, his face froze into sudden lethal coldness. His hand darted beneath his jacket.

A rich voice paused him in the act of withdrawing a knife. 'The boy is mine, cully. Lay aside your blade.'

The carriage driver appeared in the secret doorway. Breathless, as if he had been climbing steps, and a little grey in the face, he met Harry's eye, a dangerous edge to his smile.

'Well, conjurer,' he said. 'You must be very keen for another audition. Stowed yourself in the luggage, did you?'

Harry said nothing. The driver's voice sounded in his mind. *You keep your mouth shut about our mutual friend, boy, and I promise not to make you cut out your own tongue.* Harry glanced around the room, awaiting the others' reaction to this threat. The driver's smile widened. *Only those we wish to hear hear, boy. So you'd best heed when I choose to speak.*

'Vicente,' said Raquel. Smiling, she went to the driver where he still stood, framed within the darkness of the doorway. He took her doll and laid it on a table, with no sign that it meant anything more to him than a toy.

'Are you well?' he asked.

'Except that I have missed you.'

'As I have you.'

They put their arms around each other, and Harry's mouth fell open and Ursula Lyndon gasped as the couple indulged in the most intimate of kisses. Wolcroft chuckled at his guests' reaction and, as his friends continued their embrace, crossed the room to sit on a sofa by the windows, the very picture of contented élan.

'My,' breathed Raquel at the kiss's ending. She seemed pleased but, Harry thought, a touch surprised. 'Such passion,' she said.

The driver, half-smiling, smoothed the heavy coils of her hair. 'The journey has refreshed me.'

She frowned. 'You do not look refreshed, *querido*. On the contrary, you look quite ragged.'

His dark eyes lifted to Tina. 'That shall change.'

Raquel turned within the compass of his embrace. Pressing back against his chest, she examined the young woman before her.

Tina did not take her eyes from the driver, who she was regarding with fury. Seemingly amused at her rage, he murmured into Raquel's ear, 'Isn't she luminous?'

'She is like a candle.'

'Cornelius found her.'

Harry felt another blaze of anger at this horrible reduction of Tina to nothing but a thing – but before he could protest, Ursula Lyndon swept ahead of him. 'Oh, but Miss Kelly is just my companion,' she said. 'I am Lord Wolcroft's guest.' She advanced on Raquel, offering her hand. 'Miss Ursula Lyndon,' she said.

Raquel retreated with a grimace of almost fear. 'What did you bring that here for?'

'Raquel,' tutted the carriage driver as he shut the secret door, 'be polite.' He gave Ursula a wry look. 'Try not to take offence, ma'am. Raquel is not keen on contact with the elderly.' He offered his own very dark hand. 'I, however, should be *quite* happy to take an introduction.'

Ursula's gloved fingers curled in on themselves. Harry was sure she was about to withdraw, but she stepped forward, her chin up. 'I seem to have been mistaken as to your identity, sir,' she said, as she and the driver shook hands. 'I had taken you for a servant – it would appear that I was wrong?'

'You would refuse my hand were I a servant?' he asked.

'I…I do not think you would have offered it, were you so.'

'Because I would have known my place? Yet you offer me *your* hand. What is your place, then? Do you consider yourself more than a servant? My equal, perhaps?'

Ursula's cheeks flared red. Her mouth formed around unspoken words.

'Let her go,' whispered Tina. 'You don't need her now you have me.'

Chuckling, Vincent put his arm around Miss Ursula. The old woman made an uncertain noise but allowed it. 'Oh, but she *is* necessary.' Vincent grinned at Raquel. 'We are to have a séance, *meu amor*. Miss Lyndon has proved quite the expert with the spirit board.'

Raquel huffed. '*Spirits*. Did we not have our fill of those during Cornelius' witchcraft years?'

'Raquel,' protested Wolcroft mildly. 'Witchcraft indeed.'

'A sliver of wood pushed about a table shall hardly provide the answer to our decline! Sorcery never yielded reward before, why should it now?'

'Because,' said Vincent, 'Cornelius has found himself a seer.'

Raquel's eyes widened, and she turned to Tina. 'Oh,' she breathed. 'Is that what she is?'

Ursula Lyndon followed her bright-eyed gaze. 'But...' she said, looking Tina up and down. 'She...'

Vincent swung the old woman towards the door. 'Go and get your things,' he urged. 'Set up the board. Let us discover what the girl can see.'

'Now?' whispered Ursula.

'When else?'

'Well...' She seemed to gather her dignity. 'Might one be offered a cup of tea? A morsel to eat?'

'I don't think so,' said Raquel.

'But we've been travelling for days!' cried Harry.

'Come now,' said Wolcroft, still sprawled on the sofa. 'It has been a long journey. Our guests are fragile. Surely we can offer them a bite to eat?' At Raquel's silence, he lost his smile. 'Raquel, I messaged in advance. You knew full well—'

Raquel occupied herself with smoothing the doll's petticoats. 'Rats got into the pantry,' she said. 'They ate it all.'

Wolcroft leapt to his feet. 'We cannot just let them starve! That would be intolerably cruel!'

The carriage driver held a hand up to calm him. 'Peadar will send to the big town, cully. There shall be supplies here within two days – unless the snow hems us in.'

'Two days? Captain, you *know* what outsiders are like! They cannot wait that long. I messaged you to order *food*, Raquel! I asked that you order in *firewood*! Tell me you at least have their rooms made up!'

Raquel refused to meet his eye. 'You said not in the house. That is what you said.'

Wolcroft spun to the driver as if seeking support, and the dark-skinned man sighed. 'Oh, very well. You go and find them rooms, cully. Let them rest awhile. I will speak with Luke. Perhaps he can come up with something in the way of vitals for them.'

Raquel looked from under her eyelashes. 'Put the crone upstairs,' she said. 'Where she belongs.'

Harry did not like her expression. Without thinking, he took Ursula Lyndon's hand. The old woman didn't object. 'Where Miss Lyndon goes, we go. Right, Tina?' He glanced at Tina, who all this time had not taken her eyes from the carriage driver. '*Right?*' he said. She finally turned her attention to him. 'We're going with Miss Lyndon, right?'

She nodded, slow and careful, and made her way to his side.

'We stay with Miss U,' she whispered.

WOLCROFT LED THE way upstairs. He took each step lightly and with grace, no longer seeming to need his cane, but the hem of his elegant morning coat was filthy, his shoulders smeared with green as if he had been flung against a mossy wall.

The walls of the stairwell were lined with paintings: Wolcroft, Raquel, Vincent and the children, their portraits repeated over and over, a multitude of faces gazing down. Even the man called Luke had his own assortment of images. There was another face, too, repeated on the walls: a young man of perhaps seventeen, darkish-blond hair, wryly smiling eyes, the same amused warmth shining from each painting.

Could this be Matthew? wondered Harry. There was no resemblance between poor Joe and the boy in these paintings, but looking around the walls, Harry couldn't imagine who else the chap might be.

The family seemed to have a penchant for theatrics, especially the adults. Vincent and Cornelius in particular seemed to have gone through quite a phase of dressing themselves in old-time costumes, like Shakespearian actors. Harry passed a portrait of Vincent grinning, a cutlass resting across his knee, a pearl earring dangling from one ear. The name of the artist and the date had been scratched from the corner.

Harry slowed. His eyes leapt from painting to painting: none were dated. He turned to look at the portraits on the opposite wall. He looked back down the way he had come. He must have passed at least a dozen paintings of each person on the way up: a dozen Raquels, a dozen Vincents, at least a dozen Wolcrofts. Yet they all seemed the same age as now. Surely they hadn't had all these portraits done at the same time?

Tina took him by the elbow, making him jump. She

squinted at him as if through a fog. 'Stay together,' she whispered.

Wolcroft had reached the top of the stairs. 'Your rooms are this way,' he said, rounding the corner and walking from sight.

They found themselves in a corridor lined with doors. Wolcroft was just bending to place a key in a lock. 'I apologise about the accommodations. But this was once Raquel's room and with luck should still prove…' He stopped talking, his head tilted as if listening to something. After a moment he nodded. 'Vincent is taking care of the horses. Once he is done, we will bring you your baggage.'

He opened the door, and dull sunlight bled into the gloomy corridor. Wolcroft regarded the room with uncertainty. 'Well,' he murmured. 'I suppose it is the best that can be done.'

Harry followed the women inside. Staleness hit him, and the oppressive smell of dust. The air had a crawling quality, as if aeons of invisible cobwebs had accumulated there.

'The old woman can sleep in there.' Wolcroft indicated a half-opened door, beyond which another bedroom slumbered beneath its own blanket of neglect. 'Do not worry about the children, they shouldn't bother you here.' He glanced at the ceiling. 'Also…pay no mind to any noises. They are harmless.'

To his guests' amazement, the man turned to leave. Ursula Lyndon found her voice before he could shut them in. 'You cannot mean that Mr Weiss shall sleep here!'

Wolcroft glanced at Harry. 'I had not meant he sleep *anywhere*.'

'Well, I seem to be your friend's guest,' said Harry. He smiled. 'Might as well get used to me.'

Wolcroft's grey eyes hardened. 'I doubt you will be here long enough that I shall need to.'

'You cannot make us share a room with a young man!' insisted Ursula.

In a storm of barely suppressed impatience, Lord Wolcroft dragged his keys from his pocket, crossed the corridor and unlocked the far door. He flung it open, some comment poised on his lips, then froze. For a long moment he remained motionless, one hand on the doorhandle, the other clutching the frame, gazing into the room he had just opened. Then he slowly shut the door and quietly, almost gently, locked it. Without looking at Harry, he moved to the next room and unlocked that.

'You can use this one,' he said. 'It used to be mine.'

He left without saying anything more. Harry listened to his muffled footsteps descend the stairs, then looked into the room that had been opened for him. It contained a small four-poster bed, its heavy drapes patterned in masculine gold and red. A heavy iron-bound chest served as a dresser; a small bookshelf held travel-sized novels. The windowsill was deep and filled with cushions, as if the occupant were used to sitting there. Everything was muted with dust, the air stifling.

'Harry?' He turned to find Tina clinging to the frame of the opposite doorway, gazing uncertainly at him. 'Come...come in here with us.'

Harry went to her. Tina rested her fingertips against his chest, as if to confirm that he was in fact real, then drew him into the room. 'Stay with me,' she whispered. 'They'll be kinder to you, if you stay with me.'

Ursula grimaced. 'Let's not succumb to delusions of

grandeur, dear. We all know what happened to Joan of Arc.' She took a small brown bottle from the châtelaine purse on her belt and indulged in a bitter little swig of its contents. 'No matter how *luminous* you are,' she muttered, 'you're still just a seamstress.'

Tina went to the window, moving as if she were feeling her way through the dark. Her attention was once again fixed on the lake shrouded in fog far below them.

'The winter stops down there,' she whispered. 'It's all around us. The whole country full of snow, except for this one small place.'

'An underground spring,' said Ursula. 'A hot spring.' Harry glanced at her. 'They should open a spa,' she muttered. 'Of course they would need to learn to be polite to their guests.' She took another swig from her bottle.

'The cold is eating its way in,' whispered Tina. 'Because... because the light is fading.' She pressed her hand to the window, covering the lake with her palm. 'There's an empty space down there. It eats the light. Just like *they* eat the light.' She turned to Harry, inspired. 'They're eating the light, Harry. Like...' She made grasping gestures with her hands, as if trying to catch the words she was unable to say.

'But you can *see* it,' she insisted, as if he had contradicted her and she was desperate to prove him wrong. She pointed into midair, her eyes following the movement of something unseen and drifting. 'It's pure, all the threads of it, and it comes together around each of them.' She joined her hands, slowly twining the fingers, demonstrating. 'They're wrapped in it. *Trailing* it. Snagging it as they walk. And they're *using it up*.

'We're...at the same time, we're giving it out.' She spread

her fingers again, bursting them apart as if demonstrating a firework. 'And it *feeds* on it. You understand?' she asked hopefully. 'It feeds on the light, through them, and they get stronger – because they've been here so long they're part of it.'

Harry shook his head, grief-stricken at how thoroughly unhinged Tina had become.

'Listen, Harry! Do you not understand? They used to be like us. They used to *feed it*. Now they *use it up!*'

'I'll get you out of here,' he whispered. 'I swear to God, Tina. Whatever they've done to you, we'll fix it.'

Her face closed up like a fist. 'I'm not leaving Joe,' she said.

'Who is *Joe*?' cried Ursula Lyndon. 'Do you mean that young man from the depot? For goodness sake, Miss Kelly. He's not here!'

Tina glared at her, and Ursula Lyndon surged to her feet.

'I'd ask you to watch the way you look at me, madam! Talk about put a beggar on horseback. I might have known. Well, let me tell you, miss *luminous*, miss *lovely*, just because a man like Lord Wolcroft makes eyes at you doesn't mean you're set for life. Take it from one who knows – as soon as that pretty face of yours begins to line, you'll be—'

'Shush,' said Harry, holding a hand up.

'I *beg your pardon!*'

'Aw, lady, just *shush*. Listen. Do yah hear that?'

The old woman stilled, the little brown bottle clutched before her, her eyes wide with the fear that Harry knew was sharpening her tongue.

He looked to the ceiling. They listened. It took a moment, but then it came again, very definite, very clear: a rustle, then a thump, then the slow, quiet sound of something dragging itself across the boards above.

'What *is* that?' asked Ursula Lyndon.

'I don't know,' said Harry. 'But I'm darned sure it's no squirrel.'

Apparently unperturbed, Tina resumed staring at the lake. She pressed her hand to the glass again, as if telling something to stay in place. When she looked back, Harry felt there were miles between them, aeons. 'Let's go,' she said.

'Where?'

'To find Joe.'

'We should stay here,' whispered Miss Ursula, her eyes on the ceiling.

Tina crossed the room and gently kissed the old woman's powdered cheek. 'You stick with me now. Don't be scared.'

She went to the door. Overhead, the noise started again: the unmistakable sound of several large things dragging themselves across the floor of the attic; the uncertain scuffing of feet; the sense of a slow crowd moving.

Harry felt Ursula Lyndon press to his side. She once again took his hand. The sounds moved from where they were standing across the boards of the ceiling until they were directly above Tina. Then they stopped.

'Are you coming with me?' Tina asked.

Harry nodded. *I don't think we're the only ones*, he thought.

The Key

VINCENT KNEW RAQUEL had been surprised by his kiss, but he did not think she had been disturbed. Certainly she had not pulled away. She had, in fact, reciprocated, and when her lips had parted in response to his gently probing tongue and her arms had tightened around him, Vincent had felt a thrill between them which he had not enjoyed for decades.

He would not like her to think it was the presence of the girl that had awakened him so. Though Raquel well knew his love of pretty things and it had never seemed to bother her, he hoped she understood that the girl invoked a response in him that was less sexual and more...what? More hunger, he supposed.

It was a different feeling altogether to lust.

Admittedly, when the villagers had first advanced upon her, Vincent's fear *had* been that they would rape her. It had taken him back, all too vividly, to the many times on his father's ship when a new delivery of slaves had brought about a frenzy in the men and they had indulged themselves with horrible abandon upon the helpless women of the cargo. At such times, Vincent would scamper up the rigging as far as he could climb – far from the shrieks and the crying; far from the catcalls and laughter. He remembered hating everyone then: the slaves, for revealing that side of his shipmates; his shipmates, for their cruelty; and himself, for retreating to the blue of the African sky and staring uselessly out to sea while on deck and in the holds below, men he thought of as family fashioned hell on earth from the only place he knew as home. Sometimes he had also hated his father, but mostly he had just hated mankind – its abominable weakness, its shameless, open, striving greed.

When, at the age of fifteen, he had felt the first stirrings of his manhood in response to the sights and sounds of the decks below, and when such sights and sounds had then begun to intrude into certain kinds of dreams, Vincent had known he was on the verge of losing himself. Shortly after, he had approached Cornelius with his idea. Within the year they had enacted their mutiny and fled from the monsters their fathers had been set to make of them.

Raquel said this history made him gentle with women. Vincent did not know about that – he never felt particularly gentle – but he supposed she would appreciate better than most gentleness in a man, her first husband having inflicted more than enough masculine torment upon her.

Raquel. Vincent missed her. He had not realised how much. Where had it gone – the intimacy, the warmth? How had he not noticed its absence?

Once Matt is restored, he thought, *things will return to normal.*

He smiled. It would be good to shake off the dust they'd been accumulating; to restore their life to the idyll it had once been.

He brushed the horses. Their muscles quivered beneath his touch, and as he worked the sun-flecked air of the stables warmed their dark hide, his dark hands, his lips.

Somehow, his thoughts of Raquel became entangled with those of the girl and that dress, and how she might look in it: turning beneath a bright light, quivering, her dark hair tumbling down, the softness of her breasts pushed up by the bodice—

'VINCENT!'

Vincent jumped, embarrassed, and then amused. It would appear that the trip to Dublin had been slightly more refreshing than even he had appreciated.

Then Cornelius came slamming in from the stable yard and stole all the lazy sensuality from the air.

'You took my key!' he cried.

Vincent's heart dropped. 'Cornelius, you cannot mean to go below again so soon.'

'What business is it of yours where I go and when? How dare you take my key!'

In a perfect storm of disgust, Cornelius flung himself at the jacket Vincent had left hanging by the door. He began rifling through the pockets, and before Vincent could stop him he had found what he was looking for and more.

'You have the iron key, too!' he cried, holding up the key to the old castle tunnels.

'Calm yourself,' said Vincent. 'Cornelius!'

But Cornelius was already turning away, apparently intent on retreating underground.

He must not find Matthew! Vincent grabbed him, and Cornelius responded with immediate fury, twisting from

Vincent's grip and punching him in the face without so much as a warning.

The blow spun Vincent against the door, the bright taste of blood on his lips. He pressed his hand to his bleeding mouth and willed himself not to succumb to the instant, almost blinding, desire to beat his friend senseless.

When he was calm enough to turn, he found Cornelius had backed into the yard, a set of keys clutched in each hand.

'Look at you,' snarled Vincent. 'Barely up out of the ground, and you want to return. You have not even taken time to change your soiled clothes or comb your hair – you presented yourself to *Raquel* in that condition – and here you are, already mindless again with need.'

Cornelius turned away without replying, heading for the orchard and the old castle ruins, the closest access available to his angel. Skewered with panic, Vincent strode after him.

'Cully,' he said. 'Cully! I cannot afford to lose you yet. Stay with me for just a while longer. You can visit with your angel for as long as you wish afterwards. For days, for decades. Just help me finish what we started here first. There is still so much to do in the theatre. And…and the séance. Yes. We must prepare for the séance. And you had something else planned for the girl, too, didn't you? The dress? You must do her up in that dress, for Raquel and me. Wouldn't you like that?'

Cornelius' fury softened, and he halted, looking about him in what could only be described as despair. Vincent gently took the keys from his hands.

'What has upset you, cully? You are not usually prone to such temper with me. The last time you raised your fist to me was the week Matthew left us. Do you recall?'

'Oh, don't,' moaned his friend. 'Don't...Poor Matt.'

Slowly, carefully, Vincent took him by the arm. When Cornelius did not shrug him off, Vincent led him to the orchard gate and sat him on the bench there.

Cornelius leaned his head in his hands. 'I found myself in his room, Vincent. I had not meant to...It was such a shock to see all his things still there. The dust of ages on them.' He shut his eyes as if against a pain. 'Matthew.'

'He will return.'

Cornelius' anger flared again, cutting bright and unexpected through his grief. 'Stop that!' he snapped. 'I'm *sick* of hearing it! I'm tired of telling you it will not happen!'

'It shall happen. And sooner than you think. Then things will be as they once were, Cornelius. We will *live* again. Raquel will laugh and walk about and come on trips as she used to; you shall not spend your whole life underground, and I shall—'

Vincent stopped talking, realising with a start what he had been about to say.

'You shall what?' asked Cornelius, straightening. 'What shall you do?'

Vincent shook his head.

'What?' insisted Cornelius, his eyes narrow, his face intent.

'It has been over fifty years since I was in the village, did you know that? I had not realised it until Peadar said as much. *Fifty years*, Cornelius. Where did that time go? What have we been doing with it?'

Cornelius got to his feet. Vincent remained seated, squinting up at him as he blotted the sun. Cornelius' face was lost in shadow.

'You are not happy here,' he said quietly. 'You want to leave.'

Vincent thought about it. 'I want more,' he admitted.

There was a moment of unreadable silence, during which Vincent shaded his eyes, trying to see Cornelius' expression. A cry of 'Captain' from the far end of the orchard made him turn. Luke was striding through the far gate, his face even sourer than usual.

'Captain,' he yelled again. 'I have apples and I have wood pigeons what I caught in the traps. It's the best I can do. If them doxies don't like 'em they can bloody well lump 'em.'

Vincent found himself filled with an almost painful relief that the conversation had been diverted. He took the excuse to step out of Cornelius' shadow, and, ignoring Cornelius' eyes on his back, he followed Luke through the slants of late sunshine and the long grass of the orchard, as if keen to hear more of what he had to say.

Cornelius stayed in the shade of the wall, and when Vincent glanced back, he had gone.

Rooms and Boxes

HARRY FOLLOWED TINA as she led the way from one side of the upper floor to the other, gently opening and closing doors as she went. Most of the rooms on their side of the house had been moth-eaten bedrooms choked with dust, but here in the other wing, Harry thought things felt more lived-in. The dust was not so deep; the wooden floor and certain pieces of furniture gleamed gently as if from regular use.

He glanced back down the sombre corridor they had just travelled. It was a brooding march of closed doors. As in the downstairs halls, stuffed animals lined the walls, and they seemed to watch as the huddled knot of intruders made their way past. Between the two wings, the top of the main staircase showed a graceful curve of banister. There was no sound from the lower floors.

'This is a sewing room,' whispered Tina, stepping through a newly opened door. The creatures in the attic above sighed as Tina crossed the threshold, then went very still overhead.

'I think the poor things have decided to wait outside,' said Ursula, her eyes on the ceiling. She met Harry's eye, tinkled a little laugh. 'How odd that I should say "poor things". And yet it feels right, does it not?'

Harry nodded uncertainly. The old woman was behaving a little oddly.

This room was much less neglected than the others. In some places there was no dust at all. Unlit candles were everywhere, some new, some half melted, hundreds of them. Tina touched everything she passed, as if grounding herself, feeling her way through reality. She stopped by a tall window, framed in low evening light, and tentatively rested her fingers against the elegant black-and-gold neck of a treadle-powered sewing machine.

'Wilcox and Gibbs,' she whispered. 'Very old-fashioned. I was saving for a Singer & Co. I never told Joe that. I was afraid it'd embarrass him, when he had so little. Such foolishness…'

Absently, she pressed a finger to a sheaf of yellowed fashion plates sitting on the work table and regarded the partially finished dress on the mannequin before her. It was covered in dust. 'Years out of date,' she whispered. 'Just like that woman…all out of date.'

She looked down at the gleaming wood of a low, scroll-backed chair that faced the window, ran her fingers along the freshly dusted windowsill, gently touched a miniature painting of the boy Harry presumed to be Matthew. 'She sits here all the time…'

Miss Ursula went to her side, gazing down at the grounds. 'Perhaps she enjoys the view,' she suggested brightly. 'Like a bird in its gilded cage.'

'Or a spider in a web,' said Harry.

'Perhaps she's a *spider* in a gilded cage.' Miss Lyndon

laughed and took another nip from her bottle. 'I'm not sure I'd mind it myself,' she murmured. 'Certainly it's a pretty cage, only in need of a *little* dusting.' Harry eyed her, frowning. He wondered if there was gin in that little brown bottle of hers. 'I wonder what's in there?' she said, loosely gesturing to a door on the far side of the room.

'The light is very strong in there,' said Tina.

Cautiously, Harry went to the partially opened door and, standing well back, pressed it open. It was a playroom. Charming in the warm light from its big windows, it was obviously a much used, well loved space.

Harry ventured inside. What Gladys wouldn't give for these toys! Entranced, he gravitated towards a great dollhouse that stood like a frosted wedding cake on a table by the fireplace. He peered through the tiny frames of its downstairs windows at miniature tables and chairs, candelabras, a piano. He smiled to see all the dolls sitting upside down at the dinner table, their legs sticking in the air, then frowned to see their severed heads placed in a neat and grinning row on the sideboard. He straightened in a hurry, and the stench from the upper rooms of the dollhouse made him reel backwards in shock.

What on earth? With sinking heart, Harry placed his handkerchief over his nose and mouth and peered into one of the bedroom windows. The curtains on the four-poster bed were closed, the painted floor beneath it stained and gummy. Harry thought he only half-imagined the sound of buzzing flies.

He backed away. The room around him seemed heavy now with dreadful possibilities, and he stood in the centre of it, his handkerchief pressed to his nose, intimidated by the now glaring dolls. A stain on the floor drew his eye. Children's footprints traced a dark circuit from it to the foot of a little bed and back again.

A furtive noise brought his attention to a wall of puzzle boxes piled by the window.

He listened, his heart hammering, until the sound came again – a dry, skittering flutter, then silence.

Reluctantly, Harry approached the boxes. Cheerfully painted, and all about six inches cubed, they were stacked carefully one atop the other, like a wall of building blocks. With dread, Harry opened the lid of the nearest box. It was filled with feathers, that was all: the fine, fluffy under-down and sleek pinfeathers of a sparrow, perhaps, all soft greys and browns. Emboldened, Harry opened the next. He slammed it shut again immediately, the sight of the gaping, skeletal beak and curled dead foot enough.

That weak little flutter of movement came again, drawing his attention to the last box on the top row.

Oh, I can't, he thought. *I can't look.*

'It's all right, Harry.' Tina's soft voice made him yelp; her hand on his back made him flinch. She picked up the box and carried it to the window. The sash squealed as she raised it. Fresh air flooded the room, dolls' dresses rustled, puppets twisted on their strings.

The box thumped within Tina's hands. 'Poor thing,' she whispered.

She placed it on the broad shelf of the outside windowsill and opened the lid. Harry stepped back, afraid of what horrible mutilation might emerge as Tina tilted the box. A sleek, speckled thrush slid out onto the granite sill. It seemed frozen with terror, until Tina lightly touched her finger to its shivering back, and in a startled thrum of wings and flicker of shadow it was gone. Tina traced the arc of its flight across the top of the windblown trees, then closed the window.

For a moment she stood looking around the room, scanning the shape of things Harry could not see. 'The light was all over that little bird.' She crouched, frowning, and pressed her hand to the polished boards as if checking for heat.

'It's all heading down there, Harry.' He almost flinched when she looked up at him again, her eyes were so concentrated and fierce. 'The light. It's all heading for Joe.'

As they descended from the top floor, Miss Ursula waved languidly to the ceiling, and bade Tina's sighing followers 'bye bye'. She'd put the little brown bottle away, but Harry thought she was far too relaxed for the circumstances – far too prone to stopping and touching things and humming.

The first-floor landing led from both sides of the upper staircase to an arched picture window overlooking the grounds. From this window, another curved flight of dark wooden stairs led down into the entrance hall. Peering over the banister, Harry could just see the rump of the stuffed horse below. The quality of the light and the cool shift of air told him that the front doors were still open to the breeze.

There were four doors on this floor, one at each corner of the landing, all set into deep alcoves. Tina made straight for the door to the left of the big window and tried its handle. Outside Harry could see the dogs. They were asleep on the grass, their blunt noses facing the house. There was no sign of any of the human inhabitants.

'It's locked,' said Tina, loudly rattling the door.

'Hey,' hissed Harry. 'Keep it down! Try another one.'

'I need *this* one,' she cried.

Ursula drifted to Harry's side and gazed wistfully down at the dogs. 'Oh,' she said. 'Puppies. I had a puppy once. Mother taught him to dance while I sang.' She rapped on the glass. 'Coo coo,' she called. 'Coo coo! Puppies!'

Tina began banging on the locked door.

'*Oy gevalt*,' said Harry. He pulled Tina aside and crouched to peer at the lock. 'Just a very old double tumbler,' he muttered. 'Piece of pie.' He slipped his lock-pick set from his sock, and in a matter of moments was twisting the handle and pushing the door. He grinned up at Tina, expecting praise, but she just shoved past, frantic to be inside.

Harry scowled. Climbing to his feet, he took Ursula Lyndon by the arm. 'Come on, ma'am. Let's leave the doggies alone.'

He ushered the old woman into a world of quietly ordered sound and movement. The room was large, taking up perhaps this floor's entire right wing. Many windows flooded the space with light, and it was packed with bookshelves, tables, display cases and desks. The activity within was a stark contrast to the rest of the silent, morbid house. Clocks ticked softly from the crammed bookshelves. Lizards and snakes and chameleons rustled in cages filled with foliage. There were many aquariums, all alive with darting fish and crabs and creeping molluscs. They were fed bright streams of air by clockwork bellows, and filled the room with the sound of flowing water and the regular, gentle *shush* of a sleeper's breathing.

Tina pushed determinedly through a maze of glass

display cases. Harry went to follow, then paused at a tall desk. Someone was obviously working on a project here: there were many reference books opened, many jotters filled with notes. What looked like a scientific periodical sat open to one side. It was well thumbed, the text in French. The opened page was underlined in many places. A piece of paper had been wedged into the spine, and on it, in the same bold copperplate hand as in the jotters, someone had written: 'De Bary's ideas on mutualism interesting here. Re-read *Die Erscheinung der Symbiose.*' And then, underlined many times, a note in different ink, presumably added later: 'The living together of unlike organisms! De Bary has hit on it. I am certain. Should I tell Cornelius?'

Harry blew a light coating of dust from these pages. He flicked the pen in its dry inkwell. Whoever had written this had not been at work in a while.

Glancing up, he saw Tina pass behind a series of specimen jars. Their lifeless contents hung suspended in amber liquid, and neat labels told their names: 'Remora', 'Leech', 'Tapeworm'. Tina's slim shape shifted and warped within the curved belly of each container as she passed it by.

'He's here somewhere,' she whispered. 'The light is all straight lines here, all clear and ordered. Because he's here.'

By the door, Miss Lyndon perused a shelf of books. 'Someone likes their Jules Verne,' she murmured. 'And *en Français*, no less.' She snatched a very old-looking book from the shelf. '*The Life of Olaudah Equiano*. Why, of course!' She ran a finger along the spines on the shelves, excited. 'No Frederick Douglass? How odd, especially considering the…shall we say *mixed* nature of our dark friend's relationships.'

Tina cried out suddenly, from somewhere near the front windows. 'He's here! He's here, Harry!'

Harry ran along the aisle of cages. Dried worms shivered and shook as he forced his way between their closely packed display cabinets. 'Tina! Wait for me!' He emerged to dust-laden sunlight and a window filled with golden sunset.

Tina stood within this radiance, her face resplendent with discovery. On a trestle before her rested a box, long and narrow like a sword case, its red lacquered wood gleaming in the dying light.

'Harry!' she beamed, her hands on the box. 'It's Joe!'

Harry didn't know what to say. He had been expecting Joe's body. Or a door, a secret passage – a cage, even – but this? 'Tina,' he said gently. 'That's not…'.

Tina bent low and whispered into the box's ornate silver lock. 'It's all right, Joe. It's all right now. I'm here.' She caressed the lid and looked up at Harry again, her brown eyes shining. 'Open it, Harry. Please. Let him out.'

Harry knelt by the box. His hands were shaking as he once again removed his lock-picks from their little canvas roll. It took him several tries to insert them into the lock. The mechanism was nothing, a mere trifle, but it took longer to undo than any he'd ever encountered. All the time Tina crouched by his side, her skirts pooled around her, her eyes fixed gravely on his clumsy fingers.

'It's the light,' she whispered as he once again failed to engage the tumblers. 'It must be very distracting, the way it keeps wrapping around your hands. Here, let me…' She swiped at the lock, as if brushing something from his way. 'I think it likes you,' she said. 'That's why it keeps holding on like that.'

He stared at her and she smiled encouragingly. 'You can do it,' she said.

Harry had no doubt he could. He just wasn't too sure he wanted to. After another moment of fumbling, he took a deep breath and told himself to be a man. He pressed up with the first pin, pushed in with the second, and the heavy silver latch popped.

Tina sprang up, flinging back the lid. Harry got slowly to his feet, watching as her expression changed from joy to sorrow.

'Oh, Joe,' she whispered.

Her eyes filled with tears and she placed her hands in the box, laying them gently on the dry and rustling thing that nestled within. Harry eyed it with a mixture of nausea and fascination. It was like a deformed snake: the desiccated body of some strange, appalling rat-king of snakes. *What P.T. Barnum wouldn't give for that thing*, he thought, taking in the tangled knot of multiple heads, the strange intestinal curl of the maggot-like body.

Tina ran her hands over it, tenderly, lovingly. Small flakes of its skin floated up at her touch and crumbled to pearlescent dust on her fingers. A tear fell from her cheek to darken the papery swell of its belly.

'Tina,' whispered Harry. 'You can't possibly think that's Joe.'

She shook her head, her hands still in the box, her face wet with tears.

'That's not Joe, Tina. Look at it.'

She stilled, frowning slightly. Harry saw confusion begin to surface through her grief. He gently took her hands from the creature's body.

The sound of a door banging open made them startle, their hands clenching round each other's. Out of sight, Cornelius Wolcroft demanded, 'What in blazes are you doing in Vincent's laboratory?'

'Why, looking for our supper, of course,' Ursula Lyndon laughed. 'Have you come to deliver it?'

Harry squeezed Tina's fingers and quietly closed the lid of the box. She looked from him to it and back, her dark eyes troubled as he pressed the latch shut. 'I promise,' he whispered, taking her hands again, 'that's not Joe.'

Wolcroft stepped into view at the far end of the room, his face sharp with suspicion. 'What are you doing?' he snapped. 'You cannot be here. Get out.'

He scanned the area as they exited, as if looking for evidence of tampering or theft, but he seemed content to follow them soon enough. Closing the door behind them, locking it from his set of keys, he stalked back up the stairs, leading the way to their rooms.

Ursula Lyndon followed close behind, asking questions he didn't give any sign of hearing.

'Your dark-skinned friend,' she said. 'He is a scientist, sir? Certainly the preponderance of equipment in his room would indicate such? The son of an African king, perhaps? Sent to Europe to be educated. Is that it, sir? Did you meet in college? Or...'

She hurried up the steps until she was by Wolcroft's side, and Harry saw her glance slyly up into his face.

'Is he a *relative*?' she asked softly. 'An indiscretion, perhaps – taken in and raised as part of the family? I knew an American fellow once. His father had black brothers and a black sister. His grandfather's children, you know, by one of his slave women. The family were quite open about it – not like Mr Thomas Jefferson and *his* children. My friend's family allowed his cousins to live on family land, gave them a little farm. All the little piccaninny-children were educated side by side with the white. Personally I think that was *wonderfully* charitable of them. I admire that kind of thing *greatly*.'

Cornelius Wolcroft slammed to a halt in the bedroom doorway. Without warning, he blocked the way with his arm, causing Ursula to come to a halt. He glared down at her. It was the first time he'd acknowledged her existence by his side, let alone the fact that she was speaking to him. His expression made it clear he wished she would *shut up*, but after a moment he simply lifted his arm from her way and Ursula Lyndon sailed past, a small, triumphant smile on her face.

'Oh,' she cried from within. 'You've brought my *dresses*! How wonderful!'

Tina came to a halt as Wolcroft turned to look at her. She had maintained a grip on Harry's hand that was both possessive and protective, and now this grip tightened as she and Wolcroft locked eyes. The man was breathing deeply, his mouth a hard, determined line.

Within the room, there was the sound of cloth rustling as Ursula Lyndon moved things about. 'This bed is so dusty!' she exclaimed. 'Thank you for spreading a sheet down before you laid these out.' She tinkled another little laugh. 'What am I saying?' she said. 'Of course *you* didn't lay them out. You had a maid do it, I'm sure.'

The day was dying, all traces of the golden sunset draining from the already gloomy corridor. In the fading light, Wolcroft's eyes glowed flat and reflective like a dog's.

Harry felt as if he were caught in a suffocating dream. The only thing that anchored him, the only thing that said, *This is real*, was Tina's painful grip on his hand; the feel of her warm presence by his side.

'You can't make me do anything I don't want to,' she whispered.

Wolcroft nodded. 'I know,' he said. 'But I suspect you know that the same does not apply to everyone.' His luminous eyes shifted to Harry, then slid sideways to the old lady still chattering out of sight in the bedroom.

Harry felt fear squeeze his heart. 'Don't you dare,' he cried. 'Don't you use me as—'

'Be quiet,' murmured Wolcroft, and Harry was.

'I beg your pardon?' said Miss Lyndon. 'Did you say something?'

Wolcroft gazed at Tina. 'Did I?' he asked. 'Did I perhaps ask her to *do* something?'

Tina shook her head. Wolcroft stepped gracefully to one side, indicating with a small bow that she should enter the room. Tina squeezed Harry's hand.

'You won't hurt him?' she said.

Wolcroft smiled. 'Of course not.' He gestured to Harry. 'Go to your room and rest. The women and I need privacy.'

Every molecule of Harry's brain was screaming at him not to leave, but his body, dear God, his body simply walked to the far room, opened the door and went inside. Once there, he couldn't quite recall what it was he was supposed to be doing, so he sat on the edge of the bed and watched as the last of the light drained from the tumultuous sky.

Something Old, Something New, Something Borrowed

As Cornelius entered the room and locked the door, the old woman removed a ring from a small wooden jewellery box and slipped it onto her finger. The girl stood watching him, her hands clenched, her expression piercing. He went to the bed and laid his hand on the heavy gold brocade of the sequin-covered gown.

'You shall wear this one,' he said.

The actress turned in surprise, the jewellery box still in her hands. He saw that her pupils were contracted to pinpoints and realised with disgust that she had been dulling herself with the laudanum.

She laughed at the sight of the dress. 'Oh, that one is very pretty,' she agreed. 'But a touch ornate for a séance, don't you think? Unless…Am I to entertain, sir? Are you expecting guests?'

Cornelius shut his eyes against a surge of violent impatience. 'Not *you*.' He looked again to the girl. 'Take off your clothes,' he ordered. 'Put this on.'

There was a moment of perfect stillness.

'But,' whispered Ursula Lyndon, 'those are *my* dresses.'

When Cornelius did not take his attention from the girl, the old woman turned and placed the jewellery box onto the dressing table with a quiet *click*. From the corner of his eye, Cornelius saw her lean on the table's edge, her arms braced, her back lifting and falling with slow breaths. After a long, silent moment, she raised her head and met her own eye in the mirror. Cornelius saw her map the contours of her aging face; saw bitterness and hatred, then cold determination take their place in her expression.

She straightened and turned to face the room. 'You'll want to stay, of course,' she said, crossing the room to the girl. 'Gentlemen do so like to watch.'

Without looking her in the eye, she began undoing the buttons on the girl's coat. Roughly she tugged it free and cast it aside on the dressing-table chair.

'It's a good job I'm here to help her find her feet, I can tell you. She wouldn't have an idea what to do without me.' She slapped the girl's side, like a butcher in a market. 'Never even worn a corset, have you, girl? Well, you won't fit into one of *my* dresses without one – so prepare yourself.'

One after another, she opened the buttons on the girl's blouse. With no ceremony at all, she stripped the garment from her and flung it atop the coat. Muttering, she bent to unbuckle the girl's belt.

All through this, the girl watched Cornelius, her dark eyes intense, warning him against harming the old woman. He bowed in gracious acquiescence, content to allow her the illusion of choice. So long as the girl behaved, he would be happy to leave her more malleable friends alone. As the actress tugged the girl's skirt from her, Cornelius turned his attention to the bed and began undoing the many tiny buttons that adorned the glittering dress.

The light was almost gone, and the dress took on a subtle, translucent quality as his eyes adjusted to the gloom. The fabric shimmered beneath his fingers, and he smiled bitterly. It was perfect – Vincent would love it. How could he not? Didn't Cornelius always give Vincent what he wanted, long before he even knew he wanted it? Hadn't he spent years finding all the things that would make Vincent happy?

He would keep the hair and jewellery simple, perhaps leave the throat bare. *Pretty, but not ostentatious – that is what he likes.*

These thoughts absorbed him as he undid the costume's many fastenings, and he didn't notice the lack of movement behind him until the silence prickled his neck. He turned to find the women staring at him, the girl a gleaming, dark-eyed vision in petticoats and stockinged feet, the crone a pensive shade beside her. Cornelius straightened from his work, unsure of the problem.

'Might you like to lend a hand, sir?' suggested the actress. Dropping stiffly to her knees, she gestured him to the girl's side. 'Here, sir,' she said. 'Perhaps you could help me?'

She was indicating the floor by the girl's heels. Cornelius went and crouched beside her, thinking a buckle needed undoing.

'Do you think I should remove more petticoats?' She lifted the hem of the girl's underskirts. 'I have left...one, two, three, four,' she counted, eyeing him as she lifted the hems one at a time until the girl's slim ankles were exposed.

Cornelius looked at the skirts gathered in her hand, looked

at the old woman, looked back at the skirts. 'I…well, what do *you* suppose?' he asked. 'What is the usual arrangement for a dress like this?'

The woman gazed at him a moment as if perplexed. Then she delicately ran her finger up the girl's black-stockinged calf. The girl's leg twitched. 'Are these stockings acceptable?' murmured the old woman.

Cornelius huffed in exasperation. 'Yes, yes,' he said, climbing to his feet. 'It's the *dress* that matters – why should I care about the stockings?' He looked around at the scattered clothes. 'You said she needed to put something else on, or the dress will not fit her…Where is that thing?'

The old woman sat back on her heels. His reaction to the stockings seemed to have thrown her. 'Do you mean the corset?' she said at last.

'Yes, the corset. Where is it?'

She got to her feet and rummaged in her bags. 'She's a big girl when compared to me. I'm not making any promises…'

Cornelius began fussing with the girl's hair, shaking it out, running his hands through it, spreading it across her shoulders and letting it tumble down her back. She was no more than a doll to him, a mannequin, and so it shocked him when she spoke, and jarred him when he once again looked into those piercing eyes.

'You're all lit up,' she whispered. 'Do you know that? For the very first time, you're giving off light.'

He paused, his hands in her hair. 'What do you mean?'

'You're all alive now. Like that man from the garden.'

'Luke?'

'And those little children. You're giving off light, just like them. For the first time since I've seen you. You're feeding it.'

The actress approached again. She seemed pleased to find Cornelius with his hands buried in the girl's hair. Smirking, she came up behind the girl and put her arms around her waist, wrapping her in some stiff bodice of boning and canvas. Still reaching from behind she did up a long series of clasps on the front of the bodice, and gradually the girl's breasts were raised, her waist pinched.

Across the girl's shoulder, the old woman lifted her eyes to Cornelius. 'You need to hold on here,' she murmured. Taking his hands from the girl's hair, she placed one on each of the girl's warm hips. 'There will be some tugging.' She began fiddling about out of sight. 'Like I said, she's a big girl when compared to—'

Abruptly, she heaved at the back of the bodice. The girl was almost ripped from Cornelius' grip, and he tightened his hold. The old woman heaved again. Cornelius met the girl's eyes. They were glittering and pained as the constricting garment tightened around her. She raised her hands to steady herself against his chest. The process seemed to go on forever, and Cornelius found himself holding tightly, looking down into the girl's face as her body was hauled at and jerked against him.

'Do you even know my name?' she whispered.

Shocked, he stepped back, releasing her, but the job was done, and the old woman came to stand by his side, admiring the strange shape into which they had forced the girl's body.

'Doesn't it do wonders for her?' asked the woman. 'Don't you like what it does for her…um…' She gestured to the top of the garment, where the creamy swell of the girl's breasts now strained against the pale fabric of her chemise. 'Oh, *do* try not to look so tragic, girl. Smile, for goodness sake. Learn some art. No gentleman wants to look at a scowl!'

Cornelius pulled away. The girl looked awful, imprisoned and mutilated, as if she had been squeezed in two. Disconcerted, he skirted the bed and backed all the way to the window.

The actress squinted at him in renewed uncertainty. 'Sir?' she asked.

'It…it has grown quite gloomy,' he said. 'I will fetch some candles. Raquel has always enjoyed candlelight – she will be certain to have some to hand.'

He left them in the gathering dark and almost ran into the adjoining room. He came to a halt just inside the door, his heart hammering. He could hear the actress whispering as he stood motionless in the shadows, and her words gradually replaced his crawling shame with anger.

'You can't do this without me, girl. Don't think you can. This is obviously a sophisticated man – you'll have to do more than drop your bloomers and close your eyes to keep your hooks in *him*. Oh, spare me that look! I've heard you, with your "Joe, Joe, Joe". And I've seen you, too, as soon as you think my back is turned, holding hands with that American boy. You think I don't know how a girl gets by? You can drop the act with me.

'But you must be careful with that man – he's no grab-handed street boy. He'll buy all the innocent eyes and fluttering virginal heart you have to offer, but when it comes down to it you'll need to know what you're doing with him. I know his type. You need to have *technique*. I can help you with that. You follow my advice, keep me close, and we could be well set up here – we could be here for years.

'Are you clean? When was the last time you washed? Here, I have perfume…'

Cornelius listened to all of this with his jaw set and his fists clenched. The filthy old *pander*. The dirty, shameless, appalling old *whoremonger*. How could she?

Then he lifted his eyes and caught his reflection in the sheen of the dusty window. *You hypocrite*, he thought. *Holding on to what you've got the only way you know how. What difference is there between you and that desperate old harridan?*

His eyes flicked away from his reflection. There was plenty of difference, *plenty*. That creature in the room next door was nothing like him. Barely sixty years old and already used up, she was, like the girl, like the rest of humanity, a flicker, a hiccup, a dust mote on the face of time. Here and gone in the blink of an angel's eye, they were nothing. They meant nothing.

Cornelius fetched a box of candles and matches from Raquel's spare wardrobe. The old woman stopped whispering when he returned to the room, and, all business, he went about setting the candles into their holders and lighting them.

'Let us put her in the dress,' he said. 'I should like to test it out in the candlelight. Then we can head down to the séance.'

You

YOU ARE WALKING down a staircase in darkness. Ahead of you walks a man. He is invisible to you in the dark, but I can see him. Through your eyes, I see him. He is carrying unlit candles. There are matches in his pocket. He passes a painting on the wall – the intelligent, dark-skinned face of the man he loves – and his fingers brush the frame as a caress. Behind you, hopeful and frightened, is an old woman. Her hopes are pinned on you. You are nothing to her but a currency.

Your heart and lungs and stomach are squeezed in the grip of a merciless giant, and you find it hard to breathe. You are thinking, *Joe Joe Joe. I will find you. I will find you, Joe.* It is this that has called me back. This and the singing, which is not aimed at me. It is not aimed at me at all, but I can hear it, as I know you can. It, too, called me back. From the cold arms of my mother; from a darkness so intense it hurt my thoughts; from eternity, it called me.

Need. Hunger. Loneliness.

And you.

You reach the bottom of the stairs, and the man leads you to a big room where there is a table set up with planchette and spirit board. The man means to test you with these things, to force open your mind so he may speak with the one who is with me here in the dark.

That will kill you. You must not allow it.

There are others sitting on a sofa in this room. They rise and the man smiles, waving them back down. He sets you up before a silent piano, behind a screen, and arranges you like a doll. He moves about the room, putting candles in holders and setting a match to them.

The old woman hovers by the door, unheeded and uncared for. Her hope is turning to bitterness. She is so close to hating you.

The man raises his head. The light of the candles is shaded from you by the screen, but his face is illuminated by them. He smiles across at the people on the sofa: the man he loves, the woman they adore.

'This is just an hors d'oeuvre,' he says.

He unshields the candles, and – as you have been commanded to do – you turn and turn and turn.

All is sparkling, all is brightness, the room about you filled with shivering light. There is a surge of wonder, and with it a howl, a scream, a vast, visceral, eternal *rush*. The creature with me rises up. It rises up. It is the one howling. It is reaching for the ceiling. Its arms, its wings, its face are turned upwards in painful need. At last. At last. At last. It feeds.

Hungry for Something

Hᴀʀʀʏ's ᴍᴏᴛʜᴇʀ ᴡʜɪsᴘᴇʀᴇᴅ, '*Ehrich, was sitzt du da so rum?*' and he opened his eyes. The room was flooded with silent moonlight. For a moment he found himself listening for the sounds of New York; then he remembered where he was.

Tina. He had left her. He had turned and walked away and left her all alone with that man.

Frantic, he jumped to his feet and rushed into the hall. The women's room was empty, and Harry came to a halt within it, frozen at the sight of clothing strewn about. With sick certainty, he picked a familiar garment from the floor. It was Tina's blouse, the sprigged cotton cold between his fingers. How long had he been sitting, calm and motionless, across the hall, and in that time what had been done here?

Harry went to the closed door of the adjoining room, certain that he would find Tina crouched, huddled and ruined, within the darkness there. He realised that her blouse was still clutched in his hand and he dropped it. Tightening his jaw, he pressed open the door.

'Tina?' he whispered.

Only stillness and shadows greeted him.

Somewhere far off downstairs someone crashed their hands onto a piano. It was a jarring, dissonant chord that made Harry jump. Angry and aggressive, the music forced itself upon the silence of the house. Harry did not recognise the tune at first; then he realised that it was the third movement of Beethoven's *Mondscheinsonate* – the *Moonlight Sonata*. A music-hall favourite. Harry had never heard it played with such rage. There was a frantic desperation to it that, in light of Tina's scattered clothes, set Harry's heart to racing.

In the attic above, the whisperers began moaning, low and yearning.

Harry made his way down to the first-floor landing. He paused in the segmented light of the arched window, staring down the main flight of stairs that led to the hall. The music was very loud down there, coming from a room somewhere to the right of the big horse. There was candlelight there, a scintillating blaze of it, which flooded the hall in warm contrast to the cold moonlight illuminating the rest of the house. The music, the sheer rage of the music, drew him downwards.

From the shadows of the hall, Harry peered through open doors into a vast ballroom. Tina sat opposite him, in a lone chair on the far side of the room, shadows at her back. A table at her elbow held a spirit board. She was dressed in Ursula Lyndon's gold-sequined costume. From the upward slant of light it would seem that much of the floor within was covered in candles, and they reflected off the dress and spangled Tina and her surroundings with shivering radiance. Her attention was fixed on something out of Harry's sight in the far corner of the ballroom, the source of the music. Her face was strained, her eyes glittering.

Are you hurt? he thought. *What has he done to you?*

A sofa was positioned between them. On it sat three distinctive figures, their backs to Harry. The carriage driver was lounging at the closest end, his arm stretched along the ornate back. His strong profile was outlined in candle glow, the soft mass of his dark hair coloured by it. Raquel nestled comfortably against him, her head leaning against his shoulder. Her legs seemed to be up on the sofa, her feet perhaps even resting in the lap of Lord Wolcroft, who sat on the far end, nearest the candlelight. His face was hidden from Harry's view, his shoulder-length hair pure, unbroken darkness, rimmed in a thin thread of gold. All three were motionlessly absorbed by the music, Raquel and the carriage driver so rapt that their faces were blank.

Harry stared at Tina, wishing she would look his way, wanting her to know that he was there. But she could not seem to draw her attention from the far corner of the room, where someone was pouring all their rage into a violent rendition of the *Mondscheinsonate*'s third movement, *Presto agitato*.

I will be back for you, thought Harry. *Just hold on.*

Silently, he backed away.

The best thing would be to head for the stables and see what he could find by way of transportation. Even if he had to perch Tina and the old woman on the back of one of the carriage horses, he'd do it. He'd put them on his *own* back if he had to – just so long as they got away from this crazy place.

Making his way through the library, he exited via the

French doors, slipping out onto the moonlit terrace. He came to a halt there, his shadow stretching long and black ahead of him on the flagstones, the moon glaring down on the back of his neck.

What about Joe? he thought. Last time he'd seen him Joe had been lying on the carriage seat, a blanket flung across him as if he mattered nothing at all. Was he still there? If he was, Harry would take him with them. He wasn't going to leave Joe's body here for these vultures – God knew what they'd do with it.

'Contemplating a walk, are you?'

Harry shrank back against the wall of the house. A chuckle drew his attention to the far side of the roses, and there, so much a part of the shadows that he was invisible until he raised his hand, was Luke. He was sitting on a bench, his back against the stone wall of the sunken garden, his arms folded, his legs stretched out before him. He grinned as Harry found him.

'Caught you,' he whispered.

'How did you know I'd be here?'

A soft snort told Harry that he had a high opinion of himself if he thought Luke was there for him. 'I come to watch the bats,' he said, and he tilted his chin to indicate the space just above the roses.

Their petals were black in the moonlight, and moths big and small rose and fell from the heavy blossoms, bright as glimmering stars. A sudden flutter of shadow disturbed the fragrant air, and Luke made a satisfied sound.

'I'm awaiting on that one,' he said, pointing high above.

A good five or six bats were swooping and diving, gorging themselves on the aerial creatures of the rose garden, but up above them, barely discernible against the stars, a single member of their species flew in aimless circles. Luke followed it with his eyes. 'It's been like this a good few nights past now. I'm awaiting on it.'

Harry glanced furtively back to the terrace, wondering if he could slip away. Luke chuckled again.

'How do you figure dealing with Himself's dogs, eh? They won't be so friendly now you're up and about, you know, and there'll be no distracting *them* with a coin pulled from their ears. Animals don't have our sense of wonder, boy; things like that don't stop them in their tracks.' The man nodded, as if agreeing with himself. 'Only Eve's fallen children are stopped in their tracks. It's the last residue of our closeness with God, I reckon, the ability to see the wonder of things.'

He fell silent, gazing up at the lone bat again.

Within the house, the pianist had returned to the first movement of the *Mondscheinsonate*. In contrast to its earlier frenzy, the music now held a graceful melancholy, and for the first time ever, Harry heard the yearning in it – the genuine, soul-deep *heart* that cheap music-hall renditions had hidden until now. Even under these circumstances, it gave him pause.

'Say,' he whispered. 'That's beautiful.'

'It's the girl is playing, is it?' Luke asked this the way one would ask after a fever patient – in the same tone one would ask, *Has she much time left?*

Harry shook his head, alarmed by the man's expression. 'It...it may be Miss Lyndon, the old woman. She's the entertainer. As far as I know, Tina doesn't play.'

The man eyed Harry from head to toe. 'What are you, boy?'

'I'm a magician. Lord Wolcroft hired—'

The man tutted. 'Not what do you *do*! What *are* you? Where are you from? Your accent is mighty strange.'

Harry drew himself up. 'I'm from New York.'

'A colonial.' Luke seemed amused by this. 'So, a Spanish settler? British convict? Some poor Dutch Puritan running from the church?'

'I'm an *American*,' insisted Harry.

'Ach, there's no such thing. What are you really? Where were you born?'

Harry huffed. 'Just because I wasn't *born* in America doesn't mean—'

'Ah, sure you don't know what you are,' the man said dismissively.

'I know *damn well* what I am. I—'

Luke waved his anger aside like a gnat. 'Hold your whisht, it nary matters. I used to think it did, and it's habit that makes me cling to the question – but after a time, you come to realise we're all just mongrels. It's the man himself that matters, not his seed and breed. The Captain taught me that.'

The Captain – the carriage driver. Harry looked over his shoulder, as if naming him could conjure him. 'Why do you call him the Captain?' he whispered.

The man's expression hardened. 'Why else would I call him Captain? Isn't that what he is?'

'Of a ship?'

'Aye, of a ship. Of *his* ship. Best cove to work for in the West Indies, that man. Had the same crew his whole time at sea, give or take. That's a rare thing, boy, to hold the loyalty of a shifty gang of scoundrels such as to be found in the islands. And him the colour he is, and them so used to seeing the dark fellas subject, and them loving it, because what else do you want when you're bottom of the ladder but some poor cove lower than you so as you can spit on him?'

Luke looked up again at the bat fluttering aimlessly over his head. 'Captain earned his title. As far as I'm concerned, he'll keep it. God knows, the disease stole everything else from him.'

Harry descended a few steps, the better to hear the man's quiet voice. It was sultry down there, the moist heat heavy with scent. The subtle burr of bat wings agitated the air. 'Why did they bring Tina here? And that man – the Captain – he took our friend Joe. Why?'

'You said it yourself, boy. You're here for the show. Because Himself chose you for the show.'

'Himself? You mean Lord Wolcroft? No, he—'

'*Wolcroft?*' Luke sneered. 'Wolcroft is long ago dulled and grey and gone to the oubliette. And you should thank your stars for it. That old bastard was wicked beyond repair – you would not want to find yourself in *his* grip.'

The man grinned at Harry's obvious confusion. 'My family and I had the gall to think we owned this place once, the nerve of us. Wolcroft – the *real* Wolcroft – was the fist the English sent to beat us down. Planter bastard. New Model Army spalpeen. He settled himself over this land like a toad, he did, and I fled his rule like a beaten whelp. Fled halfway round the world. But I didn't stay gone – not me.

'The villagers bless the day I brought Himself and the Captain here. Didn't take long for those two to change things, like I knew they would. The Captain was always one for the underdog. And even Himself, with his high blood, he knows what it is to baulk against the yoke.

'Himself is a great man, boy – no matter his quare ways. It's him brought us through it all, in the end. Through Williamites and rebels, through famines, plague and war, with his fine words and his pretty manners, playing one side off against the other. No one here's ashamed to say they love him for it. He's held this place out of the mud of history for the past two hundred year.'

'*What are you talking about?*' cried Harry, losing his patience at last. 'What are any of you people talking about? *Two hundred years?* Do you expect me to believe that? That black man, the carriage driver, your Captain, he *stole my friend Joe*! And *Himself*? If *Himself* has laid a hand on Tina, if he's so much as laid a *finger* on her, I'll—'

'If he laid a finger on her? Himself?' At that, the man began to laugh.

'Say!' cried Harry. 'Say, that's nothing to laugh about! You'd better watch it. You—'

Luke hooted. 'Oh, be quiet, you yapping pup. You know nothing, y'understand? Nothing! You will spend your short life knowing nothing, and when you die, you'll *be* nothing. Gone and forgot in the blink of an eye.'

He sat back, regarding Harry with deep amusement.

'Although you *are* an entertainment,' he admitted. 'Perhaps Himself will take you in. Make you part of his collection – like the missus and Matthew, and his two little gallows-apples. You'd be a lucky boy if so.'

The man allowed his attention to drift towards the bat again.

'Ah,' he said, getting to his feet. 'It's happening. I knew it would.'

All the time they'd been speaking, the solitary bat had

been sinking lower and lower. Now, the long careless loops of its flight had fallen well below the manicured heads of the roses. Luke watched as the little creature fluttered one more dazed circuit up and down the dappled central path before dropping, stone-like and sudden, to the ground. He went to it, waited patiently through its last feeble stirrings, and then, almost gentle, picked its motionless body from the gravel.

'It happens sometimes,' he said, spreading the membranous wings out against his hand, straightening the tiny bowed legs and feet. He pressed a fingertip to the sharp-toothed mouth. 'Things just stop.'

'What's wrong with it?'

The man looked up at him. 'Are you hungry?' he asked.

Harry pressed his hand to his hollow belly. As if on cue, it growled.

The man nodded. 'That'll fade,' he said, 'if you stay here long enough. When it does, you need to keep yourself hungry. It don't matter for what. It could be for that.' He gestured to the music coming from the house. 'For this.' He swept a hand around the gardens. 'For wrath, or pain, or whatever it is the childer are hungry for. It don't matter. You just need to stay hungry for something. You need to stay *interested*. Because if you don't...'

He lifted the little bat, as if to demonstrate his point. Then he folded the wings and put the small limp body into his jacket pocket.

He grinned at the disgust in Harry's expression. 'I'm not going to *eat* it, if that's what you're afraid of. I'm bringing it inside for Himself. For his taxiderms – not that he's been bothered with them for a while. Still, maybe things'll change now. Company brings life, so they say.'

Grimacing, the man turned and ascended the steps. 'Enough of this chinwaggery. Hours are a-wasting, and I've to go trim the back hedges before I do anything else.'

'But it's the middle of the night,' whispered Harry.

Luke chuckled and glanced back over his shoulder. Harry was not surprised to see his eyes glow like fireflies in the shadows. 'The night fades, too,' he said. 'The longer you're here, the more it fades. You'll get used to it.'

'No, I won't!' cried Harry. 'I'm not staying!'

Luke shrugged. He gestured to the stables. 'The childer are that way,' he said. 'The dogs are out front. The village is a few miles, back yonder. They'd like you in the village, boy – they'd eat you up with your magic tricks and your mummery.' He waved his arm vaguely towards the horizon. 'Out yonder? There's snow. Plenty of it. Waist-high and deepening. They're your options, boy. Feel free to take your pick. I've better things afoot than babysitting you.'

With that, he grouched off, leaving Harry belittled and anchorless, and angered beyond fear by the casual dismissal in his words.

Wonder

LIGHT SHIMMERED AND flowed around the girl as she rose from her chair, and Cornelius followed her movements with sleepy contentment. Only very recently he had been angry with her – he had been raging – but now he was heavy-limbed and sated, and she was but a spectacle to him. The velvet sofa cushion caressed his cheek as he shifted his head to watch her. She was a pillar of light as she picked her way through the flickering maze of candles, a column of radiance: Tatiana, Helen, Ariadne, entrancing in her magnificent dress.

Cornelius felt the almost painful tug as the Angel responded to his renewed enchantment. It was feeding on him. No – feeding *through* him, drawing on the girl via his enjoyment of her, drinking of her through him in long, aching draughts. Raquel had described this sensation as akin to that of feeding a child from the breast: a soul-deep connection, an emotional and physical sensation unlike any other. It left Cornelius languid and blissful. It left him awed.

The girl faltered and swayed as she felt the Angel's feeding; then she staggered on.

She had almost ruined this for him, stubborn child. Cornelius could not believe her wilfulness. It had gone so well at first. She had spun in place, just as he had instructed, and the room had filled with shivering light just as he had wished. Even he, knowing beforehand what was to happen, had been struck by the wonder of it. The Angel had responded immediately, of course, like a parched man filling himself with water. Its great agonised surge of need had been shocking in its intensity. Cornelius had staggered, and had had to grip the piano to stop from falling. He had heard Vincent gasp, and had turned to witness him and Raquel sink back into the cushions, their faces slack with awe.

Propped against the piano, Cornelius had watched the light on Vincent's face, the wonder on his face; his parted lips, his great dark eyes. With a twinge of alarm, he had felt the Angel respond to this, too: had felt it begin to draw on the pleasure he got from Vincent's joy. Vincent had frowned in discomfort, his face greying, and Cornelius had forced himself to look away, turning back to the glittering spectacle of the girl, trying to lose himself in her.

Then the girl had broken the spell. Still turning, still casting light, she had cried out: 'My name is Martina Kelly.' She had stumbled to a halt, the sequins spangling her desperate face as she seemed to try to focus. 'I...I am Martina Kelly,' she gasped.

Cornelius had pushed himself from the piano, appalled. *No, you're not! Stop that. You are a spectacle. You are a glory.*

'I...I made this dress. It took two weeks to sew.' She lifted her arms, and the room sang with a renewed agitation of light. 'There are ten yards of material. There are...there are two-and-a-half-thousand sequins.'

Stop it! thought Cornelius. *You're ruining it.*

'The girl who sewed the sequins was called...she was called Madge. I...I paid her a shilling. I pay a lot of women. Sometimes I pay even if they're no good. I...I pay them when they need money.' She had placed her fingers to her temples, squeezing her eyes shut as if to corral her thoughts. 'I made this dress,' she whispered, 'but I don't like it. It's heavy. I can't breathe.'

Cornelius had felt the atmosphere change. The Angel still fed: he could feel it, a faint insistent draw in the background. But the sensation was dulled. It was mundane. It was like replacing a bonfire with a candle.

There had been a dead silence. Raquel sat forward into it.

'Why now, *minha flor*,' she admonished the girl. 'After all of Cornelius' careful work, you've gone and lifted the veil.' She wagged her finger. 'Don't you know better than to expose the *woman* when the audience is admiring the *dress*?'

Vincent smiled, delighted at her animation. He closed his arms around her and beamed across at Cornelius. 'Do not be angry, cully,' he said. 'It was entertaining while it lasted.'

Cornelius let his fingers bite deep into the girl's arm and dragged her from her position by the piano.

'What do you think you are doing?' he hissed.

'I'm not food for your angel. I won't let you eat me as if I mean nothing.'

Cornelius released her, astounded. '*What* did you say?'

'I used to make dresses,' called Raquel, interrupting their hushed conversation. She gestured at the glittering artifice of the girl's costume. 'This is quite the piece. An exhibition of rare talent. But I do not like how pent you are in it, *flor*. In my day, we did not tailor the woman to fit the dress. We made the dress to fit the woman.' She glanced at Vincent. 'Though the world insists we tailor ourselves in other ways,' she confided. 'Remain quiet, and not proud. Do as we are told. Often one can go quite a time without hurt, out there, if one follows those rules.'

Vincent winced. 'My dear, you are not in Lisbon now. Those troubles are long over.'

Raquel pressed his hand, as if gently instructing him in some oft-repeated lesson. 'Those troubles will never be *over*, Vicente. The world is only ever waiting to hurt us. We must hide. We must always hide…no matter what.'

'There is nothing to fear here, though, *meu amor*. You are safe here.'

At Cornelius' side, the girl gasped, pressing her hands to her pinched waist.

'Oh, I can't breathe. It hurts.'

Raquel turned to Cornelius in hectic inspiration. 'Cornelius,' she cried. 'Rescue her.'

The girl groaned. 'Jesus, missus…it's him put me *in* this dress.'

Raquel dismissed this with a wave. 'From your life, *minha flor*. Cornelius can rescue you from your *life*. All you need do is trust him.'

The girl frowned. 'My life,' she whispered. 'I…I liked my life. I didn't need rescuing.' She turned as if seeking something. 'Joe, though. Joe might have—'

'Of course you need rescuing,' urged Raquel. 'Of course you do! Do you think that pretty face will protect you forever? No, better Cornelius keeps you. Wouldn't you like that, Cornelius? Wouldn't you like to keep her?' She turned to Vincent. 'Wouldn't she make a lovely mate for him?'

This was such a shock to Cornelius, a betrayal so familiar yet so out of the blue, that he stepped back from it. He was instantly back in his father's house, at one of those awful parties, his mother springing yet another young girl upon him as the neighbours nodded and smirked. As if flung back in time, he even ground out the same dusty old reply.

'Well…let us see what happens, shall we? These things can't be rushed.'

Raquel clapped her hands in delight.

Vincent gave her a pained look. '*Meu amor*, we cannot simply foist a girl upon him. He—'

'Nonsense! Cornelius had the same intention when he brought me and Matthew here. It worked beautifully for you and me, did it not?'

Tentatively, as if unwilling to disturb her fragile optimism, Vincent smoothed Raquel's hair. 'But we knew each other beforehand, my dear. There was already an affection.'

Raquel had frowned. 'She would be lucky to have Cornelius. He is wonderful! Would you give her my history? Have her endure the protection of a brute because there is nowhere better to hide?'

'Of course not,' Vincent had murmured, and Cornelius had turned from them, his carefully planned evening shattered.

Then the old woman had begun to play.

She must have approached the piano as they were discussing the girl and stood there unnoticed and ignored until she slammed her hands down onto the keys. The piece she chose was new to Cornelius, and the piano itself still such a novelty – its sound so resonant, so deep and penetrating and emotional when compared to the harpsichord. And the *anger* – oh, heaven help him, the anger of the playing. It grabbed Cornelius by the pit of his belly. It hooked the chambers of his heart.

The old woman had hunched over the keys as she played. Her long white hair, shaken loose, had tumbled pale onto her shoulders. Her fine-boned face was carved in fury, her long fingers commanded the keyboard, and she was captivating. Captivating.

Cornelius had felt the Angel surge up, had felt it latch on. He had lurched to the sofa, unable to keep his feet under the onslaught of its need.

And it had fed: through him, in him, with him, it had fed.

And the old woman had played. Out of control, beyond anyone's help or intervention, lost to the Angel's merciless hunger, she had played to the very end.

HOW LONG AFTERWARDS had Cornelius lain there, dazed and replete? Who knew. It was only the girl's movement that had roused him.

As she made her way to the piano, the blaze of candles spangled around her, the trail of her passage scintillating like comet tails in his fuddled vision. She bent awkwardly to peer into the shadows beneath the piano and, as if from far off, Cornelius heard her cry out.

He lifted his hand with the intention of comforting her. *Don't look*, he meant to say. *There's no reason to look.* But his words remained unspoken, and his hand shifted only fractionally. He became distracted by the softness of the cushions, and for a moment lost himself in spiralling his fingertips against the velvet. When he next looked, the girl had crawled beneath the piano, fighting her skirts and the constriction of her bodice in an attempt to reach the thing that lay there.

Ah now, he thought. *Leave it. There's no need to fret.*

After a moment, the girl backed out into the open, her hands empty, her face ablaze with candlelit tears. Her mouth opened and closed, speaking, but Cornelius only heard a faint sound, akin to the distant cry of gulls heard from below deck.

The girl scrabbled at the small of her back, attempting in vain to undo the rows of tiny buttons that held her into the dress. There was a flare of light as her foot toppled a lit candle, and the darkness below the piano was banished, the creature there illuminated. The girl spoke to it again, her hand out. Then she rose in a flurry of brilliance and was gone.

The toppled candle's flame guttered and shrank, and in the fading light, the thing beneath the piano seemed to meet Cornelius' eye. He became aware of Raquel's feet, heavy in his lap, and of the slow *shush* of Vincent's sleeping breath. They would not like to see that thing. He did not want them to see it.

Carefully, his movements languorous, Cornelius pushed Raquel's feet from his lap. She was dreaming, the sweet love. Vincent, too. Neither of them was as used to the Angel's power as he. They would dream for hours.

Cornelius dropped to his knees by their side. Gently, he wiped a line of spittle from Raquel's slack mouth. Her eyes were bright lines beneath dark lashes, and he pressed gently down on her eyelids, shutting them entirely. Sophie was on the floor. Cornelius lifted her and placed her in the crook of Raquel's arm.

Sophie, cradled by Raquel, cradled by Vincent. Cornelius' perfect family.

Vincent's head was thrown back against the high arm of the sofa, his cravat undone as ever, his dark throat exposed. For a while, Cornelius watched the small beat of pulse in his neck. Then, abruptly, and with almost no thought at all, he kneeled up, leaned over, and brought his face close to Vincent's.

Mouth over mouth, eyes over eyes, only inches between them, Cornelius looked down into Vincent's sleeping face. He had never been so close. He could feel the gentle ebb and flow of Vincent's breath against his lips. He smelled coriander and apples. For the briefest of moments, Cornelius dared to lay his hand on the crown of Vincent's head. Very gently, he closed his fingers in the soft and yielding mass of Vincent's hair. Then he let go.

He staggered to the piano. The thing in the shadows said, '*Muu muu muu*,' as he knelt and reached for it.

'Shhhh now,' he murmured. 'Don't worry yourself.'

He had not planned to use anyone up tonight. It had been his intention only to sip from the girl: to enjoy, as he had said, an hors d'oeuvre before getting down to the business of the séance. But this poor, foolish creature, it had given them everything. It had poured its all into the performance, and had simply been unable to stop, as they had been unable to break away.

Ah well, thought Cornelius. 'Better than the degradation of decline you previously faced.'

No heavier now than the weight of its clothes, the thing rustled as he hauled it from beneath the piano. Something fell from its hand, and Cornelius recognised the ring that the old woman had slipped onto her finger in the bedroom. He picked it up from the floor and chuckled when he saw that it was an abolitionist's ring. He held it to the light, examining the symbol of a slave in chains, the phrase 'Am I not a man and a brother?'

The thing's eyes followed the movement, no doubt attracted by the bright metal.

'Did you hope to impress him with this?' Cornelius asked, twirling the ring for it to see. 'Let him see how enlightened you were? How well you *knew* him?' Cornelius huffed. 'How dare you,' he said mildly. 'You do not know him. Only *I* know him.'

He tucked the ring into his pocket and pulled the dry remnants of the creature into his arms. It mewed up at him as he strode for the stairs, its wizened hands curling against its chest.

Cornelius thought of the old woman asking if Vincent was a king's son, or the offspring of a family slave, and his amusement grew. Vincent could not simply have been a man like any other. He could not simply have been the usual flesh and bone and will, conducting his business and living as he saw fit. Oh no, he must be a *symbol*. He must be a *burden* or a *challenge*.

'You think he wouldn't have seen through you? You and your ring. He was nothing but a colour to you, madam. You did not even know his name.'

The creature mewled again, and squirmed, its eyes overflowing, and Cornelius realised, to his amazement, that it was frightened. 'There now,' he said. 'Hush.'

He jiggled the thing in his arms, like a baby, and tried to recall what it was he had called it in its former life. He could remember nothing, only 'crone', only 'old woman' or 'harridan'. So he just smiled reassuringly down at it, and tried to be gentle as he made his way up the stairs.

The sighs and moans from the attic were audible from the first floor, very soft, almost sleepy. The creature's glittering eyes travelled up towards the sound.

'Do not worry,' crooned Cornelius. 'Those are your new friends. I have every confidence that you shall like them.'

The creature drew its hands in under its chin, staring at the ceiling far above.

By the picture window, the moonlight drew Cornelius' attention to the gardens. The fog had lifted somewhat, and the pond was quite visible through its gauzy veil. Cornelius stopped dead, staring.

There was a light burning down there. Deep in the frozen heart of the pond, it pulsed like green fire beneath the ice.

Cornelius dropped the creature in a dry heap at his feet and leaned on the sill. A movement by the trees near the bridge caught his eye. Someone short and stocky, their hair a wild frizz, was walking fast across the dew-laden silver of the grass, heading for the pond. Cornelius realised with a jolt of anger that it was the boy – Vincent's damned American boy.

He turned with a curse and stumbled back down the stairs, leaving the whisperers to their sighs, and the discarded creature to mew and rustle by the wall.

Plummet

After Luke had left, Harry had paced the terrace, clutching his head and trying to get his thoughts straight. He told himself that this was a scam – these people were working a scam. He just had to stay calm until he figured it out. He mustn't let himself be scared.

Don't be scared? They made a man melt his own fingers together, Ehrich! They made a grown man drown himself in a trough.

'Shut up,' he murmured. 'Shut up and think.'

Mesmeric suggestion, ventriloquism, phosphorous-coated muslin and sleight of hand – they were your ghosts, they were your spectres and your mind-readers and your—

Come on, Ehrich, you've seen all that, you've done all that. No phosphorus-soaked muslin is gonna make a man's eyes glow in the dark. No ventriloquist can throw his voice right inside your head – and no mesmerist is gonna make a guy plunge his face into a fire and leave it there until his eye melts.

He looked behind him at the ink-black shadows leading to the stable buildings. *Those kids made you lie there while they got a pitchfork. They made you lie there, Ehrich, while they talked about cutting you up.*

Harry shook his head. There had to be an explanation. Behind every phenomenon, there was always some grubby little man scraping for a dime. But what could these people possibly want with Tina and with Joe and with that sad old end-of-her-days actress? What had they to *gain*?

It doesn't matter. Get the women away from here, Ehrich. Figure a way out. Yes. Harry clenched his fists around his fear. *Go to the stables, face those damned kids. Get a horse.*

Perhaps if he blocked his ears with cotton? If he couldn't hear the little bastards talk…

A movement on the lawn drew his attention. There was something coming towards him through the dappled shadows of the trees, something low and broad – an animal. Harry took a few crunching steps onto the gravel, trying to get a better look, and immediately regretted it as one of Lord Wolcroft's dogs slunk into sight. Something in the way the big animal froze at the sight of him made Harry stand his ground. The poor thing seemed terrified.

'Hey boy,' he whispered. 'Hey.'

The dog seemed to decide that he was no threat and crept towards him across the lawn. Harry thought there was an air of beaten shame to the way it pressed its trembling body to his legs. A length of thick rope dangled from its neck. The end of the rope was chewed and ragged, and it trailed on the ground, leaving a snake-like shadow in the moonlit brightness of the dewy grass. Following this trail with his eyes, Harry saw that the dog's footprints led to the lake.

The dog whined as Harry stroked its head and stared towards the water. There was something down there. Barely perceptible, it gave off a dim green light. Harry would have dismissed it as nothing but an *irrlicht*, only that it pulsed slow and sure and steady, and it stayed in the same place.

'What *is* that?' he whispered. The dog drew away. 'Say,' whispered Harry. 'Stick with me. We can protect each other.'

As if in reply, the huge animal sank its head between its shoulders. With another whine, it turned its back and, staying close to the walls of the house, slunk away, low and beaten and afraid, into the shadows.

The night wrapped Harry in silence as he followed the dog's tracks to the lake. He was used to the hoot and bustle of city nights, the honky-tonks and cabs, the sprawling brawl of street life. The silence of this countryside settled on him like a baleful glare.

The closer he came to the lake, the colder it became. Soon the ground crunched with each new step, and Harry looked down to find he was walking on frozen grass, each blade glittering in the frigid light of the moon.

The edge of the lake was fringed in bulrushes. Harry shoved his way through their poker-like stems and stepped out onto creaking ice. The lake's frozen surface stretched away from him, flat and glittering as Central Park Lake in December.

How could this be? Up at the house, Harry had been watching bats flutter through rose-scented air.

Far ahead of him, dim within the fog, that light pulsed, steady and sure. Harry chanced moving towards it. The surface of the lake was slippery, his footing treacherous, and he took a moment to steady himself. What he wouldn't give for his skates.

What? Are you going to skate home? he thought. *This isn't getting you out of here.*

But he just wanted to see…He wanted to understand exactly what was going on.

About ten or so yards to his left lay an ornate bridge, across which Harry assumed the carriage road passed. A small noise there made him pause. It took a moment to register the trail of paw marks and accompanying straggle of child-sized boot prints leading across the frost-speckled surface of the ice and into the darkness under the bridge.

A flicker drew his eye to the central arch, and there within its shadows he caught a brief, hopeless flurry of movement. Something whimpered – a sound so full of helplessness and fear that Harry could never have considered ignoring it.

Carefully, his eyes scanning the shadows and the lake and the banks, Harry crossed the ice and made his way into the darkness at the base of the bridge's central pillar. Wolcroft's other dog cowered in the shadows there. Someone – Harry did not have a hard time imagining who – had hammered a metal spike into the ice and tied the dog to it with a rope. Another spike jutted only feet from where it lay, the chewed end of a rope trailing from it. Plate-like paw prints tracked a desperate circle around the tethered dog and then led away under the bridge.

'Your pal left you, huh?' whispered Harry, crouching by the dog's side. 'You can hardly blame him.'

The rope around this dog's neck was too short to allow it to stand, and the poor thing lay motionless, gazing up at him. Harry reached out tentatively. The huge creature allowed him to touch it. Emboldened, Harry scratched its ragged ears. It licked his hand.

'That's some wicked set of brats Wolcroft has,' whispered Harry. 'What was the plan? That you'd freeze to death?

Here, let me see what I can do with this rope. Don't bite me now, will yah? It'd cramp my act a bit to have only one arm...Good dog. Sheesh, I'll give those kids their due, they know their knots. Gosh darn it, my fingers are cold.'

Beneath his hands, the dog stiffened, and Harry froze in response to the sudden surge of renewed tension in its body.

A hushed giggle drew his attention up to the bridge, the wall of which arced twenty or so feet overhead. There was nothing to be seen there, but a movement drew his eye further out onto the ice where the moonlight was cut by the sharp black sweep of the bridge's shadow. He waited. Again, a giggle came from above. Then a flicker of movement at the edge of the shadow became the silhouette of a boy hoisting himself into sight. The shadow straightened, its hands on its hips, and Harry watched the shadow-boy lean against the silhouette of the large stone urn that decorated the centre of the bridge.

A second figure appeared on the bridge: the crisp, black shadow of a little girl. Its shape unmistakable in crinoline and bows, the girl-shadow rose to stand on the opposite side of the urn from the boy, arms out for balance.

A giggle drifted down once again from the bridge above, and Harry looked up – dumbly, stupidly, still not understanding the game.

The children, white-faced and black-eyed in the moon-light, were gazing down at him from atop the bridge. The sky was behind them, the whole panoply of stars their backdrop.

'Oh,' said the little girl. 'It is our stick-man.'

She rested her small hands on one side of the stone urn, and her brother solemnly rested his on the other. Harry scrambled and slipped on the ice, suddenly aware of their intent.

'Don't!' he screamed, slipping and falling. 'Don't do it.'

But they pushed in unison, and the huge stone vase toppled from its perch, and in a glittering cascade of frost smashed through the ice between him and the dog.

Water sprayed up in a great black geyser, the ground fell out beneath him, and Harry was sucked down in a roar and a gush of bubbles.

He was briefly aware of the dog and the urn, plummeting, then something grabbed him, some great cold hand, and he was pulled sideways into darkness, snatched into wicked cold, tumbled and racing, part of the churning universe below.

Bravissimo

RUNNING FRANTICALLY ACROSS the lawn, Cornelius howled as his dog disappeared from sight. The children did not even look up, so entranced were they by their deed. They simply crouched in the place where the vase had been, watching, enraptured, as the great flat head of Cornelius' dog came bursting to the choppy surface below. They smiled as the poor creature battered the water, fighting for purchase on the edge of the ice.

With another cry, Cornelius shrugged out of his coat and crashed through the brittle wall of rushes. The children turned their attention on him then, and to his horror Cornelius felt the Angel latch on to him and begin to feed. It was an awful, crippling sensation. Cornelius battled though it, falling to his knees on the treacherous ice, crawling to where his dog fought the water.

'Here, Beauty!' he gasped. 'Here, girl!'

The dog's white-rimmed eyes rolled to him. Cornelius flung the end of his coat to her, yelling at her to 'hold'. Somewhere in the terrified recesses of her brain the poor creature must have recognised the old order, and her strong jaws closed around the twisted fabric as they had used to close around the tarred ropes of the boarding boats. She grabbed hold and almost immediately went under again, sucked below by the strange currents that ran through the pond.

Cornelius scrambled backwards on the water-slicked ice, heaving on the sodden coat. 'Hold, Beauty!' he yelled. 'Hold, girl!'

The dog broke the surface again, her jaws still clamped around the fabric, and Cornelius laughed in horror and relief. 'Come on, girl!' he yelled, bracing himself against the pillar of the bridge. '*Try.*' And she did, struggling valiantly as he heaved, her massive paws scrabbling.

Eventually, incredibly, the animal managed to haul her drenched body over the crumbling edge of the ice. Cornelius dropped back to his knees. The dog staggered to his side, and he put an arm around her dripping neck. Overhead, one of the children gave a short, sleepy round of applause.

'Bravo, Pap,' they murmured. 'Bravissimo.'

They were lying on the central plinth where the vase had been, curled around each other like kittens. He could see the bright gleam of their eyes as they transferred their attention to the hole in the ice, their focus back on the water as they squeezed everything they could from the notion of the American boy down there, dead or dying in the frigid dark.

The Angel was feeding through them. Cornelius had felt it. His anguish, his pain, had been an entertainment to them – and thus, the Angel had fed.

This was an horrific thought. Horrific. These revolting children – these awful, awful mistakes that he regretted so very much…their cruelty nourished the Angel just as easily as any ecstasy of happiness or awe. Luke had been right all along.

The name 'Matthew' whispered soft and sly in his mind. Cornelius groaned and turned away.

Normally, such a slip of memory would be enough to send him running for the tunnels. But even as the horror rose within him, Cornelius felt it drift away – unimportant, easily dismissed. The Angel's bliss was so strong now. Bolstered by the children's glee, enhanced by his own recent wonder, it almost instantly soothed any strong emotion. He allowed it to embrace him as he staggered to his feet; felt it gift him its smooth, dreamy detachment.

The water in the hole was still now, mirror-like, a brittle crust of ice already beginning to form over its surface. Cornelius swayed slightly as he stared down into its darkness.

'You were a brief thing, American, but at least your ending served a purpose. It's not everyone can say their demise fed an instrument of God.'

He turned his attention to the dog, who still cowered, trembling, by the pillar. The memory of her rescue was a distant thing, from years ago – something from another life. He waved her away.

'Go to the house, Beauty. Go find King.'

She whined, as if reluctant to leave, but Cornelius was already turning away. Without further thought of her, or the children, or the drowned American boy, he staggered out into the fog, heading for the centre of the lake and the green light that still burned there like a beacon beneath the ice.

Jetsam

VINCENT ROSE TO the surface of himself, feeling stifled and fat somehow, overly replete. Had he been feverish again? He cracked a heavy eyelid. Overhead, a white-painted ceiling flickered with candlelight. The air was heavy with the scent of melting wax. Vincent groaned. So, Cornelius had, once again, brought him to a convent to be cared for.

Why do you insist on turning Catholic every time the disease brings me low, cully? My condition is not something to atone for. Especially not by a return to the breast-beating guilt of your tyrannised youth.

Wearily, Vincent listened for voices, for mission bells, for gulls – any sound to tell him which port they had pulled into and how far they were from the sea. There was nothing. Nothing but a warm and breathing weight on his chest and the resonance of old music vibrating through his bones.

Music.

Vincent opened his eyes, remembering. He was not in a convent. Nor was he aboard his ship. He was in the house, as he had been for centuries. The house. How could he have forgotten?

He took an experimental breath. The weight on his chest shifted and he looked down, amazed to find Raquel in his arms. He gazed into her sleeping face. She had spent so long pained and fretful that seeing her thus – calm, and fresh, and peaceful – almost brought him to tears.

Slowly, clumsily, Vincent released the plait from over her right ear and undid it. He spread the hair in glossy ripples across Raquel's shoulder and neck, letting it frame her face as it had used to.

'Love,' he whispered. The word was rare in his mouth, the only person he had ever said it to being the one now curled in his embrace. 'Love,' he said again.

She smiled and tightened her hold on the doll in her arms. Vincent regarded its bland, staring china face with the mildest spike of hatred. Cold dead thing. Sometimes he felt like they had sucked the life from Raquel – all her 'good babies'. One day he would go into the nursery and take a staff to them, all those simpering, dimpled rows of china children with whom she had replaced Matthew. He would smash them, and he would grab Raquel and force her outside. They would walk together as they had used to. They would laugh.

We shall live, he thought. *We shall all live again, as soon as…*

As soon as what? Was there something he had meant to do?

Vincent frowned. His head had found its way back against the cushions again, Raquel's warm gentle weight pressing him down as if into a giant feather pillow…deep down, where all was muffled…the world further and further away.

Gasping, Vincent snapped his eyes open. This was not good! He did not like it. It was suddenly all he could do not to heave Raquel's weight from him and send her toppling to the floor. He slipped from beneath her and slid to his hands and knees beside the sofa. Still sleeping, Raquel settled against the cushions he had just vacated.

The world tilted and spun. Vincent was reminded of the first time he'd drunk to excess, when as a boy of ten the sailors had brought him on shore leave. He'd been the crew's little mascot then – the darkie boy of the ship's captain, just as much a pet as the bevy of little green monkeys and African parrots the sailors doted on. They'd fed him rum as if it were milk, and he'd ended in the gutter, his head in a whore's lap, puking his heart out to a chorus of, 'Better out than in, laddie.'

Vincent had felt the same self-loathing then as he did now. The same desire to never again debase himself and be so out of control.

He staggered to his feet. The change in altitude broke him out in a cold sweat and sent the floor a-lurching, but he took a breath, set his sights, and launched himself into the hall and out onto the porch.

At the head of the steps, Vincent clung to one of the pillars, breathing deeply. He found himself confronted with a great round stupidity of moon. It dominated the sky and the landscape before him. Vincent followed its light down to the pond, and there he saw a figure outlined dark against the silvery fog. It was Cornelius, coatless and alone, standing far out on the frozen surface, his back to the house, his attention riveted on a strange green light that pulsed beneath his feet.

THE ICE OF the lake was humming, a deep vibration that came up through the soles of Vincent's boots. There must be a vast movement of water down there, one of the pond's strange currents. But what was the light?

Answers tried to surface through the syrup of Vincent's thoughts. Theories struggled to form. He glanced at Cornelius. The man was swaying as if intoxicated, mumbling a one-sided conversation to himself as he stared down through the ice into that slow pulse of green far below.

'Why are we like this?' called Vincent.

The words startled Cornelius, and he spun as if guilty. The sight of Vincent seemed to delight him, though, and he spread his arms in welcome. 'Do not fret, Captain! He will never find us.'

'Who?'

'God. We shall remain here as scarlet as he made us, and always beyond his reach!'

Vincent dismissed this with irritation. 'What has happened?' he said. 'I feel like some back-alley crimper slipped me a cosh.'

He lost his footing, and Cornelius caught him. They slithered a brief half circle together, turning like dancers on the frozen surface.

'Don't fret, Captain,' laughed Cornelius affectionately. 'It is but the Angel's bliss.'

Impatient, Vincent shook free. 'I…I can hardly think,' he gasped, pressing his temples. 'Why am I affected thus? Why do I feel as though I am trapped in syrup?'

Cornelius frowned, not understanding his meaning, and Vincent lowered his hands from his head.

'Cornelius, you understand that this is not normal, don't you? This is not how the rest of us usually react to a feeding?'

Cornelius took a step back, suddenly wary. Vincent sighed.

'Of course you do not understand. How could you? While we've gone about our daily lives afterwards, refreshed and renewed, you've always been a little lost, haven't you? Your mind dulled. Nothing but a smiling child in your corner. Things seem to have changed for the rest of us, though, Cornelius – I do not know how, something altered in our bodies over the years, perhaps – and we have become like you. I need you to tell me: these symptoms I am experiencing, are they what the opium feels like? Certainly you have always exhibited the same behaviour under the creature's influence as you do under the drug's.'

With a cry, Cornelius turned and began to stumble away.

Exasperated, Vincent pursued him. 'Where are you going? I need to know this! Talk with me! Is this what the opium feels like?'

'Oh God!' cried Cornelius, as if this possibility were some great horror only now revealed to him. 'Oh no.'

Vincent grabbed him. 'I must figure this *out*, cully. It would not do, should we all become like you. What would befall us then? We should be so dull and useless, it would make us vulnerable to all.'

Cornelius shoved him backwards. 'Let me *go*, you ungrateful churl. What good is it to ask me questions when I am so *dull*, when I am so *useless* and *broken* and *vile*!'

'Cornelius! I never said—'

Cornelius tried to turn and almost fell.

'Oh, calm down!' bellowed Vincent, grabbing him again. There was real anger rising in him now, an element of brutality beyond his control, and he felt Cornelius' rage blaze hot in response. With it came a thrill of fear, the understanding that they were on the edge of something with each other: something sharp and dark and violent. Something that had been brewing for lifetimes. Cornelius clutched Vincent by his jacket, his fists clenched in the lapels. He bared his teeth into Vincent's face.

Vincent was just realising that he was ready for this – had been *wanting* it – when there came a loud *thump* beneath his feet and the ice leapt, as if struck by a cannonball. The shock jolted the anger from them and they stared down, great wads of each other's clothes still bunched in their fists.

Something was falling away from them, a pale thing dropping from the surface of the ice down into the darkness. Then, *bam*, it came again – the impact of something big hitting the ice right below them – and suddenly there was a boy, his wiry hair streaming out with the current, his eyes staring wide and unseeing as he clung to the ice below. He was backlit by the glow of that green light, his face beaded with bubbles, his hands starfish against the under-surface.

Vincent dropped to his haunches, amazed. 'Well, look at that,' he cried. 'Where did he come from?'

The boy began a slow, painful upside-down crawl on the underside of the ice. There was no indication that he knew Vincent was there or that his water-blinded eyes could see up through the ice as well as Vincent could see down. But when Vincent moved, the boy faltered, his eyes seeking, as if he had seen Vincent's shadow above.

Cornelius, oddly indifferent, met Vincent's eye when he looked up.

'It is the magician, Cornelius! Did you know he was down there?'

Cornelius did not answer. Vincent looked back down.

'How can he still be alive? It must be freezing down there. Surely he has not been on the estate long enough to have attained our own endurance?'

He laid his palm flat against the ice, and to his delight the boy responded by slapping his own hand against the opposite surface. 'He sees us!'

Standing, Vincent began to stamp hard against the surface, hoping to crack the ice and get to the American.

'It is too thick,' said Cornelius flatly. 'You shall never break it.'

Vincent looked around him in a mix of desperation and excitement. 'He must have fallen in somewhere! Perhaps we can guide him back to the hole? Cornelius! Can you guess where it is he went in?'

The boy slapped the ice again, demanding attention.

'We should guide him to the bridge!' cried Vincent, beginning to back slowly away, his arms spread to make as large a shadow as possible. 'Let us see if he can make it that far! If he does, we may well be able to throw something over the side and break through for him!'

The boy began to follow, and Vincent, almost boyishly delighted at the adventure of it all, led him on.

'He is certainly a determined fellow, cully! I wager he might even make it!'

He continued backing away, leading the boy to shore.

Cornelius watched unhappily for a moment before trudging in their wake.

You

You cannot stop crying, and your heartbeat is like a hammer against the cage of your ribs. You need a knife so that you can cut yourself from this dress – so that you can liberate your heart and lungs, and release a scream and stop the tears and terror from getting in your way.

You are heading up to the room and your bag, wherein lie the scissors of your trade. But the darkness is aswarm with light, your mind a dissonance of noise, and so you stumble on the stairs. You roll to your back, the dress rustling about you, and scrabble at your ribs, terrified at all you have seen and at how little you can breathe.

It is as if you faint, then, though you do not faint. Your mind remains alert, but your body ceases to move for a while, as if it has had enough of this frantic panicking. You lie glittering on the dark stairs, your hands motionless against your imprisoned waist, and watch the ropes of light twist above you. I can only dimly perceive the web of thickly pulsing lines that are so bright to you. I want you to look away from them, to close your eyes, because I am frightened by them.

I can feel your mind examining the light – feel your calculations as you trace and follow its movement. You realise that it is not tangled like before, no longer tentative and seeking, no longer lost. Now it is *directed*. It is purposeful. All straight lines, it is pouring through that woman in the ballroom – the one with the doll – and the two men out on the ice. It is pouring through them, strong and certain and specific, and roaring back from them to the place where it originated.

You struggle to your feet, gazing upwards. You have forgotten your quest for a blade. You are following the light. It misled you last time – brought you, in the tangles of its grief, to the poor lost soul in the box. It will not mislead you again.

You descend the stairs. You pass into the silence of a book-lined room. I feel the press of your hands against cold glass: you push open a door that is like a window, and you are out in the misty air of a warm night. It must be summer; there is the scent of flowers. You stumble down steps and follow a path into trees.

It is time for me to move. I roll to my side and my hands sink into harsh sand. My body is stiff and cold; my joints creak. It takes all I have to climb to my knees. From the corner of my eye, I see the thing. It moans and sways on the other side of this place, its reflection bright in the still waters at its feet. All its attention is on the ceiling. It does not seem to notice me. It is the only source of light. Once I have crawled away from it, I will be in darkness.

You stumble through dappled moonlight, your hands pressed to your constricted ribs. Overhead, stars blaze in a moon-silvered sky. Heavy skirts glisten in your fists as you hoist them above your knees. You see ropes of light, and you follow them through long grass.

I begin to crawl.

You slam into apple trees, snag on branches, stumble on roots.

I crawl into a passageway black as the abyss you have called me from. On my hands and knees, through warm pools, I follow my hunger to where you are.

A structure looms above you. It blots the stars, and you stumble into the tumbled remains of a ruined castle. You cross flagstones worn by time, the straight lines of light drawing you on.

The darkness presses like thumbs against my eyes as I am drawn through winding tunnels of blindness: left, then right, and right again. You draw me on, as I draw you down into the black.

You descend damp stone stairs. Those people put your feet into gold slippers, and they are wet now, and filthy. I remember your feet: ten perfect toes cased in black wool. Warm. Tasty.

Your hands press against wet rock as you grope your way, blind and not blind, downwards at the behest of the light. I crawl upwards. Faster now, slipping up the spiralling steps on hands and feet, my face turned up as if testing the air. I think I may be smiling; certainly my teeth are bared.

Behind me the thing pauses. It has been feeding; now it hesitates. It senses us drawing close to each other, you and I. Coming together with the irresistible force of magnets, we are a completion: one thing belonging to the other. It recognises this. It lowers its head like a scenting dog, but I pay it no heed – I am focused only on you.

You descend, and you descend, and suddenly you are *here*.

I crawl up the steps towards you, quick and low and four-legged. You run into a gate, which blocks your way. Your hands close around the metal bars. Your eyes search blindly. You cannot sense me, though I am here, crouched at your feet.

I pull myself up the bars, drag myself up, my teeth bared.

You stare unseeing into the dark, your face inches from my cold face.

I press forward, wanting you. Wanting you. Wanting to eat you.

You whisper, 'Joe?'

My hands close on your warm face, and I remember everything. I remember everything. I pull you in, and bared teeth and greed become a kiss. We kiss. O, love. O, heart. We kiss at last. Your arms come through the bars and we are close, even with the metal between us. You are as warm as I am cold. Your lips, your breath, your tongue on mine – shocking and natural and lovely.

I remember. I remember. I am here.

The Candle
and the Knife

JOE'S FACE WAS cold between Tina's hands, the fullness of his lips colder still. She was frightened by his silence. 'Joe,' she whispered. 'You died.'

He nodded.

'Are you alive now, Joe?'

Under her fingers, his mouth curved into that smile he'd always kept so rare and just for her. She pressed her palm against his chest, to assure herself of him, and ran her hands down his arms, feeling the strength he'd kept hidden from everyone but her.

She would never forget the thrill of first discovering this strength – the summer day Joe had reduced her to laughter and she had bent double, clutching him. The solidity of his arm through the cotton of his shirt had amazed her. The masculinity of it. Thereafter, she had often pretended to need steadying, just so she could hold on to him. Was he so innocent that he believed in her poor balance? Tina didn't think so. It was just their gentle secret. Their unspoken story.

'It would kill me to lose you,' she whispered.

Joe pulled her tight against the bars; then he seemed to lose the strength in his legs, and together they slipped to the ground, the cold metal between them, closer than they had ever been.

I wish you would talk, she thought, *so I could be sure you were alive.*

As if to please her, his voice came rasping from the dark. 'There is something in here with me. An animal.'

She clutched him tighter, her eyes straining into the energy-threaded darkness. 'I know,' she whispered.

This was where the ropes of lights came from, pulsing and threading through rock and air and sky, emanating from the creature she sensed far below. She had been part of that creature's mind – she was part of it still – and it was a lonely thing. Broken and starving. She suspected it was mad.

She fumbled upwards, seeking a latch or a bolt, desperate to get Joe out. He clung to her. Joe had never been one to restrain her, it hurt to push him aside, but it was difficult enough to breathe in this terrible prison of a dress.

As soon as he released her it became difficult to think. The noise closed in, the lights stitched themselves through her mind, and she was no longer alone inside her skull.

'It…' she gasped. 'It has lost you, Joe…'

No, that is wrong.

'It has lost,' she amended, 'something *like* you…*its* you: what you are to me.'

Shaking her head, she groped to find a latch. 'You have to get out.'

She found a heavy padlock securing the gate, and she shook it, desperate. Joe's arms snaked through the bars again.

She could feel his hands exploring the deformity of her waist.

'You're trapped,' he whispered.

She pressed her palms to the corset, which was denying her lungs their right to expand. What she wouldn't give for a pair of scissors.

'I can't breathe.'

His fingers scrabbled at the dress as if it were the hard outer shell of a crab, and Tina realised he was trying to free her. She turned awkwardly and presented her back to him.

'Hurry, Joe.'

He found the rows of buttons that were out of her reach and gouged at them, ripping them apart. The bodice fell loose, the heavy fabric peeling away like petals, but it made no odds because it wasn't the dress that was trapping her, but the terrible bone-and-canvas construction beneath.

She felt him pluck at the lacings, unable to figure the knots in the dark. Suddenly he went still. He seemed to be listening. He turned from the gate, and she could feel him staring down the steps.

As soon as his hands left her the confusion poured back, and with it a clear vision of the creature in the rock-hewn caverns below. Bright and terrible, it was rushing towards them, hurtling upwards through the dark.

'It's coming, Joe! You have to run.'

He reached for her. She pushed him.

'Run! Before it traps you against the gate!'

There was the brief clutch of his hands, icy and desperate on hers, then he was gone. Tina pressed her face between the bars, calling into the darkness.

'I'll be back! I'll bring Harry!'

But he had fled from her. And there was no sense of

him at all; there was only the creature racing upwards, light trailing behind it, light pushing ahead...focused for the first time in centuries – *understanding* for the first time in centuries, that there was something here other than itself. Running forward. Rushing forward. *Longing.* It began to howl, in a voice that could unravel worlds.

Tina scrambled backwards, her eyes fixed on the writhing air below. The lights were so bright, now that Joe had left her. Thrashing. A chaotic, riotous disorder of the air. Her thoughts and the creature's thoughts were all mixed up, and it felt as if her skull was about to rupture with a million tiny fissures. Her legs tried to push her away, but the skirts of the dress knotted and snared her.

The thing was directly below her now. With layers of rock between them, it pushed itself through an entrance of stone and into the shaft of steps. Its head dropped between hunched shoulders, its body curled, and it insinuated itself into the spiralling passageway like a snail into its shell. Its wide spread of tentacles trailed behind it like a bridal veil. Its feet and hands left fading prints where they gripped the stone. It flowed past the crevasse where Joe curled like an insect, and he convulsed within the confines of his hiding place.

Tina could feel a seizure coming on: the fierce butterfly-frenzy in her temples that signalled an impending loss of control. *Oh no*, she thought, *not now.*

Light pushed itself up from the steps below her – the cold and buzzing luminance of a creature not made for this world. At the same time, light made itself known on the curve of stair above, warm and earthly: the golden radiance of a candle.

Someone was carrying a candle down the steps.

Tina fell back, her body already beginning the jittering dance of a convulsion.

As she fell, the creature exploded from below. It seemed not to expect the gate nor understand it, and its great body slammed against the bars. Portions of it surged onwards – ribbons and tendrils and eels of light flowing through the bars like weed pushed forward on the tide. Then the outflung surge flowed backwards above Tina's head, slipping against the stones of wall and ceiling as light and tentacles returned to gather around the creature that moaned and hunched and pressed itself against the gate, uncertain and trapped.

Tina stared up into its heavy face-not-face, and the creature seemed to pause. It looked down at her. There was a sudden stillness, a moment taken after centuries of pacing. Even the relentless movement of the light seemed to hesitate. The creature's song changed in pitch: a high, silver question being asked.

Then someone was shouting overhead. A woman. She came into view around the spiral of the stairs, a candle held high in her hand, and with a frantic kind of joy she leaned across Tina and shouted into the creature's face.

'Protest all you want, Angel! Your master can't hear you here!' With the candle still held high, she grabbed Tina's wrist. 'Come along, child! Have no sympathy for God's dread soldier.'

The woman was incredibly strong. It cost her no effort to drag Tina up the stairs.

The creature's voice became frantic as they left it behind. Calling without words – calling in feelings – it screamed its rage.

Tina was dragged up and up, on her back, stone steps bumping sharp against her hips. She wanted to shake free, to take to her own two feet, but the seizure was rising, strong and relentless, and every part of her was clenching tight.

She felt the darkness close its fist. Her head battered the woman's skirts. The glow of the candle was a brief comfort; then the convulsion locked down, and everything was stolen in the familiar nightmare dance.

'WHAT A SURPRISE to meet you down there in the dark. I had expected to find Cornelius.'

The woman was speaking from somewhere out of sight at Tina's back. She tutted, reminding Tina of Fran, and Tina opened her eyes to candlelight and moonlight and those incessant ropes of wavering light that only she seemed to see. The air smelled of apples. She was lying on her side in long grass.

There was no moment of confusion on returning to consciousness. She knew exactly where she was: in the orchard by the ruined castle. Below her lay a hundred feet of rock. Beneath it, the creature pressed itself against bars of iron. Joe had just tumbled from his cramped cell. He lay a moment on the damp stone, then crawled away. The creature did not hear nor sense him.

It only senses me, she thought. *It only senses what Joe is to me.*

Its voice was mercifully silent to her.

There were a series of small sharp tugs along the length of her back, someone cutting the laces on the corset, then cold air as the garment was unclamped from around her ribs. Tina lay still and quiet, allowing herself to breathe, her body too jittery yet to risk movement.

For the first time since the séance at the theatre, she felt sure and part of herself. She recognised the feeling as that strange clarity which often came after a convulsion. People thought she was stupid after, but she wasn't – she was just far away, and too comfortable to want to talk. She took stock of herself.

She was not about to vomit. There was no nosebleed. She had not pissed herself. This was good.

The woman's skirts rustled as she came around to peer into Tina's face. 'You are awake,' she said. She sat down in a puff of dark fabric and glitter of jet beading. She had a knife in her hand, the kind of small lethal folding knife that some of the Dublin prostitute girls carried. Tina eyed it.

This is what she cut my stays with. It must be sharp. She looked the woman in the eye. *I'll get that knife.*

The woman gestured the torn bodice. 'Who did this to you, *flor*? It was not Vincent, surely. Certainly it was not Cornelius. They are not men prone to inflicting themselves on women. Was it that American boy?' She weighed the knife, grimacing, as if considering what she'd do to Harry when she got him. 'You took refuge with the Angel, I suppose. Well, fear not. You will suffer no more of that unwanted jerking and thrusting here. I promise. No further intrusions will be made upon your person.'

Tina pushed herself up with shaking arms. The corset fell to her waist, and she flung it away with a groan. She shoved the remains of the dress to her knees, kicked it from her and sat back in her petticoats and stockings, breathing deeply for the first time in what felt like a very long nightmare.

'I am so glad to have you here,' said the woman. 'Cornelius has been so lonely. I almost thought it might kill him.'

Tina eyed her warily.

The woman smiled. 'We shall be wonderful friends.'

Tina punched her in the jaw.

It was like hitting stone, but the woman rocked back anyway, surprised, and Tina leapt to snatch the knife from her shock-slackened fingers. She twisted the woman's hair and straddled her, and pressed the knife to the slim arch of the woman's neck – as quick as any stall-woman ever grabbed a thieving urchin or turned the tables on a cut-purse in the dark.

'Listen to me,' she said. 'I want you to get me the keys to that underground place – the place with the creature. I want you to get me the keys to the gate.'

The woman regarded her from the corner of her dark eyes, strangely unperturbed.

'Release my hair,' she murmured. 'Have some decorum.'

To Tina's horror, wavering brightnesses began weaving themselves back into her vision as the post-convulsion clarity faded. The piercing voice – the song she now recognised as that of the creature – intruded once more on her thoughts.

With a gasp, she tightened her grip on the woman's hair and pressed the knife harder. 'The key,' she insisted, blinking to stay focused. 'The *key*.'

'Well, aren't you a rum girl? Full of defiance and your own grand purpose.'

The woman took hold of Tina's wrist. Her grip was not brutal, but her flesh was hard, and hot as water-scalded china.

'There is no need for knife-wielding here,' she said. 'Though I forgive you the assumption – it took me long enough to realise it myself and, as you can see, I never lost the habit of carrying one. But release my hair now, *flor*, before I take offence.'

The voice of the creature was rising – tearing and probing at Tina's mind as if, having been unheard for so long, it was now determined to be understood.

The woman squinted keenly at her. 'What is it?' she asked, her voice muffled beneath that of the creature's. 'What do you see?'

Fingers of light pressed themselves to the woman's face, rising and falling, curious at her curiosity, interested in her interest.

'It is frightened,' gasped Tina. 'It is terrified.'

'What is? The Angel?'

An angel. Yes, of course. An angel. Something in Tina's brain slid into place, something relaxed. The creature straightened in her mind: waving tentacles spread to glistening wings, splayed appendages became elegant hands. An angel – how had she not seen?

'He is frightened.'

The woman's dark eyes read her face, intense. 'Of course it is. Its Father has abandoned it, as He does us all.'

'No…no. There is something…He is…'

The Angel's voice was screaming within her: *Someone to talk to! Someone at last! Help me. Help me. Help!*

She staggered to her feet. The woman rose with her.

'There,' said Tina, pointing, her other hand pressed to her head. 'There!'

She stumbled forward. The woman followed her through

long grass and darkness, past hedge and white gravel, across flagstone and moon-shadow, until – standing on a plain of dew-soaked grass, gazing down towards a frozen lake – Tina pointed through fog and frost to two men in the moonlight, pulling someone slack and powerless from a hole in the ice.

Alive

I AM NOT DEAD, thought Harry. *I am not dead.*

He watched his water-blurred hands flex and probe as they pulled him along the under-surface of the ice. There were tiny bubbles on his knuckles, tiny bubbles fizzing against his cheeks. The world was reduced to a rush of bubbling darkness around him and the unfocused light of the moon right in front of his nose. He was not even remotely cold, and he had yet to consider taking a breath. How was this possible?

I should want to breathe, he thought. *How is it I do not need to breathe?*

He had been slammed down *hard* against something on the bottom of the lake. There had been flashes of ornate metal, glass, green light, a low pulse-deep throb as, still held fast within the grip of the current, he had been rolled helplessly. Then he had been caught in an upsurge and shot to the surface like a cork from a bottle, to slam against the roof of ice. He had not even felt the pain of the impact, and now he crawled like a bug on a window trying to find a way out.

I am not dead, he thought.

The men's silhouettes appeared above him again. One

of them beat down hard on the ice with his foot, and Harry felt the vibration in his hands as they once again tried to lead him into the shadow of the bridge. No matter how vehemently they insisted, he would not go back there and risk getting caught in that current. Instead, he headed for the shallows of the reed beds.

The current gradually fell away as he neared the shallows, and the water grew completely still. Harry did not like the sensation of it; it felt as if it had closed more tightly around his face. It was not cold – not at all – but for the first time, Harry realised that it felt dead. The water felt *dead*, and it pressed like corpse hands against his ears and cheeks and mouth. Harry felt a sharp thrill of fear and grabbed, limpet-like, to the ice. He did not want to be trapped down here in this motionless place. He did not want to be abandoned to this pallid half dark.

I'm not dead! he thought. *I'm not dead.*

The men moved from sight, and Harry battered the ice.

I'm not dead!

They returned in a pounding of feet, a sudden blur of shadows. There was an impact, a dully muffled *bang*, and the ice overhead star-burst with cracks. It came again, a sudden downwards shadow, and the cracks brightened with another resonant *bang*.

More pounding followed. The ice fell through. Hands reached under, grabbed and pulled.

His breath came out in a vast cloud – 'I'M NOT DEAD!' – and all of a sudden, Harry was agonisingly cold. His teeth began to chatter. His arms and legs curled in on themselves.

'Not dead,' he chattered. 'Not...'

A man laughed above him. 'And quite the feat that is!' he said.

There was a quick movement, and Harry was covered in something that afforded him a moment of intense, blissful heat before the water from his clothes soaked it through and he was freezing again.

'What is amiss with you modern boys, that you wilfully fling yourselves into any available water? Is it a fashion now? Or some new ploy to separate bystanders from their jackets?'

Harry looked up into the grinning face of the carriage driver. Over the man's shoulder, Cornelius Wolcroft watched with tight-jawed suspicion. Both men were in their shirtsleeves; neither seemed bothered by the terrible cold. Harry opened his mouth to tell them that it had been Wolcroft's brats, that they had killed Wolcroft's dog, but all that came out was the incoherent burr of his chattering teeth.

The carriage driver offered his hand. 'Up you get, little magician. Tough as you are, I would wager this cold will get the better of you.'

Harry tried to move, but his body seemed locked tight. The carriage driver frowned.

'We must get him inside, Cornelius. Perhaps light a fire. We cannot reward such resolve with a shivering death upon the ice.'

'The chimneys will not take a fire,' said Wolcroft. 'It's beyond memory since they have been swept.'

'Then we shall wrap him in blankets and chafe him dry. Come now. He has at least earned the right to another audition.'

'He was no great wonder as a conjurer. Another audition would do little towards proving him otherwise.'

Harry jerked out a hand and grabbed the carriage driver's ankle. *Vincent*, thought Harry dimly. *His name is Vincent*.

'I escape…' he chattered. 'I'm an…I'm an escapologist.'

The carriage driver savoured the word. 'Escap*ologist*,' he said. 'Why, that sounds marvellous. I should say the children would enjoy that immensely.'

Wolcroft's lip was just curling around a reply when his attention was taken by something up on the shore. Vincent twisted to follow his gaze, and Harry saw surprise and then concern cross his dark face. He stood, and Harry found himself staring helplessly at his polished boots. Wolcroft's shoes came into view, and the men stood side by side gazing towards the house.

'Raquel,' called the carriage driver, his voice ringing out in the frozen stillness. 'What is the matter?'

Wolcroft stepped from sight. 'You cannot bring that girl out in her underthings – she will catch her death!'

The woman's voice called out in reply. 'I did not bring her out. That boy drove her into the Angel's arms. It seems to have robbed her of her mind.'

Tina, thought Harry. He tried to sit but, like his thoughts, his actions were disorganised and dim. Vincent disappeared from view. A blur of conversation drifted to Harry through the chatter of his teeth.

'The boy did nothing to her. He was here, busy drowning himself.'

'Well, who else could it have been?' said the woman. 'It matters not, in any case – it is the result, not the cause, that is of interest.'

There was a small breath of silence. Then the woman's

voice came again, much closer this time, snapping an order: 'Leave her! She is on a mission from the Angel.'

Harry marshalled every inch of endurance he had within him and rolled to his elbows. His fingers scrabbled spastically as he tried to push himself up. Soft footsteps padded towards him. The filthy lace of a petticoat flashed past and was gone. He flung out an arm, fell flat on his face.

'Tina,' he croaked.

The men's feet came into view, following behind the girl. They were accompanied by the woman, wide skirts of rustling green sweeping frost in her wake. She spoke in a fascinated whisper. 'She is driven here by the Angel, to show us that which frightens it.'

'It has spoken directly to her?' asked Wolcroft. 'Without aid? Without the board? Raquel! What did it say?'

The carriage driver said, 'She is heading for the light.'

They passed Harry as if he were no more than a bundle of rags.

Don't forget me, he thought. *I'm still here.* He tried to crawl after them, but his body had its own ideas and curled back into a juddering grub-like huddle. 'Come back,' he whispered. 'I'll…I'll show you a trick…' He could feel his fingers shivering against his chin. The water that had dribbled from his clothes was freezing – fanning out around him in hard, curved patterns on the moonlit frost.

Through a blur of encroaching darkness Harry saw Tina, quite a distance away. She was dressed in nothing but her petticoats. Her long, dark hair was straggled loose across her shoulders, and her eyes were horribly wide. She had one hand pressed to her temple, and she was pointing at the gangrenous light that pulsed beneath her feet.

'Here,' she was calling hoarsely. 'Here, here.'

The woman called Raquel clung to Wolcroft's arm. 'It is the Demon,' she said.

'No,' whispered Harry, his eyes slipping closed. The ice had become the softest of pillows beneath his cheek. All he wanted to do was sleep.

Voices sounded, far off in the fog: Wolcroft and the carriage driver, arguing. The woman said something unintelligible, then her voice rose impatiently above the men's: '...*nevertheless*, now that she's given us her message, the seer cannot *remain* here. She must come inside, at least until we fetch her some furs.'

Footsteps came again, clunk-clunking towards him. Harry gasped and forced his eyes open in time to see Tina's snow-crusted black stockings. She was dragging one foot after the other, her petticoats framed against the woman's immensity of skirts, and it was obvious the woman was supporting her. They swished past with no acknowledgement of Harry's presence, leaving him to his worm's-eye view of the men following slowly behind.

Wolcroft was animated. 'A *demon*, Vincent! Like I have always told you! Like the other seer told you! Now do you believe? We are dealing with instruments of the divine.'

'There is nothing at all in what has happened to suggest the divine.'

'The Angel *spoke to her!* It *sent her here!*'

'What of it? I do not deny the Bright Man *exists*, Cornelius. Merely that it is a creature of your fantastical god!'

'Two *separate* seers, two *hundred* years apart! *Both* told by the Angel that there is a *demon in the lake!* Explain to me, what else can it be?'

A machine, thought Harry.

The men were within inches of him now, their boots gritting the frost as they passed. He heard the carriage driver sigh. 'Do not always be so ready to think in terms of the divine or the profane when there are so many other possibilities.'

'Like *what*?'

'A machine,' croaked Harry. Vincent paused and Harry, desperate to keep his attention, flashed out a hand and gripping his boot. 'A machine,' he croaked. 'A machine, Vincent. It's a machine.'

Searing hot fingers grabbed his chin and raised his head. 'Boy!' cried Vincent. 'Boy! Tell me of this machine! What was its nature? Describe its appearance.'

Harry gazed stupidly at him. Someone, perhaps the woman, called that they should get inside before the seer caught her death. He was dimly aware of the men lifting and dragging him, as the women led the way.

Frost glittered beneath him; reeds brushed him; then grass.

The carriage driver continued to hurl questions at the top of his bowed head, until Wolcroft snapped, 'For goodness sake, you will get nothing from him in that state! Wait until he has defrosted.'

The air grew fragrant. The toes of Harry's boots made harsh sounds in gravel. Stone steps jarred his shins. He was inside. The woman tutted. 'He is leaving tracks on the floor.' He lifted his head fractionally but could not find Tina. He let his head drop again. They passed through a warm rectangle of light, the scent of candles drifted through a door, then they were on the stairs, bumping upwards.

Suddenly they halted, and Harry found himself momentarily buried in Raquel's skirts. The fabric smelled vaguely unpleasant – dusty and old. Jet beads scraped his cheeks. Her skirts disappeared from view as she and Tina took the last of the steps to the first-floor landing.

Harry managed to lift his head. The women were above him now, outlined in silver against the moonlit arch of the picture window. Both were gazing down at something that lay on the floor beneath the sill.

'What is *that* doing here?' asked Raquel.

Wolcroft made a strangled sound, and Harry fell to one side as the man abruptly let him go and ran to the women. He was saved from smacking to the hard steps by the carriage driver's arm clamped around his chest. Out of his range of vision, Wolcroft said, 'Oh, Raquel, I am so sorry. I had meant to dispose of it, but—'

'Get *rid* of it,' cried the woman. 'I cannot bear it!'

'I shall put it in the attic,' Wolcroft assured her.

There was a rustle of skirts, as Raquel pulled aside. This was followed by a hesitant silence. Then Wolcroft said, 'You…you are in my way.'

Harry half-raised his head again. Wolcroft's shoes and the mud-stained cuffs of his trousers, and the bottom tiers of Raquel's skirts, were on eye level with him. Standing firmly between them and the window, Harry saw Tina's small, black-stockinged feet, the filthy lace trimming of her petticoat. Water pooled where the snow melted from her stockings. On the floor behind her lay something crumpled and still.

'You're to carry her to my room,' Tina whispered.

'No!' exclaimed Raquel, utterly appalled. 'No! Absolutely not!'

'Carry her to my room,' Tina insisted. 'And…and Harry, too. All of us. In my room. Or I won't talk to your angel anymore.'

Wolcroft dithered a moment, apparently torn between the two women. Then he dodged past Tina, lifted the rustling bundle from the shadow beneath the sill, and led the way to the second staircase. Tina followed.

Raquel and Vincent stood in silence punctuated by the steady dribbling of water from Harry's clothing.

'He cannot mean to,' she said eventually. 'In my room. In my *bed*. I can't…it can't be allowed.'

'Raquel,' sighed Vincent. 'It will do you no harm. It is only—'

'*It is disgusting!* It is *old* and *vile!*'

'It is only for a while, Raquel,' he replied. 'And only to please the seer. After the extravaganza, everything will be back to normal. In the meantime, can you not muster even a moment of patience? For Cornelius, of all people? He asks so little of us, and does so much. Just keep away from your room for the time being, *meu amor*. I promise that when this is over, I shall dispose of that thing in whatever way you wish.'

The man's arm tightened around Harry's chest, and Harry allowed himself to be hauled along the landing and hefted up the second flight of stairs. As far as he could tell, the woman remained behind.

'Put her in the bed.'

Wolcroft sighed. 'I assure you, girl, this creature is not in any way the person you once—'

'Put her in the bed.'

'May I be permitted to remind you of her vile plan for you? Her complete willingness to prostitute you to my whim? There is not an ounce worth saving about this creature. Surely you—'

'You've no right to judge her, mister. Put her in the bed.'

Vincent dragged Harry into the adjoining room, which was pitch-black, the moon having abandoned this side of the house, but Vincent seemed to have no trouble finding his way about. It took all of Harry's self-control not to protest as the man, holding him up with one strong arm, stripped him of his clothes and scrubbed him dry with some coarse and dusty fabric. He was laid down onto chokingly musty sheets and pillows. A blanket was drawn across him.

He felt surprisingly well – it was as though the house had wrapped a healing cocoon around his body. He kept his breathing steady and his body lax, waiting to be left alone. To his frustration, Vincent instead sat down on the edge of the bed, apparently listening to the conversation in the next room.

Wolcroft said, 'The Angel spoke to you?'

Tina gave only silence in reply.

Wolcroft said, 'I should very much like to hear what it had to tell you.'

Suddenly Vincent's voice spoke in Harry's head. *Little magician? Are you awake?*

Harry couldn't help but flinch at this, and the man leaned across him, hopeful.

Magician? Are you?

Harry made a feeble stirring on the pillows, as if disturbed in his sleep, and then went still.

In the next room, Wolcroft, his voice hesitant in the wake of Tina's persistent silence, said, 'Luke has caught some game. After you have rested, I could cook you something. I...I used to be quite the cook. We have bergamot in the garden – I could fix a little tea, if you think it might restore you?'

'For the others, too,' said Tina softly.

'Of course.'

Listen to him, whispered Vincent's thoughts. *So engaged after so long asleep.*

He shifted his weight on the bed, and Harry barely kept from crying out as Vincent's hand, blazing hot, absently pushed the damp hair from his forehead.

I knew he would blossom again, once you were restored. I knew you would bring him back to life. It will be so good to have you home, Matthew.

As if realising his mistake, the man's hand froze. He surged to his feet. Harry waited through a moment of breathless confusion.

'Apologies,' said Vincent. 'I get confused.'

He left quickly, closing and locking the door behind him. There was a brief rumble of voices before the women's room fell silent.

Harry forced himself to count to one hundred before creeping from the bed. He spent a moment listening at the door; then he rescued his lock-pick set from the sodden pile of his clothes and coaxed the lock. Carefully, he cracked the door.

Someone had lit candles. Tina was standing on the opposite side of the room, her hands clenched, gazing at him as if she'd been waiting for his arrival.

'Harry,' she whispered. 'You need to hurry. They won't leave us alone for long.'

He kept the door between them, his head just peeping around. 'I'm not decent.'

She couldn't seem to understand this; he got the impression she had to focus very fiercely just to keep him in sight. 'Turn your back,' he whispered.

It took only moments to unlock her door and let himself into Wolcroft's room. The man's clothes were folded neatly in a locker at the end of his bed. Harry took an undershirt, shirt and trousers. He stole a warm woollen jacket. He helped himself to two pairs of socks. He couldn't bring himself to take underwear. Wolcroft's boots were too small – he would have to pull on his own wet ones.

He crept across the corridor like a furtive mouse and sat to pull on his boots. Damn, but they were soaked. He had to roll Wolcroft's sleeves up on his shorter arms.

'We gotta go, Tina. I've got a feeling you only stay alive here for as long as you're useful or entertaining, and neither of those things seem too good for your health round here. It's gonna be *darned cold* outside the gardens. You'll need to wrap up warm. Where is Miss—'

Harry froze, horrified at the creature Tina had just finished tucking into bed like a child. The creature's oversized eyes followed Tina's hands as she took something from her travel bag. It was a rosary. Tina wrapped the glittering beads around the creature's wizened claws, tucking the crucifix into its palm.

'There now,' she whispered.

'Tina,' warned Harry. 'Come away from that thing.'

'This is Miss Ursula, Harry.'

Harry's heart sank, recalling the horrible maggot-creature in Vincent's laboratory, and how Tina had called it

Joe. 'Tina,' he said firmly. 'You come away from that thing now.'

Tina smoothed the thing's wispy hair off its wizened face. 'It's all right,' she told it. 'We'll come fetch you as soon as we've found Joe.' She bent lower to whisper, 'Don't worry about what you expected me to do with that man. I know you were frightened; I know it was the only thing you could think of.'

To Harry's confusion, a tear rolled down the creature's cheek. It moved its fingers to touch Tina's arm. Tina just kept stroking its hair, until gradually it seemed to sleep. Then she straightened.

'Harry,' she said, 'I need you to pick some locks.'

He followed her down the stairs to the first floor, hissing protests all the way. 'Tina, I'm not leaving without you, so you've gotta listen—'

'This door, please, Harry.'

'Aw, kid. We've already been in here. Please don't tell me we're gonna find Joe in there, because—'

'This door, please, Harry.'

He grimaced, and knelt to once again unlock the laboratory door. 'Was it the old lady playing the piano?' he whispered. 'Where'd she go after that? Let's find her.'

Tina pushed past him and into the familiar, living quiet of Vincent's room. To Harry's dismay, she made straight for the windows and the long, narrow box that held the snake creature. 'Tina, that's not Joe.'

'I know,' she replied. 'It's...it's the *Angel's* Joe. It's...' She breathed frustration through her nose, her fingers travelling the red wood of the box as she searched for the right words. She looked up to meet Harry's anxious gaze, and he saw that her eyes had once again filled with tears.

'Harry,' she said. 'I love Joe.'

This stopped Harry in his tracks. Uncomfortable and moved, he searched for a reply, but Tina pressed her hands flat onto the gleaming lid of the box and said, 'This is the *Angel's* Joe. He yearns for this. He pines for it. I can't...I don't think he can live without it, Harry.'

He stepped closer. 'What angel?' he whispered.

Tina didn't seem to hear him. 'But this poor thing is dead. Really dead, forever dead, not like Joe.'

'What do you mean, *not like Joe?*'

She crouched so she was at eye level with the wood, watching as something invisible rose and fell before her eyes.

'The light led me here – see how it's all straight lines here? How it all travels through this thing before going back to the Angel? I thought it was bringing me to Joe. I thought...'

She pressed her hand to the side of her head, grappling with her thoughts.

'Because...' she whispered. 'Because our *feelings* are the same: the Angel's and mine. His feelings for this, my feelings for Joe...the same. We...we got confused. We confused each other.'

She squinted up at him again.

'I need you to undo this lock now, Harry. I'm taking it back to the Angel, and...and the Angel will give me back my Joe.'

Fair Exchange

It CANNOT SEE me, but it is chasing me: the feel of me, or the smell of me – something like that. I run from it because it frightens me.

Parts of me have been coming back as I run, and I almost completely recall who I am supposed to be now. I am Joe – aren't I? I am *her* Joe. She loves me.

I stumble through darkness on yielding pathways of sand, head ducked to avoid the low snatch of ceiling. I run from its searing light, the shredding thunder of its voice. At one stage, I am herded back into the cave where I first came to life, and I run without thinking into the shallows of the glowing pool. The water grabs me as if it is hungry; there is a clutching at my heart, a deadening of my legs below the knee, and I fall.

It is dead, I think. *The water is dead.* And it is killing me.

I flounder to shore, where I fall facedown, my heart slowing to a standstill. Then the creature draws near and my body stutters to animation again, filling with sparks and flashes. The creature's voice raises, and I push myself up and run. I must keep my distance. This creature's touch will unravel me as surely as the water deadened me.

I run. My footsteps ring hollow on wooden flooring. I bump a wall, my hand closes on something metal, cold and ornate, as I round a corner: a wall-mounted candlestick. I slam against an obstacle – it is a door. I push through, and I am in an open space that smells of fresh, planed wood and paint. I trip, tumble down thickly carpeted steps and come to a halt against a velvet cushioned seat.

I listen, panting. There is something familiar about the atmosphere of this place. I grope about, and realise I am crouched between rows of seats. I look up into the pitch-dark, half-expecting the glitter of a distant chandelier.

An anemone of light opens in the darkness as the creature follows me through the open door. The space around me comes alive with the subtle winkings of metal fittings, the soft glow of illuminated velvet. Below me, rows of seats lead to the silent maw of an ornately appointed stage. Above me, the creature rises to its full height, swaying and moaning and feeling all about for me.

Far above, through layers of stone, Tina descends steps in darkness, a dead thing in her arms, a boy at her back. She tells me not to be afraid; that she is coming for me. I tell her that I am not afraid. I tell her she must stay away.

Tina tells me this creature is an angel. Immediately, her image of it tries to impose itself on mine – the curved body straightens, heavenly light casts from outspread wings. Its face is tragic with desperation.

Part of me wants to accept this picture, wants Tina's vision to erase the fluid entity before me: the heavy head and arched back, the arms that act as forelegs, the vast swarm of eel-like protrusions. But I did not wait all those years outside churches for her simply because I was too stubborn to go inside. I have not been secretly longing for my moment on the road to Damascus. I can no more believe in the existence of angels than I can be persuaded there is a God in heaven weeping for the damaged innocents of this world. This is not an angel, and in the end, I see it for what it is.

I sink between the seats, hoping it will leave. I think it might. It is groping about and seems to neither see nor sense me where I crouch. Dimly layered over this, I see the image of Tina's angel searching in growing hopelessness, as if about to give up.

When it goes I will be left in utter darkness, but I have noticed a little door by the stage. I have already mapped my route to it.

Nearby, Tina reaches the last step of a deep staircase. It led her from a library, where strewn books guided her to a secret door. The boy with her lifts a latch and raises a candle above their heads.

We're here, Joe! Tina whispers. *I'll be with you soon.*

The creature, already turned to go, hesitates and raises its head, sensing her through all the layers of rock between.

I call out to her in panic, *Shhhh. It can hear you.*

The creature whips around. Doubling back on itself like a silverfish, it flows down the steps towards me with a high, bright call of interest. It pauses face-to-face with me, its tentacles arched above, its heavy head swinging back and forth as if scenting for me. The air between us crackles, and my eyes are dazzled by its presence.

I keep my thoughts dim and low, trying not to think of Tina at all. I hope and hope and hope in my heart that she knows not to think of me. There is only it and me in the world now. Only it and me.

'Matthew!'

I cut my eyes right, past the upper seats to the door above. A man is in the theatre. Black-skinned, thin and noble-looking. His grip on the doorframe shows his terror for me.

'Matthew,' he whispers. 'Crawl away. It cannot see you. It will not hurt you on purpose, but crawl away from it now before it touches you.'

I start backing slowly between the seats, retreating from the creature as it seeks blindly for my presence. At that moment the door by the stage opens and Tina steps through, a dead thing cradled in her arms.

She looks straight at me. *Joe*, she thinks.

The creature rears high, roaring, and I realise that it *sees* her. Unlike me, who it can only sense through my connection with her, it sees Tina.

It rushes towards her, all its focus on: *Tell. Warn. Danger. Help.*

I leap to my feet, screaming at her to run. She only has eyes for the creature, her face lit up with wonder. The boy behind her freezes, the candle still held high, his eyes brimming with the impossible as it advances towards him down the steps.

I remember who he is: that dark, wild hair; those intense eyes.

'Harry!' I scream, scrambling across seats towards Tina. 'Get her away.' I launch myself at the creature and am tackled from behind, tumbling head over heels with a hot, iron grip around my chest.

The man presses me to the carpeted steps. He covers my

body with his own as the creature's shivering veil of tentacles passes overhead, a cathedral of living light.

Tina shrugs free of Harry's grip and steps into the creature's path. The dead thing in her arms rustles as she raises it high.

Here, she thinks.

The creature stops in its tracks. Only feet from Tina, it surges to its full height, rising up on those multi-jointed back legs, lifting those leg-type arms in a gesture unreadable to me. Its vast comet-tail of tentacles curl, then spread wide, rigid and shivering as if galvanised. They seem to fill the theatre, and the man holds me down as their tips hover just above our heads. Each tentacle is segmented like an iridescent worm. Each ends in a sucker that opens and closes like a searching mouth.

The creature bends forward. Its blind, heavy face reflects in Tina's shining eyes as it nuzzles the dead thing in her arms. She offers it tenderly, her face eloquent with shared grief. A bouquet of papery snakes trails to the ground; a grotesque maggot body spirals the length of her arm.

Here, she thinks. *Here*.

She sees a shining angel, his swan-like wings quivering with sorrow, his delicate hands poised, not daring to touch the fragile corpse. She sees his eyes overflow, and knows he is consumed with despair. The black-skinned man tugs at me, urging me to leave. I shove him aside and begin to crawl to her.

The real creature is poised above us all, rigid as a glass star. Transfixed by emotion beyond human expression, it regards the dead thing in Tina's arms. Without warning, it releases a long, piercing wail of rage.

Tina sees the Angel bare its teeth, and the creature surges forward. It snatches the thing from her, and there is howling and screaming; a violent thrashing of light that fills the theatre.

The man snatches me by the ankles and drags me between the seats. Harry grabs Tina around her waist, hauling her in the opposite direction. She stares up into frenzy, into centuries of grief. The creature's voice is fire, it is chaos. It has burned my mind.

I feel the man's arms around me, the bump of each step as he escapes and drags me with him. I find I cannot move. The creature's light is fading. Burnt out and hopeless, empty and lost, it has fallen to the floor and curled around the body of the thing it loved.

It is dying, I think. The thought fills me with terror.

Burnt Out

Harry's legs were like jelly. He felt he might fall down.

'Let's...let's sit down for a minute, will we, kid?'

Tina sank to the stone steps, wrapped her arms around herself and laid her head on her knees. Harry dropped to the step beside her. The candle he held out against the darkness cast just enough light to show that they were at a junction on the staircase. Below them lay the steps they'd ascended from the underground theatre; far above, the door that led to the library. To their right, a passage sloped steeply up into darkness.

Harry switched his attention back and forth between the passages, feeling crawlingly vulnerable. That had been Joe down there – pale and wild and crouched at the feet of...

Harry's mind showed him what Joe had been crouched at the feet of, and his thoughts veered from it, terrified. He returned to the facts. He had seen Joe; had witnessed the black man save him. *Vincent – I saw Vincent save him.*

Tina had told him Joe was dead. But Harry had seen him crouched at the feet of the Angel, and—

Harry's eyes opened wide. An angel. He had seen an angel. Just like Tina had said. And not just any angel, either – Uriel, the burning eagle. Uriel, the protective lion, the flames of his blazing body filling the theatre with heat and light, descending the steps of the theatre, taking that thing from Tina's arms; roaring, roaring, and then weeping in rage.

Uriel, who had saved the world from the Nephilim. Uriel, commander of the Army of Angels. Uriel, one of the four protectors of the throne of God, here, *here*, the tears of defeat in his eyes.

Magician.

Harry jolted, the candle held high.

I am here, magician.

His attention snapped towards the passageway that curved away to his right. The candle illuminated only a few paltry feet of gritty flooring and rock walls, but beyond that the now familiar twin phosphorescence of eyes watched from the darkness.

Is the seer unharmed?

Tina turned her head, resting her cheek on her folded arms as she looked in Vincent's direction.

'Joe,' she whispered. 'Are you there?'

There was a moment's silence, then a dry whisper came down to them. 'Yes.'

'I can't sense you at all.' There was no reply to this, and Tina's back rose and fell in a sigh. 'I think I need to sleep,' she whispered.

Bring the seer back to her room, boy. Make certain she rests.

There was a barely audible scuffling far up the passage, and Harry leapt to his feet, the candle thrust forward, straining to see.

'Where are you taking Joe?'

His voice echoed back to him in mocking non-answer. After a few moments, he heard the door at the top of the steps opening and closing, and he realised that Vincent had taken a different route up to it. The ground below the manor must be a labyrinth of rooms and tunnels and doors. How many entrances and exits must there be?

Looking up at him, Tina's face was very pale, and her eyes seemed bigger than Harry had ever seen them, dark as midnight. He crouched and gazed into her face. 'Can you make it back upstairs?' he whispered.

She sighed and rose to her feet. He cinched his arm around her waist, and they slowly climbed the stairs to the house above.

THOSE TERRIBLE LITTLE kids were crouched at the door to Tina's room, trying to look through the keyhole. They straightened as Harry and Tina came around the corner, and Harry felt his stomach shrink at their small wicked faces floating in the near dark – at the pinpricks of their glowing eyes.

The little girl took a step towards him and he couldn't help it, he shrank back. She smiled in sly happiness and swished her skirts to and fro.

'Hello, stick-man,' she sang. 'We were checking to see if you were home before we paid you a visit. What's that you have on your bed?'

He summoned some backbone. 'You bored with torturing helpless dogs?'

The boy pointed to Tina's door. 'Come inside with us,' he said.

To his horror, Harry found himself stepping forward, already reaching for the handle. He was halted by Tina's arm around his waist. 'Stay with me, Harry.'

She pulled him back and Harry moaned, torn between her command and the boy's. It was a nauseating feeling – an intense, itchy panic – and he bent double, overcome with confusion.

Tina tightened her grip on him and took the candle in her free hand. 'It's all right, Harry,' she said, and he instantly felt better. She lifted the candlestick high, looking at the children. 'Go away,' she said.

The boy's eyes hopped between them, a foxy curiosity welling up. He opened his mouth to speak, and Harry turned his face away, terrified. The door opposite Tina's opened a fraction and Vincent slipped out into the candlelight. He seemed unnerved at the children's presence. They seemed fascinated by his.

'What are you doing in that room?' asked the boy.

'Pap doesn't like people going in there,' said the little girl, awed at the very thought of it.

Vincent closed the door behind him and stood with his back pressed to the wood. 'You...you go off and play,' he told the children. 'You are not allowed up here.'

'We only want what's in there,' said the little girl, pointing to Tina's bedroom. 'We weren't going to play with Pap's seer.'

'There is only an old one in there. You know you're not allowed to play with the old ones.'

The girl pouted. 'That's only when they're in the attic.'

'Nevertheless, you cannot *have* it.'

'But it is *not in the attic*.'

The little boy was watching Vincent very speculatively, his eyes hopping between the man's face and the grip he still had on the handle of the closed door. 'What *are* you doing in there?' he asked.

Harry was amazed at the discomfort that rose up in Vincent's face – he had never seen the man look anything but fully in command. 'Nothing.'

The boy took a step towards him, seeming to listen intently for sounds from the room. 'Pap doesn't like anyone going in—'

'Do you know what your pap is doing right now?' asked Vincent brightly.

The children perked up like spaniels. 'No,' said the little girl. 'What?'

'He is *cooking*.'

They seemed a little confused. Then the boy's face opened in sudden wonder. 'With *fire*?' he breathed.

At Vincent's nod, the little girl squealed in delight. 'Where?'

'In the kitchens. Go on – quickly. I am certain he will let you help.'

Vincent shooed them away and they ran, tumbling and squealing and arguing happily as they raced each other down the stairs. Vincent listened quietly for a moment, then he glanced towards Tina and Harry.

'Sometimes they seem almost normal. Is it any wonder Cornelius did not believe the accusations flung against them?' He scrubbed his hand across his mouth and shook his head. 'Had I been in his place, even I might have saved them from the mob and the gallows.'

'Why do you let them stay?' asked Harry.

Vincent frowned, as if the answer to that question were obvious. 'Why, they are Raquel's. Cornelius brought them for her. Why on earth would I want to get rid of them?' He opened Tina's door for them, gesturing them inside. 'I will not mention that you were abroad,' he said. 'We need *none of us* mention that we were abroad.'

He closed the door, and they listened to him locking it. There was the quiet opening and closing of the door opposite. It was hard to tell if he had left or if he had gone back inside, and Harry pressed his ear to their own door, listening for retreating footsteps. He heard nothing.

'Is he gone, Tina? Can you tell if he has Joe in that room?' He turned to her. 'Tina? Is he...'

She was leaning on the bed, the candlestick perilously tilted, wax dribbling onto the floor. Her face was dead of expression. Harry gently took the candle from her and placed it on the bedside locker.

'Maybe you should lie down, kid, huh? It might do you some good.'

He sat her on the bed, removed the coat she had flung on over her petticoats, and hung it on the back of a chair. He hesitated at the sight of her ragged, filthy stockings, looked up into her blank face, then, looking away, reached beneath her hem to release the stockings from their garters.

'You can't get into bed covered in mud like that,' he murmured.

He pushed the covers aside. It felt very strange to lay Tina back against the pillows. He was acutely aware of her being a girl: the soft shape of her beneath the cotton of her petticoats; the dark spread of her hair on the yellowed pillowcases.

Her feet were freezing as he lifted them onto the bed. Her dark eyes followed his every move as he pulled the covers across her. He sat down, took her hand.

'I won't leave you, Tina,' he said. 'I promise.'

She gave no indication that she heard him, but there was some look to her, some *sense* to her, that told him she knew he was making promises he couldn't keep. He squeezed her hand.

'I'll do my best to fight them,' he whispered.

The faintest of smiles tugged at her lips and her eyes slipped shut.

Beside her, the strange, wizened little creature that she insisted was Miss Ursula burbled, its big eyes watching the candlelight wink and gleam on the rosary threaded through its claws.

Harry sighed. 'I guess I'll fight for you, too,' he whispered.

Wrapping himself in a blanket, he went and sat in the chair by the window, looking down towards the lake. He listened to Tina breathing and the old thing murmuring to itself, and tried to think.

Uriel: fire of God; the light in the west. Harry tried to come up with a more earthbound explanation for what he'd seen, but there was none. He had been looking for music-hall tricks, the cheap and tawdry machinations of man, and all the time it had been so much more than that. So much more. Uriel, an angel of the presence, trapped here and powerless at the mercy of these – his eyes flicked to the door – these what?

Shedim? Mazzikim? Harry shook his head. *Men*, he thought. *He is held captive by men*. This was not right. This was not good.

Behind him, Tina slept fast within the ring of golden candlelight. Her skin was paper-white, the flesh beneath her eyes as bruised as if she had been beaten. She had gone through so much to try to rescue Joe. It had been heroic.

Harry thought of all his father had told him about God and the world, and about mankind's ancient duty to both: every human being's responsibility in actions big and small to heal the world – *tikkun olam*.

He could not let this go on here. He had to at least try to stop this terrible thing.

Did it matter that he would fail? Was there not also honour in a valiant defeat?

Harry pulled the blanket tighter, closed his eyes and, though he knew he would not sleep, recited the *Kriat Shema al Hamita*. Then *Adon Olam*. By the time he had finished, he was calm and sure, and resigned to die in his efforts to free the Angel.

Matthew

THE MAN BY the window runs his fingers across something on the windowsill, a scar or an ornamentation in the wood; I cannot tell from where I am lying. He traces the shape tenderly, then lifts his eyes to take in the slowly brightening sky. I am unsure of how long we have been here. He appears to be waiting for me to wake.

I close my eyes and remember. The underground theatre. The creature. Tina.

I search and find her nearby, a fizzing brightness, like a silent Catherine wheel on the edge of my thoughts. She is dreaming. I reach for her, and she draws me in. There is a surge of nausea, the world shifting suddenly around me in colours my eyes can't understand, sounds my ears can't hear. I am afraid, but Tina squeezes me tight, wrapping me around her, and we are no longer Tina and Joe – we are something *other*: one and the same, separate but inseparable. We.

We bend and flex together, sure and certain, performing familiar tasks. There is a calm sense of order to Us. We are doing Our duty. It is a matter of routine.

I realise I am a memory. I am the living memory of something long ago. We are tearing through purple and yellow vastnesses, faster and further than I could ever have imagined possible. We carry a burden with Us, terrible and urgent. Our duty is to return it from whence it came; to push it through to its own space; to close the door behind it; to repair the world. We know there is no danger – as long as We live, it will sleep. Still, We wish the journey was done. Somewhere down deep in Our shared soul, We must confess We are frightened.

I try to disentangle from this – it terrifies me to be so little myself – but it is impossible to pull away. The other half of Us does not want to let go. We should never be parted! How can We survive if We are parted?

Then Tina releases me, and my mind almost splits at the dislocation. It is a terrible, painful rending, the division of something that should never have been divided – blinding in its horror.

But then I am myself again, and I can breathe.

I open my eyes a slit. The man is still watching the sky. I can recall him carrying me here. He removed my clothes. I think he washed and combed my hair. Then he dressed me again. The boy I used to be would have been appalled at that – how *dare* he – but the thing I am now sees it for what it was: a desperate attempt at transformation.

Something heavy is resting on the bed behind me. I can feel it weighing the mattress down at my back. The man's eyes glance to it, then drop to me. He frowns, and comes to sit on the edge of the bed. Watching from beneath my lashes, I can see that he has a book in his hand. It is Jules Verne's *From the Earth to the Moon*. He places it on the pillow by my head.

'I have brought you my copy,' he says. 'To replace yours that was ruined. You developed the habit of reading while you were away, I suppose?' He pauses, as if considering the thought, then whispers, 'Yes. That must be it.'

The weight behind me shifts as he adjusts the object on the bed. 'You...' he whispers. 'You *have* been gone for over seventy years. After all this time, I probably look very different, too. No doubt you hardly recognise me. I am sorry I thought that American was you...Can you imagine it? That short, bull-shouldered boy? It gave me quite the start. For a moment, I thought this would be like the other times – those other boys.' A hand tentatively brushes the hair from my face. 'You are real, Matthew? You are...'

Something makes him pause, and get to his feet. 'Ah!' he whispers. 'Cornelius.' He crouches by the bed, urgent now. 'Cornelius is on his way up from the kitchens, Matthew. I do not want him to catch me in your room. I must leave you alone for the moment, but I will be back. Please try not to wander about until I have laid the groundwork for your reconciliation.'

He locks the door behind him when he leaves.

I wait, as I know that he is waiting in the hall.

He speaks warmly, as if greeting a friend. 'Cornelius,' he says. 'You look tired.'

'There was a disturbance with the Angel in the night – you do not feel it?'

'You have investigated?'

There is a hesitation, and the new arrival says, 'I am attempting to stay upside for a while.'

'Why, that is wonderful, cully! I am pleased to—'

'What are you doing here?'

'I was worried for the seer. The children were prying at her door and—'

'They shall not bother us. I left them with Luke, burning things in the kitchen. Raquel...Raquel has retreated with her dolls.'

The man who was with me speaks gently. 'She will return to good spirits soon, Cornelius. I promise. Very soon, we—'

Again his friend cuts him short. 'Let us go inside.'

There is the sound of a door being unlocked. They go in to where Tina is. She seems undisturbed by their presence, so I let her go and sit up.

Every inch of me feels creaking and unused, as if my limbs have been assembled the wrong way around. I run my hand through my hair and am thrown by how soft it feels. I recall it being coarse and stiff, the legacy of years of scrubbing with carbolic soap.

I drop my hand and a movement across the room startles me. It is my reflection, staring from the dressing-table mirror. I touch the cravat that swaddles my throat, the high collar, the rich fabric of my fine blue jacket. I look like a drawing from a book by Dickens.

I lift my eyes to the thing that dominates the bed behind me and recognise it at once. I recall the man holding me against a wall on the staircase beside it, his eyes hopping between me and it, his dark forehead creased in uncertainty. He must have carried it here as I slept, and propped it against the headboard, all the better to compare me with.

It is a painting so large and bulky that I am astonished he could have lifted it from the wall. The boy in it is wearing the clothes I now find myself in. There is mischief and worldliness in his eyes, an open, honest adventurousness to his expression. Next to him, I see myself as I am: an underfed, over-hungry, wary-eyed alley-haunt. We are nothing alike, Matthew and I, and for the first time I truly understand the insanity of the man who has saved me.

I listen at the door. There is nothing. I try the handle, and the door is locked. I go to the window: it looks down on a riot of crumbling stable yards and overgrown orchard. The ruins of an ancient castle crouch like a monument over it all.

I can sense the creature beneath us. I sense it because Tina senses it. They are dreaming – the creature lost in hopelessness, Tina exhausted. The currents that pass between them are barely perceptible to me, but they are as strong and as deadly as the ocean's tides.

Tina reaches for me, and I close my eyes as if she has caressed me. She is beginning to wake, and as she does so our need to be together grows. It is an almost physical desire – the need to be in contact; the need to be close.

My fingers brush the windowsill, and I look down at what had so absorbed the man. It is a carving, barely the breadth of my palm: a heart. Within it, the initials 'M&C' entwine. The man's fingers have cleared the dust from it, and it shines like gold against the neglect that surrounds it.

I am aware of the boy again, watching from the bed, and am suddenly embarrassed to be here: a stranger wearing his clothes, intruding on the quiet ghost of his life. I rip off his necktie and fling it to the floor; I struggle free of his jacket. I replace his expensive boots with my own, and it feels good to do so. The rough leather, the mended soles: these things are mine. I *know* who I am.

I glance up as I jerk the laces tight and see a second door, half hidden beneath a wall-hanging. I lurch to my feet, hoping to escape through it. It leads to another bedroom, a man's by the look of it.

I am halfway across the next room when something makes me stop. I glance back at the boy. He is almost lost in shadow, but I can just make out his face, the mischief in his teasing smile. I step back into his room, and stay long enough to gather his jacket, the fallen banner of his necktie, and fold them carefully on the end of his bed.

All Together Now

VINCENT PAUSED ON the threshold of the seer's room, struck by the atmosphere within. Overhead, the old ones were restless, and the room was filled with the whisper of their papery sighs. The girl was laid out in the bed like a corpse, her hands folded, her dark river of hair spread around her face. She was so motionless Vincent had to look carefully to be certain she was breathing. In some obscenity of balance, the remains of the old woman were huddled beside her: it was as though Snow White had been laid out next to the carcass of the witch.

Cornelius had brought a tray, and he carried it to the dresser. It was loaded with a covered dish of food, one of the house's fine china teapots, a matching cup and saucer. The American boy, rising from his chair by the window, cocked an insolent eyebrow at the single setting.

'Where's mine?' he drawled. 'Surely you don't expect Miss Kelly and me to eat from the same plate?'

Cornelius scowled, then startled when he recognised his own clothes on the boy's shorter, stockier body. The boy grinned, and made a show of adjusting the rolled-up sleeves.

'I think I'll wear my cuffs turned back like this from now on,' he said. He flourished his fingers like a conjurer and smiled slyly at Cornelius. 'They emphasise my nimble hands.'

'How did you get my clothes?'

'I gave them to him,' said Vincent quickly.

The boy held Cornelius' eye. 'I helped myself,' he contradicted.

'Do not pay him any mind, Cornelius,' said Vincent. 'The boy is playing childish games. His own clothes were wet, and I gave him some of yours.'

He speared Harry with a look. *Betray me again, boy, and I will have you throw yourself out that window.*

The boy made a show of slowly meeting his eyes, but said nothing.

Cornelius turned to the bed. He was apparently intent on seeing to the girl, but was brought up short at the sight of the murmuring thing beside her.

'Oh no,' he said. 'No.' He pushed the boy aside and bent towards the creature. 'This cannot be here.'

He was frozen in mid-action by the boy's hand on his wrist. 'You're gonna leave that poor thing alone,' said the boy.

Cornelius straightened to meet his eye. 'Release my arm.'

The boy tightened his grip. 'Leave that poor thing alone.'

Vincent stepped forward, amazed to find himself utterly offended. It had been bad enough from the vermin in the city – this appalling, this *galling* disregard for their authority – but here? *Here?* In the very *house?* 'Release his arm!' he ordered.

The boy ignored him completely. He kept his eyes locked on Cornelius. 'Have you no shame?' he asked. 'Don't you understand how *wrong* this all is? It is not the place of mankind to make slaves of angels.'

Cornelius jerked back as if stung, breaking the boy's grip on him. The boy pressed on.

'You can't just bend God's order to your own benefit and the expense of others! Look around you. Can't you see how broken this place is? Those evil brats? That woman and her *dolls*? And you two?' He flung his hands out. 'Your eyes *glow in the dark*. Did you know that? What are you? Wolves? And your skin is hot like coals – you burn to the touch. *Vey iz mir!* This is *wrong*! You are all wrong here.'

That is enough, boy!

Vincent roared this directly into the boy's head, and the boy flinched, clutching his temples.

'What do you know of the Angel?' asked Cornelius. 'You have not been underground. You have no concept of its existence. What did you see under that water? Is there...' He stepped forward, his voice lowered. 'Is there another presence there? Were the seers correct?'

Still hunched over, the boy ignored him. Cornelius grabbed his arm, seeming to startle him. 'What did you *see* under that water? *Answer me!*'

A whisper from the bed stilled them all. 'It is the Demon.'

They turned to find the girl watching them.

'It is the Contagion. The...the Contagion of Worlds...'

She squeezed her face up in confusion, pressed her head back into the pillows.

'Joe,' she whispered. 'My mind hurts.'

Overhead, the old ones grew agitated, and the room filled with distressed moaning. The thing in the bed squirmed like an overturned beetle, and Vincent realised that it was trying to turn to face the girl.

'Joe,' cried the girl. 'I need you...I can't think!'

'Who are you calling?' whispered Cornelius.

'No one,' said Vincent. 'Her beau, from the city. No one.'

Then the door opened, and Vincent's heart dropped like a stone as that boy – that boy? Was that how he thought of him? Yes, already he was admitting to himself he had been wrong – *that boy*, wearing Matthew's trousers, Matthew's fine lawn shirt and Matthew's gold-and-cream embroidered waistcoat, and looking nothing at all like Matthew, stepped into the room.

Cornelius knew at once. He knew *at once* what Vincent had done. 'No,' he moaned. 'Not again.' He turned to Vincent. 'Not again,' he said.

Vincent could find nothing to say, and when Cornelius pushed past the boy and fled the room, he did not even try to stop him.

How can I have done this? thought Vincent, staring at the boy. *How? What is broken in my perception, that every single time I make the same—*

These bitter recriminations fell away and fascination took their place as the boy in Matthew's clothes crossed the room. There was something different about him. What was it?

He was still the same tall, raw-boned youth, but all his furtive caution seemed to have been burned away somehow. There was a strange calm to him, a stillness, as he approached the seer. She was huddled tight, her hands pressed to her temples. Without a word, the boy put his arms around her, and to Vincent's astonishment, she instantly relaxed.

'Joe,' she breathed.

The boy called Joe looked across at the American standing on the opposite side of the bed. 'Harry?' he asked.

The American nodded warily, and the boy seemed pleased. 'I knew that.'

Joe glanced at Vincent, and his arms tightened protectively around the seer. A strange expression crossed his face – an oddly embarrassed kind of sympathy – and Vincent realised with a flare of outrage that the boy was sorry for him.

'You brought me back,' said Joe.

'An act of gross stupidity. I am mortified by it.'

The girl glared at him from beneath her dark hair. 'Your angel is dying.'

'We will fix that, soon enough.'

She laid her free hand on the brittle creature beside her. 'You have no right to do this.'

Vincent huffed. 'We are not responsible for that. That is your so-called *angel*. That is what it does to keep itself alive. It is no fault of ours.'

The girl shook her head. 'You let him feed through you. But you know he needs more than you alone can give him.'

Vincent shifted uncomfortably.

She smiled, guessing perhaps how long he had suspected this. 'He needs *bigger things*.'

'A spectacular,' said Vincent, almost hating the word. 'Yes. I know.'

'He needs you to be—'

'Entranced,' he interrupted. 'Captivated. *Awed*. Teach me something I don't already know, girl!'

'And so you *use people up*,' she said.

'That is *life*! People get used up. Do not be so—' Vincent bit back the words. What was he doing, justifying himself to this scrap-of-nothing girl?

{ 293 }

She gazed down at the burbling thing by her side, stroked its wispy hair. 'It didn't used to be like this,' she whispered. 'People didn't used to have to wither just to feed Us. Before Joe died...' She paused, frowning. 'No...not Joe...before the creature in the box died...'

She pressed her hand to her head, clenched the other in the waistcoat of the boy called Joe. He gazed down at her: calm, supportive, silent.

'I'm confused,' she whispered.

'The creature in the box?' prompted Vincent carefully. She seemed so fragile. He must try not to break her too soon. 'The creature from my laboratory? That is what you were carrying with you last night? That is what you brought to the caverns?'

'It is dead! How can We survive without it?'

Vincent stared into her desperate, slightly feral face and wondered if the child had already been driven insane. 'How do you know this?' he asked.

Her hand tightened in the boy's clothes. 'I *remember*. We...it...*We* remember.'

'You *remember*? You remember what the Bright Man – what the Angel – remembers? Is that it?'

The seer nodded tightly. Vincent could barely contain his excitement. The seer shared the Bright Man's thoughts. So many possibilities opened at this revelation. The amount of knowledge that could be gained from it! He leaned across the foot of the bed.

'What else do you remember?'

'We must contain the Contagion,' she cried urgently. 'The *Demon*. It must not wake!'

Vincent straightened. Again they returned to the Demon. The American had retreated to the corner of the room as they spoke, his eyes hopping from one to the other of them.

'What did you see down there, boy?' Vincent asked. 'You said it was a machine. What kind of machine?'

At the boy's silence, Vincent lifted his hands in exasperation.

'Spit it out! What are you afraid of?'

The boy just kept staring, and Vincent dropped his hands, suddenly understanding. 'You saw nothing,' he said. 'You wanted my attention, and you said what you thought I wanted to hear – but in reality, you saw nothing. I am right, aren't I?'

The American's eyes flicked from him to the others, then back again. He nodded.

Vincent groaned in disappointment. Striding to the window, he stared down at the distant pond.

'The green light, the pulsing beat: your mind put these two things together and came up with a machine. A good guess, for someone whose perception is addled with angels.'

He glanced back at the American, suddenly fascinated.

'Why *do* you see an angel? Were you told it was so, before you witnessed it? Is that it? Answer me, boy. I am fascinated by this. Why do so many of you see the Bright Man as a creature of the divine?'

'It's not an angel.'

Vincent spun to face the boy called Joe.

'It's not an angel,' repeated the boy. 'Angels don't exist.'

Vincent nodded fervently.

'God doesn't exist.'

'Yes!' cried Vincent, overcome to have, at last, someone who might confirm his own vision. 'Yes! So what did you see? What *is* it?'

The boy seemed to struggle for a word. After a moment, he shrugged. 'Something other?'

'Other.' Vincent nodded. *Other.*

He looked back down at the pond. 'I am going down there,' he murmured. He looked across at the American. 'Thank you, boy. For all it was a deception, I think you might have taken a step towards solving a centuries-old mystery. I am grateful to you.'

The boy regarded him with an uncertain frown and then nodded, slow and wary, as if afraid of what he might be agreeing to.

What an amusing group these three were: the pugnacious little magician, the fey, defiant girl, and…

Vincent hesitated. He made himself look again at the boy called Joe, made himself acknowledge exactly who he wasn't and exactly who he was: a gutter-boy with ragged clothes, and a love of books, and an unusual disregard for angels.

For a moment, Vincent almost felt sad for these children. For a moment, they were almost real to him.

Then he shook them off and left the room, locking the door as he went.

An Agreement

HARRY WHISPERED, 'HAS he gone? That man? We're all alone?'

Joe, his face mask-like and strangely still, nodded.

Harry scratched and scrabbled at his ears until he'd dislodged the wads of paper and wax he'd plugged them with. The sounds of the world became immediate and accessible again – a relief and an anxiety all at once.

'So,' he said, shoving the earplugs into his pocket, 'what's going on? Tell me everything.'

'SAY!' HE CRIED, pounding down the stairs after Vincent. 'Say! Wait a minute there!'

Surprised, Vincent spun to a halt on the first-floor landing. Harry came to a stop a few steps above him. He gripped the banister, trying to seem imposing. With his ears plugged again, nothing he touched felt real. His feet didn't even seem to contact the ground, his breathing sounded panicked in his head.

Vincent was stalking towards him, demanding to know how he kept escaping the room. Harry blessed the crotchety old mind-reader who'd taught him to read lips, and all the pre-show audiences he'd spied on from behind the curtain, gathering those morsels of information people gave when they thought no one was watching. This man would be a damned sight harder to fool than a hall of country bumpkins, though. The best thing Harry could do now was to keep talking so Vincent couldn't get a word in edgeways.

'I lied to yah about seeing nothing in that lake.'

Vincent halted.

'I did see something. Something big, filled with lights, made of metal. It *is* a machine.' Vincent went to speak and Harry leapt in ahead of him. 'I was afraid you'd make me go down there again. But I've decided that I *want* to go with you. I want to see what's down there.'

The man raised an eyebrow at Harry and said something like, '*Why would you want to do that?*'

Harry hoped he was reading this right.

'Why do you? I just want to *know*. Isn't that enough? I'm pretty certain I'm not getting out of here alive, mister, and I'm not gonna sit around like some *zeyde* waiting for my end. I want to *understand* – to know what's going on.'

This seemed to appeal to the man. He said something Harry couldn't catch, and then stood looking up at him as if expecting an answer. When Harry remained silent, the man lost some of his amusement. He made a shooing gesture up the stairs.

Harry nodded and turned, trying to hide his relief. He didn't even feel the man rushing up the stairs behind him, so when he was caught and spun and slammed against the wall of the upstairs landing, he was momentarily paralysed with shock.

He found himself pushed up onto his tiptoes, held against the wall by Vincent's arm across his windpipe. The man was talking, his face calm and cold, his head tilted downwards. Harry couldn't make out what he was saying, but considering that he was efficiently and methodically turning Harry's pockets inside out, it felt safe to assume he was searching for something.

It only took moments for Vincent to satisfy himself that Harry hadn't got what he was looking for. He leaned a little more of his weight against Harry's neck, frowning curiously into his face.

'...*do it?*' he asked.

Harry responded by looking as defiant as possible.

Raising his eyebrows in patient warning, Vincent tweaked the collar of Harry's borrowed jacket. '...*think I...allow you...wander...stealing clothes. How...locks?*' ·

Ah! Harry twisted his chin against the man's forearm and forced a smirk onto his face. He flourished his hands. 'Magic!' he said.

The sudden dark rage this brought to Vincent's face sent a spear of ice through Harry's heart. It was just a flash, the briefest slip of the man's patience, but it was enough. Vincent leaned closer. '...*think I am?*' he asked, his dark eyes piercing Harry's. '...*superstitious savage...sangoma-ridden peasant?*' He gripped Harry's face in one terrifyingly strong hand and squeezed, forcing his lips and teeth apart. '...*don't know a common pick-a-lock when I see one?*'

Vincent's scorching fingers probed beneath Harry's tongue, behind his teeth and around his gums, hunting for the lock-picks that Harry was eye-wateringly glad he'd chosen to hide in his shoe. The search seemed to go on forever, and Harry was just thinking the man would shove his entire fist down his throat when, suddenly, Vincent dropped him to the ground.

He crouched against the wall a moment, his hand to his bruised face, shaken and mortified and trying to swallow down his fear. Then he straightened to meet Vincent's eye. 'Well? Find anything interesting?'

The man just tightened his jaw and jerked his head for Harry to lead the way back to the room.

TINA WAS SITTING in the chair by the window. She had put on a pale-blue wool dress and was pulling on her boots with one hand, holding fast to Joe's with the other. Both she and Joe looked up as Harry was shoved through the door. He stumbled a few steps, and grinned his showman's grin.

'Our friend has agreed that I can join him,' he said. Straightening his jacket, he turned to Vincent. 'Isn't that right, sir? We are all set for our voyage of underwater discovery?'

The man just swept the room with his eyes, nodded to Tina and left, shutting the door behind him.

Harry waited.

After the briefest moment, the door opened again. The man stared at him as if not knowing whether to laugh or scream. He held out his hand.

Harry wrinkled his brow, affecting not to understand.

The man just stood there, silently waiting.

Feigning puzzlement, Harry patted himself down, turning all his pockets inside out. At last, and with pantomime amazement, he found the man's keys in his trousers.

'Well now, how did *they* get *there*?' he cried.

He palmed the keys to his left hand while offering the man his empty right. Palmed them right while offering his empty left. Then he lost them up his sleeve, before producing the entire set from his mouth.

The man's expression did not flicker, his hand did not move, and eventually Harry laid the keys into his waiting palm. Vincent did not close his fingers until Harry's had withdrawn. Then he spoke quietly into Harry's head.

In our youth, Cornelius' father would have rewarded such a performance by asking my father to cut off your hands. When you had recovered – and you would have recovered, because my father was a very fine surgeon – Cornelius' father would have strapped you to a plough and made a mule of you. You would have eaten your meals from an animal trough for the rest of your miserable life. These are the methods Cornelius and I were taught to use when confronted with defiance. I want you to remember that. I want you to think about it the next time you are tempted to be insolent.

With that, he nodded politely to the other occupants of the room and left.

Harry stood motionless, regarding the blandly painted wood of the door. Then his knees failed him and he staggered back to sit on the edge of the bed. He removed his earplugs, sick of this vulnerable deafness.

Joe went to the door and tried the handle. The door opened a crack. He peeked outside. 'He's gone,' he whispered. Sounding slightly surprised, he added, 'He didn't bother to lock us in.'

Conversations on
the Threshold

By the time Vincent had reached the bottom of the second staircase he had to stop and lean against the banister, completely given over to a fit of silent laughter. This caused him an unusual amount of discomfort, and so he sat on the last step, grinning up at Cornelius' beloved horse, waiting for it to subside. He twirled the keys on his finger, thinking of the boy popping them from his mouth.

'Such defiance,' he said. 'It has been years since I've enjoyed the like.'

Vincent lost his smile. It *had* been years.

Slowly he closed his hand around the set of keys, thinking of the American boy, and how even with his head deep in the lion's mouth, he'd had the nerve to clown about. Vincent got to his feet, patted the dull, dead flank of Cornelius' horse, and headed for the place he knew his friend would be.

CORNELIUS WAS SPRAWLED on the floor by the lower door. He did not look up as Vincent descended the steps, merely picked at a splinter in the doorframe, his head leaning against the wall at his back. Behind the door, the Bright Man sighed and moaned, beams of its light slanting through small gaps in the wood.

Vincent took a seat a few steps up. Resting his elbows on his knees, he threaded his fingers together, and considered what he was about to say.

Cornelius spoke first. 'You have disposed of him, of course.'

Vincent frowned. His thoughts had been on the Bright Man – the revelation that the seer shared its thoughts; the possible answers presented by a machine in the pond. It took a moment to realise that Cornelius was referring to the boy called Joe.

Distracted and dulled by his proximity to the Angel, Cornelius continued to pick at the wood. Gradually it seemed to dawn on him that his statement had not been answered, and he looked at Vincent for the first time. 'You have disposed of him?' he asked.

Vincent winced apologetically. 'He seems to calm the seer, cully. I thought perhaps—'

'He is wearing *Matthew's clothes*. Do not tell me you left him up there for Raquel to see.' At Vincent's silence, Cornelius groaned. 'How many times are you going to do this to us? Every time you return from a trip, now, I am on tenterhooks thinking I may round a corner and, all unsuspecting, walk into some stranger wearing Matthew's things. It's *torture*, Vincent. Do you not understand that?'

Vincent huffed. 'I have not been on a trip in decades. I think—'

'Over and over I have had to convince you! Each time, again and again. Matthew is *gone*. He will never be back. Please will you reconcile yourself to this? Please.'

Vincent shifted uncomfortably, wondering how it was that he had once again managed to cause pain, when he only ever desired to make things better.

'It is never my intention to distress you. It is just…the life they lead is always so appalling and squalid, and they always seem so likely to be him. Then when I get here…they are never anything like him.'

'Nor will they ever be.'

'You are wrong,' said Vincent quietly. 'Matthew will not stay away forever. He would not break his mother's heart that way.' He hesitated, and then said, 'Neither would he break yours, cully.'

There was a stricken silence. It was clear that Cornelius understood exactly what had been meant by that last sentence, and Vincent saw him freeze under the weight of it, motionless and terrified, waiting.

Just take one step further, Vincent told himself. *Just one more step and we may, at last, be truly honest.*

This was the closest he had ever come to saying it. The words were already on his tongue, already in his mind, poised: *Matthew loved you, Cornelius. You loved Matthew. So much happiness you could have given each other. Why did you push him away?*

But as usual, he faltered. He had lived his whole life indulging Cornelius' charade. To speak now would feel like a betrayal, like the breaking of a pact made in silence long ago. Only Matthew – in all his freshness and confidence, all his self-knowledge and certainty – only he might have been brash enough and sunny enough to end this tired and poisonous game.

The silence between them stretched on. When Vincent dropped his eyes, there was a moment of almost disappointment, almost betrayal in Cornelius' face; then he shut himself off. He sat back, his expression bland.

'If you do not dispose of this latest mistake, I shall take him myself and put him in the oubliette with what is left of Wolcroft. Is that what you would like for him?'

Vincent grimaced. 'Do not make yourself out to be crueller than you are, cully.'

Even slumped against a dungeon door, his clothes three days crumpled, and soiled with cavern slime, Cornelius could summon effortless élan.

'Do not test me,' he drawled, wagging a reproving finger. 'I may delight in proving you wrong.' He grew serious. 'I will not have Raquel disturbed by this, Captain. Not when her humour seems so recently set to improve. I will tie a block to the knave and cast him into the well if I must.'

Vincent shrugged. 'I shall give him a change of clothes and he will be just another boy. Raquel does not have to know that I...mistook him.'

Cornelius' eyes narrowed. 'Why am I having to persuade you to rid yourself of him? You had no qualms with his forerunners. What difference is there in him?'

Vincent hesitated. He almost said, *I like them, this sorry little group. They appeal to me.* But in the end, he told only half the truth. 'The seer is fragile. He calms her.'

'How so?'

Vincent rose to his feet. 'This is one of the many things I hope to discover when I explore the pond.'

Cornelius pushed himself to sit up straighter, his face dropping. 'What do you mean, "explore the pond"?'

'I intend to go down there, cully. Today. I want to investigate the American's machine.'

'Don't be ridiculous! That will serve no purpose! Why would you put yourself at such risk?'

Vincent turned and jogged up the steps. He smiled as Cornelius began staggering up behind him, calling out, 'It does not *matter* what is in the pond – the extravaganza is in *six days*. For God's sake, slow down! Come back and listen to reason!'

Vincent ducked his chin and put on a bit of speed, drawing Cornelius up into the house, out into the daylight, and away from the numbness and the torpor of the Angel.

The Things That Were

HARRY STARED INTO Joe's same-but-different face. 'So,' he said. 'So...I guess you're better, huh?' He awkwardly patted Joe's arm. 'Nice to see you again, pal.'

'Joe,' gasped Tina. 'Will you hold my hand?'

Harry and Joe turned from the door to find her crouched in the chair by the window, her hands white-knuckled fists in her lap.

'I'm sorry. Really I am. But the Angel is so frightened, Joe – it's hurting me. I can't seem to hold it back without you.'

Joe went to her side, and she took his hand. All the tension left her, and Joe smiled gravely, squeezing her fingers.

'What have those men done to us?' she whispered. She eyed his outfit as if for the first time, and then Harry's. 'They're keen on people changing their clothes here, aren't they?'

'I have me own boots on,' murmured Joe.

The three of them spent a vacant moment gazing down at the scuffed toes of his boots.

'The rest of me has changed, though.'

Harry didn't like the way Joe said this. He had an uncomfortable feeling they weren't talking about clothes anymore.

'I'm never going home,' said Joe.

Harry nodded. 'You're right. We haven't a hope of getting out of here. But I'm telling yah, Joe, I'm going down swinging.' He threw a gesture at the creature in the bed. 'I'll burn this *farkakte* house down before I let them do that to anyone else…and as my last act on earth, I will set that angel free.'

Tina slammed her palm down on the arm of the chair. 'Never going home?' she cried. 'Last act on earth? What are the two of you *like*?'

In a rage, she shook off Joe's hand and surged to her feet, intent on storming to the dresser. Halfway there, she bent double, her face blanched. 'Oh,' she breathed.

Harry leapt to help, but Tina flung out an arm for Joe. He took her hand, and after a second or two she was able to straighten. 'Thanks, Joe,' she whispered.

She led them to the tray that Wolcroft had left on the dresser. One-handed, she lifted the cover to reveal what looked like two roasted pigeons and a small heap of apple sauce. There was a moment's hesitation; then Tina laid the cover aside.

'We're going to eat,' she said.

Harry eyed the strange, dark little carcasses of the birds. Tina cut him off before he could speak. 'We're going to *eat*,' she insisted. 'We're going to stay *strong*, we're going to stay *together*, and we're going home.'

'Tina—' began Joe.

Tina abruptly pressed her fingers to his lips, silencing him. It was such an intimate gesture – so private and true – that Harry almost looked away from it.

'We're important, Joe,' said Tina. 'We matter.'

Gently, Joe took her hand from his mouth. He kissed her small, rough fingers. Then he bent to kiss her lips.

'I waited too long to do that,' he whispered.

She shook her head, her eyes filling with tears. 'These buggers aren't the first to try and tell us we're nothing, Joe. They won't be the last, either. We're getting out of here. You and me. Harry and Miss Ursula. We're getting out of here. And then we'll start to *live*. All right, Joe? We'll go home and we'll figure things out, and we'll start to live.'

Joe just tilted his head, not answering.

At his silence, Tina's eyes grew momentarily wider, then she turned sharply for the tray. 'Right,' she said, digging her fingers into the little carcasses, pulling the meat into three portions.

Joe kept his hand on her back. 'I don't need mine,' he said softly.

She stopped putting the meat into its little piles. Her hands tightened on the plate.

'I don't need it, Tina.'

Without looking up, she slapped the three portions back together, divided it neatly down the middle and shoved half over to Harry's side of the plate. 'Eat,' she said.

The meat was strong and dense and clay-like, the apple sauce almost too sharp to bear. Harry thought they complemented each other. It was the kind of dark, bitter meal warriors might once have eaten in Syria or Babylon: pre-battle fare. He ate determinedly, the girl grim and focused beside him. Joe stood over them both, silent and calm, his hand on Tina's back.

When they were done, Tina wiped her hands in the fancy cloth Wolcroft had left for the purpose and went to look out the window. 'Are you really going under the water with that man, Harry?'

'Sure am.'

'Why?'

'There's something down there. I want to see what it is.'

'What if you drown?'

He paused, not wanting to think about it. 'I won't. I was under there for a long time last night, and I didn't even want to take a breath. I just didn't seem to need to.'

Tina leaned on the sill, apparently thinking hard. Joe's hand rested against the dark tumble of her hair, keeping her with them.

'What's in that lake is wrong, Harry,' she said at last. 'It feels all wrong for this world. Like it will *infect* it. Like…I keep thinking the word "contagion". It's a *contagion*. The Angel is terrified of it.'

A contagion. A disease. Harry shuddered, images of boils and pustules and open sores spreading in his mind. 'Maybe I should forget the lake,' he murmured. 'Maybe I should just let the Angel out…see what happens then.'

'You can't just let him out, Harry,' said Tina. 'He's mad. He's *hungry*. If you let him out, he'll come straight for me and Joe. He'll rip us apart. Do you understand?'

Harry nodded, dry-mouthed. She was so matter-of-fact. 'Okay, I won't let it out,' he said. 'But you two should leave while I'm under the water. Take advantage of the distraction and get as far away as possible.'

'Sure, couldn't we all just leave?' said Tina, staring at him with a knowing kind of gentleness. 'Couldn't we all just sneak off, right now, and take our chances in the snow?'

'I'm not going to abandon an angel to these madmen,'

said Harry. 'But *you* should go. You're used to horses, Joe. Take one of them from the stables – make a break for it!'

Joe shook his head. 'I can't,' he said. 'But Tina—'

As if to silence him, Tina turned back to the window. 'Harry,' she said, 'if you're going underwater, you'd better get moving. They're starting to burn their way through the ice.'

'*What?*' Harry rushed to see.

Far out on the frozen lake, Vincent was straightening from a crouch. He pointed something out to the man called Luke, who was nodding and tugging at his whiskers, deep in thought.

They had constructed a large tripod and were just finishing the process of suspending a brazier below it. As Harry watched, Luke tossed something into the brazier, and its contents roared to sudden flame. The men stepped back, waving smoke from their faces, and yes – it was obvious – they were planning to burn a hole into the frozen surface.

Harry swallowed hard at the sight of the children sitting on the wall of the bridge. They were chatting and swinging their little legs, full of the innocent joys of youth.

Wolcroft was also on the bridge. He seemed to have put as much distance between himself and the children as possible while still taking advantage of the elevated view. His arms were folded, his posture tense, as he watched the proceedings on the ice.

The woman was occupied on the lake shore. Despite the overcast sky, she had stuck an ornate sun umbrella into the frosty ground and was busy placing a folding chair in its shade. She had a pram with her, filled with dolls. It seemed the entire family was set to watch the show.

'It's a circus down there,' whispered Harry.

'You don't have to do this,' said Tina.

Harry didn't like how much he wanted to be persuaded by this. 'Say now,' he said, gesturing to the man on the lake. 'If that guy can do it, then so can I.'

'These people aren't like us, Harry. I don't think they can die.'

'I wouldn't mind testing that theory,' murmured Joe.

Harry wet his lips. He had a question he very badly wanted to know the answer to. It was a hard question to ask, but it wouldn't leave him alone. Especially now.

'Joe,' he ventured. 'Tina told me…Tina told me you died. Is that true?'

Joe turned his calm, strangely immobile gaze to Harry. 'Yes,' he said. 'I died.'

'What was it like?'

Joe thought a moment. 'Lonely,' he said. 'Empty. It got very dark.'

Harry's voice felt too small and too dry when he asked, 'But…did you see nothing? No heaven?'

Joe smiled gently. 'Don't let that bother you, Harry. If heaven exists, I'm pretty sure they wouldn't let me in. Sure, why would they, when I never had the manners to believe in the place?'

Tina, her eyes still on the lake, tightened her hand in his. 'Joe,' she murmured. 'Do you remember when I was sick, and all the neighbours were scared of me?'

Joe winced. 'Stop,' he said.

'Nana and Fran were so good to me, Joe. But they wouldn't talk to me about it. Do you remember? They never talked about it, and they were always bringing priests to the gaff, and holding novenas…and for a long time, it was like I was a stranger everyone was praying would go away, so their real little girl could come home.'

She looked up at Joe.

'But *you* talked to me about it, Joe. You talked to me as if I was still the same person. And when it happened again, you and Saul went and found Dr Taxol's epilepsy book and Mr Aristotle's list and all them other things. You made me see I wasn't on me own; that it wasn't the devil doing these things to me. You showed me there wasn't anything wrong with me that other people hadn't already gone through. Do you remember all that, Joe?'

'I remember,' he whispered.

'Good. I'm glad you do.' Tina stretched up and kissed Joe on his lips. 'Any god that wouldn't let you into heaven deserves a kick in his arse,' she said.

'Now.' She turned from him. 'You and Harry are going to have to help me sort something out, because we're not leaving without Miss U.'

Burning Down

VINCENT SHIELDED HIS eyes from the billowing smoke and steam and examined the shoreline, trying to map the shape of the boating pond in his mind.

'Luke,' he murmured, 'have you ever read Jules Verne?'

'Pah!' spat Luke, crouching to check the padded feet of the tripod. 'Fiction is for women.'

Vincent huffed softly. 'Fiction is the human mind exploring all the possibilities of what is and what might be, Luke. Every progress ever achieved began as a fiction, in one form or another.'

As he spoke, he pondered the ripple of hills that bordered the southern end of the pond, and then turned his attention towards the north shore. The breeze blew the smoke away in that direction, a stream of acrid darkness tumbling across the ice until it was swallowed by the fog.

'I cannot believe that I have never noticed this,' he murmured.

'Noticed what?'

'The pond. The shape of it.'

'Oh, aye,' said Luke. 'You could see the shape clearly from

atop the monastery tower before Wolcroft tore it down – like someone plunged their fist through a field of mud and left a great big hole. Old folk named this lake *Stad an Púca* – said the divil ploughed it up with a smack of his hurley; that the lights over it were himself looking for his lost *slíotar*. Story was that the Bright Man was sent by God to find it and deny the divil the satisfaction of collecting it.'

He grimaced up at Vincent from where he was crouched. 'But you know all that, Captain. Sure I bored the trousers off you many a night on board with these tales. Trying to tempt you and Himself back here to free my land.'

'I confess, I never thought too deeply about it. My mind was always occupied with the Bright Man, and plans for his capture and preservation.'

'Huh. May chance had I writ it down as *fiction* you would have paid more heed.'

Vincent let himself smile. 'May chance.'

'It's strange to be crouched here o'er the lights that featured in so many stories from my childhood,' said Luke, laying his fingers against the surface of the ice. 'I hadn't ever thought to see them myself – allus believed they were nothing but a tale inspired by marsh gas or such. What brought 'em about now, do you think, Captain?'

'Perhaps they have always been here – perhaps the presence of the ice concentrates them somehow and makes visible that which previously the waves hid from us.'

'It's said they once shone bright as stars,' murmured Luke, rising to his feet. 'That the surface glittered at night like scattered emeralds. If so, they lost their lustre long before I was born. Perhaps the extravaganza will restore them, Captain? It's said…'

His voice trailed off when he noticed that Vincent had switched his attention to the bridge, where Cornelius brooded and scowled.

'Himself is in a right scorp, ain't he? Doesn't fancy your present enterprise much, I reckon. Too *dangerous* for you.'

'At least he is above ground for once, and engaged. It gives me hope that he might be improving. And Raquel! Look at her, out and about.' Vincent slapped the nearest tripod leg. 'I should do more public experiments, Luke, if they will animate the others so. Why, I can feel it in the air myself, can't you? A renewed vibrancy – a freshness. It is quite gratifying. And there is very little hunger today, did you notice? Even the children seem content. It makes me…'

He trailed off at the look on Luke's face. It was a miserable look, filled with reluctance and uncertainty; it turned Vincent's happy zeal to wariness.

'What is it?' asked Vincent.

Luke shook his head and waved a hand, went to turn away.

'What?' Vincent grabbed his arm. 'Say it!'

Luke seemed to squirm internally. 'Captain…' he said. 'Captain, you know it ain't just Himself and the missus. Don't you?'

Vincent released him. Luke went on apologetically.

'Who is it you think has kept that laboratory of yours going these past fifty years or so, sir? Who is it you think has topped the water up in all those tanks, and kept all those bellows working? Clockwork don't wind itself, you know.'

Vincent backed away. He tried to recall the last time

he had maintained the aquariums, or checked the cages. He came to a halt against a leg of the tripod. Smoke and steam gushed from the slowly sinking brazier, the roar of the flames and hiss of melting ice filling his head. Luke gave him a fleeting glance of pity, and Vincent was too frightened to even be angered by it.

'Where...where do I be, at such times?'

'Sitting. Just sitting. Sometimes it feels like the childer and I are the only people left on earth, Captain: walking those dusty halls; seeing you and Miss Raquel so still and quiet; knowing Himself is down there somewhere, just the same, with his angel watching over him.' Luke shook his head.

'And the villagers?'

'Just the same, sir. Was a time they tended their gardens and their animals, and went *a-céilídhing* even, out into the world. But not this long time since have they done anything but sit. It's only when the hunger began to set in that folk started stirring again, and then only to moan and feel bad.'

Vincent sagged against the tripod, his mind stretching back and back for some tangible memory that wasn't from around the time Matthew had left, or since the hunger of the Bright Man's decline had begun to ache within him. He could think of nothing. Nothing.

'In fairness, Captain, you and the missus've been the best of 'em. Every now and again I'll bring you a new delivery of periodicals and she her bookkeeping, and you'll rouse yourselves awhile to work at your projects and such...'

'But not for long,' whispered Vincent, recalling.

'Not for long, sir. And not for a long time. It may even be as much as ten year since you last stirred yourself in such a way.'

Vincent felt like sinking to the ground. He felt like losing himself in the smoke and steam that now rolled about their feet as the brazier shuddered and sank into the ice. He looked up at Luke from beneath his brows. 'How is it that *you* are not affected? What is so special about *you*?'

'Me and the childer,' Luke reminded him.

The children. Vincent glanced across at them. Laughing in that tinkling, high-pitched way of theirs, they were busy flinging stones from the parapet of the bridge, attempting to shatter the new ice that had formed since they'd tried to drown Cornelius' dogs.

'The childer always find something to occupy them,' murmured Luke. 'Though it burns my heart, sometimes, to acknowledge what it is that pleases them most.'

Vincent looked to him, questioning: *And you?*

Luke shrugged. 'I can't tell you, Captain. All I know is I just want to keep moving – just keep working my land. It never fails to please me: the working of the land, the walking of it, the knowing that it is mine. But shall I confess something, Captain? I haven't ever felt the Angel's presence – not the way the rest of you seem to. Even now, I can see you feel it, but this "freshness" you speak of, this "renewed vibrancy"? I don't feel that, sir. Today is just a day, to me. That's all. A day like any other. Maybe that has something to do with why I haven't…haven't ever fallen away?'

Vincent's expression must have told him that he didn't know, because Luke nodded. 'Matthew was the same, you know. I suspect it shamed him somewhat, because he only ever spoke to me of it once and never again. I told him it was on account of him being already so full of happiness – what need had he to borrow that of the Angel's?'

Luke fell silent, and his eyes slid to the horizon. 'Reckon I feel a bit awkward now,' he said at last. 'Reckon you might be angry with me, for speaking out so true.'

Vincent shook his head, his mind in turmoil.

Luke cleared his throat. 'Will we lay out more slack for the chains?' he suggested. 'Winch them loose a bit so as—' He squinted past Vincent, up towards the house, then gave a half laugh. 'By God, Captain, but here comes a quare trail of ducklings!'

Vincent turned to look. It was the seer and her friends, treading their way carefully across the lawns, obviously intent on joining them. Vincent's heart gave a startled little *bump* when he noticed what the girl was pushing. At the same time, Luke emitted an anxious whistle, and his eyes dropped to Raquel. She was poised like a china doll within the shelter of her umbrella, her back to the approaching threesome, her eyes shaded with one lace-gloved hand as she watched Vincent go about his work.

'Jesus son of Mary, Captain. Tell me the missus gave them permission to take that baby-carriage, or there'll be blood on the water before we can blink an eye.'

Vincent hopped his gaze from Raquel and the seer to Cornelius, who was standing tight-lipped and unaware on the bridge. He put a hand on Luke's arm. 'Leave it,' he said. 'The discomfort will do us good.'

Behind them, the chains sang, the tripod creaked, and at last the brazier fell through the ice, its fire extinguished with a roar of steam as it began plummeting on its chains into the depths below.

Vincent turned from the oncoming storm and, with his eyes on the churning water, began unbuttoning his shirt. 'Stop looking up at the house,' he said. 'You will alert Cornelius to their presence.'

'But they're halfway down the hill now, Captain.'

'Stop looking, damn you, or I shall push you in to test the depth.'

Luke moved a little further back from the hole, purposely averting his eyes from the gardens. Vincent removed his boots and his trousers, adding them to his shirt in a growing pile of neatly folded clothes on the ice. He untied the lacing at the knees of his underbritches but kept the garment on. Then he stepped to the edge. The water was black and choppy and depthless, the chains racing down into it, swallowed, link after link, by darkness.

The cold of the ice gnawed up into the soles of Vincent's feet. The air clamped itself around his naked chest and arms. His skin began to steam. Still the chains paid out, rattling madly through the winch head as the brazier sank away from them.

'Will we have enough to reach bottom, Captain?'

'Even if we do not, I shall follow the chains as far as they go, then follow the lights from there.'

'What if you run out of rope?'

Vincent did not look up.

'Captain, don't act rash down there. If you run out of rope, come back for more. You can't be down there without a lifeline.'

The chains ran to the end of their length and came to a jarring halt. The tripod moaned, the winch creaked, and the chains began to turn and sing as, far below, the brazier swung its weight at the end of them.

Vincent lifted the coil of fine rope intended as his lifeline and looped the end over one shoulder. He pointed to the second coil. 'That is for the magician,' he said. 'He may join me if he wishes.'

When he sat down on the edge of the ice, and the water closed around his lower legs, Vincent shuddered. It felt dead: like dead hands gripping his flesh. He could not see his feet.

'Captain,' said Luke, but Vincent slipped over the side and into darkness before the man could finish his sentence.

Dead Water

TINA CROSSES THE lawns with me, Harry striding ahead, determined and terrified. The light is pressing hungry fingers against them, the creature attempting to force its grief into Tina's mind. But I am holding Tina's hand, and so she is calm, because I am her anchor.

We are pushing the pram with our free hands. The thing within blinks up at the passing sky, the beads of Tina's rosary twinkling between its fingers.

I remember this rosary. It is made of Austrian crystal, and Fran and the Lady Nana gave it to Tina the day she made her first communion.

I remember that day. She and all the little girls of our parish paraded down the street, happy and proud in their veils and dresses. There were white crepe ribbons on all the buildings leading to the church. White paper bunting hung from one side of the street to the other. I stood on the corner in my scruff, and Tina grinned at me from behind her veil.

That was when she was seven.

I remember when she was fourteen, and suddenly it was like she was made of crystal, she was so bright and shining and alive. I couldn't keep my eyes off her. She had already moved from our street, but we were always together. I remember Mickey began following her with his eyes, then. He began to go quiet when she was near. I knew if I wasn't hanging around her, she wouldn't be in his vision. I knew I should remove myself from her life. But I didn't want to.

I remember Mickey followed her to her building. I watched the door swallow him while I stood paralysed on the street. It was just a moment's hesitation, but even now the shame of it burns me up. By the time I ran in, Tina was descending the stairs like an Amazon, whipping him ahead of her with that selfsame rosary. I remember the fierce glittering arc of it, swinging through the sun from the skylight. It must have been the first thing she'd snatched up, and he was lucky it wasn't a poker, because she nearly took his eye out with it.

That night, Mickey bounced me off the wall so hard I left an imprint in the plaster. Daymo, dragging potatoes from the ashes of the fire, snickered. Ma turned her face to the wall. The ladies moved to the other side of the city very soon after.

Now here I am, with Tina's hand in mine. I've kissed her, and she has kissed me; a boy who could turn out to be my best friend is striding ahead of us, and it is the most included, the most loved, I have ever felt in my life.

But we are walking through a torment of light, towards a great black hole of nothing; I can barely look at the contents of the pram that Tina and I are pushing; the people who live here are no longer human, and I am empty. Inside my chest, I am empty – there is a small, suspended space where my heartbeat should be.

I need to get her out of here.

Harry marches straight past the frilled moon of that woman's parasol and out onto the ice. He sheds clothes as he goes, a trail of small bundles, as if he hopes they will lead him back to shore.

The creature in the pram gurgles happily. When I look back up from its contented face, Harry has already disappeared, following that black man underwater.

The light is gushing overhead, pouring into the ice, where it disappears without return. Some of it comes and goes from Tina, bringing messages to the creature underground, but most of it, *most* of it, is sucked into the ice and dies there. I can see all this through Tina's eyes. If she lets go of my hand, I will not see even a fraction of it.

The wheels of the pram whisper through frozen grass as we near the shore. The closer we get to the water, the stranger I feel.

The air is dead here. It pushes dead fingers into my eyes and ears and onto the top of my head, pressing me down. Surely I am sinking?

At my side, Tina takes a long breath and releases my hand. I turn to her in panic, feeling as if I am plummeting away from her. She smiles at me, the strain no longer evident in her face. Her voice comes from far away. 'It's much quieter down here, isn't it, Joe? I think I can manage by myself down here.'

I release the pram and she pushes resolutely forward, heading for the water. I feel like I have sunk knee-deep into the yielding ground. But I take one step, then another, and I am moving and walking and following on behind.

We round the screen of the parasol, and a woman is

standing there. At the sight of Tina's stolen pram, she starts forward.

Tina says, 'I wouldn't look in here if I were you,' and the woman stops.

'Why not?' she whispers. 'You haven't put a baby in there, have you?'

'It's not a baby,' says Tina.

The woman relaxes. 'Very wise, *flor*. Babies are messy and fragile. They break your heart. Only one in eight ever survives, you know, and even then he leaves without…'

She looks confused. She starts again.

'I did not give you permission, though, *flor*. One should always ask before…'

Her eyes flick to me, and she stops talking. She seems struck dumb by me. Can she see I am sinking into the ground?

'This is Mr Joe Gosling,' says Tina. 'Your friends stole him at the same time they stole me.'

'But…but who is he for?'

Those little children are running towards us from the bridge, shouting. They are angry, and – something that at first is difficult for me to read – they are *delighted* to be so. The joy of it fizzes off them.

'Mama!' screeches the girl. 'She has your things! How is she allowed? Who is that boy? What is he for?'

Her brother runs beside her, his face a savage twist of determination. Cornelius Wolcroft strides behind, his hair flying, his eyes fixed on the woman as if anxious for her.

She is looking me up and down. 'What is *wrong* with you?' she whispers. 'You are so dark.'

Tina grabs my hand, and my mind is filled once more

with the light gushing overhead. She pushes the pram through the rustling reeds, and I force my feet to follow as she leads me onto the lake. I feel the ice beneath my feet, and I am *so heavy*. I am lead.

Tina releases my hand and bends to retrieve the first of Harry's discarded clothes. I am pressed down even as I feel like I am rising above myself. Heavy and light at the same time, I look into the sky, expecting to see the balloon of my thoughts float away. Darkness is seeping up from the ice, filling me from my feet to my empty head. I am falling. I am falling. The darkness has sucked the light from me.

I am dead.

There is a dull and distant *thud* as I hit the frozen surface of the lake. Tina's face fills the clouded sky as she bends across me. I am gone.

Beloved

'Joe?' whispered Tina. 'Oh, Joe, don't!'

Footsteps thudded dully on the ice, and the woman's skirts came into view. The last of the light went from Joe's eyes as she bent to look into them. 'What ails him?' she asked.

Tina snatched Joe's arm and stood. He was unbelievably heavy – even accustomed as she was to hauling sacks and boxes at the market, she could barely move him.

The woman took his other arm. 'Allow me,' she said.

Shoving the pram with one hand, dragging Joe with the other, Tina made for shore. Suspended between her and the woman, Joe seemed to float on the green and blue billows of their skirts, his face turned peacefully upwards as if in sleep.

Those children were coming from shore now, pushing through the reeds. Light was sparking and wheeling from them – they were so wickedly alive. Lord Wolcroft followed them, his attention riveted on the woman, who was gazing down into Joe's upturned face, rapt.

'So young,' she murmured.

Tina tightened her grip on his arm. 'If those brats come near him, I'll batter them.'

The woman lifted her dark eyes.

'I'm not joking,' said Tina. 'You'd better keep them away from us.'

'I would never allow the children to play with you.'

'I'm not asking for your *protection*, missus. I'm telling you what'll happen if they lay a finger on my friends.'

The woman grimaced at the contents of the pram. 'You consider *that* a friend?'

Tina jarred to a halt. 'I swear to Jesus, missus. You let them children near her and I will gouge out their eyes.' She held the woman's gaze for a fierce moment, then concentrated on getting to shore.

It was a hundred times easier to focus down here. Though the light still roared around and through her, her mind was her own.

She was fully aware of Joe as a dead weight on the end of her arm – *Joe. Oh, Joe* – and of the ice as a dead surface beneath her feet. Harry and the man named Vincent had faded as soon as they sank into the lake, dropping from her awareness into a nothingness of silence below. But she could still feel the Contagion, coiling in its sleep down there – tenuously contained by the last flickering remnants of the Angel's strength.

Not for long though, Joe. Not if we can't help him.

Joe did not reply. Tina lengthened her stride. She was frightened as to what would become of her back at the house. She did not want to feel her mind fracture again, she didn't want to slip away. But she had to get Joe back there: back to the fragrance of roses, and the mist-softened warmth; away from this dead water.

The children were racing towards them, Wolcroft striding in their wake.

'Cornelius,' called the woman. 'Best you keep them away!'

The little girl howled at that, and sped the last few yards, screaming and grasping for the pram. 'Not *fair*! I never get to play with Mama's things! Give that to me!'

Tina thrust the pram forward and the child bounced off it, tumbling to the ground in a flurry of ribbons and frills. Tina's skirts swept over her where she lay. The woman glanced back, but did not stop.

The little boy halted, apparently stunned. 'Wh…why did that girl not do as she was bid?'

'Get out of the way,' said Tina. 'Or I'll walk right over you.'

'Pap!' The boy turned to Wolcroft. 'Why does she not do as she is *bid*?'

Wolcroft, his eyes on Tina, gripped the boy's shoulder. 'Come away,' he said.

The little girl, still tumbled on the ice, wailed. 'She pushed me *over*!' Tina was grimly satisfied to hear fear in her voice.

'Find them something to do, Cornelius,' murmured the woman, then she and Tina swept past, heading for the reed beds.

AT THE SHORELINE, Tina struggled to manage the pram one-handed. 'Missus,' she snapped. '*Help me*.'

After a pained hesitation, the woman averted her eyes from the contents, gripped her side of the pram handle, and pushed. Between them they manoeuvred it up onto the grass. Soon they were striding across the field of glittering frost, their skirts billowing, Joe dragging between them, lifeless as stone.

The woman spoke. As if responding to a question no one

had asked, her words were sharp with exasperation: 'Well, what would you *have* me do?' she snapped. 'Regardless of their impulses, they are still but children. One cannot very well drown them like unwanted puppies.'

Tina's attention was riveted on the seething tangle of light at the house. 'I don't care what you do with your brats, missus. As long as you keep them away from me and Joseph.'

'Joseph,' said the woman, as if tasting the name. 'He is your beau? Is that why Cornelius brought him here?'

My beau, thought Tina, *my beau*. All the things she had ever wanted for Joe and from Joe rose up like pain. The plans she'd had: the sewing machine she'd been saving for, the seamstresses she'd been gathering, the workshop she'd been planning to rent – a cooperative workshop, a manufactory. *My factory*, she thought. *And then…and then…* She thought the word *together*, tightened her grip on Joe and began running towards the house.

They crossed the threshold of frost back onto soft grass, and once again the light pressed in, seething and chaotic when compared to the orderly rush of the frozen places. Tina hunched her shoulders, anticipating a renewed assault of the Angel's thoughts. But as she passed into the radius of his influence, there was no pain – just an increased thickness of the air and the familiar, probing inquisition of the light.

It was as if the Angel's face were turned away for the moment, his urgency and grief laid aside as he sought to understand what was happening beyond the confines of his prison. Tina could sense him crouched below ground, his head angled close to the reflections of a glimmering pool. He had his beloved wrapped around his neck, and he clung to it, wishing it would translate for him, as it had always done; wishing to see again, and hear again, to feed properly again – wishing to be We again, instead of this blind and crippled, solitary, lopsided I.

He was listening to messages from the water. It told him that something was happening – some tiny movement where previously there had been none, a ripple of life newly intruded on centuries of slow decay.

Harry, thought Tina. *And that man.*

The Angel was tracing their descent to the bottom of the lake: two tiny insignificances pulling themselves down through a well shaft of pollution that oozed from…from what? *The Ship? The Friend? The Burden?* Tina could not untangle the feelings the Angel had towards this vast dying thing. The closer Harry and Vincent came to it, the better the Angel could feel them, and he waited, dreading and hoping at once, for the moment when they would touch its flesh.

The woman asked, 'What do you see?' and Tina realised she was standing on the edge of the driveway, her mouth hanging open, her eyes hot from not blinking.

'They…' she said, 'they're nearing the bottom of the lake. Something is down there. Like a ship. It belongs to the Angel.'

The woman seemed to search an internal landscape. 'I sense no such thing.'

'The Angel's ship can feel them. And because of that, so can the Angel.'

The woman regarded her resentfully. 'And therefore, so can you.'

'And therefore so can I.'

The woman helped her force the pram out onto the gravel and over to the house. They laid Joe in the shelter of the porch, where Tina knelt at his side.

She tapped his dead cheek. 'Joe?' she whispered. 'Please, Joe.'

Absorbed, the woman knelt, watching as if they were an exhibit. 'Ah,' she said. 'You are in love.'

Tina shook Joe gently. 'Wake up...'

'I know what love is,' confided the woman. 'Vicente thinks I have forgot, but how could I forget? Looking up from the accounts and seeing him for the first time, all business and smelling of the sea, ready to speak to my husband of taxes and excise duties and dues.'

She hugged her knees.

'O *pirata negro* – my husband used to call him that. As if Vicente were incapable of being anything else. As if legitimate business were beyond a man like him. How could I not love him? So sure and calm. So undeniably himself in the face of the world.' Her face fell. 'You can imagine my husband's rage, when he finally realised my feelings.' She shuddered. 'Such rage.'

Tina closed her fists in Joe's waistcoat. He was lifeless and cold beneath her hands. 'Oh, Joe,' she whispered. 'What about our plans?'

The woman chuckled softly. '*Plans*,' she said. 'But of course. Because you are pretty, and because you are in love – you still believe those things are an armour against the world.'

'Be *quiet*,' cried Tina. 'Stop *talking*!'

The woman glanced wryly at her, then turned her attention to the lake. 'Never mind,' she said. 'Cornelius will save you.'

At that moment, Joe's body jerked. He made a startled noise, his hands fluttering, and the woman smiled. 'There,' she said. 'See? He returns.'

Joe came alive in an abrupt series of jumps and shudders,

and suddenly Tina found herself looking down into widely alert eyes. They regarded each other for a moment, a tragedy of understanding passing between them. 'I'm sorry,' he said at last.

'You only fainted.'

'Ah, Tina.' He struggled to sit.

'You only *fainted*. You wouldn't eat your dinner, so you fainted.'

He pulled her into an embrace. 'I'm sorry,' he whispered.

She squeezed her eyes tight against knowing what he was apologising for. She could feel that new, strange calmness emanating from him. His mind was cool water, the circle of his arms a still, dark cave. Tina tightened her hold on him, rested her forehead on his shoulder, and refused to admit that this was the stillness of death.

'You didn't eat your dinner,' she whispered. 'I told you to eat your dinner.'

'I'm dead, Tina.'

'You're not! You're *not*! Sure, amn't I holding your hands, Joe?' She grabbed his hands, the fine lace cuffs falling back as she dragged his fingers to her lips. 'Amn't I kissing you?'

She pressed her lips to his, to the softness of them and the warmth, to the taste of him, which had surprised her by being like apples, only sweeter – peaches maybe, or how she imagined peaches might taste. 'How could I be doing these things, holding you so close, and kissing you at last? How could I be loving you *this much* if you were dead, Joe? It wouldn't be fair.'

And they were clutching each other again, her fists in his shirt, as she whispered, 'You're alive, Joe. You're alive. I won't let you be anything but alive.'

Something rested lightly on her back, hot and dry and intrusive. The woman's hand. She was leaning close, regarding them with an intense fascination.

Tina shrugged her off with almost thankful anger. 'Stop it! Stop *watching us*!'

The woman tried to gently brush the hair from Tina's face. Joe slapped her hand away. 'Get your own life,' he hissed. 'Stop pawing at ours.'

The woman smiled. 'So tender.'

Someone rushed up the steps, startling them. Wolcroft.

'Raquel?' he asked anxiously. 'Are you well?'

She turned to him with a decisive gesture. 'Cornelius, I would very much like to keep these children.'

'Keep? But...'

Wolcroft sank to his haunches on the step at the woman's feet. He tentatively took her hands. His eyes flicked to Joe's borrowed clothes and jerked away again, as if afraid to draw attention to them.

'Raquel, does that boy not...does that boy not *disturb* you?'

The woman shrugged. 'I had hoped the girl might give you joy, Cornelius, and I admit the boy quite stymies that plan. Nevertheless, they make a tender little couple. I want you to rescue them for me.'

Wolcroft's expression drew down, and his grip on the woman's hands tightened. 'The boy's *clothes*, Raquel. Do his clothes not disturb you?'

The woman turned to Joe as if inspecting his clothing for the very first time. She laughed in amusement. 'Cornelius,' she said, 'I think even I can withstand the youthful impropriety of a shirt worn without cravat and jacket. Besides' – she playfully tapped Wolcroft's stained waistcoat – 'you are hardly in a position to judge.'

Wolcroft drew back, his expression tragic, and she smiled at him in puzzled concern. 'Why, *meu caro*, what has upset you?'

'There is not one item of his which I would not know on sight,' he said. 'I remember every *button*, Raquel. I remember every thread. Surely as his mother you should…'

Wolcroft bit his lips, as if to kill his words, and abruptly turned his back to sit at Raquel's feet. Raquel immediately leaned on his shoulder, gazing down to where Luke and the children were playing on the ice. At her touch, Wolcroft clenched his hands and squeezed his eyes shut.

Raquel seemed to have no reaction at all to his obvious distress, and Tina began to suspect that this woman saw only what she wanted to see, understood only what she wanted to understand – everything else was just so much mist to her, so much meaningless birdsong.

Wolcroft, however, was aswarm with darkness. Dense and heavy, and sickly sweet as if compressed by aeons underground, his emotions rose through the surrounding ropes of energy. Tina knew this was how her own feelings must look as they travelled to the Angel – sorrow so intense it darkened the light.

She pressed back against Joe, anticipating the return of the Angel's howling greed. But – despite the nourishment he received from them – the Angel seemed to feel only the merest flicker, only the faintest suggestion of Tina's and Wolcroft's pain. Without an audience to marvel at them, their feelings were negligible, it seemed, and the Angel turned away again, focusing all his concentration on the lake.

Joe gazed over Tina's shoulder, fascinated at what he saw through her eyes. 'It's feeding off them.'

'It's not enough,' she said.

These people took far more than they gave. Even now, the woman was growing numb and still as she absorbed her share of the meagre sustenance the Angel had taken from her friend's anguish.

She mumbled, 'The seer claims part of the Angel resides in the lake, Cornelius. She claims it allows her to see Vicente as he journeys under the water. Do you think this is true?'

Wolcroft opened his eyes and looked straight up into the clouds. 'I do not know, my dear. I have sensed nothing of him since he submerged. He is a blank to me.'

The woman sighed. 'Isn't that Vicente, through and through? Always keeping the kernel of himself withheld.' She smiled and whispered into Wolcroft's ear. 'And don't we love him all the more for it, *meu caro*? Doesn't it only serve to deepen our yearning?'

He sat forward, away from her touch. Tina thought he looked marooned, all alone in the world.

'Seer,' he said dully, 'tell me what they are doing down there.'

She closed her eyes, welcoming the chance to concentrate on something other than his sorrow and her own, and the Angel's disregard for it.

'They're...they're nearing it.'

'It?'

She opened her eyes. 'The ship – they're being drawn to it. Time is very slow for them. It's like they're moving through a dream.'

'A dream,' he whispered. 'If only.'

Raquel pulled him back into her, closed her eyes and laid her head against his shoulder. Wolcroft's brow creased in pain as her breathing deepened into sleep. Tina clutched Joe's hand. Out on the ice, the children tired of playing with Luke, and retreated to the trees. Luke resumed his vigil over the tripod.

Slowly, slowly, underwater, Harry and Vincent neared the poisonous hulk of the ship.

Dead Angels

THE WATER WANTED to float Vincent upwards, and he had to pull himself along the brazier chains in order to descend at all. The chain was visible for a scant few yards below him before fading to nothing in the dark. Deep below, the dull green light endlessly pulsed.

Except for the moderate chill of the metal against his palms, Vincent did not feel in the least bit cold, and he had absolutely no notion yet of needing to breathe. Prior to the plunge, he had entertained the experiment of inhaling a lungful of water – just to see what would happen – but once submerged he had quickly discarded the notion. He did not much like the idea of this water intruding into his body. Its touch was…what was an appropriate word? Clammy? Yes. Clammy. Unpleasant.

No wonder the pond had never featured much in the leisure pursuits of the family. Thinking back, Vincent realised it had never factored much even in their thoughts or conversations. How strange. It was as if, in all the time they had been here, the pond had existed only vaguely for them, its presence acknowledged but ignored by the human occupants of the estate.

The deeper he went, the darker it became. Vincent waited for his eyes to adjust, as they would have underground, but they never did, and soon he was dragging himself through total darkness, with only the feel of the chains and the dull green pulse of that distant light to guide him. The old illogical panic began to swell, his fear of small spaces gnawing its familiar hole in his chest.

You are not confined, he told himself. *You are surrounded by space – it is simply space that you cannot see.*

The water began to press on him like a vice. He must be imagining that. He must. It was not nearly deep enough for such crushing pressure.

But it is. It is. I am trapped. I am going to die!

Vincent came to a halt, clinging childlike to the cold security of the chains, staring desperately into darkness. Chains and darkness. The dull, dead press of the water. He was trapped. He was trapped. He had been confined.

It was all he could do not to heave a lungful of cadaverous water and scream. Then Vincent looked up, and high above him, for as far as he could see, stretched the shining vault of ice. All was space, all was light. He had been staring blindly into blackness while, overhead, such beauty glowed in silence.

Vincent gazed upwards as the hammering of his heart subsided. Arching pathways curved into the distance – the passageway of those violent currents that had borne the magician down, then back again. Now that he had calmed himself, Vincent could hear the vast, mutinous rush of their progress through the otherwise still pond. He could feel the steady vibration the American had described as the throb of an engine. Vincent thought it felt more like the beating of a heart. Most certainly it was coming from the direction of that gangrenous light below.

He looked down again, into pitch, into fear.

He would do this.

A disturbance on the chain caused him to look up. The point of entry was so distant now, it was barely a fingerprint of light. Vincent waited, unsure, then smiled as the starfish shape of a person spread briefly against it. There came the subtle tug and shiver of someone travelling along the chain.

The American had joined him.

It gets dark down here, boy. But I have yet to feel the need to take a breath.

There was a hesitation in the movement on the line. Then a tapping: *one, two, three.*

If you begin to feel closed in, look up and the light will comfort you.

Again a tapping. Then the tug and shiver again, as the boy made his way down. Vincent resumed his descent. When he neared the brazier, he released the chains and launched himself down towards the light.

He descended into grave-like stillness and a bilious pulse of green. The water here neither floated him up nor sucked him down, and when he stopped swimming he simply hung suspended in the lifeless dark, the dull throb of that engine sounding below. Uncertain, he stared down. *I know what I think I am seeing*, he thought. *But in truth, is that what lies below me?*

If the American had not said this was a machine, if Vincent's own mind had not already been influenced by Jules Verne, might he now be seeing something other than the curve of ornate metal and glass that bulged from the mire below? Would he be seeing a creature, perhaps, the heart of which could be heard pounding, slow and failing, within the mud of its final resting place?

If this is a creature, I am about to swim through a gap in its very ribs. I shall, all unknowing, be drifting about its broken body; seeing wires and pistons where in fact there are organs and veins; touching metal and glass where in fact there is membrane and bone.

Vincent shuddered and dismissed this. He was not about to come so close only to allow some squeamish fancy to turn him aside. Determined, he jackknifed down and into the jagged opening in the ship's side, which pulsed light out into the morbid dark.

The interior seemed entirely composed of narrow twisting tunnels, spiralled with copper ribbing. Vincent pulled himself along them, his body bending and curling, as if negotiating the curved recesses of a snail's shell. The walls between the metal ribs were gelatinous, almost permeable, but the merest press of Vincent's palm would cause their surface to harden. A metallic imprint would remain long after his hand was removed, fading only very slowly as the wall lost its temporary rigidity.

The water around him was thick as jelly – warm against the skin. The light and that pulsing noise throbbed in unison. Vincent found it comforting. As comforting, perhaps, as the beat of a mother's heart to the child within her womb. Vincent knew nothing of the womb in which he had been seeded, except that his father had kept her for more than one voyage, and that one day she had leapt to the sharks with Vincent's infant sister in her arms.

Vincent frowned. It had been a long time since he had

allowed himself to remember that. How strange – the memory did not bother him as usually it would. Thoughts seemed to come and go very peacefully here. Vincent felt he might be perfectly happy to go on forever like this, pulling himself along one hand after the other, the thick water parting gently ahead of him and closing gently behind, his body sliding as through warmed oil, comfortable, sleepy, content...

His hands were pushed into the open, then his shoulders and his waist, and he was propelled outwards as if from an oesophagus. Released into warm and yielding space, he tumbled through a softness of light until he gently bumped against a floor.

Overhead, the corpses of angels floated and spun like specimens in a jar.

Oh, thought Vincent. *Cornelius was right.*

How long did he lie there, gazing up at the mesh of wings, marvelling at the great immobile hands, the perfect, stony faces of the creatures above? How long, before realising that his own heart was slow, slow, slower than molasses, and that he was looking up at visions borrowed from the childhood he had long since shoved away? He bit down on his lip, hard enough that blood swarmed upwards and pain sent a flare into his stupid brain that screamed, *You are drugged.*

Instead of wings, he saw a widespread net of tentacles; instead of angels, the hunched bodies of dead creatures, multi-jointed legs curled into lifeless bellies, heavy heads tucked onto motionless chests, all bathed in that nauseating light so they almost seemed alive with the pulse of it.

Directly above him, part and parcel of the roof – or floor, door, wall – of this vast chamber, a huge membranous blister bulged. Inside it, something thick and segmented, ominous and diseased, coiled slow and steady and eternal, round and round and round itself like an apocalypse waiting to be born.

Symbiote

BOY...

Harry paused, one hand in front of the other, his body twisted like an Indian acrobat within the spiral of a tunnel.

Hello? he thought. *Vincent?*

There was nothing but silence, and Harry waited within it, uncertain. He tried again – though it had never been proven to him that the man could read his thoughts. *Vincent? Where are you?*

That deep voice, usually so self-assured, sounded again, slow and dreamy as if its owner were battling sleep. *Dead...floating...go...*

Go? Was he telling Harry to go?

Then, with desperate volume, as though the man had raised his head from his death pillow and yelled with his last breath: *GET OUT!*

Harry was retreating before he even knew it. Hand over hand, backwards through the tunnels – determined to go. He would get back to the surface. He would grab Tina and Joe. They would battle their way past the dogs, past those kids, past the woman and those men, and run and run and run into the snow. It was okay to do this. Whatever was happening to Vincent, it was okay. He was a crazy, unnatural, broken man. He deserved whatever he got. He was wrong, he was wrong, he was all wrong. He was wicked.

But Ehrich, murmured Papa. *You are not wicked. And what of the Angel?*

Harry stopped crawling and pressed his forehead to the faintly glowing floor. *Don't*, he told himself. *Just leave.* But he knew it would forever haunt him – not knowing the fate he'd left Vincent to. It would forever haunt him if he didn't try to save the Angel. With a resigned clench of his teeth, he began, once again, to pull himself forward through the ship.

He was expelled into the open with dreamlike abruptness: one moment pulling himself hand over hand, the next tumbling down through soft green light.

Rolling head over heels into what felt like a yielding tangle of ropes, Harry grasped one, hoping to stop his fall. The rope had a repulsive, fleshy texture, and it gave with his weight. Too late, Harry realised it was attached to some huge floating thing that he was now dragging towards him.

A great, blind, heavy-browed face loomed close as the curtain of ropes parted before it. Appalled, Harry kicked it away. The head twisted aside, leading its serpentine body in a slow arabesque back through what Harry now understood to be a curtain of floating tentacles. Dislodged by the movement, something uncoiled from around the creature's neck and fell onto Harry. He found himself entangled with it, the two of them tumbling though liquid space and falling together to land with a *bump* against the membranous resilience of the far wall.

Even as he was struggling free of it, Harry knew what the thing was. There was no forgetting that disgusting curled body, nor the Medusa-like trail of snakes coming from its head. This was unmistakably the pale maggot-brother of the thing Tina had taken from Vincent's laboratory, the sight of which had caused the Angel to rage and mourn and finally fall to its knees in defeat.

Harry kicked the thing from him and watched as it floated upwards to rejoin the tangled forest of corpses above.

Vincent's voice sounded in his head. *Boy...*

Harry lurched to his feet. The floor curved steeply up on either side; sticky-strange and faintly luminous, it made Harry feel like a bug on the inside of a lampshade. The water here drew his hair up off his face, but it did not float him upwards as it had done the maggot creature. Instead, he had the strangest impression of being sucked gently downwards.

Was he imagining it, or was he losing the feeling in his feet?

Bending, he pressed his palm to the membrane of the floor. The skin of his fingers immediately went numb, and Harry snatched back his hand, trying not to panic.

Vincent, he thought. *I don't think we should hang around here.*

Overhead, the tangle of corpses turned and drifted in response to minute currents in the globe. Harry gazed up at them. Could these be the demons of Tina's vision? If so, it was hard to imagine what threat they posed. In fact, they looked very beautiful with the light shining through their translucent skin. The ballet of their movement was almost hypnotically peaceful. They reminded Harry of sea creatures – slow, stately, magnificent. He could watch them forever and not...

Boy...stand up...

Harry startled. When had he lain down? He lifted his arm and glassy threads stretched between it and the floor, releasing it slowly. He raised his head and there was a sucking feeling, as if he had been caught in a pool of jelly.

Boy...

Harry peeled himself free and forced himself to his feet, staggering from the boy-shaped imprint he had left in the floor's gluey surface. Vincent's voice was barely audible, just the one word repeated at intervals: *Boy...boy...boy.* Whether it was a warning or a plea, Harry could not tell. He looked around once again for the man.

It took a shift in his understanding, but once Harry spotted Vincent, it was difficult to believe he had ever missed him. Despite the membrane that had blistered up to cover him, the man's long dark figure was perfectly visible, spreadeagled against the wall, which, as Harry trudged around the side of the globe, became the floor. Soon he was staring through a transparent covering into the face of the man at his feet.

The direction of Vincent's dark gaze shifted towards a point directly above, and Harry looked up. The sight of the slow-coiling presence overhead almost caused him to scream. Then something clamped down hard on his calf and he *did* scream, air bubbling from his mouth and nose as he dived away. His action drew Vincent from his translucent grave, hauled forth by one strong black arm and the relentless grip he had on Harry's leg.

Boy, he thought, flopping limp as a newborn onto the gelatinous ground. *You came for me.*

It was then Harry knew for certain that Vincent could

not read his thoughts. Otherwise, he would have known that Harry had still not decided on rescuing him.

Feeble and uncoordinated, Vincent struggled to get to his knees. Everywhere that his bare skin touched the floor, colourless strands attached themselves, and Harry could see that membranous cover already beginning its not-too-slow crawl across Vincent's strongly muscled body. Soon the man would again be part of the floor, subsumed facedown this time, blind and helpless to free himself.

Harry shuddered at the thought and, almost against his will, stooped to help.

Vincent rose in his arms, clinging and slippery, his thoughts a jumble. *Kick off*, he thought. *Kick off...* And Harry did, cursing himself for not having thought of it earlier.

Almost immediately a gentle weight began drawing them back to the floor, and Harry had to swim up through the viscous liquid, nearer to the tangle of dead creatures and the terrible thing that coiled and twisted in its prison on the wall above. There, he treaded water, his arms wrapped tightly around Vincent.

As the man slowly returned to his senses, Harry searched the walls for the spot where he had come in. It must have been somewhere close to that repulsive blister and its roiling occupant. Surely there would be a door visible? Some kind of indent, even? A hole?

Vincent's curly head lolled, his legs bicycling feebly as he struggled to regain control. Suddenly he shuddered and shrugged loose of Harry's grip. He sank only a little before summoning enough coordination to tread water.

You returned for me, he thought.

Harry grimaced and continued scanning the wall – there was an odd discolouration around the upper parts of the globe, which seemed—

Vincent swam around to peer into his face. *How do you feel?* he slurred. *Are you…distracted? I feel dull as ditchwater here.*

He was too close, his movements loose as a drunkard's, and Harry pushed away from him. The gesture sent them floating backwards and Harry found himself entwined once more in that clammy net of tentacles. Vincent watched with interest as he thrashed free.

What do you see them as, boy? Are they still angels to you?

Were they still…Harry spun to regard the slow-moving corpses with horror. Still *angels*?

Vincent swam around to look again into his face. *Ah, they are not. Do you see what I see, then? Serpentine bodies? Four limbs with many joints? Spiderish paws? Tendril-shaped growths from hip and shoulder?*

Harry met his eye, and the man nodded.

You do. How interesting. He turned clumsily in place and they treaded water together, gazing up into the nest of gently rotating corpses. *No one told you what to expect here, and so you see with a clear mind. But look, what is…*

Vincent pushed his way deep into the tangle. Harry hung back, staring at the now horribly, horribly familiar creatures. He felt his recollection of the underground theatre change. His vision of the Angel – the Lion of God, descending the steps in glory and despair – shifted. Like an image from a dream, his memory of the Angel resolved itself and became not Uriel the Protector, not an Angel of the Presence, but…*this*. One of *these*.

Oh, Papa, he thought. *Where am I? What has happened to me? I cannot even trust my own mind.*

Vincent had pulled himself closer to one of the big heavy heads. Fascinated, he shoved aside the chin, revealing another of those grub-like things nestled at the creature's neck. At the sight of it, Harry realised that one memory had stayed true and clear in his mind: the Angel's pain had remained, its sense of loss, and its terrible, grinding fear as Tina had presented her offering of one of these dead maggot-things.

Vincent touched the dull curl of the thing's tail. *Why, it is the very twin of the corpse we found by the pond. The time we lured the Bright Man from the woods and had it dragged below...See how its tendrils seem to plug in at the base of the larger creature's skull? What can that mean?* He pressed his forehead to the creature's spongy skin. *So many questions...Tell me your secrets, Bright Man. What are you? How do I keep you alive?*

Still clinging to the creature's corpse, Vincent turned his cheek against its bulging forehead and looked about him in something that resembled despair.

Do you know what this brings to mind? It brings to mind all the creatures the crew would bring on board at every exotic bay or harbour – all the poor lizards and cavies and birds the men would dote on and cosset and in their ignorance murder with rum and ship's biscuit and salt beef. An endless collection of beautiful creatures killed by ignorance and neglect.

Vincent closed his eyes, his voice growing dim in Harry's mind.

They were jolly times though, eh? We had some rum times...

Harry caught the man as he slid from his perch. Vincent jerked awake, and pulled free with a scowl. *Damn this place!* He thrust up with a strong kick, breaking through the topmost reaches of the tentacle forest, into the open space above. Harry followed, only to find the man treading water – once again rapt.

A creature was suspended before them. But this one was not like the others. The wide spread of growths sprouting from its shoulder and hip were stretched out in various directions and attached to the wall. It was raised slightly above its companions, the kelp bed of their tentacles floating about its chest and shoulders.

Do you suppose they were all once similarly attached? Vincent wondered.

Staying clear of the creature's bowed head, Harry swam up the taut length of one of its tentacles, examining where it joined the wall. There were dimples in the surface, and the tips of the tentacles seemed to fit into them. He allowed himself to drift along the curved wall, finding more of the same indents.

Vincent, there are dimples all over the surface. And look! He pointed. *There is a staining over much of the wall – but not in the area where this creature is attached. I wonder…*

He twisted to look over his shoulder, frowning up at the thing in its blister prison. The discolouration seemed darker there.

Vincent, I think that blister is the source of this stain. I think it's spread out from…

Abruptly remembering that Vincent could not hear him, Harry turned, meaning to point these things out in dumb show. With a flare of irritation he realised the man had once again succumbed to the ship's numbing atmosphere and was drifting, limp and head-hung, in the sea of tentacles.

Wake up, you dumkop! *You're going to bump into that thing's head.*

As if determined to prove Harry right, Vincent's body bobbed against the suspended creature's brow.

Gah! thought Harry. *Why do you have to keep touching these things? You will catch something and—*

His thoughts slammed to a dead end and he came to a terrified halt as the creature lifted its heavy head from its chest.

Mein Gott, he thought. *Mein Gott. Vincent, wake up.*

The creature seemed to nuzzle Vincent's body, as if unsure of what he was. Then its head did a repulsive series of jerks and wobbles, and Harry realised the creature was not alive at all, but responding to something living that was attached to it.

There was further spastic struggle somewhere in the region of its neck, and one of the maggot-things uncoiled itself. With a pained jerk, it fell loose and lay against the creature's chest, as if too weak to do any more.

Harry let himself drift down, carefully down, until he was within reach of Vincent. Just as he reached for Vincent's slack left arm, the maggot-thing raised its head and nudged in a blind and hopeful way at Vincent's right hand.

Harry grabbed Vincent, kicking hard to get the two of them away. Too late. The maggot shot forward and, even as Vincent was pulled away, twined itself, fast as a snake, up his arm and around his neck.

So many things happened at once then. The maggot's connections to the base of the dead creature's skull stretched taut and snapped free – *pop, pop, pop*. The creature's huge body sagged as the tentacles that had connected it to the wall of the ship came loose one after another. Unsupported, the great body rolled and sank to become an indistinguishable part of the tangled dead.

The globe darkened, the bodies began to spin, and Harry found himself dragging Vincent up through a slow-moving whirlpool. He looked up; had one terrified moment to realise that the imprisoned thing overhead was moving faster and with less grace, shivering and halting and juddering against the wall of the blister, as if only now realising its confinement.

There was a revolting squirm against Harry's chest as the maggot's Medusa-tail wormed up to spread its fingers into Vincent's woolly hair. Harry yelled, a bright, violent bubble of air. Vincent bucked. His eyes shot wide. *The light!* he thought.

They changed direction. Suddenly Harry was not the one propelling them through the pulsing gloom, and all he could do was hang on as Vincent's body was directed in an abrupt swallow-arc towards an entrance that was opening like the iris of an eye in the flesh of the wall.

Then they were being channelled, twisted, dragged, round and round, up and up: into brightness, past dimness, into brightness again. A quivering moaning – a horrified sense of despair – rose around them as they were pushed through the body of the ship. Then *out* into dark, dead water; *up* towards the brightness of the sky; and *out* to breach like salmon into air and flop, quivering, onto the deserted surface of the sunset-coloured ice.

Storm

'Tina,' whispered Joe.

It was difficult to hear him, because her attention was far away: inside the ship, focused on two tiny men drifting through a forest of the dead. They were nearing something. Something very important. The Angel's breathless hope filled her mind.

Joe whispered again, his breath in her ear. 'Tina. We left your basket in the theatre.'

She turned her head to look at him. His earnest face was so close, his words painting faded memories over the searing present: the theatre, her home, two women who loved her and had raised her strong.

'My…my basket?'

'Yes. My money is still in it, Tina. I want you to have it. I want you to—'

But she was turning away from him, his words dropping into the background as something within the ship lifted its head and opened its eyes; as it struggled free from the one who had loved it and now was dead; as a thought rose loud in a mind that had lain dormant for centuries: *I am not dead.*

Tina surged to her feet. She flung up her arms and, breaking Joe's connection with her, she roared.

Far below, the Angel did the same.

Joe reached for her, but she had already staggered down the steps, her arms raised, her face turned to the sky, just as the Angel's face was turned to the ceiling of its prison.

Underwater, a long, desperate creature twisted its way up Vincent's arm, and Tina's mind was riven by the Angel's voice, her mouth stretching to accommodate his scream.

I am here. I am here. Beloved, can you feel me? I am here.

Anchor

JOE LEAPT TO his feet, his hands clapped to his ears.

Wolcroft and his woman seemed stunned into helplessness by the monstrous sound that now fountained from Tina's mouth, and they simply stood watching as Joe plunged past them down the steps.

The gravel was hopping like peas on a drumhead, the pebbles battering his ankles as he ran across the driveway. Out on the ice, the whiskered man ran and fell and then ran again, heading for the shore as, behind him, the tripod collapsed and fell. There was a booming noise down there: a heavy, ominous rush. For a lunatic moment, the entire lake seemed to bulge.

Joe grabbed Tina around her waist. She was rigid as a holy statue, her arms stiffly upflung, her head back to accommodate the noise that spewed from her. As he dragged her back to the house, Wolcroft stumbled down the steps to help.

The world was shivering with the noise coming from her – the stones and wood and glass vibrating. *This is what an earthquake feels like*, thought Joe. *The world is going to shatter.*

But the steps amazed him by not cracking, and the roof remained intact over his head as Wolcroft helped him wrestle Tina into the house.

The woman followed them, fascinated.

Joe yelled above the noise, '*Get Miss Ursula!*'

The woman did not, of course, go, so Joe pushed Wolcroft.

'Go! Get Miss Ursula!'

Wolcroft hesitated, clutching Tina.

'Do it!' ordered Joe. 'Or Tina will have your guts.'

Wolcroft strode away, but the woman remained, watching as Joe jostled Tina through the half-open double doors of a candle-filled ballroom.

Everything rattled: windows, walls, doors. Dust sifted down from the shivering ceilings. The noise coming from Tina was so loud Joe had to shout to be heard over it, but Tina showed no signs of knowing he was there.

She began to fall, and he could only help control her descent. She was difficult to hold. Her body had become so rigid. Her beautiful hair was in her face. Joe pushed it from her mouth and her eyes and held her as tight as her convulsing body would allow, trying to anchor her as he had done before.

The woman's shadow was visible through the glass panels of the ballroom door, as if she was standing in the hall outside listening. Through the rattling windows, Joe saw Wolcroft running towards the lake. Down on the ice, a geyser of water shot to the sky.

Night Falling

Cornelius rushed past Luke and out onto the rumbling ice, calling for Vincent. Vast quantities of water had been thrown up by the geyser and now lay on the surface. It reflected the lurid sunset like a mirror, and Cornelius found himself sloshing ankle-deep above his distorted reflection as he made his way towards his friend.

Out by the ruined tripod, the American boy was rolling to his hands and knees, heaving in air and shaking sodden curls from his eyes. Vincent was at his side, arching and flopping like a fish, his hands to his head. Something was wrapped about his face – his shirt, perhaps, thrown up in the violence of the explosion. It looked as if it were suffocating him.

Hold fast, Vincent. I am coming!

There was no answer, and with a flash of horror, Cornelius realised Vincent's mind was still a silent void to him. It had been over a hundred and fifty years since the talent had developed between them, and Cornelius had forgotten what it was like to be so solitary. It was terrifying.

His legs slid from under him, the ice came up to hammer

his chin, and he saw stars. By the time he found his feet again, the boy was hunched over Vincent, tearing at the fabric that swaddled him. At his back, the water roiled and bubbled within the jagged hole the geyser had thrown them from. It rumbled like a steam train beneath the ice.

'What is happening, boy?'

The American could not seem to hear above the unearthly noise that vibrated all around them, and he continued manhandling Vincent, shouting at him: '*Help* me, *dumkop*! Don't just flop about!'

Cornelius began fighting his way across. 'You insolent dog!' he roared. 'I will thrash you senseless!'

At that moment the fabric tore free of Vincent's face and the boy, lurching to his feet, spun and flung it. His intention was clearly to get it as far from himself as possible, and, all unawares, he hurled it right into Cornelius' path.

The sight of the thing – long and pale and sinuous, trailing a veil of tentacles like some ghastly octopus – stopped Cornelius in his tracks, and he stood gaping as it sailed through the air to land with a living *splash* at his feet.

The thing twisted and shivered, sending rings of brightness radiating across the water's surface. Cornelius took a step back. In the water at his feet his own face stared up at him, reflected in sharp detail, the sky a scarlet flare above his head. Aside from the creature's feeble disturbances, the water had become still as glass.

Cornelius looked up into silence. The terrible noise had ceased as soon as the creature had been ripped from Vincent.

All of a sudden, the water level began to drop. The pond, retreating back the way it had come, spiralled with the gentlest of gurgles through the hole in the ice.

The boy crouched again by Vincent's side. 'Hey!' he yelled. 'Hey, are you okay?'

Vincent bellowed and sat bolt upright, his arms straight ahead as if reaching for something. He saw the boy and grabbed his shoulders. To Cornelius' amazement, he was grinning.

'The light!' he cried. 'Did you see it? The seer spoke of light, did she not? We must question her! Where have you put the symbiote, boy?'

Feverishly excited, he began swishing his hands about in the retreating water, searching.

'Where is it? Tell me we have it!'

The boy seemed just as excited. He was running his hands through Vincent's hair, examining him, shouting questions.

'That thing had its little suckers all over you! What did it feel like? Did it hurt? What the hell *was* it? What the hell were we *inside* down there?'

Vincent grabbed him again. 'So many questions! And finally, the chance of answers!'

'We're alive!' The boy leapt up and began a hideous, clumsy, slipping dance on the ice. 'We're alive!'

Vincent laughed. 'Where is my symbiote, boy?'

'It's over there!' The boy helped him climb to his feet, and they waded though the shallows, each supporting the other on the slippery surface.

The grinning boy was shuddering already with cold. Vincent steamed like a live coal in the snow.

He called out as they came abreast with Cornelius, not even bothering to slow as they passed by, 'Such an adventure we've had, cully! You would not believe it!'

Can you hear me? asked Cornelius.

Vincent waved his hand. *Yes, yes! Everything is fine. Where is—*

'There it is,' cried the boy. 'Look at it! It's still alive!'

'Do not touch it, boy. Where are my clothes? We could bundle it in my shirt, perhaps…Cornelius, lend us your jacket!'

'Here is my shirt!' cried the boy. 'Bobbing about right here. We can use it!'

They laughed and slipped about together as they retrieved the shirt, high on adventure and the taste of survival. Cornelius stood apart and watched them, their reflections refracting and colliding beneath them as they worked to capture the object of their fascination.

'*Luke!*' bellowed Vincent. '*Luke!* Fetch a big specimen jar. Hurry! You will find one in my laboratory! And dry clothes – this boy must not get cold.'

Cornelius watched them walk away from him, the light already seeping from the sky, the fog-softened shadows thickening as the sun began to set.

The Thing We've Found

'VICENTE, WHAT DOES this creature mean for us?'

Vincent barely registered Raquel's question. He could not take his eyes from the huge specimen jar Luke had set on the floor in the centre of the room, nor the creature that now rested within it.

The American boy and he had debated theories as they carried the creature up from the boating pond. Should they put it back into water? If Vincent's theory was correct, and it was some form of cosmic animal, crashed here from the stars, was water even an appropriate element for it? Perhaps it had been slowly drowning all this time. Perhaps it was this, and not poison from the so-called Contagion, that had killed its companions?

To and fro, to and fro the debate had gone between them, as they had pulled on dry trousers, tied laces, buttoned shirts, put on waistcoats. Talking, talking, talking. Raquel re-lit the candles, and their shadows flared high against the ceiling of the ballroom, their patience with each other fraying as excitement faded to exhaustion.

In the end, it had been Cornelius who made the decision.

He must have slipped away while they were arguing, and he'd silenced them both by returning with a well bucket, from which he filled the enormous jar. He had lifted the creature and, without a word, tipped it from its shirt swaddling into the water.

As if with relief, the creature had spread to fill the shivering element, its tentacles reaching and gently touching the borders of its confinement, its grotesque body curling and uncurling as it drifted within. Cornelius had slapped the bucket down and retreated to the door, where he'd leaned, his arms crossed, his frown riveted on Vincent.

'There,' he'd said. 'Now what?'

The American had abandoned the debate with an upflung hand and seated himself over on the sofa by the seer and the boy named Joe.

Vincent tore his eyes from the jar and looked up at them. The couple had already been sitting there, hand in hand and pale as china dolls, when he had burst in with the creature. There were track marks on the floor where they had dragged the sofa back against the wall, better prepared to face whoever came in the door, Vincent supposed.

The spirit board was at the seer's elbow, the candles throwing vast shadows on the wall behind her. She had her foot on the axle of the perambulator and was rocking it gently, as if to soothe its passenger. She had barely acknowledged the American boy when he sat down, her eyes fixed on the creature in its jar.

'You all right, Harry?' Joe asked.

The boy nodded, but in truth he looked wretched. He couldn't seem to stop shivering, despite the warmth of the room. Vincent's head had begun to pain him. He noticed the boy squinting in the candlelight and figured his must feel the same.

'Vicente,' repeated Raquel softly, 'what does this abomination mean for us?'

Such a simple question. How was he to answer it without toppling all the things in which she wanted to believe?

'It is a beloved,' said the seer.

A beloved? What an odd choice of word. 'Explain.'

'A beloved,' she insisted, lifting the hand she had joined with Joe's as if that clarified everything. 'A *beloved*.'

'It completes your angel,' said Joe.

'We have seen its like before,' said Cornelius. 'After we had the Angel dragged underground, we found that very same type of creature lying by the shore. The villagers thought it was the devil.'

'Yes,' said Vincent absently. He squatted by the jar, traced the glass with his finger. 'But that was dead – already beginning to dry out. This…'

'Wolcroft lost his mind over it,' said Cornelius. 'Thinking he'd harnessed the power of the devil – such a wicked man. Had I not disposed of him, he would have brought the wrath of England down on us.'

'Yes, cully, yes, you did very well.'

'So…you aren't Wolcroft?' asked Harry.

Vincent heard Cornelius huff, could well imagine the curl of his lip. 'No, boy, I am not. Though I can arrange for you to meet the real article, if you so desire – what is left of him. *I* am just the man who talked our way into his employ. *I* am just the man who, when needed, threw the lunatic into the oubliette and took his place. *I* am just the man who has kept this estate untouched and free from trouble ever since.'

{ 364 }

He swept his hand to his head, as if removing a hat, and effected a bitter little bow.

'Quartermaster Cornelius Aloysius Mills: disinherited heir to Nevis' richest sugar plantation, erstwhile pirate, and from 1690 onwards, the man known to all delegates of King Billy, Queen Anne or any subsequent monarch, lacky, tax collector or inquiring soul as Sir Cornelius Wolcroft, the retiringly shy yet always obliging Lord of Fargeal Manor.'

'Just how old *are* you people?'

Cornelius sneered. 'Older than we look.'

Vincent tapped the glass of the jar, murmuring to the creature within, 'And you, little monster? How old are you? *What* are you?'

'All the dead angels had one,' said Harry. 'You saw them. Wrapped about their necks.'

'Dead angels?' exclaimed Raquel.

'All the dead angels had one,' murmured Vincent. 'But the Bright Man never did...unless...*Cornelius*, do you suppose the one we found by the pond was his? Do you suppose we caused its death somehow, during the chase or during the capture, and it came loose of him?'

'But Vicente,' insisted Raquel, 'how can angels be dead?' She turned to Cornelius, who looked just as startled by the idea as she. 'Cornelius,' she cried. 'How can angels die?'

'Raquel,' groaned Vincent. '*Meu amor*. Hush now and let us talk sense.' Cornelius went to protest, and Vincent flung up his hand. 'You too, cully. Let us agree to call these things what we will – creatures, angels, demons or others – but let us also decide to lay aside our preconceptions and discuss only that which we have before us. Only that which we know as fact. Are we agreed?'

Frowning, Cornelius wrapped his arms around himself and leaned back against the wall, watchful.

'Does everyone here live forever?' asked the seer softly.

Luke startled her by answering from the hall. 'We didn't used to. Not 'til the Captain and Himself came.' He stepped warily from the shadows and entered the room, his eyes on the jar.

'Luke,' asked Raquel, 'where are my children?'

'Dunno, missus. I called for them in the woods but I didn't get no reply. Reckon they—'

Raquel dismissed this with a tut. 'The *baby-carriage*, Luke. My *good* children?'

Luke's face went cold. 'I'll bring that all up in a while,' he said. Then, as if his usual disapproval of Raquel's dolls had irritated the uncertainty from him, he strode to the jar and bent to look in at the creature. The water seemed to amplify the candlelight, and the creature threw sinuous reflections across his illuminated face. For some reason, this shifting light made Vincent feel ill. He glanced across to Harry.

'Do you feel sick, boy?'

Harry nodded. 'Very,' he admitted.

It's the ship, thought Vincent. *It has poisoned us.*

Tina's quietly insistent question came again. 'Does everyone live *forever* here?'

'Folk always lived long healthy lives in the village,' said Luke. 'Place were famous for it. Back in the old times, before Wolcroft and his Roundhead scum made life a nightmare, folks used to come from all over to be cured. Rabies, leprosy, consumption – you name it. Whatever ailed you, a stay in Fear Geal Woods would cure it. But no one used to live forever. Not 'til…'

He glanced at Vincent, and then to Cornelius, obviously reluctant to continue.

'Not until we locked the Angel down,' said Cornelius. 'Something changed when we put it underground.'

'No one here has died since. No one's been born. No one's died. Things just...stood still.' Luke glanced again at Vincent. 'But now things're winding down, ain't they, Captain? Slowly coming to a halt. Do you think this thing' – he tapped the glass – 'can tell us why?'

Vincent squinted down into the light-reflecting water. 'What did we change?' he mused. 'What difference was there between the creature roaming the woods as it used to and being confined underground?'

'Oh, you've been asking that question for decades,' groaned Cornelius. 'Are you not sick of it yet?'

'No,' snapped Vincent. 'I am not sick of it yet.' He rose to his feet and began to pace. The breeze of his passage set the candle flames aflutter, filling the room with shifting, smoky shadows. 'Let us retrace our steps...'

Cornelius threw his eyes to heaven. 'Again,' he breathed.

Vincent continued unfazed. 'One: we convinced Wolcroft to draw the Bright Man out with a spectacular.'

'It were allus drawn to entertainments,' said Luke.

'Two,' continued Vincent, 'we chased it from the trees and down into what was then the cow pastures by the boating pond. Three: the men brought it down. Four: we confined it underground, that I might examine it—'

'And voila,' cried Cornelius. '*Five:* we have ourselves a captive angel. And, asking nothing in return but the occasional song and dance, it has given us eternal life. And so we live in *peace* and *solitude*, needing *nothing from the world*.' He slammed his fist into the wall, his sudden rage making everyone but Vincent jump. 'Can't you just accept the gift, Vincent? Can't you just be grateful, for once in your damned life, and not always want *more*?'

'You were the one who wanted to know what the Bright Man needed! You were the one who brought this child here, that she might be forced to speak with it and let us understand what it wants.'

Vincent went and grabbed the spirit table, setting the light a-dance again as he plopped it down in the middle of the room. 'Come on, then!' he cried. 'Fulfil your plan! Let us *commune* with your angel!'

Cornelius shrank against the wall, and Vincent nodded his head bitterly. 'Of course, you have changed your mind. You no longer want to know, now the answers may contradict your carefully constructed *truth*. Well, I am sorry, cully, but we cannot all live underground wrapped in dreams while life continues on without us. Your angel is dying. And I mean to find out why.'

Vincent turned purposely from his friend. 'So...we put the Bright Man below ground; somehow we killed its symbiote. But something else also changed. Something in the way it fed. Luke, you told me it began to affect players in a way it never had before.'

Luke tore his eyes from Cornelius. 'Aye. It was then it began to use entertainers up. Any spectacle after that...' He shuddered, glancing at the wizened remains in the baby-carriage. 'It used them up.'

Vincent hunkered by the jar again and dabbled his fingers in the water. The creature lifted its tentacles and he withdrew his hand before their flesh could touch.

'I had always thought these changes had to do with imprisoning the Bright Man,' he murmured. 'That its powers were concentrated somehow by its confinement...but I now suspect that killing its symbiote is the key. We killed it, and somehow...somehow the Bright Man transferred the mutualism to us.'

He looked across at Tina. 'We have become the Bright Man's symbiote, have we not, seer? It has been living through us ever since.'

She nodded. 'And so you live forever...'

'...by feeding off others,' finished Joe, his voice immeasurably stronger than that of the girl who held his hand.

'Which presents the question,' murmured Vincent. 'What becomes of us should I choose to hand this creature over to its host?'

Luke frowned. 'Captain,' he said. 'Maybe it's best just to do what we've allus done. I ain't—'

'You are not enough for him,' interrupted Tina. 'You are less and *less* enough for him. Soon you will just stop, and then *he* will stop.'

'You don't *know that*,' cried Cornelius. 'Everything will be *fine* after the spectacular.'

Vincent sighed. 'Cornelius, can you not even begin to consider—'

Raquel's sharp cry cut him short. 'Stop it! You are being *disgusting*, Vicente! You are being *ungrateful*.'

She strode through the candles until she was standing over him and the jar, a fierce, angry shape against the light.

'In six days' time, the entertainers will come to my theatre. They will come, and they will give their all for the Angel. Then you will be *cured*, Vicente, and Cornelius will be *happy* and Matthew will come *home*. This is what Cornelius has promised will happen. This is what *will* happen.' Vincent jumped as she kicked the jar. The impact caused it to ring dully like a broken bell. 'Take this thing from my house!'

She swept from the room in a fluttering of candlelight. There came the sound of footsteps on gravel as she crossed the driveway.

'Well,' grunted Luke. 'You've gone and upset the missus.'

Vincent sighed.

Cornelius regarded him from his position by the wall. 'You will ruin everything.'

'You do not know that for certain.'

'It is not worth the risk. We are perfect as we are.'

'By the devil, Cornelius. Tell me you are not serious!'

Vincent spread his arms as if to encompass the echoing ballroom, the dusty, silent house. 'You call this perfect?' he said. '*Perfect?*' He began to laugh, a coarse noise that surprised even him with its unhappiness. Cornelius turned from the sound and fled into the dark.

'Have people come back from the dead before?' asked the seer.

Vincent tore his attention from the empty doorway and looked at her. She was slumped into the sofa, her hand clasped loosely in that of the boy called Joe. The only thing in any way alive about her was her eyes, and they watched from beneath lids pale as marble, lashes dark as ink.

Vincent flicked a glance to Joe, then back to her. 'No. I have never seen anyone return from the dead before.'

She turned to Luke, and he shook his head. 'Why?' he said. 'Who's returned from the dead?'

Without replying, the girl heaved herself from the sofa, tentatively released the boy's hand, and waited. When there seemed to be no ill effect from their lack of contact, she left him and lowered herself to the floor on the opposite side of the jar from Vincent. Looking across the light-addled surface at her was like gazing into a dark well. There was no glitter left to her at all. Still, Vincent couldn't look away.

'If you give this animal to the Angel,' she said, 'what is it you think will happen?'

'I do not know.'

She thought about this a moment, then glanced at the two boys sitting on the sofa. The American was hunched, his eyes half closed, his mouth twisted against a nausea that Vincent guessed was considerably worse than his own. The boy called Joe was sitting forward, frowning attentively.

'Your friends seem to think something bad will happen,' said the girl.

'My friends are frightened of change.'

'What about you? Aren't you frightened you'll die?'

The question surprised him. *Am I frightened to die?* he thought.

Cornelius was, Vincent was certain of that. Poor Cornelius, so thoroughly disgusted by himself that he could conceive of nothing other than an angry God – he was scared of the torments of purgatory and of hell.

And Raquel? Who could tell what Raquel was frightened of? Her beliefs were so convoluted a tincture of all she'd been taught, and then taught to despise, that Vincent doubted even she had a clear handle on them. She simply revelled in her ongoing vengeance against God – the holding captive of one of His precious children – and the barricade it had allowed her to build against a world that had shown her nothing but pain.

'How odd,' whispered Vincent.

'What?' asked the girl.

'You ask if I am afraid to die, and my first thoughts were not my own, but those of my friends.'

She tutted. 'That's nothing special, mister. I can count on the fingers of one hand the number of people I know who think for themselves.'

'That is not what I meant!'

'Oh, was it not?' she snapped, and he recognised at once the hard, dry sarcasm of the street; the impatience of one who'd learned to trust no one's judgement but her own.

Strange girl, he thought. *I believe I could have come to like you.*

'Had I not been fodder for your angel,' she added.

He startled. *You hear me?*

She just smiled coldly. 'What do you think will happen once you sacrifice the theatre folk?'

'We'll be better again,' said Luke, who had gone to the window. 'The Angel will be strong and so *we* will be strong and everything will be fine.'

The girl did not shift her attention from Vincent. 'I asked what *you* think, mister.'

'I think the Bright Man will stagger along for another hundred years or so, sipping from whatever nasty brutalities the children inflict on the world and whatever contentment Luke gets from the gardens. I think Cornelius will eventually disappear below-ground, never to return, and I think Raquel will simply sit at her window, waiting for Matthew, until she turns to stone.'

'And you?'

I will get thinner and thinner. Blood will fill my mouth with every breath. I will lay myself down in a room somewhere, and the dust shall coat me.

He shook his head and did not reply.

'Your friends are afraid that if you give this to him, the Angel won't need you. They're afraid he'll take his gifts away.'

'Are they right?'

Troubled, the girl glanced to the boy called Joe. 'I don't know,' she said.

Joe's face hardened. 'What became of your last seer, mister?'

'She lost her mind. And died.'

'This place killed her.'

Vincent nodded. 'Her communion with the Bright Man wore her out.'

The boy glared at the girl. 'See?'

She closed her eyes. 'Stop it, Joe.'

By the window, Luke suddenly straightened, peering out into the dark. 'Captain, there are lights on the ice.'

Vincent lurched to his feet. At first all he saw was his own reflection looking back at him, then there they were: distant torches bobbing; a crowd advancing through the fog. 'What the devil can it be?' he whispered. 'Let us go investigate.'

'I'll get the pistols, Captain.'

Vincent looked at Luke in astonishment, and the man tutted. 'I might as well've been on my own here these past fifty year or more, Captain. You think I'd feel comfortable without weapons at the ready?'

Luke grouched from the room, and Vincent trailed behind, feeling uncomfortably like an admonished child.

At the threshold, he hesitated. The creature bobbed in its jar of water, silent now that it was no longer part of something else's consciousness. The girl sat in a sprawl of sky-blue skirts, watching him, her two boys like sentinels on the sofa at her back. Lost children. What danger or use were they now?

Luke called from the depths of the safe room by the front door, 'Pistol or fowling-piece, Captain?' and Vincent went to join him.

The Heart That Pushes

Tina went to the window and looked out. Wolcroft was on the porch steps, accepting a pistol from the man called Luke. Wolcroft and Vincent murmured to each other as they checked the weapons, their attention on the lake. The woman, Raquel, was standing halfway down the lawns. Nothing but a crinolined shape cut from the illuminated fog, she too was watching the lights advance.

Weapons in hand, the three men descended onto the drive and strode into the dark. Tina knew they would remain lost from sight until they reached Raquel and were silhouetted against the torchlight.

Behind her, Harry rose from the sofa. He had one hand pressed to his stomach, his face the colour of old milk. 'Let's go,' he gasped. 'Now, while they're distracted. Tina, you grab the pram. Joe, help me with the jar. After we've brought that creature down to the Angel, we can head to the stables, rig up the carriage and make a run for it.' He staggered over and crouched to grab the jar by its rim. 'Come on, Joe. I don't feel too good. I can't do this on my own.'

Tina knelt by his side. She laid her hands on his. *Harry,* she thought. *Wait.* She allowed her thoughts to caress his mind – felt him succumb and rebel at once, a fuddled, terrible mixture of affection and resentment.

Don't you do that to me! he thought. Still, his fingers loosened on the rim of the jar, and he dropped to his knees before her as if awaiting instruction.

Joe and me will take care of the Beloved, Harry. You go to the stables now, get yourself a horse. Leave while you can.

Harry tried to pull away. 'No,' he whispered.

Tina tightened her grip on his hands. She smiled. *Yes, Harry. Joe and me have things to do here. But it's much better for you to leave. Go back to the theatre – back to your plans. You've so many plans, Harry. You're going to be so famous. You're going to be so rich. You need to go back to that.*

Harry turned his head the miles and miles it took for him to see Joe.

'Joe,' he managed. 'Stop…stop her.'

Joe looked at him – one of those rare, direct looks that showed the world just how blue his eyes were. 'It's all right, Harry,' he said. 'Go to the stables. Get two horses ready.'

His words seemed to undo a thin black thread in Harry's chest, and, just like that, Harry was rising to his feet and walking from the room.

When he reached the door, Tina said, *Harry, put in your earplugs.* He smiled back at her and did as he was told. Then he was outside the candlelight and crossing a dark hall. He was in a book-lined room. He was pushing open a glass-panelled door and stepping into the moonlit night. He walked through the scent of roses and gave himself up to the darkness of a shrub-crowded path. His mind was set and sure, the clock-tower of the stable yards a beacon, guiding him through the maze of the garden.

Every step of the way, Tina was with him, her gentle assurances sounding in his mind: *It's all right, Harry. Don't worry. It's time to go home.*

JOE CALLED HER mind back to itself, and Tina sagged, drained.

'He won't be safe out there,' he said.

She heaved herself to her feet and took hold of the jar. 'Harry crossed an entire ocean on his own, Joe.' She began to drag the jar across the room. 'He dived to the bottom of a lake and back. He's well able to wriggle past some kids and steal himself a horse.'

She paused, breathless already, and looked up. Joe sat with his hands laced together, his elbows on his knees, as if calmly watching the sunset on the Royal Canal. He looked like a prince in those fancy clothes, his hair all soft and gleaming. He was something completely different now, completely different but still the same: her Joe.

Down in his lonely cave, the Angel was shifting and turning about, trying to find a connection to the beloved. He had his own dead beloved slung about his neck. He carried it with all the grief of someone carrying a dead child, but he was torn by hope, too – and by need. Any moment now, he would begin to notice her again. He would begin to touch, then paw, then hammer at her receptive mind, demanding answers she couldn't give.

This jar was so heavy; her time was so short.

'Are you going to help me or not?' she snapped.

Joe's eyes dropped to the creature, then back to her. 'What are you going to do with it?' he asked.

'I'm *hiding* it! What else? We're not going to let them give it to the Angel! What would happen you then?' She tried again to drag the jar. She felt so bloody weak and useless. Her head was starting to swim. Why wouldn't he help her?

Joe got to his feet. His expression sent a spear of rage through her, because she knew what he was about to say. The Angel paused his frenzied prowling and lifted his head. Oh, he had found her. By her pain, he had found her. He lifted his hands and his wings, feeling his own loss echoed in the rise of her panic. He began to sing, and Joe's next words were barely audible above his voice.

'This place will kill you, Tina.'

'To hell with that!' She stopped, gathered her anger, then lowered her voice, purposely using the tone she had only recently learned, the one that had turned Harry on his heel and sent him into the dark.

Help me, Joe. Help me hide this thing.

Joe just tutted, disapproving, and Tina cursed him as much as she loved him for the very same strength. He had never been one to do what he was told – sure, hadn't that been the very thing that attracted her in the first place? In a world crippled by poverty, and cowed by violence, hadn't Joe's quiet sense of his own worth drawn Tina to him like a charm?

'You're not staying,' he told her.

'I bloody am!'

She took hold of the jar again, and the Angel roared in sudden understanding. *Beloved. Here. To me.* Tina clenched her teeth against its terrible voice. Shuffling backwards, she began dragging the jar through the stands of flickering candles, squinting behind her for the trail of water that betrayed Wolcroft's earlier journey from the well. She had so little time. The Angel was so loud.

Silence clamped down as Joe's hands grabbed the top of her arms. He dragged her up so they were face to face. 'You want the theatre folk killed? Is that what you want?'

'That doesn't have to happen.'

'It *will* happen if we don't give your angel its creature. You know that.'

'We can figure that out later. It's not important now.'

She shook free of him, reaching for the jar, and he grabbed her again. Tina felt the tiniest flare of fear, as he jerked her back around to face him. She'd seen so many men turn this way. Tenement love letters, Nana called them: black eyes and bruises, the language of men who knew only one way to find respect.

But that wasn't Joe. Never Joe.

Tina pulled herself to her full height. 'Let go of me,' she said. 'You're not some back-alley bully with your mot.'

'And you're not some stupid young wan giving everything she is for some *lad*. Haven't we both seen enough of that?' He shook her, just a gentle shake, to emphasise his fear. 'You have plans,' he said softly. 'Did you think I hadn't noticed? There's so much you want to do. Are you really going to give that up just to stay here, Tina? *Here?*'

The candles were making everything about him gold – his hair, his eyelashes. Threads of light were falling and melting into him like snow. Tina took his face between her hands. He was hers: so utterly, so tenderly her own. Could he not understand that?

'You're *part* of my plans, Joe. We're a team. You've never let me down. Do you think I'm going to run away and leave you?'

He drew her hands from his face. 'I'm finished, Tina. And this place will kill you.'

He stepped back, releasing her, and the Angel's voice flooded in, shredding, roaring, deafening.

'This place will kill you,' Joe said. 'Tell me you'll leave.'

She lurched for him and he stepped back again, coming to a halt a scant two yards away. She pressed her fists to her temples, regarding him across the forest of the candle flames. Without his touch, the Angel's voice was a knife in her head, hacking the inside of her skull.

'Tell me you'll leave,' Joe whispered.

'I'll leave.'

He looked away, as if ashamed. Tina held herself in place, fists clenched against her head, eyes narrowed against the pain.

'Don't be angry at me, Tina.'

'I'm not angry.'

He came and offered his hand. She took it. He stooped and gripped the lip of the jar with his free hand. She leaned to help, and between them they dragged the jar across the musty dimness of the hall and into the library. 'It won't be easy to get this over to that castle,' Joe grunted. 'But between us both…'

'That won't be necessary,' said Tina. He straightened warily, as if suspecting she'd changed her mind. She pointed to the chill gap in the bookshelves, the books scattering the floor. 'They left the secret door open,' she said.

At the threshold of the door, they stood gazing down into blackness.

'It's very dark,' said Joe. 'Maybe…'

Her hand tightened on his. 'Joe! There's something moving down there.'

He crouched slightly, pushing her behind him. 'Where?'

She pointed a shaking finger. 'Can't you see it? There! About three steps down. I'm scared, Joe.'

He pushed her further behind him, straining to see. 'I can't see it,' he whispered. 'Are you sure?'

'I'm sure, Joe.'

She pushed just hard enough to send him stumbling down the top few steps, and was already swinging the door shut as he turned. She had just enough time to see the panic in his eyes before the latch clicked shut. He began hammering almost immediately, and she pressed her face to the door, feeling the pounding of his anger through the wood.

We'll figure it out, Joe. We'll think of something better than you dying and my going on alone.

For a moment, the hammering ceased.

I'll be back for you, she told him.

The hammering recommenced as she dragged the jar through the French doors, but once she was out on the terrace it fell from earshot. She was left only with dim and silent moonlight, and the terrible voice of the Angel gnawing at her mind. Across the flagstones, a spattered path of rapidly drying water betrayed Wolcroft's route from the well. Tina regarded it a moment, in weariness and pain, then began the slow, scraping task of dragging the jar away from the house.

The Heart That Pulled

IT HAD BEEN a long time since Cornelius had felt the reassuring weight of a pistol in his hand. A long time since he and Vincent strode out together motivated only by the simple concept of kill or be killed. The old days were so old now, so distant and covered in dust, that he could barely discern sentiment from actual memory. But this? This was the past alive again; this was the vibrancy of youth pumping like fresh blood through his veins.

Raquel fell into step with them as they came abreast of her. She had her little knife in hand – the one with which she had killed her husband, and so ended his wretched abuse of her. Cornelius was still appalled by her lack of fidelity to Matthew. But that did not stop him handing her a flintlock as they advanced together across the frozen grass. She took it without diverting her attention from the torches on the boating pond.

'Is it the world?' she asked. 'Has it hunted us down at last?'

'If it has, we shall soon see it off.' He felt a flare of happiness at the sheer straightforwardness of that thought.

The set look on Vincent's face filled him with the fiercest joy. *Yes, Captain. Yes! This place is worth fighting for, this little island of ours.*

He felt the cold air on his teeth and realised he was grinning.

They came to a halt on the shore of the pond and spread out in a close-knit line, squinting towards the lights.

'It's Peadar,' grunted Luke, lowering his fowling-piece.

'So it is,' said Vincent, uncocking his pistol.

'It is the entire village,' said Raquel. She picked up her skirts and followed Vincent out into the eddying bank of fog.

Swamped with the most intense disappointment, Cornelius watched them go. The villagers. Come to beg access to the girl, no doubt – and now he would have to talk them all into going back home. He closed his eyes, the glorious anticipation of battle replaced with the tedious vista of diplomacy.

Damn my life, he thought, wearily plunging the pistol into his belt.

The ice was thick with frost and it crunched like snow beneath his feet. Voices came murmuring through the muffling fog, then Vincent's slim figure resolved itself in a halo of torchlight. The villagers gathered around, their eyes flat coins of firelight.

'What do you mean, you chased them here?' Raquel asked Peadar. 'Why would you drive them onto the estate?'

'We didn't drive them in, missus. We followed them, after we noticed their horses tied at the church gate. We were hoping the sight of the torches would panic them.'

'Is it the seer's family?' pondered Vincent. 'Could they have traced her here so soon?'

Cornelius groaned. It was possible. They could have taken a train from the city, and then horses from the nearest town. *Damnation*. 'We had best search the grounds. Douse those lights; they've done their job. The sudden darkness will better serve to unsettle the intruders further, and give us the advantage.'

There came a series of violent hisses as a dozen or more brands met their death. The villagers' eyes now blinked back green from hazy darkness. Peadar asked, 'Do we drive them off, or put an end to them?'

Cornelius glanced at Vincent. Intruders were not as common as they had once been; the hordes of pitiful skeletons that the great famine had driven across country were already a distant memory. Even in this remoteness, however, vagrants weren't unheard of – the occasional family dispossessed by the land wars, the occasional pedlar. He and Vincent simply drove those kinds of trespassers from the place. But if this *was* the girl's family, the girl's inevitable fate and that which they planned for the artistes would quickly become clear to them. It was impossible that they could be allowed free to spread tales.

Complication upon complication, he thought.

'We must do away with them,' said Raquel.

Cornelius stared at her a moment – her clear, handsome face, the calmness of her expression. She was absolutely correct. So why did this pain him? He could not answer, but there was no satisfaction to it when he nodded his agreement.

'You are right, of course, my dear. Let us make a clean sweep of this. Vincent, Luke and I will take the house and its immediate grounds. Raquel, will you take a group around the topiary gardens and the maze?'

'The rest of us will split between the drive and lawns and woods,' said Peadar.

'Thank you, friend. Be careful in the woods. I think the children may be there.'

Raquel and the villagers drifted away. It was not the first time they had done this; they knew their roles. Soon Cornelius was left in fog and silence, Luke by his side, Vincent at his back.

'The children are not to be allowed to amuse themselves, Luke.'

There was a small, resentful silence.

Cornelius sighed. 'I am adamant, Luke.'

With a tut, Luke nodded, and trudged away.

Cornelius looked back at Vincent. 'Best to it, I suppose, Captain.'

To his night vision, the fog was beautiful, billowing around his motionless friend in softly luminous veils. The brightnesses of Vincent's eyes flashed towards him, then away.

'Captain?'

'When was it we began to so casually use people up?'

'Tell me you are joking.'

Vincent didn't answer.

Cornelius' stomach tightened in inexplicable fear. 'Have you forgot where we came from?'

'I recall the youth we escaped. I recall the mire from which we freed ourselves.'

'Aye, by stealing your father's ship and crew, Vincent! By clearing my father's strongroom. By becoming *pirates*. Murder and theft were the very foundation of our present fortune. Our entire livelihood has been based on the misuse of others.'

Vincent looked off into the swirling emptiness of the fog. 'I cannot help but think that was different.'

'Different!'

'Yes. Different. What are we doing here, Cornelius? Eating children up. Hunting old women in the dark. For what? That we may continue to live like leeches in a bog?'

Cornelius' heart began to pound. *What are you suggesting?*

'I do not like what we have become.'

'What are you *suggesting*?'

'That this is no longer worth the price, cully.'

'You will die if you leave.'

Vincent shrugged. 'We do not know that for certain.'

'Things are going to improve. Once the Angel is—'

I can no longer do this, Cornelius. I can no longer live this dusty, empty life.

Vincent's eyes once again flashed towards him. 'Come with me, cully. We can resume our adventures. We have many ships at our disposal these days, centuries of accumulated wealth. Let us travel the world with it – take Raquel and head to South America, sail up the Amazon and see what we can see. Let us travel to Africa. Or we could tour Europe! Do you know that on the Russian steppes there are—'

'No.'

'Cornelius, we could—'

'No. I will not go with you.'

Vincent hung his head in defeat. He sighed. 'Very well. I will speak to Raquel about dividing our fortunes into—'

Cornelius laughed. The harsh sound of it frightened him; the anger he felt frightened him; but he couldn't stop. He couldn't. It was like a tide rising. A great black rush of bitterness, and he *couldn't stop*. 'You don't honestly think you can go without me, do you? How in God's name would you manage?'

'What are you talking about?'

'You? *Touring Europe?* No doubt you would set yourself up in the finest hotels? Visit the great houses, perhaps – view their collections of art? A Byronic dilettante sampling the highest of culture?'

Vincent chuckled. 'I know it seems out of character, but I—'

'I can picture you now, sitting in a café by the Rhine, ordering yourself a dish of cheese and a glass of good wine. Dear Raquel, how *nice* it will be for her to sit there with you. How long do you think it will take for you to get served? Oh, and what shall you pretend to be? Her cab driver? Her servant? The amusing wild-man act from a travelling circus?'

Vincent went very still and quiet. Cornelius could feel his own heart battering his ribs as if panicked by his words; as if appalled by them. But his mouth kept moving. It just kept moving, and this vileness poured out.

'Or perhaps you plan to take to the sea again? How easy do you think it will be to find a crew? We own many ships, Vincent, and the men who sail them are content to take your anonymous penny in wages. But do not suppose they would be so happy to tug their forelocks and call you Captain to your black face.'

Such silence fell after this, and such a stillness, that Cornelius almost reached to make certain Vincent was there. When Vincent finally did speak, his voice was immeasurably cold.

'This is your understanding, is it? That everything I am, or can ever hope to be, exists only thanks to your intervention?'

'You cannot deny,' said Cornelius softly, 'that you carry your colour wherever you go.'

'I see.'

Thrusting his pistol into his belt, Vincent strode past him, heading for shore.

After a hesitation, Cornelius fell into place at his back. 'Where are we going?'

Vincent did not reply.

'Are we going to find the intruders?'

Vincent just kept moving forward, heading for the house, and Cornelius spoke no more. He hoped his silence might afford his friend some time to think; some space in which to reason things through and see the sense in what had been said. But when they came to the driveway and, still wordless, Vincent marched up the front steps of the house, Cornelius knew that everything was broken between them; everything was lost.

He came to a halt on the gravel. 'Do not leave!'

Vincent strode through the door.

'If you leave, you will die! You will end up like Matthew!'

Vincent turned. Within the dark interior of the house, his eyes were the brightest thing about him.

Cornelius spread his hands to him, in offering maybe, or pleading. He felt he could admit anything now. Here in the confessional of the moonlight, at the cusp of losing everything, he could offer up his sins. Oh, it was almost a relief. It was almost, *almost* a relief to finally say the words.

'He came back, Vincent.'

'Matthew?'

'He was so old. He was so frail. I hardly knew him.'

'And you sent him *away*?'

'He stood right there. Right there in that doorway, and

he smiled at me. Such an old man. He said, "I came to show you, Cornelius, that you don't have to be afraid."'

Vincent moved forward to stand above him on the steps. 'And you sent him away *again*? You think I don't know about the first time? You think I did not hear the vile things you called him? Tell me you did not repeat that!'

Cornelius heard Vincent's words only vaguely. At that moment his mind was filled with a blaze of autumnal sunlight, and he was gazing down into the gentleness of Matthew's smile. These things were more vivid to him than anything.

'He was so old,' he whispered. 'He had travelled such a long way. He wanted to tell me about his life…'

'How could you have said those awful things to him? All because he loved you, Cornelius! Because he dared to be what you could not bring yourself to be. And then he was *gone*. You had driven him away!'

Cornelius pressed his fingers beneath his eyes, felt the scald of tears he had not shed for decades. 'I closed the door in his face. I said I could not see him. I said I could not see him, and I left him standing there. A frail old man. Alone.'

Their eyes met, and Vincent knew. He knew. The terrible truth of it. He slowly sat down on the top step. Cornelius could not take his eyes from him. Finally, Vincent said, 'How long did they have him?'

There was no good answer to that. Cornelius just shook his head.

'Yet you kept them here.'

'I took…I took what remained of him to the fields. I buried…I buried him in the fields.'

'And you kept *them* here.'

'They are Raquel's. What would it have done to her to lose them, too?' At the expression on Vincent's face, Cornelius paused – then he told the truth, the *real* truth of it. 'How could I get rid of them without admitting what they had done? What could I have—'

It was not really a noise that drew his attention, more a fluttering of the shadows within the hall. He thought he himself might have made a sound at the sight of her – a small, agonised groan – which caused Vincent to turn where he sat and stare helplessly up as she edged her way into the porch.

'I sent the others ahead,' she said. 'I needed to bring my babies back inside. Out of the frost.'

'Of course,' whispered Vincent.

'Are you taking a rest?'

'A little one, *meu amor.*'

She nodded. 'Well. I'd best return to my task. Good night, my friends. Good hunting.'

She gathered her skirts, her knife glinting in the moonlight and, with no further comment, made her way down the steps and around the far side of the house.

Vincent rose uncertainly to his feet as her footsteps faded into the night.

'She didn't hear us,' whispered Cornelius. 'She could not possibly have, and remained that calm.'

The look Vincent gave him was so replete with disgust that Cornelius could barely stand to register it. Vincent descended the steps, and Cornelius could only whisper, 'Where are you going?'

Vincent gave no answer, and soon he too had gone, following Raquel around the house and out of sight.

The Girl Who Blazed

THE WELL WAS down a flight of narrow stone steps by the sun terrace, not far from the house. Hemmed by dense woods, it was a cloistered area of ivy and moss, redolent of peace. Tina intruded on this in a torment of agony, one part of her battling the frenzy of the Angel, the other holding at bay Joe's overwhelming sense of betrayal. She scraped and bumped the jar down each step and hauled it through clasping ivy to the coolness of the well mouth.

The creature within the jar cast a gentle glow, which illuminated the softly weeping stones of the well. This would not be difficult. Wolcroft had already pushed aside the wooden lid; all Tina had to do was lift the jar onto the wall. All she had to do was tip it over. Then the thing inside would slide out. It would fall away. It would be gone forever, and Joe would be safe.

She was trying very hard to hold on to everything: the glass curve of the jar's rim beneath her grip; the solidity of the wall; the cool drip of the water. But it was a struggle to focus.

If only I had a stronger mind.

She'd said that to Joe once, after a seizure. *I should be able to stop myself from doing this.* She remembered clearly the look he'd given her.

Tina, he'd said, *do you think Billy the stable boy grew up crooked because he didn't work hard enough at not being a cripple?*

That had been a shocking thing to say. Poor Billy, with his twisted legs.

Do you think if Saul just tried hard enough, he'd be able to see without his spectacles?

She had understood what he was saying. The expression on her face had made him squeeze her hand. *Stop being an eejit*, he'd said. *You are what you are.*

Joe.

Tina knew she had been born rich. From the start, she'd had the Lady Nana and Fran the Apples. She'd had the life they'd given her. In a sea of women who were nothing but someone else's shadow, they had taught her to be herself. Joe had understood that. Joe had loved it.

Without Joe, Tina knew her good, strong life would continue. She would be successful. She would be herself. But – and Tina knew this as certainly as if it were written in the Bible – she would be alone. Because Joe was her best friend: truly, honestly, deeply her best friend. He had added himself to the completeness of her life, and by doing so he had made that life bigger, made it brighter, made it stronger, just by being Joe.

How could she give that up?

Tina heaved the jar onto the rim of the well. The creature within stirred gracefully, its soft light radiating. It was such a gentle presence. While the Angel moaned and thrashed and tore within her brain, this creature simply tapped gentle inquiries against the jar. Even just looking at it soothed her mind. They were like the disparate parts of a divided whole, this thing and the Angel – balance divided.

'That is it exactly, isn't it?' whispered Tina. 'You are the other half. You are Beloved. Without you, he is not complete.' She ran her fingers against the round belly of the glass, and the creature followed with its own fingers of light.

Joe had ceased his panicked battering of the door. Even the Angel had paused, his presence a great bursting firework in her head, but standing still, as if a firework could hold its breath. She could feel Joe's mind trying to figure out the change in her. She felt him reaching out, speaking to her as he had at Miss Price's, just before he died all alone in that snowy street covered by a horse blanket like some piece of meaningless rubbish.

Tina?

She shook her head, not wanting to hear.

Tina. Nothing lasts forever.

Nothing lasts forever. That was a tune you didn't have to play twice to a tenement-dweller. Didn't every dawn bear witness to the last fluttering of another life: a loved baby, a smiling mother, a gentle dad? In the tenements, love was a paper shield against death; it meant nothing, and even a beloved life could be the briefest of candles.

Please leave, whispered Joe. *I'm already gone.*

She closed her eyes and gripped the jar. *I'm sorry*, she whispered. Down in the darkness of his prison, the Angel fell to his knees, not believing.

'I'm sorry,' Tina said aloud.

Without opening her eyes, she placed her hand into the warm water. *Come on. I'll bring you to your friend.*

The tentacles unfolded from the mouth of the jar and trembled for a moment in grace and beauty before spiralling shut on Tina's arm. Her mind filled at once with order, a coolness of numbers tumbling down and clicking precisely into place. Two-dozen-apples-at-a-farthing-apiece-sold-for-a-moonbeam-a-pair. The-weight-of-depth-outside-space. When-a-clock-measures-distance-and-time-has-form. *There are no more apples until I and He are We because He is the belly and I am the mouth.* I understand. *I am the mind and he is the heart.* Yes. Truly. I understand.

A cascade of numbers, a gentleness of numbers, a soothing of numbers; this creature was calmness itself, and it took its time, now there was no poison to escape, it took its gentle time insinuating itself along her arm. And the light poured through it, oh, so beautiful, plummeting from the sky to converge in the curled body, roaring back out to return to the Angel, who wept in joy as he fed.

The mosaiced canopy of the sky. The living scent of the roses. The filigree of ivy over damp pillows of moss. All was a wonderment.

'Everything is so good,' murmured Tina. 'Behold the glory of everything.'

Awe is nourishment. Glory is food. The resonance of being. We live. We feed. Yes.

A familiar man broke through the shrubbery and, at the sight of Tina, jarred to a halt.

'Mickey,' she whispered.

Mickey's remaining eye, glittering through stained bandages, dropped to the creature on her arm. He saw a lantern, nothing more. 'Might have known you'd be here, *Miss Kelly.* Where's Joe?'

Somewhere down in the human heart of her, Tina knew she should run. This was a terrible man. He would do terrible things. But the creature on her arm did not know how to fear, only how to marvel, and so Tina stayed.

Mickey closed the distance between them, his knife a vengeful slice of moonlight in the glory of his one good fist, and Tina found him beautiful.

'You know,' she said, 'Joe didn't do anything to you. It was that black fella.'

'Don't be annoying me. The little shit drowned Graham. He threw a bucket of coals in my face. I'm going to slit him from belly to throat.' He squinted at her. 'What the...Are your eyes *bleeding*?'

My eyes? Tina lifted her free hand to check. Then another man tore from the trees in an explosion of leaves, and she was captivated once again as he barrelled into Mickey, almost knocking him over. She knew this man, too: a big, stupid gouger, another of Joe's cousins. Daymo.

Mickey shoved him aside. 'Quiet, you eejit! You'll draw them buggers down on us.' He glared at Tina. 'Where's Joe? He can't hide behind that darkie's coat-tails forever.' But even as he spoke, his companion was dodging past, intent on escape. Mickey grabbed him. 'The fuck you *running* for?'

Daymo groaned, an ecstasy of bewilderment on his face.

Mickey shook him. 'Why are you *running*?'

'They *told* me to.' Daymo pointed across to the trees.

Two small figures emerged from the darkness, the little boy a solemn watchfulness, the little girl all frills and smiles. She clapped her hands. 'Oh! Now there are two!'

'We would like you to run,' said the boy.

'But you must stay together,' sang the girl, wagging her finger. 'No fair splitting up.'

The two men hesitated, their eyes wide.

'*Run!*' roared the boy. And they did.

The little girl bent to retrieve Mickey's fallen knife. Tina thought she and her brother were magnificent, the clarity of their evil as pure and bright as the tolling of a silver bell.

'How lovely,' she whispered.

'Aren't you pretty,' sang the girl, twirling the knife in her fingers. 'You're all shiny like the moon.'

'I like your tears,' said the boy. 'They look like blood.'

His sister tugged his sleeve. 'Come along, brother. She's Pap's, remember. We can't have what is Pap's.' They strolled away, arm in arm, following the trail of broken brush left by the fleeing men.

The creature resumed its slow, sweet crawl up Tina's arm, and, as if in a dream, she brushed her free hand beneath her eyes. Her fingers came away scarlet. *Oh,* she thought. *You are killing me.* But by then the creature's tentacles had found their way into her hair, and it was much too late.

She blazed. Teeth clenched, arms spread, head back, she blazed in the dark.

Gently, the creature steered her onto the path and they began to follow the light.

The Heart That Pleased

Harry THREW UP on the path, then stumbled on, his stomach in turmoil, his mind torn. Why was he so conflicted in his heart? Tina had asked, and he had obliged. It was *good* to please her. It was always good to please. It was Harry's fondest wish that he could please everyone; that the whole world could look on in happiness as he went about his wonderful life, marvelling at him and applauding. He was a champion. He was…

Wait.

What?

Desperate to get his bearings, Harry tore the plugs from his ears. There were cobbles beneath his feet. Red brick walls surrounded him. He was in a stable yard. Yes! He had to take a horse and get away. Tina had said so. She would be proud of him then. He would be rich and famous then. She…

No. He had to get *two* horses. Joe had told him that. Two horses.

No! Where was his own mind? He had his own mind, didn't he? He…he had to get a *carriage*. Yes. He had to rig up the carriage. He wasn't leaving alone. He wasn't abandoning...

Harry staggered into the fragrant gloom of the carriage house. Horses whickered softly in the darkness and he felt his way towards them. How was he going to manage this? He'd never rigged up a carriage in his life. Joe was the one who should be doing this. Joe was the one who knew how. None of this made any sense, and yet Harry kept going, trying hard to finish a task the aim of which mostly eluded him.

His hands had just settled against the splintered boards of a stable gate, and the first curious huff of horse's breath had taken him by surprise, when a sound in the courtyard sent him ducking. It was a familiar noise, reminiscent of Harry's time in the boxing ring: the smack of flesh against flesh, the thump and scurry of big men fighting. Then over it came another sound, terrifying enough to send Harry cowering into an empty stall. Somewhere out there, a child was giggling.

The carriage house's double doors slammed open, and the sounds of wordless fighting continued as the men rolled into the interior. Two small figures darted after them, and there were squeals of happiness from the dark.

'Give them some light!' cried the little girl. 'I should very much like them to see each other.'

Harry groped fruitlessly in his pocket for the earplugs. He had dropped them onto the cobbles outside. There was the scrape and flare of a match being struck, and the girl squealed again as the far side of the barn was illuminated by candlelight.

'We should give them *weapons*,' she cheered.

'No,' said the boy. 'I like this.'

'Then...hit each other *harder*! Oh! Bite each other!'

There was grunting. The sharpness of flesh on flesh again. A man howled.

'No noise!' snapped the boy, and the struggle grew muffled again. There followed an avid, avaricious quiet as the men groaned and strove and tussled about on the floor.

Oh God, who is it? thought Harry. *Who is it?* He crawled to the edge of the stall, dreading the sight of Joe in mortal combat with some poor tramp, or two members of the theatre group maybe. Fear would not allow him to look around the corner. He could distinctly hear one of the men weeping as he fought.

What are you going to do, Harry? Sit here and listen as someone is tortured? Just be strong in your mind! Be strong in your mind! There's no such thing as mesmerism.

He stood up in the darkness, his whole body screaming at him to stay down. He forced himself around the corner and stepped into the light.

The little girl was perched on the edge of a neglected work table, swinging her feet. Her brother was leaning casually beside her, his little legs crossed. On the ground, a couple of big men were mutually strangling each other.

The girl pouted. 'It'll be over too soon if they do that.'

The boy, his face impassively absorbed, leaned forward and said, 'No more strangling.'

The men released each other's throats with gasps and sobs of confusion.

The boy said, 'More biting.'

The smaller man sank his teeth into the filthy cheek of his opponent. There was a flurry of desperate violence, and the two men struggled their way across the floor until they smacked against the stable wall.

'You're going to be in terrible trouble,' said Harry.

The children looked across with simultaneous surprise.

'Those men work for your pap,' said Harry. 'You'll be in terrible trouble if you hurt them.'

The little girl slid from the table to land lightly by her brother's side. 'Stick-man!' she cried.

Before Harry could stop himself, he stepped back.

Control yourself! he thought. *These are just kids!*

Somewhere inside him there was a core, a centre, an absolute understanding of who he was. Harry knew he had to find that part of himself. He had to grab it. He had to hold on tight, and keep it.

There were gnawing sounds coming from the men now. One of them was sobbing. The children's eyes flicked to them. The little girl smiled.

'Your pap is already angry that you tried to kill his dogs,' cried Harry.

There was a palpable hesitation. The little boy looked hurt.

'But we told him we were sorry,' he said.

'We were just playing,' pouted the girl. 'We didn't mean any harm.'

There was a long, wet tearing noise from the men, and a squeal of hopeless agony.

'You need to let them *go*,' cried Harry. 'They're your *pap's men.*'

The little boy shook his head. 'No, they're not.'

'Yes, they are! They *are!*'

'Oh my,' said the little girl. 'He is telling such big lies.'

'Lies are very *bad*,' said the boy. 'We should wash his mouth out.'

The little girl seemed to have a seriously wonderful idea then; it lit her up with delight. 'Stick-man,' she cried. 'Have a nice drink of lamp oil.'

Harry moaned and bent double, and tried to turn away. Suddenly, all he had ever wanted was to know what kerosene tasted like; all he had ever wanted in his *whole damn life* was to unscrew the lid of a kerosene lamp and drink its contents down.

'No…' he whispered. 'Don't…'

The little girl was by his side now. Oh, she was very sweet, really, this close: her smile so wide, her eyes so very clear and blue. She took his hand.

The part of Harry that was completely himself screamed and raged. It clawed and struggled. But it was a very small part, really – very tiny – and his desire to please this little girl – this charming little girl, who held his hand and looked up at him with such admiration – was quite over-whelming.

'Come on,' she sang. 'Come on, stick-man. Come over here.' She led him to the work table.

'I'm your pap's,' he whispered. 'I'm your pap's.'

'Oh, you know, I don't think Pap likes you all that much. But I do.' She hopped up and sat on the edge of the table again. 'I enjoyed your magic trick.'

'Oh yes,' remembered the boy. 'That *was* good.'

The part of Harry that was absolutely Harry stopped struggling and smiled.

It was good, wasn't it. Simple but good. Sometimes it's the simplest things that work the best.

'You're a very entertaining fellow.'

I am indeed.

'Here you go.' The girl nudged a battered can towards him. It was covered in cobwebs and had 'Paraffin' stencilled on it. 'Drink lots and lots now. It'll be delicious.'

The boy snickered. Harry unscrewed the lid. His audience of two concentrated only on him, and he revelled in their fascination. In the adjacent booths there was some frantic pugilism going on, but it didn't seem to distract them. In Harry's mind a calliope began to jangle.

Roll up, ladieees and gennnntlemen. See the wonderful Houdiiini – watch him drink from the poison cup!

The candle flame glimmered like gaslight in his eyes as he flourished the can first one way and then the other, showing it off.

The audience burst into applause. 'Hurrah!'

Harry put the can to his nose and made a show of inhaling deeply. Fumes rose thick and sweet to snag his breath – *yum, yum, yum.*

Grinning, he turned to bask in the audience's delight. Their lack of attention hit him like a slap. They weren't even looking his way! They were, in fact, frowning off into the distance, utterly distracted.

Oh no. He'd lost them!

'Ladies and gentlemen!' he cried. 'If you'll direct your attention to this can. I am about to drink a gallon of flammable oil.' (*Wait. What?* What was the act here? What was the pay-off?)

He sloshed the contents enticingly, but the delightful children in the front row remained captivated by some different sound. (Was it those fighters in the corner? Damn them! Hadn't Harry told Dash to position the curtains so no one could see the other acts?)

He glared across at the pugilists. Thankfully the match seemed almost at an end, one combatant merely hunched over the other, now, gnawing.

The charming little girl jumped to the floor. Seemingly delighted and surprised by something Harry could not see, she clapped her hands. 'Oh, Mama,' she breathed. 'I would very *much* like that. Thank you!'

'Hey,' cried Harry. 'No talking in the audience.'

The girl's brother caught her by the hand, and with a surge of anguish Harry realised they were about to leave. No! The calliope music swelled, loud and insistent and off-key.

'With one swallow,' he cried desperately, raising the can, 'I shall empty this can!' (What was the pay-off to this act?)

'We're coming, Mama!' cried the boy. 'Don't start without us!'

'Wait!' cried Harry. 'Behold!'

The children were already out the door. Harry lifted the can to his lips, and paraffin filled his mouth. The heavy, roiling fumes clawed at his eyes and his nose, burned cold in his mouth, and the pay-off rose in his mind, as bright and clear as the calliope jangle. It was the easiest, the most effective, and the most beloved act in the world. No lowly fire-eater he: Harry Houdini would breathe fire!

Bending forward at the hip and flinging his arm out behind him, Harry sprayed a long jet of paraffin onto the candle. A magnificent plume of flame roared out to illuminate the dark. Bright and fierce, it seared the shadows from the air. The sights and sounds of the penny museum exploded into flakes of rusted metal, and the calliope deflated in a hiss of steam. Harry tumbled forward into hay and ancient cobwebs, gagging on the taste of kerosene, fully aware again, of the night and the nightmare world.

Oh God oh God oh God what did I almost do?

The sound of whimpering filtered through the panic in his brain. The men by the wall had separated now. One was sprawled motionless and silent. The other, huddled in a ball beside him, was weeping. Harry stumbled across to them, carrying the misshapen stub of the candle, huge shadows trembling in his path.

'It's okay,' he rasped, crouching by the weeping man. 'They're gone.'

The man shrank back against the wall, and Harry recoiled in recognition of Joe's cousin, Daymo. His face was bearded in blood. Thoroughly unravelled, he bared his scarlet teeth. 'I ate his face,' he whispered. 'Jesus help me. I ate his face.'

Harry reluctantly raised the candle to illuminate their motionless companion. A featureless glistening mess greeted him. Daymo reached a fever pitch of hysteria at the sight. The barn spun as Harry heaved himself to his feet. He felt as if he was dying. He really did. It felt like he was going to die.

'Get up,' he groaned, staggering from the sobbing man. 'Get up. Get over to those horses. Show me how to rig a carriage.'

Undoing

i. Tina

TINA WAS A small, calm insignificance at the heart of the flame. Around her, numbers collided and flowed, painting memories of cool expanses, of light-reflective serenities, of magenta skies: a home for which the Beloved ached. Or, at least, Home as it had been before the Contagion destroyed it.

It comes, remembered the Beloved. *Birthing itself by accident through a rent in everything. Wriggling and squirming through an emptiness of space until* – horror – *it reaches Home, where the gentle crowds of Us amass in togetherness. Writhing into our sky, it realises We are not it. This is a disgust. It must fix us. For what is not it is wrong. The Contagion, the Disease: it begins to change everything.*

She walked with burning feet on illuminated ground, brightening the shrubbery as she passed. Beside her, the orchard walls unspooled in inky blackness; behind that, a ruined castle – her destination – spewed fountains of hungry light to the moon-greyed clouds. She could feel herself coming undone: everything that was truly her expanding out

{ 405 }

beyond her body's capacity to hold it. Soon there would be no her at all, no thoughts or memories, no fear or hate, no ambition, no love. She would be gone. The very touch of this creature was unravelling her.

It was a fascinating experience, to feel her soul disperse.

The Beloved's memories of the Contagion wavered before her, like a gauze curtain billowing atop the everyday landscape. Numbers broke down and broke down and broke down into tiny fractions, then slipped back and slotted together, rebuilding themselves into another, darker, form: the Contagion, touching everything, reassembling it in its image. The gradual darkening of a world.

The small portion of flame that was Tina's mind thought, *And you brought it here.*

We rise a blister in the remains of the world and We hold the Contagion within it. We sing it to sleep there – the other Chosen and We – and We grow a ship around the blister and tear ourselves from the remains of the world, and so we depart, seeking the rift from whence came the Contagion. Seeking to rebirth it into its own place.

You brought it here, thought Tina again, anger flaring tiny within her very tiny soul.

Its dreams poison Us. But even through the sickness, We sing. So it sleeps. Even as corruption spreads through our ship's flesh and We tumble helpless through the void, even as We plummet and crash and begin the long rot, We sing. Over time, the others fall silent – one, then another, then another – but We sing on. Then my Heart dies, and We become I, and I am alone in a poisoned world. The darkness is growing near; still I keep the lullaby alive. But not for much longer. Without my Heart I starve. I weaken. I will die. And it shall wake.

'But there is another Angel.'

Thrown aside during the plummet.

'He has no Beloved anymore.'

I have no Heart.

'Can you help each other? Can he take another's Beloved?'

The shifting veil of numbers rose and fell in a luminous shrug. The Beloved did not know.

There was a *thud* and they stopped moving. The sky disappeared. It took a long moment for Tina to understand that she had fallen to her knees. The sky had disappeared because she could no longer hold her head up to see it. The grass, however, was captivating, the blood that dropped onto it shining like jewels in the glimmering of the light.

Rise up, murmured the Beloved.

When she could not respond, the Beloved prodded her, a horrible, intrusive pressure on some buried portion of her mind. Her legs unfolded with the suddenness of spring traps and she was set lurching once again towards the orchard gate and the castle ruins that roared their impatience to the sky.

ii. Cornelius

CORNELIUS TOLD HIMSELF that he was going to explain everything and make things right. He told himself that he was seeking Raquel. He told himself this even as he stumbled through the woods far from where he knew she had gone; even as he purposely kept his mind silent and closed; right up until the sight of Luke sent him ducking behind a tree, where he hid his body and his thoughts until he was once again alone. Only then, hiding in the quiet shift of the darkness, listening to the distant whistles of the hunt, did Cornelius finally admit that he was not seeking Raquel.

Some small, honest portion of him sneered. *Of course you are not*, it said. *What would you say to her? 'I called your boy a whore, my dear. I dubbed him an abomination.'*

Cornelius shook his head and pressed his hands to his face.

As if awoken by his own touch, the damning memory leapt unbidden to his mind: a hot and lazy day; he and Matthew sitting together in the orchard, reading. The others had been nothing but the distant sound of a croquet game on the lawns. Matthew spoke his name and Cornelius glanced up. Smiling, the sun behind him, his hair all golden in it, his face gently illuminated by light thrown up from the page, Matthew had leaned across and, as natural as breathing, pressed his lips to Cornelius' mouth.

This is a child, Cornelius thought, startled. *This is Raquel's child!*

But Matthew was not a child. He had been a worldly and knowing seventeen when they met; was now, despite his looks, almost fifty-seven; and his kiss was filled with such certainty, such sweetness of intent, such absolute confidence that it speared Cornelius to the core.

Next he knew he was gripping Matthew by the back of his neck and rolling him over onto the warm grass, and Matthew was grinning into the kiss, his mouth widening, his arms closing around him, and it was *so sweet*, God help him, it was *so damned sweet* that Cornelius almost wept.

There came a frantic urgency, and Matthew was suddenly tugging Cornelius' waistcoat, and slipping his hands beneath his shirt, all the time craning up into the kiss, his body strong and slim and demanding beneath Cornelius' own. His leg came up between Cornelius' thighs as his hands worked fire and magic on his bared chest, and Cornelius groaned into the softness of Matthew's neck.

Matthew smiled into his ear. 'I knew it,' he whispered. 'I knew it. I knew it all along.'

And then Cornelius was shoving himself back and crawling away, his shirt hanging obscenely open, his chest and belly exposed. How could this be? This was not possible – not here. This did not belong here.

Matthew followed, laughing reassuringly. He attempted a caress, and Cornelius pushed him aside. 'Where do you think we are?' he snarled, trying to close his shirt. 'Some harbour-side cock shop?'

Matthew's certainty slipped a little at that, but he smiled again, and reached once more. 'It's all right,' he whispered. 'Don't be afraid.'

'Touch me again and I will kill you, you shameless little trug.'

There were more words – Cornelius could not believe he had said such words – but it was the memory of Matthew's face that was the worst: the slow loss of light from it, the growing hurt, then the anger and, finally, that cold, dead blankness as he took the abuse, the summer sun blazing around him in all its glory, the sounds of laughter drifting from the games down on the lawn.

In the darkness and cold of the present, Cornelius ran from this memory – the way he ran from every memory of Matthew and Matthew's loveliness and his love, and Cornelius' wasting of it. He ran the familiar path, wanting only oblivion, not caring what brink his world was teetering on, not caring what would be lost in the forgetting. He wanted his angel. And so it was he entered the orchard in time to witness the girl rise from her knees in a blaze of blood and glory and stagger from the apple trees like a living candle, into the shadow of the ruins.

He knew at once that she was taking Vincent's creature to the Angel. That she was about to break everything. He thought that maybe he cried out, but afterwards all he could properly recall was curling his lip and clawing his hands and leaping for her.

iii. Tina

SHE SAW, THROUGH a warp of numbers, a man running towards her. She lifted her hands, a gentle gesture of thanks and refusal. But he grabbed her with the brutality of a thug, and ripped the light from her. There was a tearing in her throat and behind her eyes. The light was flung from her, a comet-blaze arcing away to impact with the ruins ahead. A great wall of ancient stone flared with luminance; then the comet dulled and slid to the ground, where it glimmered among the nettles, like a dying star.

For a moment Tina remained standing, staring at the man. *You've ruined everything*, she thought. *What will happen now?* Then the sky revolved, the ground leapt up, and she was lying in the rubble and the grass. She tried to say, 'Help me,' but something caught in her throat, and she choked on it. The man turned his head slightly, as if tempted to look at her, then he tugged his cravat and squared his shoulders and walked away into the ruins.

Tina watched along the twitching length of her useless arm as he crossed the ruined courtyard and came to a halt at the very place for which she had been headed. Light was roaring up from the steps below. Wolcroft's slim figure was ablaze with it, his tangled hair and his grim face all lit up. But Tina knew he had no concept of the magnificence that raged and wheeled about him. Looking down at the entrance to the Angel's realm, Wolcroft could see nothing but blackness.

You poor man, she thought. *Your world is so dark.*

He took the first few steps downwards. Then he sagged against the wall, covering his face with his hand. After a while, he turned his head and reluctantly looked over at Tina.

Help, she thought. *Bring it to him.*

She could not move her head as he came towards her, so she ended up staring at his shoes. It should have been terrifying, this lack of control over her body, like being trapped inside the corpse of herself, but she was calm and serene.

Help him, she thought. *Unite them.*

The man knelt, turned her face to him and brushed her hair back. With an expression of revulsion, he wiped her mouth and nose with the cuff of his jacket.

'I am so sorry,' he said. 'It was never my intention—' He grimaced and hung his head. 'No. Even now I am lying.' He looked her in the eye, took her face between his hands. 'I had nothing but evil intentions for you. I am sorry for that.' And he gathered her in his arms and lifted her, helpless and voiceless, and carried her away from the one thing she knew she was capable of saving.

In her mind, Tina cried out and screamed. In her mind, she hammered his chest and told him to put her down. But her body remained still and quiet, her gaze directed up at the moon-tumbled clouds. As he walked her through the orchard, snow began to fall, and she could not even blink it from her eyes.

Convergence

JOE HAD BEEN with Tina until her hand touched the water. What had he believed would happen then? He hadn't known, hadn't given it a single thought. He had simply been entranced by Tina, by her bravery and her strength; by her determination that the Angel would not die alone. So he had not uttered a word of protest, and had simply watched through her eyes as the creature rose from the jar and closed like a gentle trap around her arm. By the time he understood the coldness of it, the vastness, and how little Tina meant in the grand scheme of its perception, it had been too late.

The creature had bent its mind to hers, and Joe experienced an instant loss of energy as the light that fed everything here found itself strongly diverted through the creature's body. It felt as though the whole world had dimmed. Tina's voice came clear and loud in his head: *Oh. You are killing me.* Then her thoughts disappeared behind a veil of alien calm, and she was gone.

He spent a stupid amount of time battering himself against the door, screaming her name and straining his mind to find the thread of her, before he realised he had another option – he could make his way into the underground tunnels and find Tina by finding the Angel.

He had just begun a blind and awkward descent into the darkness when the latch clicked above him and golden light spilled down from the opened door. Raquel was outlined there, all crinolines and flounces. She stepped back in a gesture of invitation. 'Come up now,' she said. 'It is time for you to leave.'

Joe advanced cautiously, not knowing what to expect. Before he had reached the top Raquel stepped from sight, her grave profile catching the light as she turned to go, and he ran the last few steps, afraid she would slam the door in his face. But she simply crossed the room and stood in the library doorway, staring back at him. Her children were waiting in the hall. They had multi-branched candelabras in their hands. The many flames, blazing high, illuminated their little faces with almost painful brightness.

'Mama is going to play with us,' whispered the girl, obviously delighted.

'You may take that,' said Raquel. She gestured, and Joe turned to find the pram waiting by the French doors. 'The girl can keep it.'

She lifted her skirts and gracefully made her exit. The children followed her down the hall. Joe heard the soft tap of their heels and the susurration of Raquel's skirts as she led the way up the stairs. The light from their candles threw a bright nimbus of light on the banister and ceiling, which vanished as they passed onto the middle landing. He stood, breath held, waiting for the creak of their passage overhead, but all was silent.

Miss Ursula burbled in distress and Joe went to the pram and bent over it. 'I can't find her, Miss U. She's disappeared from my mind.'

Ursula Lyndon paid him no attention. She just waved her crooked claws and mewled like a child in need of food. Joe frowned in sympathy and tried to tuck her in, jiggling the rosary to make her happy. But she struggled free of her swaddling and once again grasped and mewled. Joe looked in the direction she was reaching. He looked back down at her. Experimentally, he pushed the pram through the opened doors and out into the night. Ursula Lyndon reached, fingers flexing, towards the path that led to the trees, and Joe, his heart hardly daring to hope, followed her lead.

He travelled blindly into the maze of the woods, trusting completely the compass of Ursula Lyndon's reaching arms. Pushing his way through tangles of undergrowth, he broke into the open with unexpected abruptness. A wall rose up ahead of him, the branches of trees peeping above it, and beyond that the craggy teeth of a ruin. Joe knew this place; he had seen it from Matthew's window.

Miss Ursula was in a small frenzy now. Straining her arms over her head, she scrabbled her crooked fingers into the hood of the pram, as if trying to scratch through and reach to the orchard that lay on the other side of the wall. Tina must be in there. Why could Joe not feel this? Even the ropes of light were invisible now, as though the girl whose eyes he had seen them through were…

'TINA!' he roared. 'Tina, where are you?'

He jolted the pram through the gap where a section of the wall had fallen down. The orchard was all stillness, filled with ghostly trees. A man emerged from between them – Wolcroft.

At the sight of the limp figure in his arms, Joe rushed forward. Wolcroft shifted his burden, and from beneath the tangled cover of Tina's hair and dress he aimed a pistol.

'I am not sure what you have become, boy. But you have not spent so long in the Angel's sphere that a shot to the brain will not end you.'

Joe regarded him with jaw-clenched rage. 'Is she dead?'

The man shook his head. Joe thrust out his arms. 'Give her to me.'

'To what purpose?'

'Are you mad? So I can get her *home*! Look what this place has done to her!'

In the dim moonlight, it was not easy to see Wolcroft's expression. But there was something about the way he hesitated then, some kind of diffidence and regret, that made Joe afraid.

'You give Tina to me, mister. We're leaving.'

'I do not think you *can* go home, boy.'

'*Give* her to me.'

'I...I am not certain that she can either.'

'Jesus!' Joe ran the last few steps between them, slapped Wolcroft's weapon aside and jostled Tina from his arms. 'Tina,' he whispered. 'Hey. Tina. It's me.'

Her head lolled into the crook of his arm, her blood-filled eyes staring at the sky. She was nothing but a weight in his arms. He groaned and gathered her close, backing from Wolcroft.

'I'm taking your carriage,' he said. 'Don't try and stop me.'

At the pram he faltered, not knowing how to handle it and Tina and make it across the uneven ground. A soft sound at his back made him whirl. Wolcroft was right behind him.

The man put up his hands in a gesture of peace and, bending over the pram, gathered its contents. Miss Ursula cooed and sighed as he laid her into the cradle of Tina's lap. 'There,' he said.

He looked up into Joe's eyes. Joe cut him off before he could attempt the travesty of an apology. 'How do I get to the stables?'

Wolcroft pointed. 'Follow that path.' Before Joe could run, Wolcroft grabbed his arm. He withdrew from his pocket what Joe recognised as Miss Ursula's ring, and laid it into the old woman's hand, closing her gnarled fingers around it.

'This was hers.'

'I know it was,' hissed Joe. 'She loved that ring. She's had it since she was thirteen – got it at an emancipation rally run by some black fella and Mr Daniel O'Connell. What are you doing with it?'

'I stole it from her.'

'You stole a damn sight more than that, you shameless bastard. I hope your fucking angel kills you. I hope it eats you alive.'

Wolcroft nodded. 'I've poisoned everything,' he agreed. 'All the good things…I let them all die.' He flinched suddenly, as if startled by a shout only he could hear, and looked to the house. 'Are the children within? They…they tell me Raquel has locked the doors.'

'What did you do with the thing from the lake?' asked Joe.

Wolcroft, his attention on the upstairs windows, did not answer.

'Tina was trying to save it, you know. She thought it was important. She wanted to bring it to the Angel.'

The man just kept staring at the house, his brow furrowed in concern, and Joe, sick to the very core of him, walked away.

THE STABLES WERE filled with scuffling, desperate whispers. The stub of a misshapen candle threw guttering light. Joe laid Tina on a nest of hay and warily rounded the stalls. Harry was stumbling about, trying unsuccessfully to back the horses into the traces of Wolcroft's carriage. Joe took him by the arm and Harry spun, wild-eyed, his fist cocked.

Joe lifted his hands. 'It's me,' he said.

To his astonishment, Harry grabbed him into a hug. He was trembling. Joe could feel his feverish heat. He awkwardly patted Harry's back. 'It's all right, Harry. I know how to do this.'

Nothing

Vincent called out, *Raquel? Raquel! Answer me!* But there was not even a flicker of a response.

When he got to the back of the house, none of the villagers had seen her. He dismissed them to the hunt, and they left eagerly, communing with the hoots and whistles whose purpose was solely to frighten their prey. Vincent closed his eyes, quelling the urge to simply scream Raquel's name into the night.

Luke, he thought, *where are you?*

In the woods to the south of the house. Got the dogs with me.

Have you seen Miss Raquel?

No. The childer still ain't answering me, neither.

If you see her, tell me.

Himself not about?

Vincent allowed a long pause between them, and Luke's next thoughts were tight and disapproving: *I see.* He assumed Cornelius had retreated underground and left them to deal with the crisis alone. Vincent was perfectly happy to let him think the worst. Luke was almost certainly right – Cornelius was most likely, at this very minute, slumped on the lower steps, gazing up at the Bright Man and doing nothing.

Are you really going to speak of doing nothing? You who have spent your whole life closing your eyes and turning away? 'Shut up,' Vincent told himself, snarling at the empty air as he stalked back around the house and onto the gravel drive.

Just like you did nothing that day in the orchard, when you heard those awful words and saw poor Matthew's stricken face?

'Shut up!'

Or do you consider turning on your heel and sneaking away 'doing something'?

'Shut up!' cried Vincent again, only marginally aware that he was yelling.

Or the next day, when Cornelius came to you and said he had done something wrong and that he needed to speak to you, and you told him 'perhaps later'? Or the next, when you found Matthew crying and you, once again, turned away?

Vincent groaned, turned full circle on the gravel, and bellowed into the night.

'RAQUEL! ANSWER ME, WOMAN!'

This was it. This was absolutely it. He was leaving. As soon as he found Raquel, and by the devil he would find her, he was taking her and they were going. He had had enough of Cornelius' inaction and Cornelius' silence and Cornelius' poisonous fear. He…

Ah, yes, Raquel. Raquel, whom you left trapped in that cesspit of a home with that animal of a husband until she was driven to murder. It was Cornelius who saved her. Not you. Cornelius who broke her from prison, Cornelius who brought her here. Cornelius who gave you the new life you had wished for but would not act upon. Matthew and Raquel, your new family – Cornelius' gift.

Vincent came to a halt by the front steps, shook his head. 'Shut up,' he whispered. 'He only did it because he knew I was restless.'

All these years his friend, and you have done nothing, said nothing, fixed nothing when he needed you most.

Vincent recalled the look Cornelius had given him only this afternoon, slumped on the dungeon steps, on the very brink of finally speaking – that hopeful, terrified, yearning look, from which Vincent had dropped his eye. How many times over their lifetime had he turned from that look? And how many things would be different now, had he responded to it as a friend and not retreated from it nor allowed Cornelius to retreat from it, like the cowards they both were?

'Oh, Matthew.' Vincent pressed the cool metal of the pistol to his forehead. *Matthew. I am sorry.*

But what use was sorry? What was lost was lost. Vincent was not about to beggar himself for the forgiveness of the dead. With a scowl, he glared out into the fog-shrouded garden.

I will not stay, Cornelius. You may continue this travesty if you wish, but I am tired of being prisoner to my disease. I am leaving.

A minute fluttering of the air startled him. Peering upwards, it took him a moment to realise that it was snowing. The liberal dusting on his jacket suggested it had been doing so for quite some while. Holding his face to the sky, he closed his eyes and let the flakes numb his skin.

The air had grown markedly cooler. Soon the roses would be crusted with frost. Soon winter would be here. The thought filled him with an almost savage happiness.

Let it come, he thought. *Let everything die. Let everything crack. It is time.*

A heavy rumbling sent him spinning, and he raised his pistol as a huge bulk of darkness lurched around the far side of the house. For a moment Vincent thought it was death, come in response to his bitter command. Then he was ducking and shielding his head from a storm of gravel as the great wild shape of his own horses and carriage thundered past. The carriage swayed dangerously on the turn and careened off up the carriageway at tremendous speed.

Vincent lowered his chin, bared his teeth and started running. *The intruders are out the front*, he called. *They have stolen my carriage.*

Flight

i.

JOE BENT OVER the reins and mercilessly cracked the whip. He usually despised whips, but in this case, with this cargo, he would bare these horses to the bone if he had to.

There came the faintest brightening of the air as the trees thinned, and the humpbacked bridge loomed ahead. The lake. Joe was so terrified that he closed his eyes. Sounds hollowed out as the carriage crossed the bridge. His thoughts beat to the rhythm of the horses' hooves: *Let me live, let me live, let me get her home.*

There was a jolt as they crossed the hump and then they were rattling over cobbles once more, and he was looking over his shoulder as the bridge faded into the fog. He was alive!

He turned forward again. He was alive. And he felt fine. There was none of that floating heaviness he had suffered on the lake. He felt perfect! It had been the water, that was all! It had made him sick. Sure, poor Harry could hardly stand after being down in it, God love him; he was weak as a kitten.

Joe stood in the box, bared his teeth in a grin, and cracked the reins. They were going home.

Flight

ii.

Harry clung to Tina, his legs braced to prevent them both from bouncing off the seat. Every bump in the road lurched his stomach and brought kerosene-tasting bile into his mouth. He hadn't felt this ill since he'd had influenza and had missed the New York boxing championship.

'I ever tell you I'm a champion boxer, kid?' he whispered.

Tina's head battered his shoulder, her dull eyes fixed on the ceiling. He gathered her closer.

'I'll...I'll show you my medals when we get outta this. You can help me polish them.' He belched kerosene again, and groaned. 'Of course, I might have made some of those medals out of bottle tops. But I'm not admitting to which...'

In the seat across from them, Joe's cousin was crying like a baby. *Shut up*, thought Harry. *Just hold on to that poor old woman and stop crying.* Truth was, though, Harry wanted to cry himself. He'd never felt so useless and scared.

They bumped violently over the hump of the little bridge and Daymo screamed with terror. Miss Ursula was curled in his lap, wrapped in the blankets from her pram. She was gazing at Tina, perfectly content so long as the girl was in sight.

What was going to become of the poor thing? What was going to become of Tina? She was like a warm corpse in his arms. She seemed completely broken.

'Kid?' he whispered. 'You still in there?'

He wondered if she had saved the Angel. He had tried to find out, staggering after Joe as he had rigged up the carriage, asking again and again what had become of the creature in the jar, what had become of the Angel, until Joe had rounded on him.

'Do I look like I care what happened to the Angel?' he'd yelled. 'Look what it did to Tina! She was trying to help it! She was trying to *help* and she meant *nothing* to it, you understand? Nothing.' He had pushed Harry aside and gone back to snapping things into place. 'The Angel can choke for all I care.'

'But Joe,' Harry rasped. 'That thing in the lake. If we don't fix the Angel...'

He'd rambled on, dizzy and sick, barely keeping his feet, trying to make Joe understand just how *apocalyptic* that thing felt, how terrifyingly end-of-the-world.

Joe had laughed, a harsh and bitter laugh. 'End of the world.' He'd grabbed Harry by the scruff and bundled him into the carriage. 'Every day is the end of the world for someone, Harry. But I'll be damned if today is hers.'

He'd pushed Harry over to Tina, who lay on the rear carriage seat like a bloodstained fairytale. He'd snarled at his cousin, who was already cowering inside. Then he'd slammed the door on their faces and banged his way up onto the driver's box to send the carriage lurching from the yard.

Once they'd crossed the bridge, the air grew much colder. Harry was aware of the lake to his right. He peered out, trying to get some inkling of the creature that lurked there, twisting and turning under the placid water. There was no sense of it at all. It was as if it did not exist.

Harry remembered standing on a snowy New York street at Christmas. He had not been able to understand how it could still go on – the crowds smiling and jostling, the glittering prettiness – when his brother Armin lay on the other side of the wall, coughing his life up in gobs of blood and pain. Harry had wanted to grab the laughing crowds and shout, *Listen to me, listen! He is real! His life is real! He's not a dream!* Then Armin had died, and it was as if the world had been right, and he had never existed.

'But he wasn't a dream,' whispered Harry. He put his hand to the window. 'And neither are you.'

He did not think this creature would let the world ignore it.

There was a grind of brakes, and the carriage halted with a suddenness that almost flung Tina from his lap. He held her tight, staring across into Daymo's crazy eyes. Had they been caught?

Three knocks from above sent them cowering. Harry looked up. 'Joe?' he called softly.

The knocks came again. *Rat, tat, tat.* Then nothing.

'They've caught us,' groaned Daymo. 'I'm not going out there.'

Harry slipped from under Tina's weight. Out the window there was nothing to be seen but a lamplit circle of fog. He could hear the horses panting in the stillness. He opened the door and stepped down into the cold.

Joe was a dark blob perched high in the driver's box; Harry could barely see him through the glare from the carriage lamps. 'Joe?' he whispered. 'What's wrong?'

The young man lifted his arm, pointing forward. 'The lock,' he said.

Harry shielded his eyes to look. Ornate gates hung suspended in the fog, blocking their way. 'Joe, what about the Angel? What about the creature in the lake?'

Joe shifted above him. Harry thought he might be looking back at the avenue of trees. There was a strange flatness to his voice when he said, 'Vincent is coming.'

This spurred Harry forward like a poker in the ass, and he staggered to the gates. He clung to the elaborate metalwork as he examined the lock. The chains were heavy and chill in his hands.

Joe's voice floated down from behind him. 'Harry, can you drive a carriage?'

'No,' he mumbled, trying to insert a trembling pick into the keyhole. 'So stay right where you are. You have no hope against that man. I don't think he's even human.'

Shit. It felt as if he was going to fall over. He could barely focus. What if...*ah!* There it was: the lovely satisfying give and *clunk* as the lock succumbed to his charm.

'I love you,' he whispered, kissing the cold metal. 'Marry me.' Then he was lurching about, hauling first one then the other gate aside and stumbling back to the carriage. He hesitated on the step, staring back into the dark.

'Get inside, Harry.'

Sure enough, there they were – the familiar, terrifying pinpricks of light: Vincent's eyes, far off but getting closer as he ran towards them in the dark.

'Shit, Joe. He's faster than a steam train.'

'Get inside.'

The door hadn't even swung shut before Joe urged the carriage forward again and they were through the gates and out on the road. Harry clung to the window frame, gazing backwards. There was a foot or so of snow on the road, and a wintry stillness to the world that spoke of miles of frozen wasteland.

The carriage lurched and Harry sank to his knees on the jolting floor, clasping his stomach. Even the roughest Atlantic crossing had never crippled him like this. It seemed the further they travelled, the sicker he became.

The carriage bumped again and Tina, all skirts and elbows, fell from the seat to land on top of him. Gasping, Harry wrapped himself around her unresponsive warmth and hung on.

They seemed to be picking up speed. It felt like they were about to rattle apart. On the seat above him, Daymo was making a high, terrified whine. He was staring down at the bundle in his arms, holding it out as if to distance himself from it. All Harry could see was Miss Ursula's crooked little hands, which she was holding up to the ceiling, her fingers moving slightly like she was reaching for a gift. Daymo was fixated on her face. Whatever he saw there was causing him to make that horrified sound.

'What is it?' asked Harry, his voice vibrating like a harpsichord note. 'What's happening?'

Daymo thrust the bundle at him, begging him to take it. Harry drew back, not wanting to see. There was grey dust rising from the cowl of blankets. Puffing up with each bone-jarring lurch of the carriage, it was snatched by the wind through the open window to mingle with the snow as it was sucked out into the cold.

Harry yelled as the carriage lurched again – a massive bump this time, as if the wheels had left the road. The floor tilted, sending him and Tina sliding in a heap. They rattled along like that for an alarming moment: the floor tilted, Harry and Tina tumbled against the door, Daymo yowling. Then it felt as though the carriage fell off a cliff, and they were all suspended in the air until, *bam*, they slammed down onto the floor again.

Harry saw a blaze of stars as his head hit the foot-warmer, and then there was nothing, or nothing that he cared too much about, except the carriage jolting along beneath him for a while.

HIS SENSES CAME dribbling back, along with the slow creak and moan of the carriage. He was lying on his back on the floor, and, oh, Tina's weight was squashing him.

'Get off,' he whispered. 'Tina. Please.' He pushed weakly until she slid from him; then he just lay there, gulping at the cold air, which streamed down from the window above.

After a while, he reached to find her. 'Sorry,' he rasped. 'Sorry.' He closed his hand on her hair. Through the window, dimly illuminated by the flickering carriage lamps, he could see the ivy-covered stones of the big estate wall passing by with a stately lack of urgency.

Why were they going so slow?

Daymo was huddled on the seat above, his eyes shut and his lips moving in prayer. There was no sign of Miss Ursula – just a thick coating of ashy dust on the lacy coverlets, and a scattering of red crystals from Tina's broken rosary.

As Harry stared at these paltry remains of the vibrant, tragic old woman, the carriage slowed and juddered beneath him, and then came to a gentle halt. Somehow, he found the strength to drag himself outside.

The air was brutal and still, snow falling lightly in the golden circumference of the lanterns. They were at a corner of the estate wall. Just ahead, the fragile ruins of a church rose delicate shapes against the scudding clouds. The road turned sharply left there, and made its way through a village of neat, dark houses. Everywhere, the blanketing snow caught the diffused moonlight like a reflecting mirror and made the world seem ghostly and impermanent.

Harry groped his way around to the driver's gate. 'Joe?' he whispered, fumbling the latch. 'Joe, we need to keep going…' He crawled into the box and knelt at Joe's feet for what felt like the longest time, his burning forehead rejoicing in the snow-covered leather of the seat. Then he straightened.

Joe was bolt upright in the middle of the seat. He had wedged himself in with the driver's blankets, and had tied the reins to his hands so the horses would keep going in a straight line. But a dead driver gives no signals, and so, with no one left to urge them on, the horses had eventually come to a halt, waiting to be told what to do.

'Ah, Joe,' whispered Harry. 'Ah, Joe, come on, pal.' But Joe's hands were colder than ice and his face was crusted in snow. Harry brushed the crystals from Joe's cheeks; they melted instantly on his own feverish skin.

There was a sweeping sound from the road behind them, and a jolt as something hit the carriage. A shape launched itself from the luggage-rack to the roof, then up to the wall on their right. It was Vincent. Perched on the wall, clinging with one hand to the bare branches of a great oak and pointing a pistol with the other, the man glowered down in fury. Harry couldn't even summon the energy to be afraid, and when Vincent saw who they were, he lowered his weapon.

'He's dead,' said Harry. 'He got us this far; then he died.'

Vincent thrust the pistol into his belt and jumped lightly into the driver's box. He went to gather Joe in his arms. Harry pushed him away. 'No!'

'There may still be time for him.'

'No!'

Vincent tutted, and stooped once more. Harry put his arms around Joe's cold body and held on. To his surprise, Vincent sat back.

'You cannot make this choice for him, boy.'

'He's here, isn't he? He made the choice himself. Leave him alone!'

'You *want* him to be dead?'

Harry shook his head, gasping. He was so confused. The world was swimming, everything coming in waves. He realised he was sobbing into Joe's shoulder. 'Don't take him back there. Please don't.'

Vincent sighed. 'He only sacrificed himself to save another. How do you know what he might have chosen had she not been in danger? Are you really willing to reward him by taking him from here as a corpse?'

Harry shook his head again. *Yes. No. I don't know.*

With another sigh, Vincent pushed him to one side and gathered Joe in his arms. Harry slumped against the seat, helpless, and openly crying now, the snow falling down on him in gently cooling drifts. In the carriage, Daymo's prayers continued, selfish and useless, as Tina lay broken on the floor below.

Vincent rose to his feet, a tall dark shape cut from the night. 'Do you think you can manage to take the girl home?'

Harry didn't answer. He was staring at Joe's pale dead face.

Vincent huffed. 'At least do him the justice of *trying*,' he said. 'If you drive through the village and then take the right-hand fork, you will be in the big town by evening.'

The man seemed to think for a moment. Then Joe's hair brushed Harry's face as Vincent leaned in to look into Harry's eyes. 'Tell everyone there has been an outbreak of the cholera here,' he said. 'Warn them not to come. And, boy, if you ever, *ever* say anything more than that, I will find you, understand? I will make you do things you would wish yourself dead for. By protecting my family, you will be protecting your own. Do you understand?'

Harry nodded. The man held his eye just a moment longer. Then, with Joe's body still in his arms, he sprang to the roof, then to the wall, and was gone.

Goodbye

TINA WATCHED THE lacquered wall, listened to Daymo pray, and sensed Harry shiver and moan as he tried to keep the horses moving. Now they had passed beyond the Angel's sphere, the poison in Harry's system was running riot. He had begun to talk to himself, and laugh and cry. Sometimes he paused to get sick. Still he stayed up there, the cold eating at his face and hands, stubbornly guiding those horses through the deepening snow, trying to get her to town.

She had been broken in some way she was not certain could ever be fixed, and she floated within herself, calm as a lily on a pond despite the great depth of her grief; despite the knowledge that everything was lost.

Joe was gone. She had felt him go. As the light had grown weaker and the distance between him and the Angel increased, he had simply faded away. When the man took him, there had still been the smallest spark of him left – just the tiniest, tiniest fragment – and then the carriage had moved on and he had disappeared from her entirely.

Still she had kept calling out to him, as she had been calling since he'd wrestled her from Wolcroft's arms, hoping that he would hear her, hoping that her thoughts would reach his across the growing distance and through the storm of damage that Cornelius and the Beloved and the vast torturous pain of the Angel had done to her mind. *I love you, Joe. I love you. I love you, Joe. Save him. Save him. I love you. I love you. I love you, Joe. Save him.*

The carriage stopped moving again, and she listened as Harry spoke to people who were not there. He was saying the same thing over and over: 'There's cholera. Don't go to the village. There's cholera.'

Come on, Harry, she thought. *Get moving. You can make it.* The carriage lurched as he opened the driver's gate. *Ah no, Harry. Stay up there.*

He was babbling as he made his way to the carriage door. 'Promise me, okay? We can't go back.'

A deep, familiar voice said, very gently, 'Why don't you stand back now, son?' and the door opened in a blast of snow and cold. A woman's voice cried out, and there was a great confusion of shadows as someone piled into the little space beside her. She was turned onto her back. The woman groaned, 'Oh, *acushla*. Oh no.'

Tina felt herself being lifted into a sitting position.

Daniel Barrett was frowning at her from the door, a shotgun propped on his shoulder. 'Cholera,' he said. '*Cholera*, Fran. If folk hear that, they'll never let us back into town.'

The woman's arms tightened around her, and Tina was comforted by the smell of apples. 'We'll say nothing 'til we get her home, Danny. No one need know. And when we warn the theatre boss, he won't have to tell the performers the truth. Sure, he can make something up.'

Daniel's eyes hopped from Tina to Daymo, who still

moaned and sobbed on the seat above her. Fran the Apples squeezed Tina even harder. 'You're scared of some germs, is it, Daniel Barrett?'

The man smiled, a gentle, adoring smile, and shifted the shotgun so that he could reach in for Tina. 'After travelling the length and breadth of the country with you, woman, I'll be scared of nothing again.'

The sky was falling down in soft pieces, filling her eyes, as they carried her to a covered cart and laid her down on blankets there. Fran bundled Harry in beside her, a blanket round his shoulders. Tina heard Daniel bully Daymo up onto the driver's seat. She felt the cart begin to move.

Harry kept mumbling to himself and trying to leave, and finally Fran put her arms around him. 'Shush now, *acushla*,' she said. 'Shhhh, now. It'll be all right.'

Harry started to cry, very quietly, his face turned away. Fran rocked him and murmured to him, all the time gazing across his shoulder to Tina, who could not turn her head or look away from his defeat, nor take a breath to say the name that echoed in her mind.

Endings

i. Vincent

Taking the long walk back from the church gate, Vincent shifted the weight of the boy in his arms and savoured the tranquilly falling snow. No matter how weak the Bright Man, he still had hopes this boy might revive. 'It will be good for Cornelius to have you around. You may even find that you are happy here – certainly I was for long enough.'

It felt good to have finally decided to leave, but for once in his life Vincent was not going to turn away without speaking. He would talk to Cornelius. By force, if he had to. He would turn his friend's face to the mirror and make him look himself in the eye; ask him how many lifetimes he intended to squander on this existence of dust; how much love and life and opportunity he would continue to waste. *Better one brief life lived to the full than an eternity of fear, cully.*

Then Vincent would leave. He would take his chances, with the disease and with the world, and he would live – really live – for as long as his body would last. He would take Raquel with him. Gently, kindly, he would show her that the world held more than the brutalities it had previously revealed. What a life he would give her – he would fill every day with wonders.

The children would be difficult. They must be disposed of – but how best...

Vincent hesitated as he emerged from the last of the southern woods, the smell of burning timber pulling him from his thoughts. He paused a moment only, not comprehending; then he saw the top windows all ablaze with light, and he ran.

The entire village was arrayed on the grass, staring up at the brightly lit top floor, their faces slack. The atmosphere was thick with awe. Vincent ran into it like a wall of hot syrup, and it stopped him in his tracks.

What can it be that is amazing them? he thought. *It is only fire.* But he knew, the devil take him, he knew already: it was the thought of what the fire consumed, the *spectacle* of its tragedy, that held them entranced.

Vincent searched in vain from face to upturned face. 'Cornelius?' he called. 'Raquel? Where are you?'

Luke came running from the house, trailing smoke and coughing. He staggered across to the nearest villager, Peadar Cahill, and grabbed him as if repeating an action he'd already tried in vain. 'Help me!' he gasped. 'Help me. I can't get him to leave!'

Suspended as the Bright Man fed through him, Peadar did not react.

Realising the boy was still in his arms, Vincent dropped him to the gravel and ran to grab Luke. 'Where is Raquel?'

Luke shook his head. 'I can't get Himself to leave her. I tried. He's determined to break down the door.'

Vincent spun for the house. Luke staggered after. His eyes were swollen with smoke and he could hardly breathe. 'She's barricaded herself in,' he gasped. 'I can't hear the childer anymore.'

As he ran into the house Vincent heard the villagers make an awed sound, and he felt the violent, coring sensation of the Bright Man latching on to him and beginning to feed.

Smoke was pouring down from the upstairs landings. Vincent ripped his cravat from his neck, tied it across his nose and mouth and battled the stairs. Even his eyes could see nothing in the blinding air, and he had to grope his way to the upper floors.

In the sewing room, everything flared with light. The playroom door was a sheet of flame, and Cornelius was hurling himself at it, bellowing and snarling as he tried to break it down. His sleeves were ablaze when Vincent hauled him away. He had to be punched in the jaw to prevent him struggling free. Vincent threw him across his shoulder and fled for the hall. He could feel the heat on his back as they descended the stairs – from Cornelius' burning coat or the advancing flames, he could not tell.

By the time they reached the porch, Cornelius was thrashing blindly, all aflame. Vincent threw him to the ground and stripped him of his coat. He hurled the blazing garment away into the gravel. It illuminated a ring of watchers there, their avid eyes all fixed on him.

Vincent staggered back from them as if from a blow. Luke was running from one to the other, slapping them and screaming, 'Stop! Stop looking at them!' But he could do nothing to break the spell, and the villagers continued to drink deep from the wondrous circus of anguish and fire of which Vincent and Cornelius had become the heart.

Vincent barely had the strength to turn from them. He fell onto Cornelius, who was attempting to crawl back into the house, and clung tight. Cornelius' hair had begun to streak with white. Vincent's strong hands were beginning to age.

Cornelius' thoughts were loud in Vincent's head now, directed only at him, screaming and crying and calling over and over: *Help me save her, Vincent. Help me save her. She cannot end like this.*

But there was nothing that could be done. Raquel was not even a whisper inside their minds. She was gone. So Vincent wrapped his arms around his friend and gathered him in, and with all his strength held him in place as the spectacle of their pain fed the Angel, and smoke poured from the doors, and the flames overhead ate the only person left who they had ever loved.

ii. Joe

JOE JERKED TO life on hard gravel, flames lighting the sky above him. He was sprawled at the feet of heedless men and women, their attention fixed on a smoke-filled doorway. Tina's voice was in his mind, or the echo of it was, or the memory, because she was not here. She had gone. But her insistence remained, the desperate plea that she had been drumming into him since the bridge. He rolled to his elbows, crawled from the smell of fire and ring of rapt watchers, and followed his memories into the darkness of the trees.

The symbiote was where she'd remembered leaving it,

lying in a dim shiver of light at the base of a stone wall in the ruin of a castle. Joe wrapped it in his waistcoat and carried it to the place Tina had been heading before Wolcroft had saved her life by breaking her contact with it. Down into the dark throat of the earth he went with it, fathoms underground, through depths and depths of darkness illuminated only by the nacreous glow of the creature in his arms.

He turned a corner into a much brighter light, and there behind the thick bars of a rusting iron gate stood Tina's angel. It paid him no heed at all, and it seemed not to even notice the creature in his arms. Its great spider hands were pressed to the ceiling above its head, its sea of tentacles held upwards like a cup. It filled the tiny space of the stone staircase with its presence, and it was, as it had been when Joe had first seen it, intently feeding.

'Here,' whispered Joe, holding the Beloved up to the bars of the gate. 'I brought this for you.'

The Angel did not respond. But the Beloved, as if reacting to the Angel's light, raised first one, then another, then all of its trailing arms. Almost too weak to move, they groped and wavered, then finally, finally, made contact with the Angel.

It was so graceful, in the end. Such an elegant, peaceful, tender union. After all the wailing and pain and need, it was like a gentle song, the way they came together.

Joe put his hands against the bars as the Angel straightened and expanded and became whole. He could feel the power withdrawing from the air, the focus of energy shifting as the Angel withdrew its yearning light and began, as was its proper nature, to feed through the consciousness of the creature that had curled around its neck.

Its own Beloved, that poor dead thing, was pushed aside,

and it slipped to the floor, unheeded and unmourned. These were the things left behind when the Angel walked away into the tunnels: the body, long dead, of a casually discarded soul; and Joe, alone and lonely in the dark.

iii. Vincent

IT WAS MORNING when Vincent found the boy. He was sitting on a jumble of fallen stone, his head tilted back against the wall of the ruined castle yard, watching the sun rise above the smoking roof of the house. The air was bitter, the grounds bright with frost, and for the first time in many decades Vincent truly felt the cold. The boy watched his approach without lifting his head from the wall, and did not react in any way when Vincent offered him the blanket he had carried from the house.

'Put it around you, boy, or you shall be ill.'

'You look older.'

Vincent sat stiffly onto the stones, the blanket bundled in his lap. 'I feel older,' he said.

They watched the smoke rising and, not for the first time this morning, Vincent wished that he could cry. 'My wife is dead,' he whispered.

'And Wolcroft's kids?'

'They were not Cornelius' children. He brought them as a gift for Raquel when...' Vincent glanced at the boy, who stared coldly back. 'Yes,' he answered flatly. 'The children are dead.'

'Is your house ruined?'

'The upper floors are gone. The attics. The structure can be rebuilt, of course, but the occupants...' He looked down at his hands, the already healing burns on his fingers and palms. 'Not even the Bright Man can resuscitate ash.'

'I gave the creature to your angel. I took it down those stairs.'

Vincent nodded dully. 'I think you saved our lives doing that, mine and Cornelius'. Had you not done so, I think the Bright Man would have sucked us dry.'

'I didn't do it to save you. I did it because Tina wanted me to. I thought I'd die afterwards…Why didn't I die?'

'I do not know. Perhaps because that particular creature and that particular symbiote are not meant for each other? Perhaps they do not fit quite perfectly and there is, even now, still something of the Bright Man's power reaching out to us.'

'I don't want to live here forever, mister.'

Vincent got to his feet and dropped the blanket into the boy's lap. 'That is up to you,' he said. 'You can always just walk away.'

Joe squinted up at him, the rising sun in his eyes. 'Are you leaving?'

'It's time. I've had my fill. I need more, or I need nothing. Either will do. How about you?'

The boy shook his head. He seemed terrified. If Vincent had been a different type of man he might have stooped and gripped his shoulder, or embraced him, or offered advice. But Vincent was what he was, and he had given all that he could give. The rest was up to Joe.

'Here,' he said, dropping the iron key into the boy's hand. 'In the old days, I'm told the Angel used to wander the woods. It used to stand sometimes by the pond and touch the water, and the old folk say it used to sing. Let it free. I cannot guarantee it, but I suspect that if you do, the pond will thaw and the creature within it will remain asleep – at least for so long as the Angel lives.'

The boy closed his hand around the key but gave no sign that he would act. Once again, Vincent found he did not much care, and he turned away with no more words.

Leaving the boy in the shadow of the ruins, Vincent took the path through the apple trees and down through the woods. Once he reached the lawns the whole world seemed to open up in frost and snow, a wide and careless, glittering expanse waiting but not caring either way if he came or went. Smiling, Vincent kept on walking, the house at his back, the world at his feet, not choosing a direction, just happy to be gone.

The Persistent Woman

Fargeal Manor, 1900

THE GIRL DID not flinch as the door slammed open and the doctor ran out onto the porch. She had been expecting this violent exit. They had heard him within, running all the way from the top of the stairs, and the panic in his footsteps had been hard to miss.

Cornelius, sitting on the top step on the opposite side of the porch from the girl, had to smile as the doctor passed between them. The terrified man was down the steps, out onto the gravel and halfway to the carriage before he could bring himself to a halt. Miss Kelly simply watched from the wrought-iron chair that Cornelius had had installed at the top of the steps for her, her expression resigned, as the doctor gathered his dignity, straightened his necktie, then rounded on her.

'It is a poor thing, madam,' he said, 'to bring a professional man all this way, simply to play a practical joke upon him. Did you suppose I had nothing better to do with my time these past two days than to travel to the middle of nowhere for the amusement of you and your wealthy friends?'

'You can do nothing for him, then?' she asked.

The doctor flung out his hands. 'Do nothing for him?' he cried. 'There is nothing to be done! I do not know how you have managed it – I do not know *why* – but whatever your aims, young lady, whatever trick of confidence you hope to pull in order to separate the gullible from their money, I shall not be a party to it. That boy is as alive as I am,' he yelled, pointing a shaking finger at the house. 'He is as alive as I! I do not care what my eyes or ears or instruments tell me! I shall believe no other truth!' He flung himself at the carriage and, in a storm of clumsiness, sealed himself inside with a slam.

The girl sighed. 'What is it he thought I was doing?' she said.

Cornelius shrugged. 'That you were setting him up as witness to a phenomenon, perhaps, in order to cash in on the current trend for the supernatural?' He looked gently at her. 'It is for the best, Tina. What would you have done, had he actually believed himself to be examining a dead man?'

She winced and looked away. 'Don't,' she said.

Examining her profile, Cornelius thought she looked much the same as the day he'd first met her. Except for her eyes, of course; her eyes were far older than those of the average twenty-seven-year-old.

Not that I am one to talk about ancient eyes, he thought.

'He won't see me?' she asked.

'It has been ten years, Tina. He has never once come down to see you. When are you going to accept that he does not want you coming here?'

'I really thought medicine would have caught up with him by now,' she said. 'I really did.'

Cornelius did not bother to answer, and the two of them sat in silence a moment, looking out across the peaceful lawns and boating pond. The carriage horses huffed gently as the driver awaited his mistress's orders. No doubt the big-city doctor was stewing away in there, anxious to be gone.

Cornelius found himself smiling again. He never smiled so much as on these brief annual visits, sitting here with her on the porch. He would have liked for her to come inside, but he had long ago given up offering the courtesy. She would not enter the house until Joe himself invited her. Hence the wrought-iron seat.

'I see Luke went ahead with his plans for the sheep.' She indicated the lawn's new fences and the flock of contented animals grazing there.

Cornelius nodded without answering, his eyes travelling as a matter of course to Vincent's beautiful horses grazing further down the land, closer to the pond. They had not aged at all in the last ten years, and neither had Cornelius' dogs. Neither had Cornelius, for that matter. Neither had poor Joe.

Tina was still talking about Luke and his precious sheep. 'I'm glad he followed my advice,' she said. 'It's a good flock to keep on this land: animals you can make cash from without having to kill. The villagers get an excellent crop of wool, I suspect?'

He nodded again, thinking how much he had come to love this girl, and how close he had come to destroying her, and how she was wasting her life on all these long years of waiting.

'Tina...' he began.

She spoke over him. 'You're looking well, Cornelius,' she said.

He shrugged. 'I am an old man. That is all.'

'You are a handsome and elegant man of about fifty or so,' she said, smiling gently and looking at him from the corner of her eye. 'You'd turn the head of any cat, dog or divil as looked at you.'

This brought his eyes back to the horses again, and she followed his gaze. She seemed to hesitate, then she said, 'He writes to Harry, you know.'

She must have seen the shock in his face at that, the punched-in-the-belly hurt, because her mouth quirked up in sympathy.

'I'm sorry. I've never known if it would be the right thing, to tell you. But I always suspected you'd want to know.'

'How...how is he?'

'He is *really* well!' she exclaimed, raising her eyebrows at the surprise of it. 'Life on the yacht seems to be good for his condition. He doesn't write often, but the last Harry heard he was docked in the Mediterranean, travelling Italy, I believe.'

Cornelius did not know what to say. To his terrible shame, his eyes had filled with tears.

'You never hear from him, Cornelius?'

He shook his head. 'Our men of business communicate. That is all.'

Tina leaned across the wide space between them, squeezed his shoulder, and then sat back.

'Have you...' Cornelius cleared his throat. 'Have you read his latest novel?'

'I've read *all* his novels,' she said. 'But only in English. Saul tells me they're much better read in their original French?'

Cornelius couldn't answer, and she looked away, giving him a moment.

'It amuses me how everyone thinks he's writing fiction. But I suppose the sea-going adventures of an immortal African pirate might be a little difficult for some to swallow as fact. He and Harry started corresponding after the first book was published. Harry was so surprised to hear he was still alive. They both realised the lake had changed them a little – changed their constitutions – and, well, you know what they're like, them and their science. They began exchanging notes. I do think it's become a friendship, though. Certainly Harry speaks fondly of him. "We Indestructible Men", that's how he refers to the two of them.' She chuckled. 'Harry and his titles. Everything must be a show.'

'Tina,' said Cornelius quietly, 'you cannot keep returning here. It is not right.'

She took a deep breath, as if gathering her patience, and tightened her hands on the head of her walking stick. The walking stick was very beautiful. One of his own, it was fashioned of silver-chased ebony, and hid a blade as sharp and light as a shaft of morning sunshine. Cornelius had given it to her when it became clear that she would never fully recover from the Angel's damage. He had given it to her to steady her and to protect her – and because it reminded him of her.

'I spent over two centuries trying to hold the people I love here, Tina – trying to make everything stand still, for myself. It poisoned everything. Joe doesn't want that for you.'

'Has he tried to leave again this year?'

Cornelius nodded. 'We got as far as the big town before I had to bring him back.'

'So he's getting better, then. Last year he couldn't get half that far.'

Cornelius spread his hands. 'Tina, it's been *ten years*. He will not *see* you. Are you going to keep doing this for the rest of your life?'

She shook her head. 'No,' she said. 'I can't. This is my last time. I told myself if he didn't come out to me this year, I'd stop. I've had enough.'

That was like a blow to him – the suddenness of it, the bluntness. Tina stood up, putting on her jacket, and nodded to her carriage driver that she was ready to go. Cornelius just sat there, looking up at her, unable to fathom the fact that she was leaving. That she was finally giving up. There would be no more.

She stood with her hands on her cane, looking out over the grounds as if saying goodbye to them with her eyes. The sun showed a hint of her real age now: the lines that pain and long nights of hard work and a constant readiness to laugh had begun to etch around her eyes; the experience in those dark eyes; the depth of knowledge that those outside their little circle would never have.

'It's very peaceful here. Very calm.' She said this every year. It was her way of letting him know that everything was well – that the creature which roamed the woods and which at night could be seen crouched above its reflection in the pond was still singing the monster to sleep.

He almost reached for her then; almost said, *Don't go.* But that was not what was needed here. That was not what was right. And so he remained silent while she pulled on her gloves, and said nothing when she lifted her bag.

'Lord Wolcroft,' she said, 'I believe I have made good many times over on the investment you and Mr Vincent made in me. The factories that we own together and the cooperative workshops are all doing extremely well. My aunt's grocery shops and her husband's coal dealers are all ticking over nicely.'

Thrown by the unexpectedly technical and business-oriented nature of her goodbye, Cornelius rose to his feet. 'Uh, yes,' he said. 'Yes. Very nicely.'

'Very well. Then I suspect that you and Mr Vincent shall have no difficulty part-funding my latest enterprise?' At his confused agreement, Tina nodded and began to make her way carefully down the steps.

She was already on the gravel when he thought to ask, 'What is the enterprise?'

She turned to look back up at him. 'I am moving to the country, Lord Wolcroft. I am setting up a wool mill, where I plan to produce quality tweeds and woollen cloths. I believe there is a village near to here where I might be successful in finding suitable properties.'

'Tina!'

'There are excellent sheep locally, and a good supply of clean water. The local landlord is kind to his tenants, so I hear, and much loved by them. I have a strong feeling that this particular village will survive whatever turmoil the future might bring us. In this turbulent country, that kind of stability is good for business, sir. I intend to exploit it.'

'Tina, Joe would never allow you to move into the house.'

'I've no intention of moving into the house. I'm moving to the village. I already have rooms booked in the guesthouse, and I have arranged with Luke to begin the construction of a home.'

Cornelius was utterly lost for words, and in the face of his ongoing silence, Tina softened. She stepped forward and spoke gently, just for him.

'It's a perfectly sensible plan, Cornelius. He can't go out into the world, and so, for as long as it's necessary, I'll bring the world to him.'

'You cannot do this, Tina. He will not allow it.'

She huffed, and turned to go. 'And when was the last time, Cornelius Wolcroft, I let anyone tell me what to do?'

She was at the carriage when the front doors opened. The boy stepped out, and they regarded each other in stillness across the shade and sunshine, ten years' worth of silence falling down between them. Already he looked younger than her. But Cornelius thought that was all right: their eyes were very much the same.

The girl lifted her chin, not smiling in the least. 'Well,' she said. 'You took your time.'

The boy nodded. 'Should have known it would be a wasted effort.'

She continued to stare until he said, 'I'm sorry.' Then she nodded.

He hesitated, not quite certain what to do. 'Would...would you like to come in?'

She looked from his face to the hall and back. 'Actually, Joe, I think I'd prefer a walk.'

He came down the steps to join her. He did not comment on her cane.

She took his arm. 'I still have your purse, you know.'

'My...my purse?'

'It's in my handbag. I suppose you'd like it back?'

They left her carriage in the driveway and her handbag on the steps and strolled away across the drive. Entering the shade of the tree-lined path together, they began a walk. It would take them back through memories, forward through dreams – the resumption of a conversation that had only ever paused and was, from that moment, destined to never end.

Grace Hospital

Detroit, 29 October 1926

'HARRY, WAKE UP.'

Harry opened his eyes, and for a very long moment he looked at them without knowing who they were.

'Dash?' he asked.

'No, Harry, it's not Dash.'

'Bess, what are you doing? The doctors say you're not well enough to be here.'

The girl smiled, and crouched down by his bed and took his hand. 'It's not Bess, Harry. It's me, Tina. Your other Catholic girl.'

'*Mein Gott*,' he whispered, reaching to touch her dark hair. '*Mein Gott*, look at you.'

She pressed his fingers to her lips, her eyes filled with sympathy, and he was suddenly horribly aware of his grey hair, his terribly wasted condition. 'How I must look,' he whispered, raising a shaking hand to his face.

'You look just fine, Harry.'

But Harry knew the truth: even before this illness, he had looked much older than his years. He lifted his eyes to the young man standing behind Tina, and for one startling moment he was sixteen again, brushing snow from a cold dead face, and mourning a friend he'd never really got to know. Then Joe smiled. 'Hello, Harry,' he said.

'Hello, Joe. You're looking well.'

'I wish I could say the same for you.'

'Aw, I'm a bit of a mess…They're opening me up again in a few minutes. I think they're afraid they left something in there.'

He chuckled, and Joe did, too.

Tina stroked his hair. Her hand was very sweet and cool, and Harry closed his eyes. 'I think I'm all out of fight,' he whispered.

'Don't say that.'

'Okay. I won't…' He squinted up at them. 'Say, how'd yah manage to get past my rottweiler of a sister and those brothers of mine? Even my manager has had a time of it today.'

Tina smiled. 'Oh, Joe and I have become very persuasive over the last thirty-odd years. We just asked nice.'

Harry eyed her, not quite happy. 'Please don't tell me your eyes glow in the dark.'

'Okay,' said Joe. 'We won't tell you.'

He smiled at Harry's troubled frown, and crouched down beside Tina.

'Listen, Harry,' he said. 'This is no good. You're not going to make it.'

'Oh, nice,' whispered Harry. 'If you came all the way across the world to give me a pep talk, I gotta tell yah, Joe, you should have stayed home.'

'We came all the way to see you and Bess,' said Tina. 'It's not our fault you're too lazy to get out of bed.'

'You just wanted to show off your amazing travelling man, here.' He took Joe's hand and squeezed it tight to show how happy he was for him. 'It's great to see you out and about, pal. I'm so glad for you.'

'Come home with us, Harry.'

Harry allowed his eyes to slip momentarily shut again. 'Nah,' he whispered. 'I don't think so…Thanks, though.'

There was a long stillness in the room, with just the sound of nurses' shoes squeaking in the hall and the rattle of equipment from the next ward. An orderly came to the door, looked at the three of them in confusion and walked away. It would not be long until it was time to go.

Harry looked at Joe's hand gripping tightly onto his. It was so alive-looking, strong as only a very young, very hard-working man's hand could be. Harry's own hands were covered in many small scars. Even relaxed with the drugs they'd given him, his body was singing with pain. His stomach, his hands, his leg. Harry had done his last three shows with a fractured bone in his leg. It was not unusual for him to do this. Bess said that sometimes, after a show, she found it hard to look at him his pain was so obvious.

In truth, it almost felt good to be finally lying down.

Joe leaned forward and, apparently reluctant to break the peace, very quietly said, 'Harry?'

Harry met his eyes.

'Was it worth it?' asked Joe. 'Have you had fun?'

Harry didn't even hesitate. 'Oh, yes,' he whispered. 'All of it, Joe. All of it was, *ganz gewiss*, worth it.' As he said it, Harry realised that he meant every word.

Joe nodded. Harry looked from his face to Tina's and back again. 'And you?' he whispered. 'Was it worth it for you?'

Tina's hand found Joe's, and she smiled a calm, grave smile. 'Every minute,' she said.

'Come with us, Harry,' urged Joe again. 'It may not be too late.'

Harry shook his head.

'But why?' asked Tina. 'We can make you better. Bess can come, too.'

The orderly arrived with some nurses, ready to prep Harry for the table. They began fussing around, and Tina and Joe were pushed back as the staff prepared to wheel the bed to the operating theatre.

Joe, his back pressed to the wall, asked again, 'Why, Harry?' and Harry smiled.

'I kinda want to see what happens next, Joe. It's too interesting an adventure to pass up.' And he realised that he meant every word of that, too. He wasn't afraid. Let it come, let it not come – he was ready either way.

As the orderlies were pushing him for the door, their stiff white coats hiding the room from view, Joe called, 'Harry, come back and let us know, all right? Let us know what happens next!'

Harry waved, his scarred hand almost too weak now to lift from the snow-white linen, then he was gone around the corner. And soon he would be gone for good: passed onto something bigger, maybe, something more exciting; or perhaps to nothing at all. No one but Harry would ever really know for sure, because once Harry was gone he never came back.

THE END

Acknowledgements

HEARTFELT THANKS TO all who encouraged and supported me along the way with this story. In particular I would like to thank Professor Richard E. Hess, Chair in Drama at the University of Cincinnati College – Conservatory of Music, for his patience and time in ensuring my theatre references were accurate; Ana Grilo for her help ensuring that Raquel's use of Portuguese was as accurate as possible; Sam and Jo Samberg for their help with Harry's Yiddish and Hebrew, and for ensuring his prayers and perception of the afterlife were plausible; to Astrid Finke for ensuring that the German dialect used in the book was accurate for the time and for Harry's origins. Thank you all for putting up with so many checks and cross-checks and multiple emails over the many years it took to write this baby and then put it to bed. Any mistakes are mine, all mine.

Special thanks again to Erica Wagner and Elise Jones of Allen & Unwin Australia, who believed in me every step of the way, and whose dedication, patience and skill were invaluable in getting this behemoth of a story to the stage it is now. Jumpers over heads, ladies, jumpers over heads.

THE MOOREHAWKE TRILOGY

The Poison Throne

'A fascinating historical fantasy characterised by vivid, colourful writing'

The Irish Times

'All the ingredients of an international bestseller'

Sarah Webb, Irish Independent

'It races the reader along at breathtaking speed and doesn't release its grip until the very last page'

International Youth Library

The Crowded Shadows

'Compelling and complex, romantic and suspenseful, populated by memorable characters'

US Publishers Weekly

'Excellent ... a cracking theatrical historical fantasy'

Irish Independent

The Rebel Prince

Passion and violence, plus plenty of skullduggery and intrigue combine to make this a compelling read'

Bookfest